Paradise

Sam Frykenberg

Paradise
Published through fiveapples

This is a work of fiction. Names, characters, places, and incidents are the product of the author's imagination or are used fictitiously. Any resemblance to actual persons, living or dead, events, or locales is entirely coincidental.

ISBN: 978-0-578-76995-0 (Paperback Edition)
ISBN: 978-0-578-82264-8 (eBook Edition)

Library of Congress Control Number: 2020924843

To parents. For holding on. For letting go. For your mistakes. For your refusal to make mistakes. For being gods. For being mortal.

For the echo, the ripple, the essence that expands beyond this story to whom it will touch, and whom they will touch in turn.

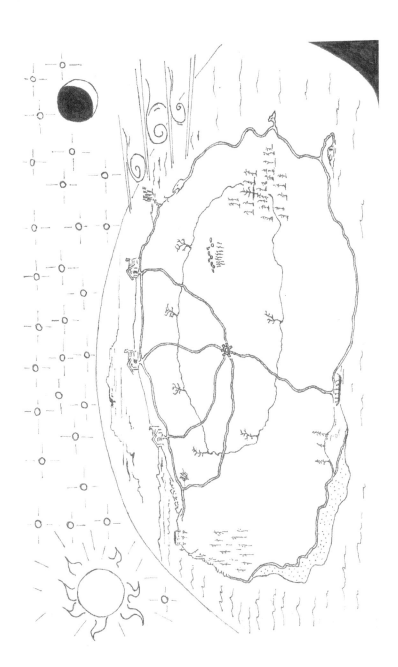

PROLOGUE

Being was. Unbounded by time and place.

Being was all. What was not being was naught.

Present in Being was consciousness, potential, and desire to be and to be more.

The decision to be more brought forth change, time, and division. For what came to pass was something different from what was.

The consciousness which brought about the decision to be more was the Former. It came before. It gave form to being which was not itself.

And thus Being was separated into the Former and the formed, Creator and creation.

The Former was broken. Ravenous to be whole again, It swallowed up form so that Being might once more be complete.

The Former lamented. It could never be truly whole, for It knew itself to be apart from all else. It knew what It had brought forth and had loved in its separateness.

Still, It desired to be more. So again, Being was divided into Former and form.

2 | SAM FRYKENBERG

And again the Former, overcome by brokenness and hunger, consumed creation.

When It next brought forth what was other, the Former separated Its consciousness further, into entities. The Former's love and desire for love were even more powerful.

Yet again the Former consumed them. And the Former wept.

Once again the Former separated Itself.

And in the new creation were now several conscious forms, enraptured with the world and with one another.

The Former again devoured them. And in restless completion It again thought and remade them. The entities assumed shapes, like and yet distinct from those they had embraced before.

Now the world had established rules. It was built to balance and to last.

Yet to sate Its desire for love, the Former demanded tributes be made so that It might feed on the essence of the formed.

For a time the entities wondered at their world and explored it, loving the world as they loved each other.

Hunger grew in the Former.

The others resisted.

One by one the Former consumed Its creations.

However, the Former grieved even as it triumphed. And already It thought to the next world. When the Former found the last entity, It charged him with the task of safeguarding the new creation.

And even as It consumed and unmade him, the promise was irrevocable.

In Its last creation the Former threw itself completely into brokenness. And the new world was beautiful. It carried traces of the old, for the formed took on their own desire.

The formed ones had likenesses to what they had been. They were new, and yet echoed the past. The world and its beings were their own, but the presence of the old was in them.

The Former now lay beneath the world, a brooding shadow of desire.

The new world was made with a structure and laws that withstood the Former. The created ones, too, possessed wondrous gifts that allowed the world to be and to grow. The first of those new ones was also the last of the old.

The Former had also created six to keep and guide the world and each other. They were young, as the world was young.

And so six children were borne into new the world.

PART ONE - AWAKENING

She wondered who had awoken first, the stars, or herself. She had a feeling that their silver light illuminated the world only as she opened her eyes. And here they both lay, she looking up, and they looking down. Was she to them as they to she? She hoped so.

They all had their places. The stars, herself, Ara, and the others. Right now Ara lay against Lenya, her eyes closed, her arms crossed. Lenya held Ara's hands while she slept: their hands belonged together.

Orin was next to awaken. He opened his bright hazel eyes and grinned at Lenya when he noticed she was awake. He put a finger over his lips, a gesture of silence. Lenya rolled her eyes, but smiled in reassurance. For a moment, they held each other's gaze, but then Orin turned forward to where the boat was headed, and Lenya looked skyward once more.

The boat was a simple vessel. It was formed from a hollowed tree. The outside was rough and watertight, but the inside was smooth and comfortable to lie against. There were no oars, nor any means of steering. There was nothing in the boat save for the children. The waves were gentle and the course of the boat was straight.

Neither one of them noticed when Namin awoke. His gaze wandered across the two remaining sleepers beside him, then to Lenya and Ara at the back of the boat, and finally to Orin who continued to stare into the distance from the front of the boat. Beside him, Namin saw Idra's head resting against Kuthan, moving gently to the rhythm of his light snores. Eventually Namin focused on the lapping of the waves. The sound almost lulled him back to sleep but he started to hum, adding his song to the music of the water. Idra turned, her head drifting onto his shoulder. He smiled.

The sky grew lighter, and the stars hid in the brightness of the coming day. Lenya released Ara as she started to stir. As Ara became fully awake, Idra opened her eyes suddenly. She leapt to her feet, screamed, and almost fell in. Namin quickly grabbed her and steadied the tilting boat. Orin yelled in surprise as well, more from the rocking of the boat than at Idra's scream. Namin and Ara laughed. Lenya smiled. Kuthan snored on.

"Is he still asleep?" Ara asked.

"I think so," Lenya said, smiling. Idra and Orin giggled. Just then the sun rose above the horizon, and they were engulfed in a wave of heat and golden light.

"I think so," Kuthan echoed. He sat up with a broad smile, and the boat shook slightly. The young day was filled with the sound of laughter and rolling waves.

They were still laughing when Orin shouted, "There's something up ahead!"

Namin's eyes shifted forward. Kuthan frowned a little, his brow creased. Sure enough, there was a dark spot on the horizon.

"What do you think it is?" Ara asked.

They were all silent as they stared into the distance.

Finally, Kuthan answered, "We'll worry about it if it becomes a problem." He put a reassuring hand on Ara's shoulder.

The response was unsatisfying. However, since no one could guess what it was, they passed the time talking—about the different shapes of clouds, the weather, and the condition of the boat itself. They laughed when Idra observed her reflection and got hit in the face by a wave. But soon enough the mystery of that dark smudge looming ahead pressed on their minds, and each lapsed into a separate silence. The sun progressed steadily across the sky, and the boat moved forth.

It took quite some time before they were actually able to see what it was. As the day passed, the waves grew choppier, the wind picked up, and clouds formed a hazy film over the sun, darkening the sky. A few of the waves splashed over into the boat. Idra began to shiver in the accompanying cold. The boat seemed to move faster as it approached its destination: ahead stood a small rocky island heavily wooded with pine trees.

"It's be-be-beautiful," Idra stammered through chattering teeth." Kuthan pulled her close to share his warmth.

As they moved closer to the island, more features became distinguishable. The island had a rocky coast, which disappeared quickly into thick foliage. While pines were prevalent, some deciduous trees were also visible, and scrub-like bushes and grasses filled the clearings. To their left, the island rose up into a cliff-face which curved around to the other side of the island. To their right, it seemed relatively level. Elsewhere, it sloped gently upward and the rise was not overwhelming. Directly in front of them was a small expanse of sand. It was toward this little beach that the boat was being carried.

The beach was a collection of sand, shells, and a few large rocks. At the edge of the beach a massive rock protruded into and over the water. As they got closer they could make out something perched atop that rock. It was not until they drew quite near that they were able to distinguish it as a person. But before they could make it out properly, the figure vanished. Their boat glided past the looming outcrop where the human form had been.

"We're not alone," Kuthan stated. Although this was obvious, the others were glad the silence had been broken.

"Where do you think he went?" Lenya asked. The answer was clear before anyone else had a chance to speak. The shore was close now, and emerging from around the rock was the figure, in plain sight, but still out of hearing range. Orin was the first to notice.

"What's wrong with him?" he blurted, his voice shaking.

"He's not ... right," Ara said slowly. Idra shuddered, and even Kuthan let out a breath he had been holding. Namin and Lenya exchanged confused looks.

The figure was tall and slender, with sharp features and elongated limbs that gave incongruous impressions of authority and gracefulness. He had deep grey eyes, darkly tanned skin, wavy light-brown hair, and a narrow face. His skin was smooth and devoid of any blemish. But beneath his long nose was a smooth patch of skin where his mouth should have been.

"What do we do?" Idra voiced.

The hull was now in the shallows, scraping against the sand. In answer, Namin hopped out of the vessel, unbalancing it. Moments later they were all climbing out. The water was frigid, and Lenya and Idra were soon shivering again.

They hurried out of the water, dragging the boat along with them onto the shore. The mouthless figure stood waiting. Now that they were on level ground with him, they could see that he was taller than any of them, even taller than Kuthan. They stared at each other. The wind picked up, and the waves continued to wash onto the beach. Finally, Ara broke the silence.

"I'm Ara," she said boldly. Following her lead, they all spoke their names.

"Kuthan." "Namin." "Lenya." "Orin." "Idra."

"Who are you?" Kuthan asked. The figure did not answer, nor had they expected a reply. Instead, he beckoned, turned, and walked to where the beach gave way to trees, and the sand to soil. For a moment the six of them were still, but then Orin followed the tall shape and the rest fell into step behind him.

They were led up a steep curving dirt path. Flanking each side of this were glass lanterns resting atop rods and grouped in pairs, each pair about ten paces from the one before. The sky was visible directly above their path; however, the ground alongside that trail was sprinkled with pine needles or covered by overgrown shrubbery and wild grass. Every so often, another path would cross theirs. At these crossings there were always four lanterns, one at each corner made by the intersecting paths. The pine trees themselves appeared to be almost identical to one another; each of them rose high into the air and could not be encircled in one person's embrace. The trunks and branches were a deep grey-brown. What did vary were the spiderwebs; large with their many sided circular shapes, they crisscrossed between the branches in unique patterns.

It came as a surprise when their path was interrupted by an earth-covered clearing with a single leafy tree at its center. After seeing so many pines, the leafed tree seemed exotic with its light- colored bark and wide, flat leaves. On the other side of the clearing, the path continued, but after the clearing, the forest seemed darker. The sun had begun to descend in the sky. Eventually the forest cleared again, this time revealing a grassy slope. The figure climbed without effort, leading the little group to the top of the hill, where he stopped abruptly. At the center of the summit stood a stone table.

The table was perfectly circular. The edge was coarse, but the top was unusually smooth. It stood just high enough so that Idra could lean comfortably against it. Strange markings spiraled from the edge of the table towards its center. The figure gestured to the table, and wordlessly they gathered around. He held his hands over the table and then placed them on its surface. As before, it was obvious that the children were to do the same. As one they placed their hands upon the table. And they understood.

You may choose to ever wander
or remain and call this home
If you stay, then you must honor
rules engraved upon this stone

Never roam in dark of night
off the path of lantern's light
But in the brightness of the day
the island's yours for work and play

By each sunset you must hone
a crafted piece of island stone
Of this tribute made each day
you may work with sand and clay

shells and sap, roots and mud
berries, bones, but never blood

Furthermore, each one of you
has an island service due
In this task that you provide
Enetheal shall be your guide

Welcome, guest, to your new home
for this is where you shall reside
To be safe, to laugh, to grow,
by these rules you must abide

None of them was certain whether they had heard it, or merely thought it. Regardless, it was clear that each member of the group experienced the same message. Ara had shut her eyes tightly and bowed her head during the ordeal. Idra and Orin stared blankly across the table toward the tree-lined path, as if they were letting the message wash over them. Namin and Kuthan both gazed intently at the strange markings. Lenya just smiled. Except for the whisper of wind in the trees, and the faint mutterings of Ara, who was repeating some of the phrases from the 'Welcome' to herself, there was silence.

Finally Namin lifted his eyes to the figure and spoke. "Enetheal." It was a statement not a question. Enetheal nodded once and blinked.

"Who are you to tell us what *service* we must provide?" Kuthan asked coldly. Enetheal stared at Kuthan with his grey eyes. They looked at each other, until Idra interrupted.

"Relax," Idra pleaded. Kuthan relented, breaking the eye contact. Lenya spoke before they could lapse into silence again.

"Do we accept?" Lenya asked, looking around. Namin eyed her curiously. Kuthan gave Enetheal a severe look. Enetheal bowed just slightly and departed, walking down the hill.

"Do we have a choice?" Kuthan intoned after Enetheal was out of sight.

"I think this is where we were meant to be," said Orin, looking down the different paths that came up to the hill. Idra looked at the forest and the winding dirt path.

"It's beautiful," Idra quickly agreed.

"I am willing to accept as long as we all are," Namin said, and Ara nodded.

"We do have a choice, though: we could choose our own way." Lenya eyed them all. The wind picked up, blowing pine needles about them. She waited a moment—a moment that dragged on for a while—before she accepted that no one was going to answer. She smiled. "Alright."

Enetheal returned moments later, carrying a large stone goblet. Suddenly they realized they were hungry. It had been a long day with no food. Eagerly they passed the vessel around. It was surprisingly light for an object made of stone. The liquid within tasted like water, yet it was thick like sap, and surprisingly warm. The warmth suited them; the sun was slipping toward the horizon and the temperature dropping. When they had finished, Enetheal took the goblet and set it down in the middle of the table.

The little group had no difficulty in understanding that Enetheal wanted them to follow him away from the table. This time they traveled a different path. Despite the still glowing early evening sky, the forest held its own darkness. The path cut in and out of trees until at last they arrived at a small cabin. The door to the cabin was darker than the surrounding wood. In front of the door was a single stone step. The frame overhung the door, giving the entrance a sunken-in appearance. Across the frame were strands of spiderwebs, crisscrossing so that, although the door was clearly visible, it was hard to access. Orin moved to brush off the webs, but Enetheal quickly caught his hand.

Ignoring Kuthan's angry look and Orin's intake of breath, Enetheal carefully peeled back the webbing and opened the door. Inside there were two small beds across from each other, each next to a window. Beyond the beds, however, the little cabin was empty.

Ara took Lenya's hand and led her in. Orin motioned as if to follow, but Enetheal held out his hand. Namin gave Lenya an uneasy look, but she shrugged it off.

"Only 'til morning," she smiled reassuringly. Then Ara and Lenya simultaneously reached out and hugged their companions goodnight, halting awkwardly when they came to Enetheal. Then Ara gently, but deliberately, closed their door. With precision Enetheal placed the delicate web across the door frame so that it formed a thin covering protectively over the door. Despite being moved and manipulated, the web seemed undamaged. Enetheal led the rest of them down the path.

The next cabin was for Kuthan and Idra. Dusk had descended by the time they reached it. Idra was exhausted, and even though it was only a short walk between the cabins, by the time they reached her cabin she could barely keep her eyes open. Once again the door was covered with a spiderweb, and again Enetheal carefully pulled it back before opening the door. Enetheal pointed a long finger first at Kuthan, then at Idra. Kuthan glanced at Enetheal, and then turned to glance at Namin, worry etched on his brow. He started to usher Idra inside, but she halted abruptly to give Namin and Orin each a sleepy hug before going in and collapsing on her bed. Kuthan peered over the threshold at the pair who huddled uncertainly by the stone step.

"We'll meet first thing in the morning. You and Orin should come here and then we'll meet up with Lenya and Ara after that and begin our day at the stone table."

"Sounds good," Namin replied, his voice hollow. "Until tomorrow then ...."

Kuthan closed the door firmly, leaving Enetheal to lead Orin and Namin further down the path. Starlight was now the primary illumination in the sky. Enetheal was walking much more briskly than he had when they had approached the last two cabins.

"Are the lanterns supposed to be lit?" Orin asked.

"Must be why we're in a hurry now," Namin answered.

Recalling the conditions of their welcoming words, *Never roam in dark of night off the path of lantern's light*, they hurried forth. Orin took the lead and soon afterwards they arrived at the last cabin. Enetheal peeled back the web nimbly, but with somewhat less care than he had shown before. When Orin opened the door Enetheal practically pushed them in. They got another glimpse of his grey eyes and mouthless face before he grasped the door handle and shut them in.

Separated into pairs within their cabins, each child drifted off into sleep. Images formed in their minds as the darkness blanketed them: images of each other, of the island, of the mouthless figure, Enetheal. Wind and waves sang a lullaby. Idra found sleep almost immediately, and Kuthan soon after her. Orin tossed and turned until Namin hummed them both to sleep. Ara and Lenya cuddled in the same bed, Lenya stroking Ara's hair as she gazed out the window at the stars. At last, she too closed her eyes.

LENYA - DAY ONE

I hope they don't close theirs. Her thought echoed ….
The stars shone, their light filling the sky. Water surrounded them. The waves pushed the boat gently. Idra slept between Kuthan and Namin, Orin was curled up at the front, and Ara lay against her. She knew that Orin would wake soon. She smiled in anticipation. A gust of wind blew from the as yet invisible island. Orin should wake any second. The gust rose into a squall, and the waves started pulling them back the wrong way. "Orin!" She called out. He didn't respond. "Namin!" They slept on, oblivious to her shouts. She shook Ara, but Ara would not wake. The noise of the wind and waves was cut off abruptly, and her cries were silenced. For a few more moments she tried to call out, but her efforts were in vain. The starlight began to fade. And as the stars dimmed, their watery reflections vanished, leaving the waves black. Just before the light was gone she saw that Enetheal had been in the boat too. How had she not noticed his presence? They locked eyes and

suddenly it was completely dark. She felt a coldness in her chest. Her thoughts were slipping away and she struggled to keep them, but it was like holding onto water. I hope they don't close theirs ....

She felt a hand on her shoulder and opened her eyes. Her muscles tensed instantly. She pressed her lips together to prevent a scream from escaping. Enetheal was leaning over her. As he gently pressed her shoulder again, she saw the silhouette of his long nose no more than an arm's length away from her own.

"Get away!" She whispered as loudly as she dared with Ara sleeping beside her. Ara moaned and muttered something incoherent, but she did not move. Enetheal backed to the far corner, his hands held up in an apologetic gesture. As he gazed across the darkened room, his face—features accentuated by shadows—remained frozen, and she found herself wondering absurdly whether he could form facial expressions without a mouth. They stared at each other, she from her bed, and he from the corner. Her racing heartbeat gradually slowed, her breathing became even, and her muscles relaxed.

"Why are you here?" she asked softly. Enetheal walked to the door and opened it. It emitted a loud creak, and then was silent. He held out his right arm, palm upward, and gestured out into the night.

"I can't leave Ara." Lenya hesitated. Enetheal gave no indication that he heard her. He just stood there. After another few moments had passed, Lenya carefully untangled herself from Ara and crept out of bed. She gently tucked a strand of Ara's light hair behind her ear and pulled the blanket over her shoulder. Ara sighed in her sleep and Lenya exited quietly through the door that Enetheal held open. Then, soundlessly, he closed it behind them. Despite Enetheal's care to replace the protective web, a single strand of it had come loose. He freed the entire filament, rubbed his fingers and thumb to release it, and let the gentle wind lift it away. Then he took her hand, guiding her down the stone step and onto a path leading away from the cabin.

The way was lit by starlight but was nonetheless hard to see, particularly when looming trees formed shadows over their path. Lenya would have tripped and stumbled into the brush without Enetheal's steady hand. The direction they took was not the one that led to the stone table, nor was it the one Enetheal had taken when guiding the others to their cabins. This new way cut into the woods, and around the slope that was crowned by the stone table. Except for the muffled sound of their footsteps along the soft earth, the woods were still. Only the distant sound of waves penetrated the silence.

A twig snapped. Enetheal caught hold of Lenya instantly, stopping her in her tracks. They waited a moment but there was no sound, save the distant waves crashing the beach. A soft breeze blew through the trees and the upper branches swayed a little. They continued. As they walked, the sound of waves grew louder. Gradually the trees thinned, and finally they opened up completely to a familiar sight. They were back at the beach where they had disembarked. Once under the open sky, the starlight allowed them to see the land and the waves clearly.

"Why are we here?" Lenya asked. Enetheal led her beyond a stand of boulders to an area of bare sand. He smoothed the sand and gestured to it. Wordlessly Lenya laid herself down, and gazed skywards. The stars shone down, amazing, and infinite. Enetheal stretched down beside her. She wondered what he wanted. It was a beautiful night, but the breeze made her shiver, and she was exhausted from the day's journey. Despite the beauty of the sky, she let her gaze wander away until her eyes rested on Enetheal. He definitely had a jaw, it just never moved. His mouthlessness was hard to look away from.

He must have sensed her watching, because he turned to her and lifted his long index finger toward the heavens. She followed his gesture and turned her eyes above. It was marvelous. Lenya began to count the stars, carefully noting their positions in relation to one another. There were twenty eight. Each was bright and big. The moments lengthened, and despite her attempt to engage herself in her task, fatigue began to overwhelm her. The sand underneath her had adjusted to the shape of her body and reflected back some warmth. She repositioned herself and fought surrender to drowsiness. Nevertheless, her focus began to slip away from the heavens. It happened just as her eyelids drooped: A star moved. No, it didn't just move, it flew! The bright white light soared in an arc across the sky, then fell down, down toward the island. Lenya stood up quickly, watching it plummet, trying to note its landing place. Where that was exactly she could not tell, but she knew that it was far from the beach, the cabins, or the stone table.

She looked at Enetheal, who had also traced the star's path. He looked back at her, and she understood once more to follow. With so little to say, Enetheal was easy to understand. He communicated with looks and gestures. She wondered if that was how he was created. He was well-suited to this mouthless condition. Did he contemplate more than his gestures implied?

Her thoughts were interrupted by the change of terrain: the sandy beach became the dirt pathway. Once again she needed to watch her footing as she navigated the trail. They followed yet another route, but she supposed this was a good thing. She would have to learn all of the ways eventually. Instead of traveling up the rise of the island, or around to the cabins, they took a winding path that kept them close to the water, yet still in a lightly forested region.

Since the tree growth was not dense at the shoreline, the stars provided ample light. This did not last long. The path turned inward and away from the water. The trees thickened, and Lenya stumbled over roots and uneven stones in the darkness. Their travel was slowed by the extra care they had to take to avoid tripping. Time passed in nearly complete darkness, and they made little headway. Finally there was light ahead. The source of the light was a clearing in which a large tree stood alone. Their course ended at the beginning of the clearing—two unlit lanterns on either side of the entrance—and continued on the other side. Unlit lanterns also flanked the exit. They reached the opposite end of the clearing and the forest became suddenly dense again. Brush encroached upon the path, trees crowded together, and Lenya's view of the trail, and even of the heavens, was obscured. Her foot caught on a rock and she gasped in pain, looking down. Although she felt a sudden heat, darkness prevented her from seeing any injury. When she looked up, Enetheal was gone.

Although Enetheal unnerved her, being alone was far more frightening. Lenya quickened her pace, but this time with extra care not to trip.

"Enetheal!?" she whispered, now beginning to panic. Her call was quiet, but since silence had enveloped them for so long, her voice seemed almost a shout. She dare not call out again. Disruption of such a long silence seemed somehow wrong, or intrusive. A rustle in the brush startled her, but she recovered her composure quickly. She hurried down a bend in the path, and found Enetheal again. He looked at her calmly, as if he had merely been waiting.

"You can't just leave me like that!" Now she was angry. He did nothing but stare. Did he understand her? But just beyond him she could see a faint silver glow. She forgot her irritation as she stared at the glowing object on the floor of the pine forest just ahead.

She pointed. "The star?"

He nodded and turned toward the luminescence coming from underneath the thickly growing pines. The presence of the star inspired Lenya with a sudden reverence which rid her of any trace of annoyance or tiredness that had possessed her. Now it was she who took the lead and Enetheal who hurried to keep up with her. His footsteps were silent, and she kept looking over her shoulder to be sure he was following. The path was overgrown, but she was almost upon her star. A small but steep slope led her up, but then the ground leveled and she halted. She was staring directly into the star's silver glow.

It was beautiful. There was a small hollow where it had lodged in the ground. A thorny bush partially covered the star's landing spot, but could not hide its luminescence. It was a natural sphere, and small enough to hold in both of her hands. Silver-whiteness emanated from it like a pulse. Up close it seemed more like a heart beating than a star shimmering. Lenya cupped her hands around it and gasped. It was cold. An exhilarating cold. She felt alive in a way she had never been. At her touch, the light dimmed. The little star was still bright, but it was no longer a beacon. As she became used to its frigid temperature she was able to appreciate its texture: it was round, hard, and extremely smooth. It was also heavier than she had expected, but not unpleasantly so. Its heaviness somehow calmed her.

Lenya noticed Enetheal looking over her shoulder at the star cradled in her hands. For a moment his mouthless face frightened her again. But this time she purposefully swallowed back her fear.

"Touch it." Balancing the glowing sphere carefully in one hand, she held it out to him. Enetheal reached, but not to take it. He took her other hand, and closed it over the star. He gave her the look that she now understood to mean, 'follow'. She practically skipped after him, holding her star close to her heart.

She was so full of exhilaration that she did not notice time passing as they strode quickly back along the path. It still twisted and turned, but with Lenya's star clutched close, and its light illuminating their way, the trail was no longer menacing. Rocks, roots, and overgrowth posed no threat. And this time Lenya knew her way better. Soon they were back on the beach, but they did not stop there. Enetheal led her to the far side, and along another path. This one was less overgrown, and shorter than the last one they had followed. Where the last trail held rocks, roots, closely bordered brush, and densely packed trees, here the trees grew far apart, and sand and grass bordered the path. When she came upon a turn in this path there was no danger of wandering off the walkway or catching her foot on one of the lanterns. The land sloped up sharply. Sand became stone, and there were fewer trees. A cliff-side now loomed on their right, water bordered their left. The path became stone stairs cutting into the cliff, which rose high above the water.

They began to climb, and the exhaustion which had been masked by the joy in retrieving her star seeped back into her muscles from the exertion. Step after step led them higher and higher. As they ascended, the wind grew stronger, and Lenya became aware of the waves crashing below on her left. Despite being far from the forest, the unlit lanterns nevertheless flanked the steps, every twenty steps or so. The stairs cut in and out of the jagged cliff-face. The rise of the cliff and ascent of the stairs grew steeper as they neared the top, until finally the stairs stopped. They were on a small plateau, and the stars seemed closer than ever. It seemed almost as if she could reach out and touch them.

The plateau was about fifty paces across. The floor was mossy, except at the edges where flora gave way to rock. The moss was not uniform. Scattered patches of flowering plants were present, differing in size, shape, and petal color. Lenya noticed that the plants seemed to face the same star-less patch of sky. A stone well stood in the center of the plateau. Many fist-sized rocks formed the base of the well. No bucket or collection device was present.

Enetheal led her to the well, avoiding the flowering plants. As she had noticed in similar open spaces on the island, the plateau was devoid of deliberate walkways. As the two of them walked by the plants, the light from her star shone upon them. Was it Lenya's imagination, or had they turned slightly, so that now they faced her? The moss came as a relief to her feet after her hike along stone paths through the night, and she stopped briefly to look back at the flowers. Enetheal paused, but resumed his approach to the well when he saw that her attention had returned to him. Soon they were at the edge of the well, and Enetheal was gazing at her.

Lenya was starting to get used to interpreting Enetheal. It really wasn't hard. He either encouraged her to follow, or he stopped, at which time she was expected to do something. They had stopped, so it was time to do something. The question was what? She looked at him for a clue, perhaps a gesture. He stared back at her. Was he calm? His body language indicated a kind of tranquility, but his mouthless face was expressionless. Surely he wasn't impatient, yet he stared, and she became convinced that he was waiting. Lenya looked around. All the plants seemed to be watching her as if they, too, were waiting. *They are not watching me, they are watching the star.* The thought came into her mind, almost like a whisper. She looked at the well and smiled.

Placing the star at her feet, she put both hands on the side of the well, and looked into its depths. The well went down! Down into darkness, and further still. It seemed unnaturally devoid of light, and the blackness seemed to be almost tangible. She reached down to her feet, and lifted the star. It was cold, and bright, and exhilarating. She leaned over the well, allowing the star's light to bathe the inside. The light did little to illuminate the huge void below, but she could see just a bit further down. She looked around. The flowers still gazed at the star. She expected some sort of sign from Enetheal, but he watched her impassively. She peered into the well's depths once more, her hands tightening briefly about the star. And then she let it go.

It fell, and fast. One moment the pulsing light was between her hands. The next, it was plummeting into the depths of the well, vanishing from sight. She waited, listening, and finally, she heard a faint splash ... or was it nothing at all? Lenya let go of a breath she hadn't realized she had been holding. She turned back to Enetheal. Only now he nodded, inclining his head just slightly. Was this approval or merely acknowledgement? She could not say. What she did know was that any residual energy she possessed had now deserted her.

She might have given in to sleep right there had it not been for Enetheal. He gazed expectantly at her, and she knew that again she must follow. They took the path leading down from the plateau. It was a gentle slope, but even the downhill walk was daunting in her tired state. She stumbled frequently, but this time Enetheal's hands were there to steady her. The path leveled out, yet her grasp on wakefulness became ever more tenuous. She felt her mind wandering into slumber even though her legs kept moving. And then suddenly, there was the open door to her cabin. She had not even noticed the last portion of the journey— had Enetheal carried her? She hoped not. She turned back to look once more into his mouthless face and his eyes. Then she entered, and closed the door behind her. Relief filled her as the sound of the latch clicked firmly into place.

The night's adventure had caught her mind. But Enetheal's presence was unsettling. Now the night was simple again, and it belonged to her and Ara alone. Ara must have slept deeply during her absence, for she had not moved. The strand of hair was still tucked neatly behind her ear. Lenya removed the blanket from the empty bed and climbed beside her, pulling the extra cover over them both. This time sleep took her quickly.

Idra - Day One

She took a deep breath. It wasn't so much the breath, but more the fact that she was aware of it. Idra had been immersed in a dreamless sleep. Thoughts of sleep were gone now, though. The room was lit with the new day. She looked over to where Kuthan slept. His face was shaded, but she could see that his brow was lined as if he were deep in thought. She almost laughed at the idea of him concentrating in his sleep, but restrained herself. Through the window she could see the pines. They looked more cheerful than they had yesterday during their cloudy arrival. The sun glinted off their dark green twigs making them radiant. She looked further. Wildflowers bloomed where dappled light met the needle-strewn soil. And she sensed something else. Now that she thought about it, it wasn't what she saw outside the window, but what she heard, something that wasn't wind or waves.

The sound was a high chirping whistle that alternated between notes. It stopped, and then started again. Moving quickly but silently, she approached the doorway and pulled it open. The door was heavier than she thought, but still, she was able to open it quickly. She bounded out into the morning. The moment she rushed through the doorway, she remembered the spiderweb screen and the great care that Enetheal had taken to make sure it was not harmed. For a moment her heart caught in her throat; she was sure she had run straight through it.

It was a great relief when Idra looked over her shoulder and saw that the screen had been neatly pulled to the side. She relaxed. But then she started. The spiderweb wasn't the only thing she saw. Sitting on a little clump of moss close to the doorway, beside the stone step she had just leapt over, was Enetheal. He hadn't reacted to her blustering exit, or to her sudden movement when she turned around. It was his stillness that had caused her to ignore him.

They held eye contact until her heart stopped beating so fast. Her eyes moved down just below his nose and she shuddered. She could not help it, Enetheal's mouthlessness repulsed her. It was simply wrong, and she knew it to be so. Idra looked away, unable to look into his face any longer. She had to find something, anything else to focus on. Her attention was quickly drawn to the chirping once more. She looked for its source and saw birds sitting on a tree limb. As she watched, they spread their wings and flew from their branch to a different one.

Idra's delighted laughter joined their song. The short moments since waking had tossed her between excitement and surprise so many times that laughter was her only possible response.

"After yesterday I was worried that we were alone," she said to Enetheal. It was hard to look at his eyes without her gaze being drawn downward, so she looked slightly to his left. From the edge of her vision she watched him nod. She returned her gaze to the birds; they were amazing creatures. But then she felt Enetheal walking away. She started to head back to the cabin, glad that he was departing, but as she walked, she watched Enetheal. Just as he was about to exit the clearing, he stopped and turned. He beckoned her towards him. He wanted her to follow. She should have known. It would have been too simple for her to have escaped that easily. She nodded back to him: Enetheal seemed to understand nods. Then she slipped into the cabin.

"Kuthan" she whispered. His answer was a voiceless sigh as he rolled onto his side. *Best to let him sleep*, she thought, and she headed back out the door.

The path Enetheal led her down was neither of the ones that connected to her companions' cabins. This path seemed to take them in the direction of the slope where the table was. As they walked Idra continued to observe the off-path activity. The birds were not the only creatures who had seemingly appeared overnight. Several times she saw squirrels running up and down trees, and at one point she caught a glimpse of something larger running between the trunks.

"Are they like us?" Idra asked, allowing her gaze to move to his face. He blinked, but didn't nod or shake his head. Idra turned her attention back to the wildlife. *They were certainly not like him,* she thought. The surrounding forest did not seem to change much as they traveled. There were pine trees and rocks covered in lichen. There were large bushes, some with more leaves, and some with more flowers. They entered a stone way which forked off the dirt path, but the scenery was changeless. Idra's attention remained on the animals that had been absent just the day before. Woodland fauna continued to hold her attention until they came to a break in the pine forest. They had arrived at a tree completely different from all the others she had seen.

The trunk was large and had a faded grey color. The pines seemed insignificant compared to it. The new tree had thick limbs that sprouted just above an easy hand-reach. As the tree rose, these branched out at varying intervals until, at the top, the tree was as tall as any of the pines. Though equal in height, the great tree spanned out, its branches reaching in all directions. Its leaves were a bright green, more vivid and lighter in color than any needles on the surrounding pines. However, its most distinguishing feature was not its shape, color, or leaves. It was the fruit. Hanging down from the branches were green and orange fruits. At the bottom of the tree the fruits matched the green of the leaves. Higher up, the fruits were still green, but now had a yellow-orange blush. At the very top the fruits were all of shimmering golden-orange.

Idra ran over to the tree and began to climb. She had to jump and swing herself up to get onto the first branch, but after that, climbing became easier. The first few branches after her initial mount were almost like steps because of how close they were to one another. It was only when Idra reached the fifth or sixth branch that she remembered Enetheal. He stood at the base of the tree watching her. When she looked at him, however, he inclined his head, peering toward the other, higher branches. Did he want her to go higher? If so, she was happy to oblige. She started to climb faster.

She moved up and over, branch after branch. After a while though, the branches became smaller, and when she pulled herself up, she could feel these smaller boughs protesting beneath her weight. Still she climbed, climbed until individual limbs bent under her weight and she had to spread herself over several of them. She was about to stop, when she looked up. The grimace of exhaustion that was spreading over her face turned into a smile. Idra knew why she was here.

The fruit she beheld was unlike any of the others. It bore the same shape, but that is where the similarity ended. This one was golden orange-yellow in color, and had no trace of green. Most of the other fruits would have fit comfortably within her hand. This one was triple their size. It wasn't merely the size and coloring of it, though. There was something about its skin and the way the sun fell upon it that made it seem to glow. Idra knew she had to get it, and so she climbed just a little more.

The boughs grew even thinner. She had to be careful to distribute her weight between several green twig-like stalks. Every time she moved, they would shake wildly. She was almost there when she pushed a little too hard off the limb which supported her left foot. With a small crack it broke. A plunging feeling filled her stomach as she started to fall, but to her relief, the branches she held in her hands bent, but did not break. She wedged her right foot into a fork and secured herself. She stayed still for a moment or two while her racing heart slowed.

Looking up, Idra realized that there was no way the few remaining limbs could support her. It was infuriating. Her goal was just barely out of reach, but still seemed unattainable. She started again to attempt to distribute her weight so as to gain height, but at this point she knew that she could not continue. She contemplated the problem, taking a moment to brace herself, motionless, over the many little branches. As she puzzled, a gust of wind brushed the upper fronds of the tree. *Not the fruit, the branch*, she thought, and she was happy once more. Idra could reach the branch the fruit was on, which meant she could reach her fruit.

She caught the branch at its base and it bent with her grip. As she pulled it closer, the fruit came within arm's reach. With one hand fastened tightly to the supple stalk, she grasped the fruit with the other. There was a brief tug of war, but Idra was triumphant; she pried the fruit from the branch's clasp. Now with the additional strain of the large fruit as well as her weight, the several supporting limbs dipped and swayed, but did not snap. Idra grinned in triumph.

The journey down was more tedious than Idra had expected. One hand held the fruit against her chest as she clambered down. Every time she moved a foot down to another branch, she held her breath until it was securely in place. Then she would slide, her one hand moving along the trunk, using friction to support her descent, the other pressed protectively around the fruit. Having only one hand available to climb with was a challenge. Moments passed. Finally she reached thicker, more stable branches and her passage became easier. Nonetheless, it was still a good while before she reached the base of the tree. The joy she felt at her initial capture of the fruit had melted away by the time she reached the ground. She held it out to Enetheal, who had been waiting motionless below. He took it, and Idra wiped some sweat off her face.

When Idra was finished panting and wiping her brow, Enetheal returned the fruit, which again, she cradled protectively. They walked back along the stone way and onto the dirt path. However, Instead of turning left, toward her cabin, they turned right, up the slope towards the table. Idra considered protesting. It was well past the time she should have returned, and she felt almost ready to go back to bed. But she decided against it. Enetheal would not respond anyway, and she was hesitant to do anything that would upset him.

Since she was so careful to avoid looking at his face, she started to notice other features about him. He walked with grace … unnatural grace. His back was always straight, his shoulders free. His gait had an almost hypnotic steady rhythm. It was especially impressive as they hiked up the slope towards the stone table. He did not slow, did not seem to tire. Idra started to envy the birds who flew so effortlessly overhead. Despite her exhaustion, though, the two of them made it to the table in good time. Enetheal indicated a small indent at its center, next to which sat the stone goblet full of sap. Idra placed the fruit in the middle, and forced herself to look at Enetheal's face. He blinked and nodded, holding his hand out to indicate the path which led to her cabin.

Idra left quickly. With newfound energy, she ran down the path. She raced past the trees, past where the dirt path crossed the stone way, and onward until she reached the cabin. She stopped just before the door, pausing briefly to catch her breath before she reached for the latch. Prying it slowly, she tried without success to avoid the horrible squeaking of its hinges. She entered once the opening was just wide enough to squeeze through, and closed it as quietly as she could behind her.

The inside of the room was unchanged, as if she had not left. Outside, the world was so vibrant, so lively. Here it was lifeless, except for Kuthan's breathing. Idra let her eyes readjust to the darkness. Kuthan lay in the exact position he had been in when she had departed earlier. All that had changed was the angle of the sun. Despite all that had happened, the shift in lighting was very slight. It was going to be a long day. Idra crept back to her bed to lie down. She decided to let the covers rest at the base of her bed; she was much too hot for them. She barely had a chance to close her eyes when Kuthan spoke:

"Back already?" There was a cool edge to his voice. Idra started. She had been so sure he was asleep.

"Yes," she said simply. Kuthan paused before speaking again.

"Where did you go?" His tone was dispassionate.

"Exploring. You won't believe how amazing it is outside." Another pause. It irked her when Kuthan stopped before speaking. She decided to break the silence.

"I found some food, I left it on the table, it looks amazing," Idra said. Kuthan let out a heavy sigh.

"You worried me, Idra," he said quietly. He sat up, and she did the same, so that they were looking at each other, face-to-face, across the room.

"I'm sorry, I didn't want to wake you, and I had to go."

"You had to?" he questioned. Idra looked away. A moment passed in which the waves, wind, and birds were all they could hear. "Next time wake me," Kuthan added after a moment.

"Well, you were asleep, and there was nothing to do, so I went outside." She looked back up to see Kuthan's expression softening slightly.

"We don't know what's out there. And until we do we should stick together. It's bad enough that we are separated in cabins this way. At least let me know next time you want to wander alone."

"I wasn't alone—Enetheal was with me, and he does know what's out there," Idra blurted. The moment she said it, she wished she hadn't. Kuthan's expression had darkened once more.

"He's part of what's out there, Idra." He looked at her until she returned his gaze.

"We know each other. You, me, Lenya, Orin, Ara, and Namin. As of now, everything else is a potential threat. We must be careful." Idra nodded, and not just to placate him. He was right, she had been careless, and she was glad to have him looking out for her. For all of them.

"You're right," she said quietly. "Thank you." Kuthan's brow unfurrowed, and his face gave way to a smile. They looked at each other. Kuthan had a nice smile. She couldn't help thinking how glad she was that Kuthan had a mouth.

"We should get the others. They're taking too long," said Kuthan.

Idra was happy to oblige. This time they left the cabin together, and went down the dirt path leading towards Namin and Orin's cabin. They had only just started down the path when they met up with the pair of them. Namin and Orin jogged up the path towards them. Normally they didn't look alike, but with both of their faces red from exertion they did share a kind of resemblance.

"How's your morning?" Idra asked lightly.

Namin scowled. "It's been a little hectic. This one thought he should take a morning stroll without letting me know." He gestured toward Orin.

"I wasn't going to watch you sleep all day!" Orin intoned.

"He's not the only one," said Kuthan, giving Idra a light shove.

Orin and Idra looked at one another before chorusing in unison, "Where did you go?" They both laughed.

Idra decided to answer first, and she told them about her walk outside, about being startled by Enetheal, and about the apparent new life on the island. Most importantly, about her climb up the tree and retrieval of the fruit.

Orin's story was fascinating, but not as adventurous as her own:

"I woke up as it got light, and I did try to wait for Namin, but he didn't wake, so I decided to explore the island." Orin spoke quickly and in one long sentence. "I thought I'd have time to get to the shore and back because I could hear the waves from our cabin, so I took the path that led to the waves," Orin paused for a breath. "Then as I got closer I could hear this high whistling sound, and by the time I made it to the shore the sun was just rising. I think the whistling happened because of the wind and rocks out on the water. But I couldn't be sure. There's a strange looking rock out in the water. There was no other thing it could be."

"That's about when I found him," Namin said quietly.

"And now we're here together," Idra said brightly. Namin smiled.

"We have that to be thankful for," Kuthan muttered. "Let's hope Lenya and Ara had more sense than you two."

"Let's find out," Orin said, oblivious to Kuthan's annoyance. "I think we've kept them waiting."

Orin ran ahead, leaving Namin, Idra, and Kuthan to pursue him. They rushed past Kuthan and Idra's cabin, towards Lenya and Ara's. The path upward looked different from the downward path, but it was still easily recognizable. The lighting of the new day also made it look more welcoming. They were interrupted when a flock of birds rose from the treetops, startled by their running.

"Look," Idra cried. Namin and Kuthan were kind enough to stop for a moment to observe, but Orin pressed on, so they had to pursue him. After winding their way through the forest they finally arrived back at the first cabin they had seen. Orin stood just outside the door as they arrived. He grinned at them as they approached. They walked over. Namin joined Orin on the front step, and started peeling back the spiderweb net. Orin shifted from one foot to the next until it was removed. The moment it was gone, he rapped on the door twice.

They waited in expectant silence. As they became more impatient, the sounds of the birds and wind and waves seemed louder. Orin knocked again.

"Maybe they both went exploring," Idra said.

Kuthan stepped forward to push open the door, but just as he put his hand against the door, it opened. Ara emerged, her face still puffy, her hair a tangled blond mass. Her eyes, however, were alert.

"Shhhh, Lenya's sleeping," she whispered.

"Still?" Orin asked incredulously. Ara nodded.

"The sun is rising and food is waiting for us," said Kuthan. "I'm sure she's rested enough. Today will be busy."

"Should we wake her?" Idra asked. Kuthan nodded his assent.

Ara pushed the door further open, allowing all of them to slip in before letting it close. Kuthan stood next to the door, while Namin and Idra perched on the unoccupied bed. Orin started to leap forward, but Ara caught his hand and shook her head. He stopped, halfway between the door and Lenya's bed. Lenya appeared to be in a deep sleep. Her head was back, her arms spread slightly, her muscles relaxed, unmoving except for a slow, even breathing. Ara stooped over her and shook her shoulder gently.

"Lenya," she whispered. Lenya did not respond.

"Lenya, it's time to wake," Ara said a bit louder.

She remained motionless.

Orin crept to Ara's side, leaned in close, and called out her name loudly. "Lenya!" She didn't get up, but her forehead creased slightly, her brows came together, and she frowned.

"Lenya, you need to wake up," Ara said again. Lenya groaned, opened her eyes, and sat up.

"Hi," she said, somehow sounding both sleepy and surprised. She looked from person to person, taking them all in.

"There's breakfast up at the table," Idra stated, barely concealing her pride.

"And it's time to get moving," Kuthan added. Lenya glanced out the window, taking in the day, before returning her gaze to them.

"Oh," she said simply. "Okay." Idra noticed that she looked exhausted. Tired or not, Lenya climbed out of bed. They filed out through the door, Ara leading Lenya by the hand. Namin came out last, and reattached the spiderweb screen. The morning sun was now clear above the trees, and they squinted against its brightness. They had grown accustomed to the dark of the cabin. After a few moments of being dazzled, their eyes adjusted and they set out towards the table.

As they climbed the slope, Idra was filled with apprehension. Would Enetheal be waiting for them at the top, standing rigid and mouthless, ready to remind them of the rules of the table? The words that had echoed through their minds on the previous day returned to her.

By each sunset you must hone
a crafted piece of island stone
Of this tribute made each day

you may work with sand and clay
shells and sap, roots and mud
berries, bones, but never blood

Today would be their first day. Where were the stones? And how would they shape and decorate them? Were the tributes judged? Deemed worthy or unworthy by someone? Enetheal? If the others shared her thoughts, no one voiced them. The climb up the hill was silent except for the distant sound of waves, wind, and birdsong. The sun shone down on them as they climbed, and by the time they reached the top Idra was covered in a sheen of sweat. The table stood, sturdy and ancient, Idra's fruit at the center. The stone goblet stood next to it. Although the sun had barely moved since her morning adventure, it felt like an age since she had climbed the tree and claimed her prize.

Kuthan took charge. He insisted that since Idra had retrieved the fruit, she should take the first bite. She obliged, biting through the brightly colored skin. Juice spurted into her mouth, flooding her senses with a tart sweetness. She gasped in surprise at how delicious it was. Even more satisfying was seeing how the others reacted. Lenya's eyes widened, and all traces of her sleepiness vanished. Ara took in a deep breath, almost inhaling her bite. Kuthan simply closed his eyes and chewed. Orin let out a laugh. Namin hummed his appreciation while he ate, and didn't notice them staring at him. When he finally did, he laughed, and promptly choked. The laughter spread through the little group and Idra joined in. Namin coughed once more, swallowed, and smiled.

Watching them eat her fruit filled Idra with pride. Even when the others had stopped smiling, Idra could not stop. Their happiness lingered even as Enetheal emerged from the forest. But if contentment remained, their laughing and talking became hushed. As Enetheal approached, they knew their day had just begun.

ARA - DAY ONE

While they ate, Ara stared at the carved surface of the table. This was where everything had started to fall into place. She had been restless during their journey to the island. When they had first arrived and began to wander along the beach, an overwhelming sense of discontent had enveloped her. But this feeling vanished abruptly once they came to the table with its inscribed rules. The rules gave each of them something to do and the means by which to do it. That did not mean she wasn't nervous. The task before her did seem daunting. However, she had confidence that they could do it.

Although she enjoyed being together and eating Idra's fruit, Ara was relieved when Enetheal arrived. Now the day would truly begin. Quickly, they took turns drinking from the goblet, until it was empty. She stood up, and the others imitated her. Namin got up last, and they followed Enetheal as they had the day before. This time, however, they had enjoyed a night's rest and a morning's meal. And although they followed Enetheal, they kept a safe distance, close enough to follow, but far enough for comfort. Lenya occasionally wandered closer to Enetheal than the rest of the group. Ara noticed this and frowned. It was a relief to be attending to the work of the day, but a vague discomfort began to rise within her.

What was Lenya up to? Ara had awoken in the middle of the night, sure that Lenya had called her name. But she found that she was alone and with the sounds of the island. She wasn't afraid of the dark, but it was certainly more threatening without Lenya. They were in a new place with little understanding of it. Ara had planned to stay up until Lenya came back, but, unbidden, sleep had returned. What was so important that Lenya had chosen to abandon her? Whatever it was, she should not confront Lenya just now. Not in front of everyone. For now they must focus on the task at hand.

Of the seven choices for paths leading from the table, they had made use of two so far: one that led down to the cabins, and another that came up from the beach. Now they were headed down yet a third path, one which lay directly in between the two they had already walked. The slope along this one was steeper than either of the others. Although she was well aware no one would have definite answers, Ara still wanted to discuss what was coming with someone else. Idra was walking with Namin, well behind the others, chattering about birds and squirrels and the other wildlife that had appeared overnight. Orin had run ahead, but kept slipping back into sight so that he could be sure he was going in the right direction. Lenya seemed distant and dreamy, probably because she hadn't slept. But Kuthan walked at the same pace and near enough that she could question him. He seemed to share her thoughtful mood.

"What do you think it's going to be like?" she asked, quietly so that her voice wouldn't carry over to Enetheal.

"I suppose it's going to be somewhat hard, but the only way of knowing is doing."

She waited for more, but Kuthan didn't say anything. Then after a moment, he continued.

"The real question is 'why'?" he said, looking into her eyes.

"Why?" she echoed. Then she gave a proper answer. "Because the rules say we have to."

Kuthan gave her a skeptical look.

"But *why* do they say we have to?" Kuthan asked.

Ara thought about this, her expression concentrated.

"I suppose …," she said slowly. "I suppose that will also become more clear."

Kuthan nodded. "I hope so," he said.

The answer wasn't satisfactory, but it would have to do for now. The ground, which had started as such a steep slope downward, began to level out. To Ara's surprise it looked like the path inclined upwards in front of them. Instead of following the rise, however, they took another path to their right that seemed to take them in the direction of the cabins, at least by Ara's reckoning. It felt as if they were walking along the floor of a ravine. The denseness of the forest had remained uniform throughout their journey, but now that began to change too. Suddenly Orin came running back from around a bend, breathing quickly.

"You're going to like this," he panted.

"What is it?" Idra asked.

"Just you wait," Orin smiled, and didn't say more.

The wait wasn't long. Around the next turn was a spiderweb, larger than any they had yet seen. It spanned the distance between two large pine trees that edged the path.

Ara noticed that at the base of the pines were lanterns, just like the ones that flanked the paths everywhere. The web was silver-white and glistened in the sunlight. It did not look particularly strong, but Ara decided that she would rather keep clear of it for fear of disturbing its guardian. The spider sat motionless, and so did they. The web barred their path, and no one seemed keen to come closer.

Kuthan was the first to push forward. "It's daytime—we can just walk around."

The solution was so obvious that Ara let out a laugh. She had become so used to walking on the paths that it had not occurred to her. The rules specifically designated night as the time when they were confined to the paths. Kuthan had already started walking around the web, a broad grin on his face. Ara followed him. Orin leapt off the path to a rock, to a root, to another rock, and then back onto the other side of the path, clear of the spiderweb.

Namin did not swerve from the path. He went towards the web, humming as he approached.

"Careful," Idra warned.

Namin smiled at Idra reassuringly, and proceeded. As he neared the web, the spider scuttled across it, and onto the tree on the right side of the path. Namin approached the left side of the web, and pinched it gently. Slowly, he peeled it off its connection to the tree, just like the web-screen on the cabin doors.

"Well done," Kuthan said appreciatively. Orin nodded his agreement.

There was a moment in which they exchanged glances from opposite the sides of the path that had been divided by the web. Then Lenya walked across, and Idra pulled Namin along. Last of all came Enetheal, who trailed the group like a shadow. Namin looked back to make sure

Enetheal followed. He did. Enetheal replaced the web, and they continued down the path.

The forest soon ended. Earth became stone, which sloped into a rocky coast and sun-dappled water. Ara stared in awe. The shoreline was strewn with stones: large and small, smooth and rough, flat and bumpy. But it was the variety of colors which surprised her most. In addition to the grey shades she would have expected, there were blue rocks, and orange, red and purple, green and yellow, and all the colors in between. In fact, most of the rocks were variations of grey, but the colored ones stood out. And where the colored rocks had a subdued quality in the sunlight, those bathed in water, glistened, capturing her eyes.

"Beautiful," Kuthan whispered.

Ara turned to Enetheal, who opened his arms outward to the coast. Instantly Orin ran off, scuttling over the rocks as fast as he could without tripping over them.

"Wait for me!" Idra called, clambering across the field of rocks. Lenya moved at a slower pace, leaping from one large rock to the next. Namin went after her. Both Kuthan and Ara held back.

"Is there a way to know which rock to choose?" Ara asked.

The question was directed towards Enetheal. He answered with silence, so Kuthan replied.

"Pick your favorite," he said, and started to walk along the rocks.

At first Ara thought she might join him, but then decided not to. It was her tribute, and she didn't want Kuthan's or anyone else's choice to influence her. The rocks were difficult to walk on. They were uneven, and moved when she stepped on them. She picked up a flat, light-pink rock. It was pretty, but that didn't make it more special than any of the others. She let it drop and continued.

She kept at this for a while. She walked, head downward, until she spied a rock that caught her interest. Sometimes she would hold onto it while she looked for more. She found a round faded green one, and a beautifully deep red one which was smooth to the touch, and finally, a jagged blue rock that had a brilliant dark shade unmatched by any other. Soon she had too many to carry, and she let some go. Choosing between so many wonderful stones was difficult. She spent a lot of time deliberating whether or not to let certain rocks go. Eventually she had to relinquish her original choices in favor of other, more beautiful rocks.

The sun moved across the sky, and still she could not find the right stone. Her back and neck ached from looking down; she was forced to rest. Glancing around, she found a large boulder. Ara placed her contending stones at its base and arched her back against the boulder, letting out a sigh of relief as she allowed her head to turn skywards. She stared at distant filmy clouds traveling slowly across the sky. When the soreness in her neck finally disappeared, she climbed to her feet and looked around. She was surprised to see that the others had drifted so far away. Orin and Idra wandered the shallows apart from one another. She could make out Namin and Lenya even further away, still together. They did not look as if they were searching. Had they found their stones already? Kuthan had found an area where the rocks appeared larger and flatter than any of the stones Ara had noticed.

Ara turned her mind back to her task. The stones she had set aside no longer seemed as beautiful as they had at first. She walked over to the water, and tossed some away into the waves. She cast an angular red rock into the shallows, and quickly followed it with a blue-green egg-shaped rock, and then an orange rock which looked like it had ripples on it. Soon she took the whole remaining handful, and threw them out into the sea. Then she waded into the water, in the opposite direction from where she had tossed her rejected stones. The water was cold, but there was something exhilarating about it. A gust of wind blew her hair around her face so it was hard to see, but she pressed on, adjusting her head so that her hair blew away from her eyes.

Just beneath the wind-tossed water were hundreds of smooth palm-sized stones, their shapes shifting as the sunlight refracted through the rippling water. She was surprised when she lifted a faded red rock and it became even more vivid out of the water. She allowed her gaze to encompass the large expanse of the rocky shores. Again, the wind picked up, and she could hear the trees groaning in protest, the waves splashing even harder. Even as she peered away toward the distant trees, she felt an urge to look back to the water. Then she walked closer, shading her eyes and staring into the shifting shapes just below the surface: she had found her tribute.

It was wreathed by colorful stones that looked vibrant even from above the water. But Ara's was not colorful. It was a deep dark uniform grey. When she picked it up, it seemed heavy for its size, and she needed both hands to lift it. It was just small enough to fit between her two hands while the bases of her wrists were touching. Although the rock was smooth, it wasn't as rounded as most of the other submerged stones. The side that had its face downward in the sand was completely flat and smooth.

A smile spread over her face. She had done it. This was *her* stone. She wandered through the water, and then along the shoreline to where Lenya and Namin were sitting.

Although she was tired, a deep satisfaction filled her. She let out a long sigh that had been trapped inside her throughout her search. Lenya smiled and touched her lightly on the arm.

And then suddenly, without considering, she asked Lenya the question.

"Why did you leave me last night?" she said. The question hung in the air, a little too much like an accusation. Namin played with some stones in his hands, and watched Lenya. A troubled look spread across her face.

"I didn't want to," she answered quietly.

"But you did," Ara persisted. "Why?" Lenya bit her lower lip. Namin looked like he was about to say something, but Lenya spoke.

"I think I did my *service*." She said it slowly, pronouncing the word 'service' carefully. Ara took a moment before she caught on.

"Enetheal came?" she asked quietly, more a statement than a question. Her wounded feelings ebbed away. She should not have questioned Lenya. Of course there had been a good reason. And if they did not follow the conditions they had agreed upon …. Well, they needed to obey the rules.

Yes," Lenya answered. "He got into the cabin without either of us noticing."

"You could have woken me," Ara added, more thoughtfully this time.

"You were fast asleep. We'd had a long day, and it was clear he wanted only me."

Ara nodded. "You're right. I was just scared."

Namin relaxed visibly, and Lenya's disquiet seemed to melt away.

"I was sorry to leave," she assured Ara. Their moment of reconciliation was interrupted by Orin's return. In his hand he clutched a deep red rock with many furrows cut into it. It was not to Ara's taste, but she could tell by the way he held it that Orin loved it. They admired Orin's rock, and then they all shared what they had found. Lenya produced a smooth blue-white stone that was narrow and elongated. Namin pulled out a very thin dark orange stone with some pink specks, that had a slight curve and an indentation. When Ara produced her own, she delighted in their surprise. Hers was the only grey stone, and in her eyes it was the only choice.

"I wasn't really looking when I found it," Orin told them. "I mean, I was aware of the stones everywhere, but I was just wandering the shallows and I saw this one gleaming underneath. When I pulled it out from under the waves, it was even more stunning."

"Mine was more frustrating," Ara admitted. "I kept trying to compare the stones to see which one was best. I didn't realize I would just know when I found it."

"I found mine quick," Lenya said. "I saw it, and knew it."

Namin started to explain his story when Kuthan arrived carrying a massive rock. Like Ara's it was grey, but that is where the similarity ended. Kuthan's stone was a lighter shade of grey. It was flat, circular, and very smooth. The bottom was slightly rounded, but the top looked almost like glass. It had a greyish-white polished sheen.

"Part of a boulder," Kuthan explained. "I hit the boulder with a rock, and this piece fell off."

Kuthan was clearly proud of himself, and they congratulated him. They put all of their stones together, and Ara was pleased to see that none of them stood out over any other. They were each special, each unique.

"We should find Idra," Namin said quietly.

Ara was surprised, not at Namin, but at herself. She had forgotten that Idra was still searching. Namin walked towards the shallows, where Idra was still wandering, and as a group they joined. When they arrived, Idra was near tears.

"I can't find it," she choked out.

"You will," Namin said firmly.

They walked together. Orin walked ahead, searching the ground. Idra glanced around hopelessly.

"You won't find it if you're not looking," Ara added.

Idra nodded, wiping her eyes, and continued to search. Up ahead Orin bent over, and emerged with an oval stone that was light green and well rounded.

"How about this one?" he asked.

Idra took it in her hand, and then shook her head.

"I just don't like rocks," she said miserably.

Orin splashed ahead to resume his search. As he looked about, the group moved closer to where the rocky coast met shrubs. Vine-like plants climbed between the larger rocks that covered the ground, extending to the water's edge. They began to push aside these beach vines in order to see the stones. Soon Orin returned with another rock, a yellow one. Idra just shook her head sadly, and Orin splashed off again.

This time Ara followed him until they were just out of hearing of the rest of the group. She caught his arm so that he was facing her, and whispered, "Idra needs to choose her own rock."

Orin's eyes narrowed. "I was just trying to help," he said yanking his arm from her hand.

He splashed loudly, jogging even further ahead. Ara sighed. She'd have to mollify him later. The rules did not say anything specific about choosing their own stones, but she knew instinctively that this was how things were meant to be. She did notice that he was no longer searching. Soon he rejoined Lenya, Namin, and Kuthan. *At least now he gets it,* she thought to herself.

She was startled from her thoughts by a sudden cheering from the little group now several paces away. She rejoined them, and saw Idra's smile spreading across her entire face.

"I found it," she said happily. The stone was round, small, and light green, much like the first one that Orin had found for her. Ara did not comment. She gave Idra a hug, and Idra giggled.

"I was so worried I wouldn't find it," she said.

"We knew you would," said Namin. He touched Idra's shoulder lightly and she smiled.

"You're just a bit picky," Kuthan grinned. Idra gave Kuthan a slight shove, and laughed when Kuthan barely moved at all.

"We should head back now," Ara said. She hated to be the one to stop the fun, but they had work to do, and by now the sun was already more than halfway across the sky. Fortunately, no one protested, and they returned to where the path met the rocky shore.

"How did you find it?" Ara asked Idra over the sound of their footsteps on the rocks.

"It was between the stems of some plants. I don't know how it got there, but when I saw it, I knew it was mine."

That did seem to be the way it worked. Ara looked down at her own stone. None of the others seemed particularly significant. But something about each stone must have drawn its viewer's eye. At the same time there was an element both of randomness and of careful choice in the selection of the tributes. Each stone fit the chooser. She gripped hers more tightly. Of her companion's rocks, it was Kuthan's that was the most interesting. This was partly because of the way in which he had come by it. As they neared the path, Orin rejoined the group. Ara looked over at him, and he averted his eyes. They would have to sort things out later, she decided.

As they reached the path, Enetheal was waiting right where they had left him, as if he had not moved at all. He stood tall, his legs slightly apart, and his shoulders back. His gaze was upon the water, but he turned to them as they arrived. Without communicating, they formed a half circle around him. One by one they held up their tributes. He stared at each of them. First at Orin's, then Idra's, Namin's, and Lenya's. When Ara showed her stone, Enetheal's eyes met hers. Her heart leapt uncomfortably, and she wondered whether he would judge her stone to be unworthy. But after a pause, he moved on to Kuthan and she let out a breath she didn't realize she had been holding. Kuthan gave a defiant stare when he presented his stone. And just as he had with the others, Enetheal met Kuthan's eyes, before turning away.

Ara was content. She had done well. Each of them had. She could not help but feel closer to Enetheal too. He had waited patiently while they had found their tributes. He had not rushed them, nor had he allowed them to linger. As soon as they presented their stones, Enetheal walked down the path and they all fell into step behind him. His mouthlessness was still offputting, but when she saw the look of approval in his eyes, she felt contentment. Ara stared up at Enetheal, hoping she would be given her own special task soon.

KUTHAN - DAY ONE

He was no closer to figuring out why they needed to choose and decorate stones than he had been before they set off in the morning. He had not asked anyone else. No one else seemed interested. They were content not to confront the issue. As a group they had accepted the island's hospitality in exchange for adherence to the rules, but that did not mean Kuthan would not question what they were doing and why they were doing it.

They walked back along the path, leaving the shore behind them. Everyone was proud of finding their tribute stones. Kuthan had to admit he was proud of himself as well. He had not chosen from the shore of rocks, but instead had taken his task in a new direction. He was pleased with the result. His rock was beautiful in its shape and texture. He had found it in accordance with the rules, but he had accomplished the task his way. And Enetheal had accepted it.

When Enetheal had turned away after he presented his stone, Kuthan felt triumphant. In a way, it felt like Enetheal had conceded. He watched his tall figure now. Silent as ever, Enetheal walked purposefully in front of the group, and they followed closely. The distance between the group and Enetheal was smaller than it had been on the journey to the Stony Shores. They were talking freely around him too. Did they not realize that although he was mouthless, Enetheal had perfect ears? A full day had not yet passed, and already they were growing less wary of Enetheal. Kuthan would not let his own guard down. Not until he knew what was going on. What was Enetheal? Clearly he had a knowledge which they did not possess and seemed intent on making sure the rules were followed.

Well, Kuthan was going to carry them out, but on his own terms, and only so long as they seemed necessary to protect the others. They stopped at the web-draped trees once more, carefully displaced the web, and then replaced it. *The webs have significance,* he thought. But again he could not think of what that might be. Time. It would all be apparent in time. He had to focus on the present task. They took a new path, and Kuthan tried to fix it in his memory. At some point he planned to be able to wander apart from Enetheal's watchful gaze.

They walked to where the dirt path crossed the stone way. To his surprise they turned and followed the stone way. *Where does this one lead?* he asked himself. As if Idra had heard his thoughts, she walked to his side and answered him.

"I think we're heading to the tree where I picked the fruit," she said excitedly.

It appeared that she was right: Around the next bend was a clearing with a large tree. Once again, it stood out from the others in that it was not a pine tree. The bark was smooth and varied in shades of brown, from a nearly black-brown to a tawny color. The variation in hue alone set it apart from the nearby pines as a fruit-bearing tree. Large branches spread out from its base, extending horizontally, and additional branches were spaced evenly, nearly to the top. At the ends of the branches were pink and white flowers in bloom.

Namin let out a slow breath, and Idra giggled shyly. Lenya gazed with her mouth slightly open. Kuthan stared up into the branches.

"You must be like one of those squirrels you like so much if you climbed this," Kuthan laughed, his face reflecting unguarded admiration for her accomplishment.

Idra grinned but did not respond. Kuthan's happieness quickly vanished as Enetheal walked between Kuthan and Idra. Once more Kuthan's expression became unreadable. He kicked himself mentally. He couldn't let his guard down, not with Enetheal watching.

"This isn't the one I climbed," Idra commented. "But you'll like that one too."

"I'm sure I will," said Kuthan, attempting, on the surface at least, to recover his good humor. Enetheal went to the far side of the clearing, and continued along the stone way. Many pines later, they arrived at another clearing. The great tree here also had low growing branches. It was grey in color, but looked healthy. The leaves were bright green, and clinging to the branches was fruit just like what they had eaten that morning.

"Is this it?" Orin directed the question to Idra who nodded. Orin rushed forward to the base of the tree. Looking upward, he started to pull himself onto the first branch.

"Orin." Namin said his name quietly, but at his voice, Orin turned his head. "I think this is Idra's task." Orin nodded in understanding, and then frowned. He dismounted from the branch.

"Does that mean I can't climb trees?" he asked, incredulous and a little annoyed.

Kuthan answered. "At least for now." He hated to agree, but Namin was right. The fruit-gathering did seem to be Idra's task, and they should be careful while they figured it all out, especially in front of Enetheal. He did feel some satisfaction at Orin's defiance, though. *Orin should be able to climb trees.*

Enetheal started along the path again and they began to follow, but Lenya stopped. "Enetheal?" she said. Enetheal turned quickly, as if he had been startled. Then he relaxed. "I'm pretty hungry, do you mind if we stop for food?" Enetheal nodded.

"Mind fetching us more fruit, Idra?" Lenya asked. "I'm starving." Idra glanced at Enetheal for his assent, and Enetheal nodded once more. Idra quickly turned away and jogged toward the base of the tree. She was an impressive climber. The first few branches made it look like she wasn't even climbing. Her task became noticeably more difficult when instead of reaching for branches, Idra leapt for them and then pulled herself up. Kuthan noticed that she skipped over many fruits which to him seemed plenty good for eating. Soon she was obscured by branches and leaves.

Then, moments later, she appeared near the outermost point of one of the mid-level branches with a fruit clutched in her hand.

"Lenya!" she called. Lenya looked up, and Idra tossed her a large orange fruit. Lenya caught it, and immediately sank her teeth in.

"It's wonderful Idra!" Lenya called. Kuthan watched her devour the fruit and realized that he, too, was famished.

"Idra!" he shouted. "Mind finding one for me?"

The others chorused their wishes for food as well. One by one, Idra tossed down the melon-like fruits to each of them. Kuthan relished the flavor. He hadn't realized how hungry he was until he bit into the fruit. When Idra descended, they set off once more, their pace faster now after the refreshment. They left the stone way, and proceeded on a winding dirt path. No other paths seemed to cross this one, and as they walked, the little trail became more uneven. Now more tree roots grew across the trail, and they had to keep their eyes focused downward to avoid tripping. Branches of close-growing underbrush grazed their arms.

They halted as the path opened up into a vast pine grove, the canopy so dense that there were no plants or saplings on the forest floor. It was only after Enetheal stopped that Kuthan realized that this pine grove was different. Not only did the many branches above obscure the sunlight, but the needles were a deeper shade of green, the bark of the trees redder, the trunks bigger, and the roots thicker. Most curious of all were the streams of sap. Each of the pines had sap flowing in rivulets down its heavy trunk. The sap was translucent, and yet it seemed to shimmer slightly with a light that did not belong to the sun. The source of the clear liquid was obscured by overlapping branches. Encircling the base of each tree was a glistening pool of sap. And there was something else menacing about this place, something he could not understand.

"The birds have stopped singing," Idra said. She said it quietly, unwilling to disturb the stillness that enveloped the grove.

The moment she said it, Kuthan recognized the unnatural silence. Even the wind did not seem to touch this place, and the waves were so distant that they could only be heard if you actively listened for them. Kuthan thought about this. Was this why he felt uneasy, why his muscles were tense? Why he was breathing faster? The others did not appear to be disquieted. Lenya sat down at the foot of a tree just outside a pool of sap, and Idra and Namin joined her. Orin had already started to explore. Kuthan exchanged a look with Ara, before walking over to Enetheal. Just as he had at the Stony Shores, Enetheal only stood and watched.

"What do we do here?" Kuthan asked Enetheal pointedly. Enetheal stared back at him, his grey eyes unfathomable. Kuthan waited, but when it became clear that Enetheal was not going to communicate, he turned away. What was Enetheal doing? When they had agreed to the rules of the table, it had been plain that he was to be their guide. *Some guide!* Kuthan left Enetheal standing there. He left Ara, who stood, her expression puzzled. And he left Lenya, Idra, and Namin, who had gathered in a little half-circle beside a sap pool, talking amiably. Orin had the right idea: exploration.

The voices of his companions faded as he wove between the trees heading carefully in a single direction. Soon the tones of their voices were as dead as all other sounds in the grove. He knew that the sun still shone above the trees by the dappled rays that found their way through the canopy reflecting off occasional scattered twigs and pine needles. Sap flowed slowly and silently from every tree. He could hear his own footsteps softly padding against the forest floor. He looked around, noticing how the forest appeared to be identical in every direction. It would be easy to become disoriented in here. However he knew very well where the others sat in their little crescent by the pool. He passed tree after tree, each with sap trickling slowly down its length. *What am I looking for?* Kuthan asked himself. No answer came to him and he wandered on. The grove did not seem to have a center. He passed more trees; none had any distinguishing features. In the silence, even his thoughts started to seem loud.

The best way to figure out what was going on was to finish working on their tribute stones, he decided. Perhaps that was the reason Enetheal had brought them here. But what specifically did they have to do? He looked around at the sap flowing. It moved so slowly, as if it had all the time in the world, or perhaps was out of the realm of time altogether. *Too many questions*, he thought, *not enough answers*. Why weren't the others searching for the answers? *Because that's my task*, he thought grimly. It may not be the service set for him, but it was the task he was going to set for himself. Having come to a conclusion, he turned back to where the others would be waiting. Suddenly, he heard a single drip behind him. In the silence that surrounded him, it might as well have been thunder. Kuthan whirled around towards its source.

The tree was slightly off the neat line he had wandered, but he would not lose his sense of direction. He walked over to it. The pool still rippled almost imperceptibly from the single drop of sap. He looked into it, and saw his reflection returning his gaze. He glanced upward, to where the drip must have come from and saw a tiny shard of sky, softened to an indigo-grey, as if their traveling into the Sapwood had softened its brilliance. He looked back down to the pool of sap, where the slow ripples still flowed. Just as the sap's surface returned to its usual motionless calm, a distinct flicker of movement shimmered across the pool. His heart caught in his chest, and he looked around to see what could have caused a reflection in the sap. Perhaps a gust of wind?

He didn't think so. He sat down at the edge of the pool and stared until his heart slowed. It was time to return.

When he got back, the others were waiting. His vexation had melted away, and he smiled genuinely when Ara ran up to him.

"I figured it out," she told him eagerly. I just had to think about the rules.

"What did the rules say about this?" Kuthan asked curiously. He tried to think but he was absolutely sure that the rules said nothing about a section of forest with pools of sap.

"We are supposed to decorate the stones, and we can use the sap," Ara said happily.

Kuthan thought a moment, and then asked, "Do we have to?"

Ara frowned, and Lenya was the one who answered.

"I say 'no'. Not unless it needs it. Mine doesn't."

"How do you know?" Idra asked, holding her stone tightly. She looked at Lenya, who just shrugged dreamily.

Namin turned from where he had been staring into a pool to answer.

"I think each stone is ours to design and prepare before sunset in our own way." He said it quietly, but distinctly.

"But they should be the best they can be," Ara added helpfully.

Namin dipped his dark orange stone into the nearby pool of sap. It seemed it was meant for the job. When he pulled out his stone, the indent was full of sap. Idra ran over, and dipped hers, followed by both Ara and Orin. Lenya and Kuthan held back. Kuthan knew that his stone was perfect the way it was, and there wasn't anything he was going to do to change it. When they were finished at the Sapwood, they walked over to Enetheal, just as they had after the Stony Shores. They had not spent nearly as long here as they had there, but the sun was clearly descending. Ara looked up anxiously, and Kuthan noted the urgency of approaching sunset.

Their moment of departure from the Sapwood was more sudden than their entry. Birdsong filled the air, the wind blew, large pieces of blue sky peeked through branches, and waves crashed against the rocks in the distance; they felt free. Enetheal led them purposefully, and at a much faster pace than when they had entered the Sapwood. If he was so worried about running out of time, why had he allowed them to spend so long collecting stones, and wandering the Sapwood? *Another question for later*, he thought. That seemed to be the way of his questions now. Again the journey on the path seemed long, and he felt the sun sinking in the sky. Perhaps it only felt long because no one was talking. It seemed as if they had taken some of the silence of the Sapwood with them. Lenya and Ara walked side by side, not saying a word. Idra and Orin formed another silent pair. Orin did not run ahead as he had been all day. Namin walked behind them, holding his stone carefully, keeping the sap from slipping from its place in the hollow of his stone. Kuthan was about to break the silence, when he realized from the thinning of the trees that they were approaching the edge of the forest. They continued over rocky ground with its scattered shrubbery, and then, finally, they saw the earth sloping down towards the water. In front of them blazed the setting sun.

Even Enetheal squinted his eyes as golden rays shone directly into his face. Their vision blurred by the glowing ball near the horizon, they picked their way cautiously down the path towards the water's edge. Where the water met the land there was a boulder. It was only when Enetheal drew him closer that Kuthan realized that this boulder was unlike the many great boulders scattered over the island. There was a flat surface which caught the light of the setting sun. Upon the surface, words were carved much like those on the Welcome Table. The message here was different.

As the sun sets you must lay
your tribute here in view of sun
This shall mark the end of day
and for this day your labor's done

Just as at the stone table, the words of this new message sounded in their minds. Kuthan considered the message. It seemed straightforward. He glanced at the horizon, where the sun almost touched. He saw now why Enetheal had not lingered along the way once they had left the Sapwood. Initially he had been sure Enetheal would stop at other places so that they could learn other techniques to decorate the stones. Now he realized that, for today at least, sap alone would embellish their tributes. Kuthan walked forward, and placed his large flat rock upon the boulder. As he relinquished it, he felt the loss like a tiny pang of emptiness. He had labored to acquire it and had carried it with him all day. Now he must let it go. He stepped back, allowing Ara to place her stone on top of his. Idra, Lenya, and Orin followed. Each of them placed their rocks on top of his, so that they were evenly spaced. He smiled. When Namin put his rock down he was very careful to avoid spilling the sap sheltered in its little hollow. His, too, now lay on top of Kuthan's.

They stared at the stones. They stared at the sun approaching the horizon. It's light formed a shimmering golden path across the water, extending to the stones and the children. The stones were suddenly radiant, almost like they had a light of their own, as the fading sunlight touched them. Soon the sunlight shifted and their tributes became as they had been before, bright, but not radiant. Similarly, the early evening still glowed, but the sun was gone.

Kuthan was still staring at where the sun had gleamed only moments before when he felt a hand on his shoulder. A chill went through him and he felt his heart clench. Without looking, he knew that the hand on his shoulder belonged to Enetheal. How could he have lulled himself into believing that this day was just finishing? He realized that he had been both dreading and looking forward to this moment.

He shrugged off the hand and looked at Enetheal's eyes, giving him a curt nod. It took a moment for the others to understand. When they did, there were sharp intakes of breath, but apart from that, they just watched. Enetheal walked over to the stones, each of them balanced on top of Kuthan's. Kuthan walked over, too. Enetheal guided his hands so that they were at either side of his rock. Kuthan understood, and he lifted it up. It was much heavier with all the other rocks. At the base of the boulder was yet another flat stone. Enetheal lifted it up onto the boulder, and helped Kuthan transfer all the tributes onto this new stone salver. *As if mine was not good enough to hold the others.* When he looked up, he saw that Enetheal had already taken the first few steps, so he followed. The others rose to follow Enetheal too, but he held up a hand to stop them.

"We'll wait for you," Ara said.

"Be well," Namin added.

Idra looked at Enetheal's face, and shuddered. Orin waved.

Enetheal walked along to where the rock sloped into the water. Kuthan followed, balancing the the tributes carefully in front of him.

Just when they were almost out of sight, Lenya called after him, "Have fun."

At this Kuthan laughed aloud, although no one heard it but Enetheal. The laugh was more a release of nerves at the absurdity of the statement. "Have fun?" He was alone with Enetheal. He had no idea what he was doing, why he was doing it, or what Enetheal's intentions were, and he was supposed to "have fun?" His mirthless laugh died suddenly when Enetheal glanced back. Kuthan instantly got hold of himself. *Control*, he thought. He would complete his service, just as Idra had; and when he did, he would learn something new, something that would help make sense of how things worked here. Composure returned. And they walked.

Their journey took them through the shallows, because the brush on the land grew too thick and close to the water's edge for easy passage. To Kuthan the watery path seemed even more treacherous. The rocks were slippery, and there were times when he needed to crouch in order to avoid slipping on them. He made no complaint though. Instead he focused on balancing the stones. *I have to make sure the sap doesn't spill out of Namin's!* The thought was alarming and he checked to be sure that he hadn't lost any sap already. He hadn't, but still he proceeded even more carefully. He didn't know why he found this so important all of a sudden. It made no sense. He withheld a snort. Nothing made sense yet, but it would soon. He knew it would.

After a distance the shore was walkable again, and they left the slippery shallows. The rock surfaces sloped upward so that they were forced to walk at an angle. For Enetheal this seemed easy, but for Kuthan, it proved to be just as much a struggle as the slippery rocks had been. Balancing the stones was difficult, but he needed to keep up with Enetheal as well. Where was Enetheal's patience now? They walked a ways further, until finally Enetheal altered their course, moving away from the sloped rock face onto flatter land. Now another path appeared.

Kuthan took care to hold the stones steady as he clambered up after Enetheal. He was getting the hang of it; his hands were perfectly steady, and he took one slow step at a time. Just as he reached the top, however, his foot caught on the one of the lanterns that lined the path. He fell hard onto his knees, but had just enough time to angle the stones so that they didn't tumble off of the salver. They shifted, Orin's coming very close to falling off. Kuthan had been sweating before; now it dripped off his brow. He rose to his feet slowly, his heart beating quickly. Enetheal eyed him with his usual indifferent expression.

"What are you looking at?" Kuthan asked angrily. Enetheal continued to stare. "They're fine, I'm fine, let's go!" Enetheal turned and plodded on. The path hugged the coast. As they walked along it Kuthan became very aware of the gentle lapping of the waves. How could they be so calm? Kuthan's stomach gave an unpleasant twist. *Just focus on the stones and walking,* he thought, and so he did. The path sloped up, curved, and straightened. Then, without warning, they reached their destination.

Even without Enetheal leading him, Kuthan would have known that this was the place. The path curved out to where the land met the water. Before them the water extended to the horizon, but that was not where they were going. Jutting out from the rocky coast was a most unusual rock formation. It was night-black and it glistened in the twilight. The smooth surface shimmered with the reflection of shifting water. At the rock's surface was a dark aperture, clearly the entrance to a cave.

The path led directly to the water's edge, and then continued into the water as a submerged flat outcrop. Even along the path's submerged portion, lanterns rose on either side, always in pairs. Water flowed gently around their ankles as they waded. Now that they were out in the open, Enetheal walked by Kuthan's side. Despite his distrust of Enetheal, Kuthan was grateful for his presence.

Side by side they waded ankle-deep through the shallow water. They were still abreast of each other when they reached slippery rough hewn stairs that led up through the shallows to the cave entrance. Again Kuthan felt compelled to look at Enetheal for assurance that he was doing the right thing. Enetheal nodded, and Kuthan entered the cave, Enetheal close behind. The cave, at least, was dry. They traveled in single file now because of the narrow width of the passage. The light diminished immediately upon their entry. Kuthan could see just well enough to make out the chiseled stone steps leading downward into darkness. He looked at Enetheal one last time. Enetheal pointed down the steps. Kuthan did not look back again. He took a long slow breath, and started his descent into blackness.

He had thought that balancing the stones would be easy after walking over the slippery rocks, but once the darkness blanketed his eyes the task became almost impossible. Were the stones still there? He could not see them; he could only feel the salver in his hands, which he could only hope was still supporting the other tributes. He held his hands as steady as he could. Dark pressed in upon him from every side. He could crash into a wall at any moment, or he might reach a ledge and then step off into nothingness. Without his eyes he tried to focus on hearing. Were the footsteps behind him Enetheal's? Or just echoes? His stomach tightened. What if the stairs just went on forever? The idea was frightening. But maybe this would be better than facing whatever was in the darkness below. He tried not to imagine what would be down there. *Were there more mouthless people?* Footstep after footstep echoed in the darkness, and still they descended. Down, down, and even further down. *Each step I am closer to the answer,* he thought, trying to reassure himself. Then he would take another step. Sometimes he was slow, sometimes he stepped faster. Finally he found a rhythm. He closed his eyes; he saw the same thing with them closed as when they were open anyway. And oddly, this comforted him. After an eternity, his descent came to an abrupt halt.

Kuthan put his foot down, searching for another stair, and he hit stone level with his other foot. Immediately he froze. Then he opened his eyes. He could see now. They were in a large cave. From the stair extended a stone path which cut through the center of the cave. On either side of the path was water. Unlike the water above, this water was still. Hanging from the roof of the cave were large stalactites, and coming up from under the water were stalagmites. Kuthan wondered which stalagmites were real, and which were only reflections. The light that illuminated the cave was white, and constantly flickering. It seemed to come from beneath the water, but Kuthan was not sure. *How could such things come to be?* He thought of the strange stone structures before him, of the entrance far above, the eerie light, the world, and themselves. Here. Deep down. Below water and earth.

Enetheal's light touch from behind reminded Kuthan why he was here. Kuthan proceeded forward. Now that he had his sight again, he moved with confidence. He walked purposefully along the path and stopped when he came to a table. This table was short and had a flat top. No letters were visible upon its surface, and he heard no voice, inside or outside his head. Still, Kuthan knew that this was the end of his journey. He carefully put the salver onto the table, the tribute stones still balanced upon it. This time he did not feel regret in letting it go. It was time to part with it. When he turned away from it, he suddenly felt faint. His knees shook, and he broke into a sweat. Utter exhaustion swept through him. For a moment the edges of his vision grew dark. He reached back and leaned against the table, and then to his relief, the white flickering returned. Step by step he walked toward the stair where Enetheal waited.

The stairs again seemed foreboding. Kuthan wasn't eager to leave the light of the cavern for the darkness of the stair. He started to glance back, but Enetheal took his hand and pulled him onto the first step. Kuthan didn't argue. He felt numb inside. *One more step* he thought, and he took another step, and then another. As the flickering light disappeared, he closed his eyes once again, heightening his other senses. He thought he heard a single drip somewhere behind him in the watery cavern. Step by step he climbed upwards. What had he been thinking on his journey down? His mind was blank now. He was struggling to make sense even of the footsteps. Whose were whose? His thoughts returned to the dark. It wasn't just blackness, it was nothingness. And then it wasn't. Enetheal's shape took form, then the last few ascending stairs, the sloping passage-way, and finally, he and Enetheal emerged back into the strong light of the dying day.

ORIN - DAY ONE

He had tried to follow them. He had given them a head start so they would think they were alone, but Ara hadn't given him a head start. Orin scowled. Ara just had to do it, didn't she? He had almost forgotten that Ara had stopped him from helping Idra earlier that day. But that memory had come rushing back when she stopped him now yet again. Why? The answer didn't matter. Only that she had stopped him. Orin hurled a stone angrily into the water. It made a loud splash. Maybe Ara had been right, but that bugged him all the more. No one else had taken sides. Namin, Lenya, and Idra had watched the confrontation impartially. Orin searched around for another rock, a bigger one. This one made a more satisfying splash. And now Ara was talking with Lenya and Namin as if nothing had happened. Orin was about to find another rock when a small flat stone skipped upon the water's surface.

"Hey Orin." It was Idra. She sounded friendly, but Orin didn't want her company right now.

"Go away, Idra," he said irritably.

"You don't want me to go, and I don't want me to go," said Idra. "I think I should stay."

She tossed another stone, and Orin watched it skip off the water's surface. Curiosity took over, and anger abated.

"How did you learn to do that?" Orin asked.

"I couldn't find my rock today, and I was angry at the rocks, so I started throwing them. The flat ones bounced. It didn't help me find it, but I forgot to be angry for a bit."

Idra picked up a small flat rock and handed it to Orin.

Idra continued: "Then I saw everyone else was done and I really panicked. That's when you guys found me."

She tossed a stone, sweeping her arm through the air, and flicking her wrist at the end. It made two quick hops, jumped a third time, and then sank beneath the water. Orin imitated her motion. His stone bounced once before sinking into the water. Idra was already ready with more flat stones.

They skipped more stones in silence. Occasionally they would give an "ahhh" of appreciation for a particularly well skipped stone, or laugh when the waves ate up a stone that didn't even hop once. They stood there skipping stones for what seemed like a long time, but it was still twilight when Kuthan and Enetheal returned.

Namin walked over to where they stood. "They're back," he said, his relief evident.

Idra immediately jogged towards the group. For the first time that day, Orin would have been glad to stay put a bit longer, but even more, he wanted to be with Idra. He caught up to her before she reached them.

"Hey Idra," he said quietly. "Thanks."

Idra beamed, and nodded.

When they returned Lenya and Ara were gathered around Kuthan. Enetheal stood near the path that led into the forest. Is that the path they had used to return to their group? Why did they return by a different route from the one they had taken to leave? Orin lost his question at the sound of Kuthan's voice.

"Not what I expected," Kuthan said to Ara, probably in answer to a question she had asked before Namin, Idra, and Orin had met them. It wasn't what he said, but how he said it that surprised Orin. Kuthan spoke slowly, as if he were unsure of his words. Orin thought that he looked pale.

"Still," Kuthan added, "I think I might be learning how things work."

"That's good," Ara said. She sounded encouraging but also worried. Kuthan didn't seem to notice.

"We should probably head back to the cabins," Namin said.

"Sounds good," Lenya agreed.

Namin led, and Lenya and Kuthan took up the rear. Orin started to follow, eager to be part of the group and lead the way. Just as they reached the forest, Enetheal held out his hand. Orin froze. Of course Enetheal would have to lead. They had to follow *his* path because of *his* rules. Still, that didn't seem to be Enetheal's intent right now. Orin became acutely aware of his own breathing. The others continued, unaware that Orin and Enetheal had fallen behind. Orin just managed to find his voice before the group went around the next bend.

"I think ...." He paused, and found his voice again. "I think I'm going to stay behind for a bit," he found himself saying.

Kuthan, who had seemed unsure of himself only moments before, snapped back to his usual self. He gave Enetheal a spiteful look.

"After everything we've been through you want to take him *now*?" he asked.

Enetheal nodded. Orin stood by his side.

"Everything is fine," he heard himself say, this time with more confidence. He realized he didn't want to go back to the cabins. What would they do? Sit around till the sun rose?

Kuthan didn't argue further. He turned to take lead of the others.

Lenya waved.

"We'll see each other soon," Namin said encouragingly.

"Good luck," Idra and Ara spoke almost in unison.

Orin realized that he was pleased that Ara had joined Idra in wishing him luck. The goodbye was quick, and he was thankful. They had to catch up to Kuthan, and Orin had to complete his task. He looked up into Enetheal's mouthless face and suddenly his confidence faded. He mustn't let that show.

"Where to?" Orin asked.

Enetheal led the way. Surprisingly, the path they took seemed to turn in the direction of the cabins, at least by Orin's reckoning. He was fairly confident. Since they had arrived, Orin had been putting together the island in his mind. He hadn't figured out why some paths were stone, but he did know that all the dirt paths seemed to lead from one destination to another. Each of the cabins were connected by dirt paths, as were the paths to the Stony Shores, to the Sapwood, and to the rocky outcrop he had visited that morning. This path, no doubt, led to another destination. Still, Orin wondered what was off the paths.

He wasn't sure how he felt traveling with Enetheal. When they had traveled before, Orin was either far ahead of the group exploring, or interacting with them. Enetheal had been silent, so Orin had not given him much thought. Now that the others were gone, he noticed Enetheal. Enetheal towered over Orin, his expression inert, impassive. And now Orin could not simply slip away. On the up-side, he thought, they did travel faster as a pair. Orin surged forward along the new path, and Enetheal matched his pace. He wondered what lay at the end of it, and wished that someone real could share his anticipation. As they traveled, the sky truly began to darken. The glowing clouds from the setting sun had dimmed into indigo shapes in a quickly fading pale sky. Soon Enetheal slowed their pace. Before this they had been jogging, but now they moved with a brisk walk. Orin wanted to say something, but a glance at Enetheal assured him that he should contain his frustration. They still progressed, but the pace was intolerably slow. And then, just when Orin could not contain his impatience any longer, they were there.

The only way he knew they had reached their destination was that Enetheal had stopped, and held out his arm to stop Orin. In front of them was a grassy clearing surrounded by pines. The little raised field was a pale green-yellow. The grass came to Orin's waist, although it reached only just above Enetheal's knees. A light breeze moved a patch of grass, bending it slightly so that in the fading golden light it appeared as if a shadow crossed the field. Even in the fading light Orin could see a lot more clearly in this meadow than he could in forest. He caught a glimpse of a tiny brightness, a golden twinkle in the midst of the field.

At first he thought he was imagining it, but then there was a second, and then a third flashing light, within moments of each other.

"Enetheal?" Orin asked.

A shiver of excitement ran through him. He wasn't sure whether it was joy or fear, but he loved the surge of energy. Orin watched the field, transfixed. When he turned, he saw that Enetheal had a lantern. A lantern just like the ones that lined the paths. Enetheal held it out, and Orin took it.

"What's this?" Orin asked.

Enetheal gestured, first toward one of the flashes of light, and then to the lantern in Orin's hand. And Orin knew what to do. Grinning from ear to ear, he ran into the grass. As he kicked up the grass, a cloud of the flashing lights rose around him. Laughing, he cupped his hand around one, and put it into the lantern through a hole in the base. As soon as he began to consider that his little prisoner might escape, he saw a small hinged disc beside the opening and closed it neatly over the circular exit. He turned the lantern over and peered in.

Flittering around the interior was a tiny winged beetle. As it moved within the lantern, its tail occasionally filled with yellow light, like a pulsing glow. He watched, fascinated, until another flash outside the lantern caught his attention. He forgot the trapped firefly, and pursued the next one, and then another, and then another. Soon Enetheal came with several more lanterns. Orin barely noticed. These little glowing creatures were amazing. He loved chasing after a single little insect as it zigzagged through the field, but he also enjoyed kicking a clump of grass and ensnaring a whole swarm. The interludes it took to transfer the flickering insects into lanterns vexed him because it broke his rhythm, but these transfers became quick, and he immediately returned to the chase.

Once he caught five fireflies in one swoop. Even Enetheal seemed impressed, and nodded his approval. After many more relays between Enetheal with his lanterns and the twinkling grassy field, Orin collapsed, out of breath and sweaty. Only then did he become aware of the now blackened world above him. The sky had been steadily darkening as he had chased and captured fireflies, but before this he had only noticed that the flashes of light were gradually becoming brighter. After he caught his breath, he turned to Enetheal, and then just beyond him. There at the periphery of the field was a small crescent of lanterns. Each lantern was continually illuminated by many captured living lights. Orin rose to his feet. Enetheal turned to the flickering half-circle of lanterns and filled his arms with them. He looked to Orin, who did the same, taking the remaining lights. Then he turned toward their new trail. Orin did not complain that the lanterns were heavy, or that they were so bright and close to his face that he could barely make out the path at his feet.

This time they journeyed across the Firefly Field and out the opposite side. As they approached the forest, Orin could scarcely make out silhouettes of the trees. When they entered, their surroundings became even darker, and their own lanterns brighter. Enetheal stopped, and knelt by the path's edge. Orin shifted his armful of lanterns and saw the unlit pair at the path's edge. He placed his glowing burden on the ground beside one of the empty lanterns, which he examined. He gently lifted the vacant lamp from its short pole, and briefly examined the rod, noticing how it narrowed to its base. He looked back at his own lanterns with their firefly entry holes, grinned, and placed a brightly shining lantern onto the waiting holder.

Enetheal moved to intervene. As Orin watched, he gently lifted the lantern from its stalk, tilted it upward and removed a single fly. Then he transferred the pulsing beetle into the unlit lantern, and placed it back on its pole. When it came to repeating this procedure on the other side of the path, it now became Orin's turn to transfer the little insect. One lantern, one firefly: he understood. After they finished the first few pairs, Orin looked behind them to admire his work. The lanterns seemed so frail in the darkness. Those they had left behind flashed only occasionally, rather than with the constant glow made by lanterns with many flies. With these rare flashes, the light was weak, hardly penetrating the forest that loomed around them. They walked quickly along the path, arriving at a new lantern pair just as the last almost disappeared in the blackness behind them. It became easy: Orin removed two fireflies from one of his several lanterns which were still teeming with the little insects, and placed one in each of the empty orbs. Each lantern now held exactly one fly.

The further they traveled into the forest, the darker it seemed. The trees were thick, and branches often obscured the sky. Orin wondered how they could possibly see without the lanterns. Around them crickets chirped, and an occasional owl hooted. Sounds of other animals occasionally mingled in and Orin tried to identify them, but their footfalls obscured the sounds of the night forest. Gradually, as they transferred firefly after firefly into the pairs of waiting lanterns, their own lanterns dimmed. Orin hoped they would not have to make a second journey back to the Firefly Field. He knew not to complain, but he was exhausted and his arms ached.

They emerged from the woods outside Orin's and Namin's cabin. This was so unexpected that for a moment Orin was disoriented. He blinked, understood, and then smiled. Then he sighed happily and turned to Enetheal to say goodbye. But Enetheal gestured to where the side of the path continued, to a pair of unlit lanterns. Orin's stomach sank. He wasn't done, that much was clear. The lanterns in his arms suddenly became even heavier. Although they were now noticeably dimmer, the lanterns they cradled still held many flickering little insects. If each fly had its own lantern, the night was going to be very long. Dispirited, Orin finished the pair near their cabin, and trudged on.

The most upsetting thing about believing he had finished was that the path they were lighting was familiar. As they walked, Orin refocused on his task. He actually enjoyed placing flies in the empty lanterns. However, this path was known. There were so many paths that he hadn't explored—why couldn't they be placing lanterns along one of those? On the other hand, knowing the path did make the time pass more quickly. They moved from his own and Namin's cabin along the cabin-path, lighting the way to Kuthan and Idra's cabin, and then finally, the way to Ara and Lenya's. It felt odd to be working just outside cabins when he knew his friends were probably inside. He kept wondering if they might hear or see him and come out. But they did not come out. After he finished lighting the cabin path, he and Enetheal turned towards the slope and the Welcome Table.

When they arrived at the stone way that curved around the base of the slope, they followed it. They seemed to be moving faster now, and Orin was pleased. He had learned quickly. They would stop, pick up a lantern, transfer a firefly, and replace the lantern on the path-side. They moved along the stone ways, filling lanterns, switching from one path to another. Now their course moved them towards the beach they had landed on. *The Sandy Shores*. He liked naming the parts of the island. *Sandy Shores, Stony Shores, Stone Way, Dirt Path, Sapwood, Firefly Field.* He had yet to see where

Enetheal had taken Kuthan, and had not explored the rocks he had seen in the morning. Was it the wind that made that eerie moaning sound? What to name them? *Wailing Rocks?* he mused. *Shrieking Stones?*

Orin hadn't noticed their diminished supply of flies until the lanterns in their arms started pulsing intermittently instead of sending out a constant glow. He glanced at Enetheal uneasily, but Enetheal appeared unworried. Orin had almost forgotten Enetheal's presence: he had been so busy transferring the flies, and Enetheal, as always, had been silent. Now he was reassured by his companion's apparent lack of concern. They proceeded with their work, but they did not need to continue for long. They arrived at the beach, and with the beach, the last two empty lanterns. Orin smiled. He exchanged two of his dimly flashing lanterns with the empty ones, and looked up to Enetheal, pleased.

Enetheal stared at Orin. Had he done something wrong? He looked back at the last two lanterns. They looked good. Once again Orin looked at Enetheal, and back at the lanterns. This time he did notice something. Each contained several of the flickering little insects. Orin withdrew all but one firefly from each orb. Hands cupped gently around these remaining flies, he walked out onto the beach, and released them. They flitted around, continuing to emit an occasional flash. A small gust of wind swept in from the open water, and suddenly the flies were gone. The breeze was pleasant, even energizing, but Orin was exhausted. He turned back to the path.

This time there was no question. He was done.

They traveled from the beach path to the stone way to the cabin path. The effect of the lanterns was very different now that they were lit in front of them. The path was lighted, but the sporadic glowing had a strange effect on their view of the trail ahead. Parts appeared dark, only to brighten suddenly. In one such illumination, a large spider materialized and scuttled away from the new light. Sometimes the reverse happened, and a well-lit path would plunge into momentary darkness. Despite the intermittent light on the path, it was much easier to see now. Orin stared into the darkness of the wood. The absolute darkness brought forth by the night and the tree's obstruction of the sky would make nighttime passage impossible if it were not for the lanterns. *What could I see if there were lanterns off the path?* Tomorrow he would explore. For sure.

The walk back to his cabin went quickly. It was well lit, and well known. Soon his door was visible, as was the spiderweb screen that covered it. Orin carefully pulled back the spiderweb, opened the door, and replaced the web. He waved at Enetheal. Enetheal paused for a moment and then returned the wave before retreating along the path. Orin closed the door.

Namin sat on his bed watching him.

"I'm glad you're back," Namin said, his relief evident. Orin smiled.

"Missed you too." He walked over to his bed. On the bed was one of the golden fruits.

"From Idra," Namin said quietly.

"Thanks, Idra." He found himself saying it even though she wasn't there to hear. He ate the fruit slowly, savoring the flavor. Instead of waking him up as it had before, the fruit left him in sleepy contentedness. He lay down on the mattress. It was soft. Beautifully and utterly soft. He allowed the mattress to absorb him, letting out a long breath. Namin echoed his sigh. Orin was just starting to drift off when Namin spoke.

"I saw the lanterns," he said. "They're beautiful."

"Yeah," Orin answered. He did not know what else to say. He agreed. He loved the lanterns.

"Thanks for lighting them, Ore." Orin barely understood. He was well on his way to sleep.

"It was fun," Orin managed, slurring his speech a little. "How were things here?"

"Good," Namin answered. "We just talked. I'll catch you up in the morning."

"Yeah," Orin breathed out gratefully. He pulled up the blankets, and drowsiness enveloped him. Far away he made out waves, wind, and a tune that Namin hummed. He felt the darkness. A gentle darkness in the room and beneath his eyelids. Yet as he drifted into sleep, he could still see the twinkling of firefly lanterns. Namin's lullaby continued, but Orin focused on the lights. Now he could see the lanterns as well as the lights. They hovered around, forming a path before him in the darkness. Orin followed them.

NAMIN - DAY ONE

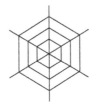

The tune wasn't happy or sad. It was the song of the present, deriving life as much from Namin as from the waves, wind, night, and Orin's breathing. Namin knew when Orin had drifted off. His breathing had changed, just slightly, but enough so that Namin knew. His tune quieted, and his thoughts became words in his mind.

Kuthan had been both upset and pleased when Enetheal had taken Orin. It had clearly troubled him that Enetheal had Orin alone and without his protection. Nevertheless, Kuthan was eager for time to talk to them without Enetheal. He had done most of the talking. As soon as Orin and Enetheal had set out, Kuthan had hurried them away. They hadn't stopped until they had all arrived, sweaty and out of breath, at the Welcome Table. He had moved them along at a quick pace, not slowing for the slope, which was a particularly difficult climb after such a tiring afternoon. He had seated himself and they had imitated him. Idra had started to say something, but Kuthan had silenced her with a look.

"Something is going on," he had said. As Kuthan spoke the tension in his jaw was evident. Enunciating each word, he continued, "And we *need* to figure out what."

What had followed was logical. He insisted that they go over what they had learned from the day. After each person had spoken, Kuthan summarized their observations. It was only when Ara had pointed out that the dark was almost upon them that they left the table in the direction of their cabins. On the way back they had continued their discussion. Namin didn't participate actively. He couldn't stop thinking about Orin. *What was Orin up to now? Was he okay? Would he react as Kuthan had?* Something had happened to Kuthan when he made his journey with Enetheal. He had returned pale and unfocused. And although Kuthan seemed as direct and decisive as ever, Namin was worried about him. And now Orin was gone.

Their journey home was delayed further when Idra insisted on getting them food. Ara was anxious about the fading light, but Lenya said there was time. After Idra descended from the tree they had broken into a run. Darkness was closing in, but the sky still held a trace of light. When they arrived at Ara and Lenya's cabin they said their goodnights quickly before hurrying on. It jarred Namin to shorten a goodbye. Why did they have to sleep in different cabins? Why couldn't they stay together as a group? They arrived at Kuthan and Idra's cabin. Despite the rant, Kuthan still seemed agitated from his experience with Enetheal. During their long discussion, he had never recounted what his task entailed. Again, it pained Namin to rush his departure from them, but he knew that he must leave. The last part of the journey was the worst: the forest was dark, and the others were gone. But it wasn't long. Namin arrived at his and Orin's cabin and waited for Orin's return.

After all the time they had taken recounting their observations at the Welcome Table Namin had expected Orin's return more quickly. The sky outside was now black save for the stars. Orin still hadn't returned. Namin had checked outside their cabin repeatedly, and then, one final time, he had discovered the lighted lanterns. He stared at the golden-yellow flashes leading up to and away from the cabin. He smiled, some of his worry now gone. This must be Orin's task. *That's perfect for Orin.* Namin went to his bed to sit, calmness now filling his mind. All would be well. Orin would return soon. Everyone would gather again tomorrow ....

And now Orin was sleeping peacefully. Namin was glad someone was content after the day. After their work figuring out the island, restful sleep was well earned. Yet sleep did not come to Namin. He was not tired at all. Something wasn't right; the day still seemed incomplete, like a song whose final notes had not sounded. He got up. As if with a purpose, he walked over the door, and opened it. A tall lean figure stood silhouetted just beyond the doorway. Namin tensed, but his breathing remained steady. The figure did not speak, and after a moment, he knew it was Enetheal. *As if anyone else would come.* It did make sense. The day would not be complete until each of them had performed their service. Had Ara completed her task yet? He hoped so.

Enetheal stood expectantly. Namin would have to leave Orin. He walked over to where Orin slept. He was safe, no doubt safer here than wherever Namin was going. Still, Namin wanted him not to be scared. He remembered how Ara had been upset to wake alone. He would be terrified if he found Orin gone in the middle of the night. He gently shook his shoulder. He hated to wake him, but knew it was right.

"Orin," he said quietly. Orin moaned.

"I'm leaving, but I'll be back soon." Orin rolled over.

"Soon," Orin echoed, and slipped back into sleep.

That would have to do. Namin walked to where Enetheal's silhouette still stood. Together, they shut the door. Namin took great care to make sure the spiderweb screen completely covered the doorway.

They walked side by side along the lit path, in the direction of the other cabins. A warm breeze blew across the pines, spreading their scent. It was a wonderful night. Somehow it seemed even brighter than the last. As they got closer to Kuthan's and Idra's cabin, the wind picked up. It began to moan, sounding almost human. Namin shivered, but remembered what Orin said about the strange coastal rocks he had explored that morning. The noises persisted as they drew near to Lenya and Ara's cabin. At first he wondered whether his task would begin there, but Enetheal took him in the opposite direction, towards the curving stone way that surrounded the slope. The wailing sounds from the open water diminished.

As they moved to the stone way, Namin was suddenly able to see why the sky looked brighter this evening. Visible near the horizon, emitting a silver-white glow, was a sliver of crescent moon. He touched Enetheal on the shoulder. They exchanged eyes and Namin pointed.

"Look," he whispered.

Enetheal nodded. They both stopped and watched the low-hanging moon. It was large and bright, and made the night feel gentle. The moment passed and they returned to their journey. They continued along the stone way until they reached one of the clearings. The large tree stood in the center.

They moved through the glade, leaving a wide berth around the tree, and reached the far side where the stone way continued in its circle around the slope. It was here that they stopped. Enetheal stood to one side, leaving Namin at the path's edge. Namin was puzzled. This was either the place where his task would be performed or, as for Orin, one of many places. What was he to do? Enetheal seemed calm, so Namin, in turn, felt no urgency. He took in his surroundings. In the semi-darkness, the great tree was a looming silhouette, its branches extending upward and outward. The way was discernible far beyond, lit by the flickering lanterns. Namin looked up. Above him, visible by the faint beams of the young crescent moon and by starlight, gleamed spiderwebs. They crisscrossed between the trees and branches and along the trunks of the pines.

The webs were beautiful. They were intricate and elaborate. No two webs were identical. Namin sat down on the edge of the path, gazing skyward towards the webs and, unbidden, a melody entered his mind. Namin began to sing. He started quietly. The melody he wove held no joy, or anger, or sorrow. It was calm, like Orin's lullaby. The song told of togetherness and completion, and of all being well. As he sang he saw Enetheal watching him intently. Was it because he liked what he heard? Did he wonder what it must be like to sing? Or lament for a voice he did not have?

Enetheal was not his only listener. The moment his song had begun, the sounds of the night forest had hushed. Now as he continued to sing, an audience gathered around him. Scuttling down the pine trees were spiders. They came in many shapes and sizes, some too small to see in the darkness, and some as large as his hands. It was difficult to make them out against the blackness of the forest.

Namin continued to sing, the presence of the spiders encouraging his song. His voice grew louder and clearer. One spider leapt over him, spanning the entrance to the clearing. As it leapt, a single silver-white strand trailed behind. Another spider sprang across the path; and another, and another, each trailing its silvery silk. They danced back and forth across the gap between the trees. Their dance matched Namin's song, his voice rising and falling as their intricate web was woven. Namin sang until he knew his song was done, and the spiders wove to his music until they, too, knew their dance was finished. When the dance and the song were complete, Namin sat on the ground, and looked at the spiders. And they looked back at him.

The web they had created was beautiful. It caught moonbeams and starlight, but also seemed to glow with a silver light of its own. Namin gazed over the creation in awe, delighting in its complexity and sturdiness. Enetheal also seemed impressed. He examined the web thoughtfully, but then returned his attention to Namin. Namin rose to his feet, and together they returned through the clearing to the side from which they had entered.

Once there, they stopped again. Instinctively Namin knew that this time the web they wove would block them out of the clearing. Again he sat down, and turned his gaze skywards. This time the spiders seemed ready. They dangled from pine limbs on their silky threads, and Namin felt their many eyes watching him, waiting for his song to emerge. And so Namin began. Again the melody started low and soft, without sadness or anger or joy. The truth and the story in the song were very like the first web-singing, but this second song was also different. The two songs were as siblings, with shared features, but each unique. Again the web was woven by song and dance. And when this web-making was complete, it was once more radiant and a marvel to behold, in every way, it's sister's equal. Satisfaction filled Namin. He did not need Enetheal's approval to know that his work was right.

Namin rose, and Enetheal walked with him back towards the cabins. As they walked, Namin's mind was pleasantly empty. It was as if all his thought had gone into the songs he had woven, leaving nothing more to contemplate. He stared at the flashing lanterns, the lights of the heavens, heard the sighing of the wind and the whispers of the trees, taking all of these in as if they were happening to another person. They echoed in his empty mind, until the wind-song changed. Its wailing had returned.

Thoughts came all at once. It was as if they had been trying to push their way back in, and now suddenly broke through. What had he done? He had sung to spiders. His song had brought the creation of beautiful, radiant webs. That did not even begin to describe the immense satisfaction, the joy of his act, and his fulfillment. But it was also unnerving. Was it supposed to be like this? He thought about Kuthan, who had returned from his service pale and distant. Other than Kuthan, however, none of the others seemed averse to their tasks.

What do the webs accomplish? The answer seemed simple: they block passage to the clearing during the night. That was enough for now. Namin was eager to get back to Orin. However, the next stop they made wasn't at their cabin. It was at Lenya and Ara's.

As soon as he saw their cabin, Namin knew what was coming next and pushed aside his thoughts of returning to Orin. They approached the front door, and stopped just before the spiderweb-screen. Namin stared at it, perplexed. There was already a web present. Should he sing as he had before? No song came immediately to mind. Perhaps he should remove the existing web and begin anew. Namin looked to Enetheal for guidance. For a long moment, they held each other's eyes, and as they each looked away, Namin felt sure Enetheal understood. Raising a long finger, Enetheal pointed to a loose strand that had broken from the web.

Namin reached for the loose silk and allowed it to rest on his finger. This web needed repair. He examined it, trying to decipher its pattern. The melody did not come into his mind all at once, but he knew its beginning. Namin lifted his head, opened his mouth, and let his song emerge. Almost as if the spiders had followed him, they were there. This time as Namin sang, he unwound the loose strand of the web. What first had seemed simple immediately became complex. He unraveled more loose strands, and as if no time passed, new silk threads replaced the broken filaments through the spiders' intricate dance.

He was aware that without purposeful thought, this melody was unlike either of the others. Still, his song held no joy, anger, or sorrow; it told of wholeness and of all being well. And then, as his mind wandered to the sleepers in the cabin, it changed. He thought about Ara with her fierce intensity and perseverance, and then of Lenya, her serenity and confidence. And as he considered them, the new web grew both in size and in intricacy. The reworked web was now larger than the one that had initially covered the door. By the time Namin finished, the door was completely cloaked with the spiders' elaborate work. It shone in the moonlight, crisscrossing patterns shimmering with small gusts of wind. This web was densely woven, without spaces between strands like those that had been made in the clearing. Turning away from this creation, Namin let the wind take away the long silk threads that had first shielded the door. They caught the moonlight as they blew away.

Namin and Enetheal walked towards Idra and Kuthan's cabin. By the light of the flashing firefly lanterns they traveled along the path until the cabin was in sight. Namin found the loose strand by himself this time, Enetheal watching. It was as if the song he sang before had never stopped. The only difference was that his thoughts wandered to Kuthan and Idra, bringing a subtle change to the melody. As he sang, he glanced briefly at Enetheal. Enetheal stared at the old web as it unraveled and the new web as it emerged, tracing a finger over the smooth skin under his nose. Namin turned back to the web. Something about the motion was distracting, even disturbing, but he needed to focus on his task. Finally, he rose in satisfaction, his work complete. This web, too, shone brilliantly. Again he released the old strands before leaving the cabin and once again, they shimmered softly as they disappeared into the night.

Once more they journeyed down the path. Somewhere in the darkness an owl hooted. Apart from this cry in the night, the only sounds were the whispers of trees and wind and waves. They reached the last cabin. When he examined the web-screen, Namin found no fraying or loose strands; but he did find a portion in which the silk fibers seemed thin, so he started the unraveling there.

He sang. The spiders danced and a new web emerged from the old. Satisfaction filled him when this last weaving was finished. Somehow the others didn't seem complete until this one was done. He looked over his handiwork and sighed. Although the young crescent moon had dipped beneath the horizon, the heavens still glowed, illuminating the web-screen he had created. He lifted the tattered strands of the old web and released them into the waiting darkness before turning to Enetheal.

Enetheal gazed at Namin. They looked at one another for a long moment before each turned away, Namin toward his cabin and Enetheal away from it. As Namin pulled the spiderweb screen aside and replaced it, he realized that he had not spoken throughout the whole experience. No words had been necessary. However, this still left Namin uneasy. His discomfort dissolved when the web-screen sealed the doorway and the door was securely closed. Orin was breathing softly. Namin let himself sink into his bed, the darkness now a comforting blanket.

As his body melted into stillness, web-weaving melodies sounded through his mind. He thought of each of his companions, how each had approached the day. Ara had been so cautious and so eager to do what she thought was needed. Namin had loved her smile when she showed her rock. Orin and Kuthan were eager to figure out the secrets of the island. Idra was so happy to feed them, so scared to become a burden when she could not find her stone. And Lenya was calm and confident. As he drifted into sleep, his thoughts turned to Enetheal—his grey eyes, his long nose, and of course his mouthlessness, his silence, and his lack of expression. He remembered how Enetheal had watched as he sang, how his finger had traced over the smooth skin under his own nose. Namin's stomach lurched, and his heart sank. Suddenly he felt sick. A dull burning filled his chest. *Does Enetheal feel incomplete without a mouth? Does he crave our speech and song?*

ARA - DAY ONE

"*Arrraaaa.*" *The voice, if you could call it that, was barely audible, but it was piercing and unforgettable. Ara looked for its source, but she could not guess which direction it had come from. It was a very windy day, and she was walking along the Stony Shores. The others were with her too. Enetheal was leading the way just as he had throughout the day, only this time his form was barely a dark grey silhouette, like the grey of her stone. "Arrraaaa!!" The voice cried out again. This time it was louder, and the piercing quality was gone. If the others could hear, they showed no sign of it. They continued to follow Enetheal, until he brought the group to an abrupt halt. He put his hand on Lenya's shoulder and pointed towards the heart of the island. Ara waited impatiently for Enetheal to continue, and eventually he did. They took a few more steps, but then stopped again. Now he put his hand on Idra's shoulder, and guided her vision towards the inner island. While they were at a standstill, Ara looked around.*

To her surprise, Lenya hadn't followed. Her form was now a dark grey silhouette, just like Enetheal's. Then Ara turned back to Idra, and saw that she, too, had transformed into greyness. "Arrraaaa!!" The voice wailed. She must find its source. They walked a few more steps, but then, yet again, they stopped. Ara gazed at her companions. All of them had transformed: she was surrounded by grey silhouettes. "We need to hurry," she told them. To her relief, they nodded, seeming to understand. They began to follow her. But they moved as if wading through water. "Arrraaaa!!" It was much closer now. Her companions trudged, with painful slowness, repeatedly glancing back toward the island center where Enetheal had indicated. Almost there, Ara thought. "Arrraaaa!!"

She woke up drenched with sweat. It took her a moment to realize that she had been dreaming. When she did, she clenched her jaw in frustration. She had been so close! She let out a long breath and allowed some of her anger to ebb away. It was the second night in a row she had been robbed of sleep. As she remembered last night, she glanced uneasily to Lenya's bed. This time Lenya was present, silent except for the slow, deep rhythm of her breathing. Ara sighed with relief. Outside the wind howled and moaned. She thought about joining Lenya in her bed, but something made her pause. The howling wind had woken her. But it seemed like there was more to its voice. She closed her eyes, shutting out the cabin, and listened. Beyond the creaking of branches, the crashing of the waves, and the howling, moaning wind, she heard … something. A wailing cry. She strained her ears, and finally, she could make it out. *"Arrraaaa!!"*

She sat up suddenly. A chill swept through her. It was the voice from her dream. It had called her from sleep not only now, but the night before as well.

Moments passed. The wind continued to howl and wail, but her name was not among the sounds. Her breathing slowed. *No.* She told herself. *It's just the wind.* She must have imagined it. She lay back and closed her eyes; but she still listened. Slowly her excitement died down. Her lids felt heavier upon her eyes. Her thoughts started to flitter to dreams … *"Arrraaaa!!"* She sat bolt upright. There was no mistaking it this time. It was a distinct voice, and it was calling her.

Her mind raced. She must respond. She looked over to Lenya, sleeping so soundly. She couldn't leave Lenya. But then again, she couldn't *not* leave Lenya. This time, however, there would be no confusion. Ara climbed down from her bed and walked over to Lenya. She touched her shoulder. Lenya's eyes opened.

"Hey," she responded sleepily.

"Hey. I had to wake you. I need to go, and I had to let you know," Lenya sat up so that they were face to face.

"Thank you. Be careful. Let me know when you come back."

"I will," Ara replied, and walked over to the door and opened it. Another shiver swept through her. She wasn't sure whether it was excitement or terror. She carefully pulled the screen webbing aside, shut the door behind her, and replaced the web up on the frame.

In front of her, her path was illuminated in small bursts of firefly light from the lanterns. A gust of wind blew her hair into her face. From far off—like the hoot of an owl or an echo—she heard her name again. *"Arrraaaa!!"*

"Where are you?" she almost said aloud. Was it coming from the coast? It came from behind their cabin. *There must be a path that leads there.* Ara walked slowly. Even with the lanterns it was hard to see where she was going. Above, wisps of clouds swept across the night sky occasionally allowing filtered starlight and moonlight to shine through. It would have to do. The paths forked outside their cabin. Ara turned down the path towards the other cabins. As she journeyed, the trees creaked and swayed, almost as if they were trying to reach the lit path. A firefly lantern flashed brightly. For a brief moment she thought she saw a pair of eyes looking back at her from the darkness.

She held very still, her heart pounding. The trees stilled as well, as if they, too, held their breath. When the lantern flashed again it revealed an empty wood. Ara continued to wait until the lantern flashed several more times before forcing her legs to move. Finally she continued down the path. She started to focus on the path itself. *I'm safe on the path.* Unconvinced, she said the words aloud. "I'm safe on the path." As if in answer, the wind picked up, and for a moment she thought she heard laughter. When she reached Kuthan's and Idra's cabin, the path opened up, but as she left she returned to the dark closeness of the thick forest. The brief respite made the return to the dense woods even more daunting.

Never roam in dark of night off the path of lantern's light. The words echoed in her mind. She had no desire to leave the path. And she was now sure there was a very good reason for staying on the path. Her mind wandered to Orin. He had lit the paths; it must have been his service. It was good for him to do something. Orin. He just didn't get it. That Idra had to find her own rock. That he should stay with the group instead of repeatedly running ahead. That Kuthan and Enetheal had to be alone when Enetheal showed Kuthan his service. She had tried to help Orin understand, but he couldn't take it. If he could just listen … to the rules, to Enetheal, to common sense, or to her … but it had only been one day. He had performed his service adequately and would soon understand the island. She would look out for him

She passed Orin's and Namin's cabin and gazed at the web-covered, tightly latched door. Again she enjoyed a brief respite from the close-growing trees, and again she returned to the dense forest growth as she left their little cabin behind. The path forked, one branch leading to the coast. The wind picked up as she moved towards the open water. Branches waved, trees creaked, and the wailing grew in intensity. Thoughts of wind and darkness filled her mind. The further she walked, the darker it seemed, and the more forceful the wind. Ara kept feeling like she heard something else, another sound within the wind. She strained her ears, but if it was there, it eluded her.

The path turned, and the forest abruptly gave way to a rocky coast. As she left the dense tree growth she was hit with a torrent of wind and noise. She couldn't tell whether it was one sound or many. However many there were, the voices moaned and wailed, whispered and hummed, howled and screeched, and mixed in with the noise was her name … *"Arrraaaa!!"*

A shift in the clouds allowed the moon to shine through, revealing a rocky outcropping from the island. The crying voice seemed to come from a rock formation at the end of this protrusion, and Ara knew she must go there. She made her way carefully down a large jagged boulder that sloped into the water. Waiting for her at the water's edge, the wind blowing about him and catching his hair, stood Enetheal.

She froze. Had he seen her? His gaze was out in the direction of the water. She considered retracing her steps, but surely he was only here for her. He was waiting. Had she done something wrong? The idea terrified her. She had been so careful during the day. What would Enetheal do if they did something wrong? If she had made a mistake, it would be far worse to turn back now. She clambered down the remainder of the rock slope until she was by his side. For a moment they stared at the source of the wailing together. Then Enetheal sprang from the water's edge, to a rock just off shore.

It was so unexpected that for the moment Ara just stared. Then all at once she understood. She hadn't done anything wrong. In fact, it was quite the contrary. She had been called to her service and had come. Although she could not see the source, somewhere out in the waves her caller awaited her, and she would answer. Expanding out before her into the water was a chain-like archipelago of rocks. The rocks just off the land were large and flat, with small gaps in-between. Further out they became smaller and smoother, the gaps between them growing farther apart. The last and farthest few rocks were partially submerged as the waves washed over their slippery surfaces. The little archipelago would take her where she needed to go.

Enetheal waited impassively on the first rock. Ara took in a breath, and leapt. She landed easily. The rock was flat, and dry. It felt good to stand there. She walked across, before leaping to the next rock, where again, Enetheal now waited. For a short time the gaps were small enough so that they almost seemed to be walking. However, the journey soon became more challenging. The gaps were now wide enough so that Ara needed to think about each leap very carefully before making the jump. With each leap the noises of the wind loudened. Sounds overlapped, and became distorted. Within the wind she could make out a piercing, whistling hum that simultaneously gave the impression of both a high pitched shriek and a low groan.

Without warning, the miniature islands became slippery. Enetheal made a graceful leap to a flat-looking rock. His foot slid forward, but he caught himself easily. Instead of leaping to the next rock, however, he waited for Ara. Despite Ara's preparation, she, too, slipped, but Enetheal's arm caught her before she could collapse or fall into the water.

Out of necessity their journey slowed. Each jump was made with caution and precision. The rocks were now a full leg-length apart, and quite slippery from the lapping of the waves. Enetheal took the lead, and indicated where it was best to land. He also steadied her when she occasionally faltered. The long leaps, and careful landings were challenging, but soon their most difficult battle was with the wind. The nearer they came to the end of the rock chain, the louder and stronger it blew. It became so strong that they could not jump, or even hold still, without being tugged towards the black water. The distorted cacophony became nearly unbearable, but still they pressed on.

At last they were huddled together on a small rock, with one more leap to go. In front of them was her destination. It was an expanse of rock rising out of the water. Ringed around its edge were large standing stones, angular in shape. They were far taller than she or Enetheal were. The wind rushed between them. Somewhere in the midst of its passage, the normal sounds of wind mixed together to produce a low hum, a piercing whistle, a wailing cry, and a resonating note. The rise itself looked to be about fifteen paces across. Compared to the rock she and Enetheal were on, it was practically an island in itself.

Enetheal put his hand on her back. He had not jumped yet, which meant this was a leap she was going to take alone. Without Enetheal waiting for her on the other side, the jump looked more menacing. It was certainly the longest jump she had attempted yet, but at least her destination looked like it would provide a solid landing. Ara glanced back. Behind them, across the water, was their island. It seemed distant, maybe because the overwhelming cacophony and the immediacy of the leap before her eclipsed all else. *Come on! One more jump!* She looked briefly at the black water, waves visible only because of moon and starlight through cloud cover. She focused on her destination, the wind whirling around her, howling, singing. And then she leapt. The waves crashed below her, inviting her to plunge into the cold depths, but she sailed through the air and her feet met stone.

Silence. A shudder passed through her. And then, suddenly, she laughed. The wind was gone; she could think again. Was it a dream? She blinked hard, and reopened her eyes. Everything she could see had remained the same. Around her the waves crashed. Trees on the nearby island swayed in the wind. The clouds moved quickly across the sky. Ara was in a quiet place, however, untouched by the wind. Enetheal stood on the last rock, standing very still, watching her. Somehow she knew he was not the only one observing her. She wheeled about. There were tall boulders at the border of her large rock platform. They were evenly spaced and dark grey, tinged with green. She noticed that they were eroded, yet had retained an angularity. Upon further inspection she decided she could not really call them boulders. Their shape was too unnatural, as if they had been shaped with purpose. Every stone was unique, with lines and holes cut into each of them, like scars. She turned her gaze from stone to stone, trying to find a pattern. She found none. As she stared, she felt the back of her neck prickle. The wind! Sound was returning.

She barely had time to brace herself, before sound and wind came back in full. The wind whirled about and through the circle, howling and wailing. Ara staggered, caught by its full force. She tried to move back to the center, but another gust sent her careening toward the edge. She dropped to the stone surface, letting the wind blow over her. Then she waited a moment, trying to gather her bearings despite the noise. *The center,* she thought wildly, and began to crawl. Gritting her teeth, she moved one limb at a time. The circle's center gradually neared. *I just have to keep close to the rock.* When she finally arrived, she planted herself firmly.

The torrent of wind was still ferocious, but it no longer pushed her in one way or another. Ara breathed deeply. *What now?* There was no clear answer. The wind screamed in her ears. Her eyes watered, and she closed them against it. *Why did I come here? What task is this?* Someone had called her, she remembered. She tried to scream out, "Why am I here?" but the wind took her voice away. The rocks around her seemed to thrum. It was impossible to focus upon the low hum because of the high whistling and singing, which were in turn constantly interrupted by wailing, moaning, or howling. All the sounds bored into her head; all her thoughts were gone. The wind swept tears across her face. She bowed her head, lying face-down upon the rock. Only then did she hear it: her name. Somewhere in the midst of the sounds of the wind, was her name. *"Arrraaaa!!"* It was a whisper, except it was loud. Now she remembered why she was here. She had been called.

The wind slowly died down within the ring of boulders. She wished desperately to crawl out of the circle and fall into the water. Was it not enough that it had pierced her mind as it had? She knew it was not. She held her place in the center of the circle, and spoke: "Here I am."

To her relief, her voice remained steady as she spoke, and as her words came, some of the wind's wildness abated. But once her voice subsided, it returned. It swept across, through and around the stones, so that they whistled and howled, moaned and hummed. Again sounds overlapped, piercing her mind. It happened so fast that all she could do was cry out and cover her ears. She opened her eyes and saw tall dark waves crashing about her.

As if in the midst of the waves, stood Enetheal. His image was blurry through the tears and wind in her eyes, but she thought she saw him cup a hand to his ear. She took her hands away from her own ears, and her mind was overwhelmed once more. Something must be hidden in the cacophony, as her name had been. She sat still, accepting the sound, receiving it into her mind. They returned again and again. The whistles and moans and whooshing sounds combined. *"Eiiiiiiiisssuun."* "I don't understand!" she called out despairingly. Again the wind died down as she spoke; but as soon as she stopped, it returned with even more intensity.

"LEIIIIIIISSSSSUUNNN!!" Ara flung her hands over her ears without thinking. She crumpled to her knees and lay face down. The wind swirled about her. She stared into the blackness of her eyelids as the waves crashed and the wind howled around her. The rocks continued to twist the wind about her: *"L-iiissssuuuun."* For a moment she heard

what could have been an L sound, and then she thought she had her answer. "Listen," she said. There was silence. "Listen," she said again, the silence giving her confidence.

She thought about it, and then something welled up inside her. She became aware of another noise, echoing off the stones. It took her a moment to realize this wasn't the wind, and then another to realize that the sound came from her own mouth. She was laughing. No, not laughing. She was cackling. Tears streamed down her face. It was absurd. Did she truly believe the wind and stones were talking to her? That she had shaped the monstrous noises into words? She laughed and laughed. The wind was gone. The waves were calm. The trees on the distant island stood still.

The night was bright. The crescent moon shone above them, and each star was a beacon. Were they laughing too? She looked over at Enetheal. He stood upon a small rock, with water all around him, his hand outstretched. He wasn't laughing. His face was still as the stones, as it always was. Her laughter died and her smile left. Her cheeks hurt from smiling. She managed to leap away from the stones that had been screaming, and into Enetheal's awaiting arms. The rocks had been soaked by the waves, but every leap seemed easy. Ara led the way now, jumping from rock to rock, never stopping to pause in between. Their journey was fast, and blessedly silent.

The next thing she remembered was Lenya sleeping. She put a hand on her shoulder and whispered, "Back." Lenya awoke. They stared eye to eye, and then Ara crawled into bed with her. Lenya held her close. She stared into the night, trying to understand what had happened, but her mind was numb. Just when she decided that sleep would not come, she thought she heard something. At first she tensed, scared of any sound other than Lenya's breath, but this new sound was pleasant. It was a song, and it was soothing, and it made her feel warm and safe. Before she knew it she was fast asleep.

IDRA - DAY TWO

Idra opened her eyes and breathed in the new day. She was ready. More than ready. She was excited. She tossed aside her blankets and climbed out of bed. Across the room, Kuthan lay still. *"Next time wake me,"* he had said. Now she debated whether or not to wake him. He looked so peaceful; he definitely needed his sleep. And she knew that she was completely safe. Most likely, she would be back before he was up. Still, it was what he had asked for. She guessed he would be happier if she followed his instruction. Walking over to his bed, she spoke his name, "Kuthan."

He slept with a small frown. At her voice his furrowed brow relaxed, but his eyes remained closed. "Kuthan," she spoke again, this time shaking his arm. Another moment later his eyes were open. He took another moment to orient himself before he was fully present. "Hey," he said in an offhand voice.

"Kuthan, I have to go. I know you wanted me to wake you."

"I see." He paused for a moment, and looked her up and down. "I suppose … that is best for now." She could tell he was trying to think, but was struggling through sleepiness.

"Yes. I'll be back soon. Don't worry." She took her hands off his bed and headed for the door.

"Be careful," he said as she left. "Especially around Enetheal." She didn't need reminding. Closing the door, she carefully replaced the web-screen. Enetheal was waiting for her on the path just beyond the stone step. This time she was prepared for his presence and managed to look him straight in the face without flinching.

"Ready?" she asked. He nodded. This time she led. They reached the stone way that curved around the slope, and made their journey around it. As they approached the clearing with the tree she quickened her pace. When it opened up in front of her, she stopped short. Something was wrong. Yesterday the tree had been full of vibrant green leaves and golden orange fruit. Now the fruit was gone, and the leaves had turned a brown color. As she looked around she noticed that many of them had fallen to the floor of the clearing. *What had happened?* She couldn't imagine. But then a worse and far more important thought struck. *How am I going to feed the others? What are we going to do?* Her throat closed, and she became very aware of her short shallow breaths. *Calm,* she told herself. There would be a way. Would Enetheal know? After all he was the one who wanted all of this. She turned to him.

"Where did they go?" she asked. He looked at her unblinkingly. "What can we do?" She said it aloud, but this time the question was more for herself than it was for him. Enetheal started to walk across the clearing. She looked at the tree, and then it occurred to her: This wasn't the only fruit-bearing tree. Yesterday they had passed another fruit tree along the stone way on their journey here. She took a deep breath. It would work. She ran, hoping to make up for lost time. Enetheal kept pace with her easily.

When they reached the next clearing, Idra gasped. She stopped short in wonder. The tree was large, just as the other had been. Its smooth bark was colored in shades of brown. The various hues intermingled across the tree forming a pattern like light and shadow. Weighing down the branches, in the light of the morning sun, were bright purple fruits.

She was just about to enter the clearing when she noticed the spiderweb crisscrossing between two trees, blocking her. She pondered for a moment before approaching the web. Then she stepped forward and carefully peeled it back. She entered the clearing with Enetheal. However, once Idra had come under the shade of the tree, she set aside all thoughts of the web. She ran to its base and stared up the thick trunk. To her frustration, the first branch was just out of reach. She had to consider the tree for a while before she realized that there was a knot she could use to boost herself. She raised her foot to it, and placed her hands securely on the bole of the tree. As she hoisted herself upward, she kept her eyes focused upon the lowest branch. Just when this came within reach, she sprang off the knot and grabbed hold of it. Then she started to climb.

Once again, the fruits on the lower branches looked less appealing than those higher up. She climbed quickly. The exertion was exhilarating, and she smiled openly. Soon she was high up. The fruit around her was now a beautiful indigo shade. The fruits on this tree were far smaller than those of the other, so she picked many. If only she had a way to carry them. Perhaps Enetheal would help.

"Enetheal," she called. And then there he was, under the tree. She tossed down the fruit she had picked, and continued to gather more. When Enetheal's arms were full, she took what she could, and descended. She had retrieved it much faster this time. Despite the time lost at the first tree and again with her hesitancy at the spider-web, she was sure the whole task had taken far less time than it had yesterday. She was not eager to return to Enetheal, but soon she would have the deep satisfaction of seeing the others eat her food. Idra landed gracefully and wiped the sweat and matted hair from her forehead.

Enetheal looked at her, and she turned away. "Shall we go back?" He followed her with silent footsteps. They brought the pieces of fruit up the slope and arranged them in small groups around the table where the goblet of sap waited. "Thank you," she said to Enetheal. He nodded, and she took his nod as both a response and an indication that she could leave. She hurried down the path. Eventually she would get used to him. She would have to. Just not yet. Maybe Kuthan would figure something out.

She arrived at their cabin, to find the spiderweb screen already pulled aside. She opened the door. Namin and Orin had arrived. Namin sat on Idra's bed, and Orin sat on Kuthan's legs in Kuthan's bed, talking animatedly.

"They're so bright when they flash, and you think that will make them easy to catch, but you only have that one moment to catch them before you lose them."

Idra joined Namin, listening. Orin continued:

"What's going to be great is when I can light up what we haven't seen yet! There's so much we haven't seen!"

"I'm sure we'll see it soon," Kuthan said. Orin grinned.

"Food is on the table. Shall we gather the others?" All three of them let out an eager "ahh," and Idra swelled with pride. They got up, Kuthan leading the way. Namin carefully replaced the web behind them, and they journeyed up the path.

When they arrived at Lenya and Ara's, Idra knocked lightly on the door. When no one answered, Orin hammered on the door. Namin and Kuthan exchanged raised eyebrows, and Idra hid a grin. "That should wake them," Orin said, oblivious.

"Definitely," Namin agreed, not bothering to conceal his smile. However, to their surprise, no one answered. Kuthan frowned, looked around them, and pushed open the door. He let out an audible sigh as he entered. Curled together on one of the beds were Ara and Lenya, still fast asleep.

Idra felt confused. It was time for the day to start. She was eager for them to eat her fruit. But she hated to wake them. Orin made the decision for her:

"Lets go!" It wasn't quite a shout, but it was very loud.

Lenya awoke, shadows under her eyes. "Ready," she answered. She brushed her fingers through Ara's hair, before shaking her shoulder.

Ara moaned, tensing her muscles, shutting her eyes tighter, and putting her hands over her ears. Lenya persisted, rocking her shoulder until Ara opened her eyes. They were bloodshot. "Okay, let's go," she echoed in a flat voice. She arose, and Lenya followed.

They stopped again outside the cabin for Lenya and Ara to adjust to the sunlight before marching up the slope towards the Welcome Table. Orin took his favorite position at the head of the group, and Idra and the others followed closely.

"Do you think we'll go anywhere new today?" Orin asked, turning just a bit so she could hear him.

"Yes," said Idra, thinking about the new tree whose fruit she had just harvested. "We still have so much we haven't explored."

"Great," said Orin between breaths. The slope was causing them to be winded and soon they were sweating and panting in the morning sun. The last portion of their climb was quiet except for the noises of the forest, wind, and waves. They arrived at the top, took their places around the table, and sat down.

For a moment they gazed at the table—at the perfect circle it formed, the rules engraved on its surface, and most of all the fruit Idra had brought. Then Kuthan took some and gestured to a piece in front of Idra.

"After you," Kuthan said with a smile. She decided against it. She certainly would eat, but she had harvested the food for them, and before she started she wanted to see them eat.

"Not my turn," she answered evenly. Kuthan raised an eyebrow.

"Oh?" he queried. "Whose turn is it?"

Idra thought about it. Orin looked up hopefully. Namin watched her. Lenya or Ara, she decided. They both looked exhausted, but Ara looked worse.

"Ara?" Idra both stated her name and asked her. Ara nodded, took the piece of fruit in front of her and took a bite. She transformed. Her shoulders dropped, she sat up straighter, and something returned to her eyes. She let out a long breath, and her face relaxed into a tenuous smile. Then Idra took her own fruit, which invited the others to do the same. Soon they were all eating. The taste was sweeter than what they had savored the day before. For a moment they all lost themselves in the rapture of good food.

"Amazing," Lenya said. Her fatigue had vanished. Ara nodded in agreement. The others exclaimed their joy as well. Idra felt herself smiling, happiness rising inside her.

"I love your task," Orin said through a mouthful of fruit.

"So do I," Idra responded, almost in a sigh.

"Do we all know our tasks now?" Namin asked.

"We must," Kuthan answered for them. "Which means we can start understanding."

"Understanding what?" Idra and Ara asked in unison. They glanced at one another and then back at Kuthan.

It was Namin who answered: "How the pieces fit together."

Orin looked excited, but still confused.

"We're working to do something," Kuthan explained. "We just don't know what. The more we know, the more we'll be able to get control of the situation." He stared at them meaningfully.

"The situation is pretty controlled as it is so far," Ara said pointedly.

"So far we're the only ones being controlled," Kuthan retorted, his voice rising. They took a moment to consider what he said.

"Knowing more could help," Lenya stated softly.

Kuthan relaxed, and Idra let out a breath she had been holding. She didn't like it when Kuthan got angry. Last night he had been agitated when he returned from his service, and then had grown angry that they had to perform their tasks without knowing why. He had vented about it after they returned to the cabin. She agreed that figuring out stuff was good, but why did he have to get angry? At least he was less angry now.

"We can start by describing the basic idea of our tasks," Lenya said, before taking another bite out of her fruit.

"And then we can try and see how they fit together," Namin added. "We should keep it short for now because it's only a little while before we need to gather stones."

"I catch fireflies and light the path with them," Orin said. "... with the lanterns," he added helpfully when no one continued.

Idra wanted to hear more, but urged by time, she pressed forward. "I gather fruit from the trees to be eaten." She didn't like saying it like this, as if that was all it took. Although she had only completed it twice, the task meant so much more. There was the hike to the trees, the climb, the retrieval of the perfect fruit, and being able to give the others sustenance. Most of all, it was a feeling that transcended words.

"I go into an underground cave and drop off the stones we gather," Kuthan said.

He said it in a matter-of-fact way and looked for the next person to speak, but Idra knew at that moment that something was not right about what they were doing. Kuthan had returned unnerved and agitated. Something had happened during his task, something had taken place in all of their tasks, which could not be described so simply.

"I sing to spiders and they weave webs," Namin said quietly.

"I listen to the wind as it passes through some boulders," Ara said slowly.

And again Idra knew that something big was missing—not only because of how Ara seemed when she awoke, but also because her task was too undefined compared with the others.

"And I bring fallen stars to a well," Lenya finished.

It took a moment for Idra to comprehend what Lenya had said. When she did, she laughed.

They all laughed. Perhaps because they were relieved to have shared even some part of their experience, or perhaps because of how incredible things were. When they stopped laughing they finished their fruit.

"Enetheal is coming," Ara said in an undertone. Idra started to rise, but Kuthan stopped her with an urgent whisper.

"Look for patterns," he said, giving them all an intense stare. "*We* can figure this out. I know we can." Idra barely had time to process what he said when Kuthan got up and walked toward Enetheal. They followed.

The Stony Shores were breezier than they had been the day before. Waves crashed, and trees swayed and dipped. After her previous difficulty finding her stone, Idra felt anxious. The little group had started to disperse and Idra had to work to control her breathing. She inhaled slowly, held it briefly and then let it out. She watched Orin, who must have seen something, because without warning he started running along the shore. Idra glanced at Namin. He smiled, and gave her a wink before turning away. Feeling braver, Idra chased after Orin.

At first they followed the coast together, but soon Orin wandered deeper into the water, and Idra stayed in the shallows. Soon she came upon some flat rocks, in the same area where she had started skipping stones the day before. Searching for a stone to skip, Idra picked up a handful of the flat rocks, and gasped. There was her rock. She was surprised that she had found it so early. It was deep brown in color, and had a light blue line that looked like a crack in its surface. It was not nearly as flat as the other rocks she had picked up, but this was her rock. The other stones in her hand splashed into the shallows. She wandered onto the dry stones that covered the shore.

She found Lenya, and watched how she walked with grace over the bed of stones, her hair blown about by the wind. Every so often Lenya would leap from one large rock to another. The way Lenya carried herself reminded Idra of Enetheal, except that Enetheal had a certain erectness in his gait—or perhaps it was just because he was so tall.

"Lenya," Idra called when she got closer.

"Hey Idra," Lenya's eyes moved down to Idra's hand which clutched her tribute.

"You found your stone," Lenya said happily.

"Yeah," Idra answered simply. She was surprised Lenya hadn't found hers, and yet she did not seem to be searching.

"Beautiful, isn't it?" Lenya was gazing out into the water. It was beautiful. The waves crashed about, some upon each other, and others onto rocks. Clouds moved across the sky allowing brief glimpses of sun. They walked in silence for a while, looking at the waves. The wind was strong but pleasant.

"What is it like, finding and holding a star?" Idra had not realized how curious she was until after she voiced the question. Lenya glowed in response, and the shadows under her eyes seemed to fade.

"Amazing," she whispered. She focused on Idra fully. Idra waited for more, but Lenya eventually shook her head. "Beyond words," she finished. They continued walking.

"I could probably take you with me some time," Lenya said, as though deep in thought.

"Really?" Idra hadn't even considered the idea. The tasks seemed too personal.

"Would that be allowed?" Idra asked, lowering her voice. No one was in earshot, but Idra wanted to be careful.

"Would it not be?" Lenya answered, not troubling to emulate Idra's quietness.

"I don't know," Idra puzzled. "It sounds fantastic, but I think we should see how the next few days go first." She felt annoyed at herself for saying it. She really wanted to go, but Kuthan had advised caution, and she wanted to keep them all safe. Lenya nodded, and they continued wandering.

Eventually they came to an area with rounded stones. Without warning, Lenya reached down and lifted a rounded grey rock. "This is it," she smiled. The rock did not seem any different from the ones which surrounded it. To Idra, it didn't seem unique in any way. But it was Lenya's clear choice. They turned together, and walked back to the forest entrance where Enetheal waited.

The others arrived shortly after them; each carrying a rock which they held close. Idra glanced up into the sky. It was sea of grey. She could tell where the sun was from a glowing patch of cloud. Not nearly as much time had passed as it had during yesterday's gathering. *I must never slow them down again,* she thought to herself grimly, remembering the catastrophe of yesterday when she couldn't find her stone. Just as he had the day before, Enetheal made eye contact with each of them before turning and heading up the path and into the forest.

Enetheal and Orin lead the group together. Idra considered whether to walk alongside Kuthan or Ara. *Ara,* she decided. Ara seemed far more relaxed after the fruit, and completely back to herself now that she had found a tribute rock. But it would still be good to make sure everything was well. She fell into step beside Ara.

"Hey," Idra said.

Ara turned. "Hey Idra," she spoke softly, and her voice wavered. Ara held up her stone. "Do you like it?" It was very small, and a very dark shade of blue.

Idra held her hand palm up. Ara looked at her open hand before placing the stone in the center. Idra closed her hand over it briefly just to get a feel for its texture. It was hard, and surprisingly rough and grainy. Opening up her fingers, she returned it to Ara.

"Yes," she answered simply. Her other hand still clasped her own tribute rock tightly. Why was her rock so important to her, and Ara's to Ara? They just *felt* right? Maybe she would ask Kuthan—he liked to figure things out. "*Look for patterns*," he had said. She was looking.

Up ahead, Orin waited at a fork in the path. Enetheal pointed Orin down one of the passages, and Orin raced on. Another new path. Idra smiled. What would Orin do when they ran out of new paths? Now Lenya walked beside Enetheal, and Namin and Kuthan were together behind them. She could just make out Kuthan speaking in an undertone through the sound of the birds. One of the birds alighted on a pine tree near them and began to sing. As soon as it had finished, Namin copied its tune with a loud whistle. Ara jumped in response, and spun around to look for the source.

"Sorry, Ara," Namin said guiltily.

"Don't be," Ara responded quietly. She laughed, "I'm just a bit jumpy I guess." She turned back so that she was walking along the path, stepping forward purposefully. As soon as she turned away from Kuthan and Namin, the smile left her face, replaced with contemplation. Idra waited until they had walked a ways more before speaking again.

"What's up, Ara. You okay?"

"I'm fine," she said shortly. "How about you?" Ara asked the question almost defensively.

"I'm great."

They walked in silence some more. Behind them Idra could still barely make out Kuthan's voice. Lenya and Enetheal continued together. Orin was back with them now, pulling on Lenya's arm.

"How was your task?" Idra asked softly. Ara took in a deep breath in response, and then let it out slowly before answering.

"I did it," she said shortly. "It was a challenge, but I did it and I will do it again." Her tone was dismissive. Enetheal took them off the path. They clambered through some brush in the forest for a time, but stopped when the bushes grew too close together to continue.

"Well, if you need me or want to talk about it, let me know." Idra said quietly. Ara inclined her head, and Idra moved on.

Idra didn't like the bushes nearly as much as the trees. They grew too close together and were prickly and unpleasant. But one thing she did like about them was the berries. At least the trees weren't alone in producing fruit. She plucked one and tossed it to Orin.

It hit him on the back of his neck. He let out a small "ah" and turned his head sharply, looking around. Idra tried to keep her face blank, but when he looked at her she couldn't help laughing. Orin's annoyance melted into an evil grin. He grabbed a handful of berries and started pelting her with them. Idra ran for cover. Orin pursued her closely, but finally she lost him among the brambles. Idra made sure she had her own handful of berries before poking her head out. He was gone.

She took a tentative step out, and suddenly heard a small snigger behind her. She whirled around. Simultaneously, each smashed a handful of berries into the other.

Juice exploded over them. Orin had a giant splotch of red, blue and purple on his chest. Flecks of the juice covered his face and arms, and by the look he gave her, she could tell she must look just as ridiculous. Together they burst into laughter. They wandered back together to where the others waited, still laughing.

Orin's smile fell as the others came into sight, and Idra felt her own smile sliding off. Ara, Kuthan, and Enetheal stared at them. Idra felt heat rushing to her face. Ara's look was accusatory, Kuthan's severe, and Enetheal impassive as always. Kuthan moved his eyes over to Enetheal and back. She understood his disappointment. He was right. She heard his voice as if he had spoken inside her mind: *"Caution near Enetheal!"*

Lenya and Namin looked at them too, but Namin looked on with kindness, and Lenya smiled softly. Idra felt a wave of thankfulness towards them despite her guilt. She should have been more careful, but she was grateful that Lenya and Namin were calm about it.

Namin broke the silence. "Looks like Idra and Ore have already figured out what to do." Idra and Orin exchanged a confused glance before turning their attention back to Namin. Namin delicately plucked a small blueberry, and squished it between his middle finger and thumb. He ran his juice-covered finger over his grey stone, and it began to transform.

Ara nodded appreciatively, and soon they were all plucking berries and painting their stones with the juice. They sat in a circle. Enetheal joined them, even though he had no rock to paint. For the first time his presence did not seem to matter as much. Idra rubbed the juice back and forth over her stone. It was therapeutic. She felt her guilt for fooling around with Orin diminishing as she focused on the task at hand. When she glanced around, the others were equally absorbed. The sun shone through a gap in the clouds, providing warmth and better lighting, and the juice-stains shone artfully on the stones.

When she finished, Idra was surprised to see that the sun had moved. Time had passed much more quickly than she had perceived. Namin glanced at her rock, and gave her a nod of appreciation. It was still much the same as it had been when she had found it on the Stony Shores, only now the light blue line that ran across the stone's top surface clearly bisected the stone. On one side it was the deep brown color that was natural to the stone, on the other side the stone was a deep red. She'd left the bottom surface of her rock untouched, and preferred it that way.

Except for Orin, the others were still working, but Idra enjoyed watching them. Juice-painting had left her tranquil. Painting the stones was more satisfying than finding them, she decided. Here there was no fear of being left behind, or of not succeeding. Everyone was content, too. Each person focused on his or her individual stone, yet they were working together. Maybe that was why she enjoyed it so much. It was like her task, because they were gathered together and happy.

Orin lay on his belly next to her, his legs bent at the knee and his feet waving slowly and rhythmically. He looked up at her, gestured to the others, and then rolled his eyes. Idra controlled the smile that wanted to spread over her face. "Relax, Ore," she said under her breath. He quietly moaned his discontent. "They'll be done soon," she added.

"We could be doing something," he said.

"Or not," she answered, slightly exasperated.

"Think about how much we haven't seen."

Idra worried his voice would get too loud and distract the others. "Later," she said quietly. He must have been somewhat mollified, because after that, he waited silently until the others had finished.

One by one, they relaxed as their tribute stones were completed. Ara finished last, and almost as one, they arose. Their journey to the stone altar was faster this time. They took a path that led them almost to the beach where they had first arrived, before following another route. Yesterday Orin had run ahead to explore and then returned to see whether he was going the right direction. Enetheal had still clearly been the leader. Orin was sharing the lead with Enetheal now. He would indicate a path, and Enetheal would nod his assent. Orin was learning his way around quickly.

Idra was surprised when they arrived to find the sun still a good distance from the horizon. Yesterday it had taken the whole day to gather the stones, explore the Sapwood and arrive here. Ara frowned, her eyebrows coming together. Orin took lead again, depositing his stone upon the altar, and then returning. Namin followed, and then Lenya, trailing after Namin with a smile. After they had all deposited their stones, Kuthan turned to Enetheal expectantly.

Enetheal gestured towards the rock, and then the sun before turning to Kuthan. They had another exchange of eyes, which lasted uncomfortably long. Eventually Kuthan turned away, and Enetheal cast his gaze upon the water. Idra turned to Orin at the same time he turned to her. By unspoken agreement, they turned to go back up the path.

"Where are you going?" Ara inquired, her eyes narrowing slightly.

"Away," said Orin, a defiant note to his voice.

"To gather food," Idra added before Ara could respond. Once she said it, she felt the hollowness in her stomach and knew that the others must be hungry as well.

"Don't be too long, my belly's starting to ache," Namin said playfully. Idra stuck out her tongue at him. He raised his eyebrows and she laughed. As soon as the others were out of sight, Orin picked up the pace, and soon they were both running. She hadn't realized that she wanted to get away until they had gone. The path melted before them. Again Orin showed excellent navigational skills. It did not take long before they reached the stone way near the base of the slope that led to the Welcome Table.

They slowed as they approached the walkway, and journeyed in a long, loop-like fashion around the base of the slope. They proceeded through a clearing with another large tree like the ones that bore fruit, and passed on to the other side, continuing to follow the stones. They lost themselves in pine trees once more. Orin kept looking at where dirt paths met up with stone ways. Occasionally he would set his gaze far ahead, or turn and look behind. They passed through another clearing with another tree, and continued on to the other side.

"What's up?" she asked Orin, as he scrutinized the path.

"I'm still trying to figure out where this one goes," Orin said, puzzled. "The other paths seem to each link up with some sort of destination: the Welcome Table, the Stony Shores, the Stargazing Beach, the Sunset Altar, the cabins …."

They arrived at today's fruit-bearing tree. Once again, Idra removed the webs before entering. She thought how each clearing with a single large tree was placed along the stone way. That morning she had walked along the stone way to find the next fruit-bearing tree. She felt her breath quicken, and it took a moment to realize why. Now she understood: Kuthan was looking for patterns. Idra had found one.

NAMIN - DAY TWO

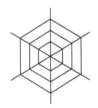

His comment about coming back soon with food hadn't been a joke. Namin was hungry. He became all the more aware of the emptiness inside his stomach as soon as Orin and Idra were out of sight. Still, he knew that hunger wasn't all of it. Something about having Idra and Orin gone made the day seem colder. He turned towards the others. Maybe Orin and Idra felt it too—something within their group was off. It was probably why they were so eager to leave. The aura of the island had become grimmer since they received their tasks. Lenya, Kuthan, and Ara had all lapsed into silence after Orin and Idra left. They each seemed lost in their own worlds. Ara's head was cast down, her eyes closed. Lenya's gaze was upon the horizon.

Kuthan stared at the trees without observing them. He no doubt was trying to piece together what they were doing, and why they had to do it. They had talked about it earlier that day: "Think through it logically," he had whispered intensely. All their conversations had been conducted in a whisper because they 'couldn't trust Enetheal'. "Someone wants us to do what we're doing with the stones, which is why we are doing it. That was established in the rules."

"I'm with you so far," Namin had answered. He appreciated considering their situation one step at a time, but didn't understand why this mattered so much to Kuthan.

"That same someone wants us to make an additional 'service' for the island, which is where our individual labors come in." Kuthan's eyes fixed on Namin's with intensity.

"And so we are trying to see how our different services and the collecting of the rocks are like each other," Namin continued, "... to figure out what we are doing."

"And what the Rule Maker *wants,*" Kuthan finished. He emphasized *wants*, and said *Rule Maker* with harshness.

"If there is a Rule Maker," Namin added.

"Yes. I think that's a safe asumption," Kuthan responded coolly. "After all, there are rules."

Namin had not known how to respond to this, so they had lapsed into silence. He reflected on it now. The rules did not bother him nearly as much as they bothered Kuthan. There was something about the individual services that did irk him, however. It wasn't the services themselves—he still felt elated from last night's web-weaving. Namin was bothered by how the group had changed since receiving their individual tasks. On the boat they had been one family. During the course of yesterday they had been a united group as well. Perhaps they had been apprehensive, maybe even a little scared not knowing what the day would bring, but they had had unity.

Things were noticeably different today. Ara in particular had been quiet for most of the day. Kuthan was sullen, and Lenya was even more detached than she had been yesterday. Now Idra and Orin had left them. Maybe they, too, felt something was off about the mood of the group. The only obvious difference Namin saw between today and the last two days was that they now had individual tasks. Could this be the source of their discomfort? *Calm down*, he thought. He was making assumptions. It was probably his imagination. But as he looked at each member of the little group, he was not convinced.

He was not the only one watching. Enetheal stood nearby, his eyes fixed upon them. At least Enetheal remained unchanged. Namin walked over to Enetheal. A small splash and accompanying cold told him that he had stepped into water. He had not noticed that Enetheal was standing ankle deep in the water. He waded through it until they were side by side.

Kuthan had looked up at the noise. He watched them for a time, but when Namin did nothing else, he turned away.

"What do you think?" Namin asked under his breath. Enetheal's eyes met his. They stared eye to eye, before Namin added "I know you can't answer, but I'd still like to know." Enetheal blinked, but otherwise their eye contact remained unbroken. Namin turned his gaze back to the others. If they would only have extra time tomorrow, as they had today, perhaps they might accomplish something beyond their tasks which would give them a break from the rules and obligations. *Not just tomorrow. Today. Now.*

"Good thinking," he said to Enetheal. It was Namin's thought, but he felt like Enetheal's presence helped him think. He had a plan now, and would make sure things did not get too out of hand. He felt Enetheal's eyes follow him as he walked back towards the others. He joined Ara and Lenya. Ara sat near the water's edge, her legs hugged close to her chest. Lenya sat behind her, playing with Ara's hair, a vacant expression on her face.

"Hey," he said. It wasn't directed to either of them in particular. There was a long pause before Ara answered.

"Hello." Her voice was tired and strained.

He sat next to her. At first she tensed, but when he said nothing else she seemed to relax. They sat in silence until a burst of sun came through the clouds. Warmth and light washed over them, and the dark water sparkled in the sun. They both squinted against the light. Lenya stopped playing with Ara's hair for a moment. Namin bumped Ara's leg lightly with his own.

"Beautiful," he murmured.

"Yes," Lenya and Ara both answered. They basked in the glow. Namin tried to think about what they should do, but his thoughts were interrupted.

"We're back!" Orin called out. Both he and Idra were laden with fruit, their arms held close to their chests, cradling the awkward bundles.

"Excellent," Kuthan answered. Namin felt his stomach leap in surprise. He hadn't noticed Kuthan come up behind them. "A feast for our bellies and a feast for our eyes," Kuthan continued, gesturing towards the sunset.

"Guess what we figured out?" Orin said breathlessly.

"Tell us, Ore," Namin smiled.

"Orin can't run and hold fruit at the same time," Idra answered.

"Only 'cause I was faster than you!" Orin retorted.

"Okay Ore," Idra laughed. Orin grunted.

Orin's discovery would have to wait. Idra and Orin passed fruit around, and they all filled their mouths. In front of them the sun set. The sky and water were suffused with light. The clouds shifted from brilliant shades of orange and pink and into the quiet indigo of impending darkness as the sun dropped below the horizon.

"*And for this day your labor's done,*" Kuthan quoted ironically. Ara let out a nervous laugh, which she stifled abruptly when it was unshared. Kuthan got up and walked toward the Sunset Altar. He picked up the stone salver to bear the stones, and gathered them carefully. Enetheal walked over from where they had been standing, and they left together.

Namin watched them go. He felt uneasy, partly because of how Kuthan had responded to his task yesterday, but even more because he did not like waiting. He turned to the others. Idra and Orin were gone. He looked around just in time to see them walk out of sight behind a cluster of trees and stone. Namin considered following them when Lenya spoke. The curls of Ara's sand-colored hair were still laced between her fingers.

"The stars are shining." She said it dreamily, but with clear excitement. Sure enough, when he looked up at the sky he could see the stars just coming into view. Lenya stopped playing with Ara's hair and gazed out serenely.

"You will be finding one of them tonight," Namin said. She turned at him and smiled.

"Yes." He was glad she had actually spoken: she had been so quiet today. He thought for a moment.

"Could you show us where you bring them?" He asked the question without thinking, but realized after he asked it that it was exactly the right thing to do.

"Of course."

"Let's go," Ara agreed, as if she felt Namin's new insight. She got to her feet.

"Idra! Orin!" Lenya called. To Namin's surprise they appeared almost immediately. They must have been close.

For once, Idra led. Orin followed, a scowl on his round face.

"Want to visit Lenya's well?" Ara asked. The scowl vanished into an eager smile.

"Yes!" he responded instantly. He glanced at the darkening sky. "Let's go quickly," he added.

"I'm staying here," Idra said. "But you guys go," she added hurriedly.

"Idra!" Orin complained.

"Orin!" she mimicked. "Be quick," she added with a smile.

The smile was for Ara, but as they left, she caught Namin's eye. They parted immediately.

They moved at a quick pace, racing against the fading light. Namin knew that Idra was staying for Kuthan, and it annoyed him slightly. He would have liked to take them all away from worries over rules and services and their labors of the day. But Idra stayed. He remembered the firmness of her voice insisting Ara should be the first to eat that morning, her pursuit of Orin the day before when he had become so upset. Well, at least between the two of them each person would be looked out for.

Lenya led the group across the beach they had arrived on. Rocks rose up to cliffs at the edge of the beach, and cut into the cliff-side. They climbed. Higher and higher, steeper and steeper. The air started to feel cooler, and Namin did not know whether it was night settling in or the breeze rising off the water that started to chill him.

He forgot the cooling temperature once they reached the top of the stairs. Even in the dimming daylight, the view was spectacular. They were atop a small plateau. The level surface was vibrant with life. Plants of every color bloomed around its perimeter. More dazzling still was the view. To one side, the water extended into nothingness. Shimmering ripples darkened into the sky, where the horizon surely divided them. The other side faced the island, and for the first time Namin was struck by the beauty of the place: not only were the greens and browns and greys of the land itself beautiful, but he also began to see how everthing fit together. The Welcome Table was visible from here, and he could see where the Stony Shores must be, and also their sleeping cabins.

Lenya waited as the little group gazed out at the water and the wondrous view of the island. Finally she led them to the well in the center of the plateau. Orin almost plunged into it in his excitement to look down, and heedless of his near-miss, craned without caution over the stony lip. Namin had his hands ready, prepared to catch him if he should lean too far.

"See any stars?" Namin laughed.

"Almost," Ore answered. Namin and Ara also looked down. If he squinted and peered beyond the blackness, he could almost make out two specks of light in the well's dark recess.

After a while Ara said they should go. Namin was glad. He was about to speak up himself, but did not wish to end their time together. They hurried down a different path on the far side of the plateau. As soon as they reached the bottom they realized it was dark. Night had not yet fallen, but the sky was a deep blue.

"We need to move," Ara said. And they did. They ran. They didn't just jog; they sprinted. Orin and Lenya took the lead, and seemed to know where they were going. It was a good thing, too. The darkness seemed to chase them as they ran. Pine trees loomed close from all sides. A few times they mistakenly journeyed off the path. Ara and Orin always caught these false steps and brought them back on track.

Sweaty and red in the face, they arrived at Lenya and Ara's cabin. Their quick goodbye reminded Namin how much he hated parting without proper words, but they were forced to press on. They ran past Kuthan and Idra's cabin. They could only hope that Kuthan and Idra had made it back safely. Finally they arrived at their own. They were almost at the door when they saw Enetheal. He seemed to materialize out of the gloom. His tall slim frame and mouthless face were somehow more noticeable as he leaned to peel back the web-screen and open the door. A shiver swept through Namin. He entered, leaving Orin and Enetheal to shut the door and depart: Orin would have to continue onward to light the lanterns. They left in a hurry, and again, Namin was left alone with his thoughts.

The cabin was dark, but this darkness was comforting. The blackness settling outside the cabin was terrifying. Why? What would have happened if they had not made it back in time? Although he had broken into a sweat as they tore down the path to their cabin, it was when he saw Enetheal that his heart had started to pound. For the first time something about Enetheal truly frightened Namin. Was he there to make sure they arrived before the sky turned black? What would he have done if Namin had not come back on time? The cabin seemed small now, and he found himself pacing back and forth. He wished he could talk to Kuthan. These were the kinds of questions that belonged to Kuthan.

He wondered whether their trip to Lenya's well had been worth it. Had they been in danger? Regardless, they had made it. So it *had* been worth it. The well and garden were amazing; even more, their journey had been deeply satisfying. He felt a serene significance in this journey that was missing from the mere collection and decoration of rocks. Now the day felt somehow accomplished. He lay back, letting out a long breath, gently took air in, and began to hum to himself, tunelessly. Once again he relaxed. He thought about the webs he was going to weave that night.

It seemed only moments later that he awakened to Enetheal's knock. As Orin entered, Namin touched his hand for a moment as they switched places. Then, as he walked along the newly lighted path, Namin studied Enetheal's face. If he was angry or worried, it didn't show. They wandered further into the night.

They reached a fruit-tree clearing. Just as on the night before, Namin wove his song until webs spanned the clearing at both entrances, sheltering the tree within. One by one he visited the cabins, reworking and repairing the webscreens on the doors with his melody. He thought of Lenya and Ara, and of the little adventure they had taken as the darkness had settled. He visited Kuthan and Idra's cabin, and prayed that Kuthan's task had gone more easily than it had the evening before. For a moment, pangs of guilt filled him at having left Kuthan. But Idra had been there. Idra was always there. He left their cabin and returned to his own. As he journeyed down the path Enetheal trailed after him, more shadow-like than ever. After he had finished singing at his own door, he turned. Enetheal stood there watching him.

"Thank you," Namin said quietly.

Enetheal blinked, and they turned from one another, Namin to the cabin and Enetheal into the darkness of the night.

LENYA - DAYS THREE AND FOUR

She wasn't sleeping. Not really. Resting was more accurate. Ara was sleeping, that was for sure. Ara breathed in, slow and deep. Outside the wind blew gently, the branches swayed, and the waves rolled. Ara exhaled slowly. Lenya felt her eyelids flickering. *She was falling. It was both exhilarating and terrifying. She had been chosen. Tonight was her night. Her silver aura lit her way as she plummeted. Why? Surely she had been in the right place. She couldn't help but feel hurt.* Ara took in a sharp breath. Lenya ran her hand over her, and Ara released the breath slowly. *The impact was hard, and once again she felt fear. What now? What was her fate now?* The door creaked as it opened. He didn't approach. He didn't need to. She was more than ready. True wakefulness started to rise inside her, but she knew it was a only shadow of what was to come.

Lenya made sure Ara was wrapped in blankets before she left the bed. She took Enetheal by the hand, and pulled him into the starlit night. The night felt cold after her warm bed, but it also made her smile. In front of her, on either side of the path, were little golden flashes. The lanterns weren't bright enough to see much, but she knew where she had to walk to stay on the path. Orin did his job well. The first night Enetheal had led the way. Last night they had walked tentatively side by side. Tonight they walked together confidently, Lenya directing their course.

The problem about trying to keep to the path was that she needed to keep returning her eyes to the ground below. When they arrived at the beach, she was relieved she could turn her gaze to the heavens. She ran out onto the open sand. Without the forest of pine trees blocking them, the silver shine of stars and moon bathed water and sand alike so that the whole beach-world was silver. She allowed herself to spin, and let the wind catch her hair before she fell to the sand, gaze turned skyward. Enetheal joined her silently, and together they stared into the sky. She realized she enjoyed his presence now.

The night was bright. The last two nights had been luminous as well. She silently thanked the clouds for not obscuring the stars. Slowly her body became still again. She would not enter sleep, but she was resting once more. Lenya kept her eyes fixed on the heavens above. She did not have to wait long. The star seemed to shiver briefly in the sky, the movement instantly drawing her eyes. Then it plummeted.

At first the light seemed to grow brighter as the star came closer. As it neared, it became as bright as the moon, although its color was a colder blue. The treeline obscured its final stretch, and she lost sight of it. However, she was sure it had landed somewhere between the cabins and the Stony Shores. Lenya got up and turned to Enetheal.

"Ready?" He rose in answer, and they headed into the pine trees.

With the sky-illuminated beach behind her, and the silvery shine of the fallen star obscured, Lenya's eyes had to readjust to darkness as she entered the forest. She focused on Orin's lanterns—flickers of gold marking the path ahead. The star appeared to have fallen near the Stony Shores, so she wandered in that direction, carefully keeping to the path.

Before long, the glimmering shoreline came into sight, and she quickened her pace.

The Stony Shores dazzled her far more now than they had earlier that day, or even the day before. She practically danced across the stones to her waiting star. The rocks surrounding it had been crushed or scattered aside forming a small circle where it had landed. In the center was her star. Lenya slowed as she reached the ring of dust and broken stones, hesitating at its edge. Enetheal halted next to her. She breathed deeply before carefully placing her foot into the circle. Tentatively, she made her way forward, stopping to kneel once she was within reach of her star. This star shimmered, different parts of it brightening intermittently, yet no part of it ever becoming truly dark.

Gently, Lenya placed her hands around her star and allowed her skin to touch it—and she remembered.

She gasped as a wave of coldness swept through her. She was utterly still, unable to move, her hands just touching the star. Its quavering glow washed over her, and Lenya stared back, unblinking. They were both still for a moment, she and the star, until something tickled the back of her mind. There was something she was supposed to do. And it had to do with her star. *The star needs to go to the well.*

It was a whisper of a thought, but the whisper persisted. Slowly she straightened up, pulling the star to herself.

The shoreline was illuminated by the light in her arms. She noticed that the beach stones gleamed differently by starlight than when the sun shone. Colored stones were indistinguishable from plainer grey or white, since all the stones reflected the blue-white starlight. They looked even more magical by the light of the star.

To her, the star also revealed Enetheal more completely. She was always aware of his presence, but it was only after she retrieved stars that he became clear. It was not so much that he appeared different from how he looked during the day, but she noticed him more. He was not unlike her. Granted, he was taller, mouthless, and did not follow the same rules. But now they were both bathed in star-shine. Everything looked better by starlight. Wordlessly they left the Stony Shores for the path through the pines.

Now that she carried a beacon in her hand, she hardly noticed the golden flashes of Orin's lanterns. The path and the woods were brightly lit as they traveled. The night was also strangely silent. Perhaps the night creatures were also dazzled by her star. She was hardly aware of the time passing as she journeyed to the plateau. She arrived not even winded. The flowers, their faces lifted to the moon, now turned towards the light of her star. Lenya remembered how sad they had seemed during the day. Now she felt vitality both in herself and in the garden. Slowly, she walked to the well, prolonging her time with her star. Enetheal walked ahead and paused beside it. She knew she ought not to keep him waiting, so reluctantly she quickened her pace and finally arrived at the well's edge.

The abyss within became a darkness even the star could not penetrate, at least not from its place in her arms. She held it tightly, allowing herself to experience its coldness and exhilaration for a few moments longer. Then she let it fall. Down into darkness it went, until all she could see was black. And as she glanced beyond the well, she saw that her surroundings were now shadowed as well. The plants seemed dazed, the flower-heads still facing toward her. She noticed her hands gripping the side of the well tightly. She let go.

A terrible dizziness swept through her. Although she remembered this from the last two nights, she was not prepared for the weakness that now overwhelmed her. Her hands shook, and she shivered. The world seemed at once too hot and too cold. By the time she recovered, the flowers were no longer watching her. Once again, their heads tilted up towards the moon, and she joined their gaze. Was the moon slightly bigger than last night? She could not tell. Enetheal moved. It was time to return. She stumbled in the direction of the cabins, Enetheal at her side.

A warm wind blew through the trees. To either side, small flashes of gold showed them where to walk. Once, a root snagged her foot and she almost stepped off the path. Enetheal steadied her and they moved on. She was too tired to make sense of what had happened or to realize that she should have been nervous, but she was thankful.

As they reached her door they paused. Behind it her bed waited. "You should join us for breakfast tomorrow," she said sleepily. Enetheal stared at her. When he did nothing else, she peeled back the spider-web screen and opened the door. "Goodnight," she called softly before closing it behind her. She crawled in next to Ara, pulling the covers around them before allowing herself to be taken into sleep.

The door opened. She heard them, so she opened her eyes. Light streamed through the open door and Ara awoke, too. The two of them climbed out of their bed and looked at Idra, who was talking excitedly about the day to come. They followed her as she lead the way out of the cabin and towards the Welcome Table. Namin reminded her to keep up, so with some effort she did. As they traveled along the path and up the slope, Ara and Orin chatted amiably. Orin described his path-lighting last night. He had enjoyed it very much, and had lit the way to the Stony Shores. She was so pleased that Ara was happy. They arrived at the table. There, waiting, was Enetheal. She sat next to him, remembering how he had looked in the starlight. It took her a moment to realize the others had not sat down with her.

She beckoned to the others. Finally Namin came, followed by Idra, Orin, and Ara. Kuthan was last to sit. As they sat together the wind swirled and lifted dry pine needles around the little group.

"Lenya, will you start?" Idra asked.

"Okay," she answered. She picked up the fruit. It was green, rounded at the bottom, and narrowed to a neck at the top. The skin was rough—it felt weird. But she suddenly knew she was hungry. She put it in her mouth and bit down.

An explosion of flavor filled her mouth. It was juicy, and unbelievably sweet.

"Oh," she gasped. "It's amazing!"

Idra beamed. Kuthan and Namin both eyed Idra when she answered, "Thanks, Lenya."

They all started eating their fruits. Enetheal did not eat, of course, but he sat with them. Ara started describing her plan to do something new with the stones today. Namin agreed, and they started talking. Kuthan and Idra did not say much. Lenya thought she already knew where to find hers.

They went down to the Stony Shores. It was a nice day. The sun was up, the sky was blue. Today was the easiest stone-choosing day yet. All the rocks were pretty, but only a few were star-touched. When Lenya reached the small crater where her star had hit the ground she already knew which one to pick. Grey-pink, rough, and a comfortable fit for her two hands. There were several deep cracks on its surface, a relic from the star. They could remember the star together, she thought, as she picked up the stone. She held it close. It radiated the sun's heat, completely able to discard the cold of the star which had touched it the night before. Lenya didn't mind, though. It was just different. She returned to Enetheal. He stood at the forest edge as he had for the last two days.

"You should make one, Enetheal." She thought it and voiced it at the same time. He stared at her and shook his head, which she guessed meant no. When he did nothing else, she lay down. The rocks weren't nearly as comfortable as the beach, but they were warm. Clouds floated overhead. Waves splashed gently. Birds sang. Kuthan walked over.

"Do you want to walk?" he asked.

In answer she got up. They walked down the shore.

"Any luck?" she asked.

"Still looking," he answered, before jumping into another thought. "We didn't get to talk today at breakfast. I am interested—did anything special happen last night?" He said it in a flat, uninterested way, but it seemed as if he were looking for something.

"I found a star!" she answered. *It had glowed, and shimmered, and had been alive.* "It was beautiful!" she added quietly.

Kuthan kicked some rocks aside, running his fingers through his hair. He turned, glancing back toward the path before refocusing on her.

"How was Enetheal?" He picked up a handful of the smaller stones, throwing one after another into the water.

"He kept me company," she said. She picked up a flat stone, as she had seen Idra do, and tossed it at the water. It splashed and sank.

"Did your service go well?" she asked. Her next stone bounced.

"It stayed the same," he said evenly. He picked up a large stone, eyed it, and then held it close. He gave her a nod, and they returned to the path where the others waited. Everyone had a larger stone today, perhaps because they were eager to paint as they had the day before ....

Enetheal did not take them to the Berry Grove. Instead they went to the beach where Lenya and Enetheal had watched stars. In daytime the Stony Shores and the beach could not be more different from one another. Here the sun seemed brighter, the world brighter. The sand was yellow and warm, and the wind was more a breeze than a gust. There were no rocks scattered about to slip or trip on. The only rocks here were large outgrowths from the sand. Lenya was surprised when she realized everyone was looking down instead of up. Three nights had passed, and already it was hard to think of the beach as anything other than a bed to lie upon while stargazing.

Shells. Scattered across the sand were shells, and that was how they were going to decorate the stones today. It would be nice, she was sure, but she couldn't help but think about what would happen that night.

They used some syrupy sticky substance to stick the shells on the rocks. Was it sap? It must be. Orin had brought it over on a piece of pine bark. The shells were pretty, and looked good when stuck to the stone. They sat in the sun, fixing shells to stones. Enetheal disappeared for a time.

Namin started playing in the sand with Orin, and Idra and Kuthan joined after a few moments. Ara kept encouraging the others to return to their stones, so eventually they did. Enetheal returned, and they set off to deliver their stones.

They stopped at a tree "... a new tree," Lenya thought. The fruit was as delicious as it had been at breakfast.

It was sweeter than she remembered. She became aware of Orin laughing as he and Namin tossed a piece of fruit back and forth, Idra in-between trying to intercept it, Ara suppressing a smile. She noticed Kuthan watching Enetheal, and Enetheal watching her. The greens of the pine needles seemed more vivid, the wind tickled her skin, and the sun got in her eyes.

They journeyed to the Sunset Altar and placed their own stones on it. Namin pointed out that the sun was still far from setting, so they returned to the beach and played with the sand some more until the sun started to set. She had enjoyed the day, but she longed for the night ....

The darkness arrived; Enetheal did not. Lenya waited and waited for him to come. When she couldn't stand it any longer, she set off. The golden flashes told her where she could step. The wind was cold this night. Not an exhilarating cold like the star she knew she would find, but a cold that seeped into her. She hurried into the night, trying to outrun the cooling wind. She wasn't aware of when he first joined her. At some point she turned to find him on the path some distance behind her. She stopped so that he could catch up. He walked to her side, but when she started walking again he fell behind.

She wished he would walk closer; at least then they might be a bit warmer together. It was even colder when she walked out onto the beach. Wind washed over her, and now the pine trees no longer guarded her. She lay on the sand and tried to forget the cold. Above were the stars. More were hidden tonight behind clouds, but there were clear patches and starshine.

Enetheal waited at the edge of the forest, shrouded by the shadow of a pine.

"Come," she called out.

He seemed to ponder for a moment before coming out to her to lie together under the stars. They watched. The clouds moved across the sky. Moonlight shone through at times, as did starlight; but the stars stayed fixed in the sky. Lenya closed her eyes, and then opened them slowly.

"What was it like before we came here?" she asked.

Enetheal slowly turned his head to look at her. He put a finger on his face where his mouth should have been and then turned back toward the sky. She closed her eyes once more—they ached to be closed—but forced herself to open them again. She felt warm. *I have to stay awake!* She realized that despite her anticipation, the sound of the gently lapping water had been lulling her into a doze.

"What did you do then?"

Enetheal gazed out at the horizon, and then back at Lenya. She wondered what that could mean. She glanced out at the horizon. Just as she moved her eyes; she caught a flicker of movement. Quickly her gaze returned skyward, and she saw the light fall. This one was not as bright as the others had been. As it fell it seemed to trail some of its light behind. It landed far away. Together they got up. Her legs protested, but she managed to get to her feet.

"Let's go." Lenya led the way.

The wooded path met the stone way at the base of the slope. The stone way was less overgrown than the others, allowing the silver light of the night to join the golden flashes of the flies in lighting the way. The path twisted, turned, and curved. Were they headed in the right direction? She turned to Enetheal. He was gone. Her chill returned for a moment and her stomach clenched.

"Enetheal!" she called. There was no answer. She started to turn back along the way, but then she noticed a flicker of light between the pines up ahead. Her star? It had vanished so quickly, though. So far, the stars she had collected had emitted light relatively constantly. She stared where she had seen the light, but there was only blackness. It was more than blackness though, there was something else. Her heart seemed to pause. *It had to have been my star.* She followed the stone way towards the trees where she had seen the light. The clouds now obscured the moon and most of the stars, so she had to rely on the golden flashes to see the way.

A cool wind blew, and she suppressed a shiver. The darkness blinded her, but she crept closer. Even the fireflies had stopped flashing. And then there it was again, a brief glimpse of something in between the trees. The air seemed still, as if the wind itself was holding its breath. She took another step, and then another, and then, without warning she felt hands grasp her shoulders.

She tried to scream, but a hand covered her mouth, stifling all sound. She spun around. Her assailant was Enetheal; he had returned. Her fear briefly turned into anger, but Enetheal pointed, first down in front of her and then into the woods up ahead. She took a moment to comprehend what he meant, but then realized: the stone way ended just in front of her, yielding to forest. But not simply forest. She could now hear something else. Silence.

She sensed what was beyond the path just before the parting clouds allowed silvery light to illuminate it. In front of her stood the tall dark pines of the Sapwood. Rivers of sap seeped down the trees, glowing in newfound light. She could just make out reflections of the nearby pines in the pools of sap where each tree stood.

They backtracked quietly. Before this, Enetheal had trailed her at a distance; now he was almost stepping on her feet. They took a different path away from the stone way. Flashes of gold led them around the wood. She gazed into its depths every time she had a chance, but saw nothing more. Whatever she had seen in the Sapwood, it was not her star.

Her star waited for her in the forest just beyond the Sunset Altar, pulsing softly. She could feel its coolness before her fingers touched it. She came closer, and the air grew colder, until at last, her fingers brushed its surface. They became one, she and her star, and she felt as if she too glowed and emitted coldness.

Together they lit the path around the Sapwood and illuminated the way of the slope to the Welcome Table. They brought light to the beach where she had first seen the star fall, and up to the plateau and the well. The golden flashes guiding them were dim beside the silver luminescence which they themselves sent forth.

The garden atop the little plateau had been waiting. The plants turned hungrily toward their silver light. Rather than go straight to the well, she moved about the garden with her star, sharing their radiance. Flowers leaned in close at their approach. *Could they unearth themselves?* They circled the garden once again, but finally Lenya knew it was time. She froze momentarily, the star's energy coursing through her as she held it poised above the abyss. Then they let go of one another.

The plants watched her a moment longer—perhaps Lenya glowed with residual light—but then they turned their gaze back to the heavens. Slowly Lenya joined them, turning her face skyward, feeling empty. A new night would come. Her emptiness lessened at that thought, and she smiled at the sky.

"Soon I will know you all," she told them. They gazed back at her in silence, but the smile was shared.

KUTHAN - DAY FOUR

"Wake up!"

The words pulled Kuthan out of a deep sleep. He knew he had been dreaming, but the dream had been dark. Not just dark, but the same blackness that had enveloped him as he descended to deliver the tribute stones. While he had been asleep it was comforting instead of terrifying. He only recognized it as the nothingness it was when he started to awaken. He tensed, panicked, but then opened his eyes … to Idra. Her eyes were large, brown, happy, and just a little too close.

He tried to push her away, but she jumped back giggling.

"I'm going to get us food now," she said excitedly. "And I'll be careful," she added more seriously. Her eyes were wide and earnest.

"Let me know …."

"As soon as I get back," she said, cutting him off and rolling her eyes.

Kuthan nodded his thanks, and she was gone. He allowed himself to rest once more, but his mind did not stop racing. Today would confirm what Idra had worked out. The stone way looped around the slope in a more-or-less circular fashion, connecting each of the fruit-bearing trees. The trees themselves took turns bearing fruit, one after the other, along the stone path.

It was a step forward. No. More than that. Not only did he have a pattern, but he now had an ally. Idra understood the importance of looking for patterns. Idra had waited while Kuthan completed his task; the others had left him. And Idra was getting food for them now. He was uneasy with her gone. Still, he wasn't as scared as he had been the last three mornings when Idra had departed. It was now routine. And so far, the routines which had been established had not resulted in harm.

However, they were still a problem. Namin did not believe there was a Rule Maker, but Kuthan could not shake the idea that someone desired their time and their labor during the day. The quickest way to figure out the intentions of the Rule Maker would be to figure out what, or who, was behind the rules. *Enetheal's rules*, he thought angrily. Enetheal was the one who gave them their services, who ensured they spent their days toiling over tribute stones. Enetheal had established the routines that they were all now following. *That I'm following.* He let out a grunt of disgust.

He had hated the rules from the moment they had first sounded in his mind. From the beginning, he had challenged Enetheal's rules. But then he had followed along. He had accepted the laws of the Welcome Table. Lenya had said they had a choice, but that was simply not true. Kuthan was disappointed with the others for being so compliant, but truly disgusted at his own weakness. *It's just until I figure stuff out,* he had told himself. That's what he had thought on their first day of tasks and tributes. Even on the second. It was not until the second night that he realized he was afraid: afraid of Enetheal, afraid of Enetheal's rules, afraid of the island, and afraid of darkness. *But I will conquer my fear,* he thought. And I *will* act once we have figured out more.

Soon he heard voices accompanying the sounds of birdsong, wind, and waves, so he arose. Opening the door, he found Orin, Namin and Idra already gathered together outside. Idra had a wide grin on her face and he felt happy just looking at her obvious joy. She gave a silent nod, indicating that the next tree in the circle had borne fruit. Kuthan shared her smile.

"Food," Idra added happily. And they left together.

Kuthan was surprised when the door to Ara and Lenya's cabin opened after the first knock. It was Ara. Orin started to say something, but Ara held a finger to her lips and he stopped.

"Stay here," she said quietly, and so they did. They waited, Orin shuffled impatiently from one foot to another until Ara returned, trailed by Lenya. Lenya looked tired, but she wore a smile. They left the cabin, and together they went up the slope to the table. As they approached, Kuthan's stomach plummeted. Waiting for them was Enetheal. He hadn't been there the first two days, but he had joined them yesterday, and now here he was here again. Why? Now they couldn't even eat in peace.

It must have been because of something Namin or Lenya had done. Neither of them seemed surprised, and both of them seemed to welcome Enetheal's presence. Yesterday Lenya had even asked Enetheal to join them in their labor, as if she wanted Enetheal to be one of them! It was clear that Namin, too, didn't oppose Enetheal's presence. Sometimes Namin actually talked to Enetheal. Come to think of it, Ara was unperturbed by Enetheal as well, but at least she was indifferent instead of welcoming. Lenya and Namin took seats on either side of Enetheal. Kuthan sat opposite. Idra, Orin, and Ara filled in the gaps.

To his surprise, Idra chose him to eat first. He took the fruit, and bit down slowly.

"Wonderful Idra!" he sighed.

It was good, and he would not let on how much Enetheal's presence poisoned his pleasure. Idra beamed, oblivious of his unease. Afterward they migrated to the Stony Shores to search for tribute stones. As usual, they stopped briefly at the spiderweb that blocked the path before hurrying on to the shore.

The waves were choppy that day, and the wind was strong. Before him were the Stony Shores, each stone varying in shape, texture, and color, and he would have to find one to make a tribute. The task no longer carried the same worry as it initially had, but it certainly took the same effort. Kuthan's search was impeded by the ever-present feeling that Enetheal was watching. However, when he looked back towards the path, Enetheal's form was absent from the treeline.

Today's stone was a large rounded light grey-green rock. He found it nestled in the shallows between some weeds. It was wide enough to decorate, which he hoped he would be doing. The beauty in collecting stones was that *they* got to choose which rock was right. At least they had *some* choice. In front of him the water expanded outward until it met the grey sky. *Lenya's choice*, he smiled mirthlessly.

Lenya had also finished her search. She stood by the path, gazing across the Stony Shores, one hand on her hip, the other holding a pale stone.

"Where is Enetheal?" he asked, walking over to her. She blinked and looked at him with her light-blue eyes.

"Not here," she answered.

Kuthan felt a surge of energy, but he said nothing. He waited with Lenya in silence. She did not seem to mind.

Namin, Orin, and Idra arrived together. Orin and Idra had finished first, and they had followed Namin around until he, too, had found his stone. They arrived as a threesome.

"Where is Enetheal?" Namin asked.

"Not here," Kuthan said, echoing Lenya's words. A smile crept into his voice.

"Does this mean no one will check our stones today?" Orin asked.

"It means a lot of things," Kuthan said. "This changes everything."

"This changes nothing," Ara responded coldly. Kuthan had not noticed her join them.

"Enetheal enforces the rules. Enetheal is gone," he told her shortly. Ara scowled, but Orin spoke before she did.

"We can do what we want now," he added helpfully. Kuthan was grateful for his support.

Ara rounded on Orin. "The rules stand." She glared at him.

Then she turned to face Kuthan, but addressed the group at large. "Enetheal has shown us how to follow the rules. It is up to *us* to uphold them." She spun around, and started to lead the way up the path. Kuthan felt his muscles tense. He wanted to grab Ara, and force her to look back at him. Instead he called after her.

"We need to remember these are not laws that we chose, but rules that were forced upon us!" Unbidden, anger was creeping into his voice. How could Ara throw aside an opportunity to take control of their situation?

"We chose them when we accepted them," Ara answered shortly. "And I think it is best to keep them." She spoke dismissively again, as if her way was the only way. Kuthan was ready to retort once more, but Idra intervened.

"Please stop," Idra pleaded. Her voice echoed in his mind. *Ara is not the enemy,* he remembered. *The rules are. Enetheal is.*

"The rules are meant to keep us safe," Namin said, almost in whisper. "I think we should follow them." Kuthan wanted to cut in, but Namin continued to speak. "We still have some control. We choose our stones, and now we can choose what to do with them. Already we are learning more and are able to do more."

Kuthan did not know how to respond to that. It was not as if he could do it alone. Ara, Lenya, and Namin were against it. But he was not inclined to listen. *Namin and Lenya might side with Enetheal.* The idea was horrifying. There was a part of him that did not want to concede. *Please stop.* Idra's voice echoed in his mind, joined by his own: *We can't afford to fight among ourselves.*

"If we make a decision, it will be together." Kuthan said slowly. "We keep the rules for now." Idra relaxed. Orin sighed. He saw a look of approval from Namin. Ara gave him a curt nod, as though she too was more relaxed. Lenya looked relieved. Although it was frustrating, it made sense. At least he maintained control of the group.

They walked in silence. Kuthan decided it was a good thing. They all needed a moment to think. Was Enetheal watching them even now? Did he want them to divide?

They would certainly make better servants that way. Even when he was absent Enetheal dominated their actions.

They came to a crossroads in the path, and it became clear that they were not all going in the same direction. Lenya was going to the beach, Ara joining her. Namin headed towards the Sapwood. Orin and Idra wanted to paint. Kuthan joined them.

"Let's meet at the Welcome Table for food when we're done," Idra said.

Kuthan recognized this as an attempt to bring them back together, and quickly added a 'yes'.

"What if some of us finish before others?" Ara asked. Idra thought for a moment.

"We'll wait at the Table until everyone comes," she said finally.

Lenya started off towards the beach, and they all began to separate; Ara with Lenya, Namin to the Sapwood, and Kuthan, Idra, and Orin to the berry grove. Kuthan waited until the others were out of earshot, before stopping.

"Thank you both," he said quietly, as they walked along the path.

"For what?" Orin asked. He looked up at Kuthan, with golden brown eyes.

"Being there for me," Kuthan answered.

"We're *all* here for each other," Idra answered. Kuthan knew that the 'all' she was referring to included Ara, Lenya, and Namin as well.

"But we *three* understand that what's best for us all is to take back control."

"And figure out the island," Orin added in agreement. Idra bit her lower lip, looking agitated.

"We've agreed to keep the rules, and we will as long as that's best for the group," Kuthan stated, hoping to calm

Idra, "but that doesn't mean we can't take extra care to find out how things work." He took a breath, and then continued. "Can I trust you two to help me to figure out the island?"

Orin nodded eagerly.

Idra was still biting her lip before she answered, "Aren't we already doing that with all six of us?" Her eyes darted between Kuthan and Orin nervously.

"We were." Kuthan answered, bringing them to a stop. "But now I'm not so sure. The others don't seem as interested."

He took a moment to let his words sink in. They were harsh, but they were true and needed to be said. "You two remain interested in protecting us as a group, and to do that we need to know how things work." They both gazed at him unblinkingly, so he continued. "What I am suggesting now is new. I don't think it's enough to simply look around anymore. We must actively explore what we can and cannot do. We won't actually break rules, but to understand what is going on, we need to push them to their limits."

For a moment, the island sounds were the only sounds audible. After a moment of wind, waves, and the rustling of trees, they began walking again. Some time passed and Kuthan had started to worry, but finally Orin answered:

"You can trust us," he grinned. Kuthan felt a warmth spread through him, and he felt a smile spreading on his own face to match Orin's. His newfound happiness melted when he saw Idra. She looked nervously between the two of them.

"I don't think this is a good idea." Her voice quavered as she spoke. "Not without the others. This is dangerous." Kuthan's hurt was like a physical pain, and he had to work to keep his voice neutral.

"What *is* dangerous is being unaware, or not understanding." His words were cut short as he caught sight of Enetheal, who seemed to have appeared out of nowhere. Tall and mouthless, his figure blocked the path that led to the Berry Grove. His nose seemed sharper, his cheekbones higher, and his eyes more narrow than they had that morning. Kuthan felt the blood drain from his face. Enetheal walked over to them. Kuthan tensed. The others presented their stones as they usually did to Enetheal at the Stony Shores. Kuthan felt himself do the same. But he glared into Enetheal's cold grey eyes. Enetheal's gaze flickered down to the stone and then returned to Kuthan. Kuthan broke the visual contact first, his eyes shifting downward, settling at his feet, and he felt anger, fear, and shame. Once he sensed Enetheal's departure, he looked at the retreating figure, and continued to stare until the sound of his footsteps were no longer audible.

Wordlessly they entered the Berry Grove. They separated, each attending to their own rock. Kuthan wandered through the bushes. At first he forgot what he was doing. His mind was numb; he could not get the image of Enetheal's cold grey eyes out of his mind. But then he looked down at the stone in his hands, and remembered why he was there. Kuthan was preparing a stone as a tribute. He was not making the stone because he wished to, but because there were rules that decreed that he must: rules forced upon him by a mouthless aberration. Each day Enetheal marched them around, pushing them through tasks, but today had been the worst. By his very absence, Enetheal was ever more present. Kuthan was a fool to believe, even for a moment, that he was gone. Enetheal had merely been hidden. He had probably spied upon them as they harvested stones, delighted when Ara defended the rules, triumphant as the group became divided.

Kuthan started his work. He plucked berries from around him and smeared them on the stone's flat surface. His movements were precise, and well-defined. Slowly he labored. The sun did not shine through the cloud cover, but the wind dried the juice as well as yesterday's sun. His finger traced back and forth across the rough surface of the stone, smudging the juice where it should be smudged, and drawing out delicate lines where they were needed.

When he was finished, he smiled. It wasn't a happy smile. It was an angry smile, and a satisfied smile. Between his two hands were the Stony Shores. There were waves, stones, and even the forest in the background. Between the rocks and in the shallows were six silhouettes. Each of the shades stood separately, backs bowed, heads turned down. Looming in the back, taller than the trees stood a seventh figure. This last figure stood erect, one arm by its side, and the other raised out over the others. In creating this tribute, some of Kuthan's agitation had diminished. As he left the Berry Grove, he clutched his newest creation closer than he ever had the others.

Orin and Idra had long-since departed, so Kuthan walked alone to the Welcome Table. They all waited for him there. Idra had provided more fruit. Kuthan did not know how long they had been waiting, but now they ate together. They even managed a few laughs. By unspoken agreement, Idra, Orin and Kuthan didn't mention their conversations with one another, nor their confrontation with Enetheal.

The day passed. At twilight, Kuthan collected the tribute stones from the Sunset Altar and left for the cave with Enetheal. He knew the way well now. However, as they approached, their progress slowed. He knew why. It was time for the darkness, and no matter how much he told himself he was being foolish, the darkness terrified him.

Enetheal kept their pace from lagging too much, and soon the cave entrance was in sight. Kuthan entered, crossed over to the far end and the stairs, and was just about to descend his first step, when he paused. He turned to find the cave empty behind him. Returning to the entrance, he found Enetheal standing outside, his gaze turned toward the open water.

"Are you coming?" Kuthan asked. Enetheal's grey eyes met Kuthan's hazel ones, and Kuthan knew his answer. Wordlessly, Kuthan returned to the stairs, and began his descent. He was alone now. Enetheal had left him alone. He wasn't sure how he felt. Pleased? Angry? The first steps melted away before him. This task now belonged fully to him, and Enetheal had no part in it! That at least made him feel some triumph. Yet despite his fear and dislike of Enetheal, the darkness soon stole any satisfaction he had gained. It pressed in on him from all sides, stifling sound and sight, taste and smell. *I'm alone.* He wasn't sure where the thought had come from, his own mind or the darkness itself, but it latched on to him tightly: *What if this is it? What if there's nothing else?* He pressed his feet hard into the steps, but still his thoughts raced on: *My footsteps are all I have. I could go down the stairs forever; I could go up the stairs forever; it wouldn't make a difference. There are only stairs and me, and the stones which I carry.* His throat was closing, and his breaths labored. The sound of his breathing joined with his footfalls and the dead silence.

Enetheal has left me to darkness. Kuthan shut his eyes. They stung as he closed them, but he also felt calmer. At least the darkness of his eyelids belonged to him. And the now invisible stones were his as well. He remembered the painting on his tribute. In his mind, it came to life: the Stony Shores, six slaves, and Enetheal, who called himself their master without uttering a word. Enetheal, who had abandoned Kuthan to the dark. *Enetheal and the rules and the island!* Kuthan gripped the salver close, the image on his tribute bright and alive in his mind.

When Kuthan opened his eyes again, that image still burned clearly. The stair was no longer dark. Still, he held to the picture as tightly as to the stones, keeping them in his mind and his grasp as he reached the bottom of the stairs. Today the flickering light was accompanied by the sound of water dripping from the stalactites. Ripples formed in the water below, distorting the reflected images. In front of him was the narrow path that led to the table. As always, the table was empty. Where were the stones of the past? He did not have any good guesses; it was another of the island's mysteries. They were gone. Slowly he removed the tributes off of his salver and onto the table. He placed his own stone there last, and fixed his eyes one last time on the image he had made. He brushed his fingers over it and then turned back to the stair.

The return journey was if possible, even worse. Once again the darkness swallowed him. Kuthan felt even more alone than he had during his descent; it was as if he had given away part of himself when he left his tribute behind. He felt the urge to run back, to retrieve his stone before it disappeared, to take it back with him out into the light. Instead he pressed on, one step at a time. The echoes of his footsteps followed him up the stairs until he reached the dying rays of sunlight.

It took his eyes a moment to adjust to the light outside. When they finally had, he almost wished they had not.

"Next time don't wait for me," he told Enetheal. They held eyes, and Enetheal nodded.

ORIN - DAY FOUR

One thing none of the others seemed to get was that there was a whole lot more to the island than merely the paths and where they led. The majority of the island wasn't the trails; it was the land between. Orin was confident that he now knew every path. He did light them, after all. The rest of the island was another matter entirely.

By now Orin had been off the trail many times. The rules of the Welcome Table specified night as the time in which they were confined to the paths. In a sense, they were almost encouraged to leave the path during daylight. The others hadn't picked up on this, but then again, that wasn't their job. Orin was the explorer, the pathmaster.

His off-path travels had been less revealing than he had hoped. There were bushes and bees, birds and trees. He had walked through areas thick in mud, covered in brush, buried in sand, and simple solid earth. The only advantage his explorations had were that he got a better idea of where the paths were in relation to one another, as well as the different destinations that they linked. There were no answers off the path so far. But maybe that was because they hadn't asked the right questions, or answered them: Why were there paths? What was their significance? Why mustn't they leave them at night? Orin hoped this last question would answer the first two. But so far his daylight travels had not revealed much.

Although night would be best for unraveling this mystery, Orin had not given up on the daytime exploration. But between tribute preparation, service, eating, and talking, there was not enough time to explore the island.

Orin also knew that, like him, Kuthan was eager to explore. Kuthan had recognized what Orin had been thinking. *"We need to push the rules to their limits,"* he had said, or something like that. Orin was glad he wasn't the only one who understood they needed nighttime exploration to find out more ....

The stone skipped seven times. The last jumps were quick, but he counted seven. The day had started with grey skies and choppy waves. Now the water was calm, and the gold light of a recently set sun reflected from the water's black surface. Idra's stone skipped eight times. Her gaze lingered where it had finally dropped beneath the waves. She wore a frown.

"You still upset?" he asked apprehensively. He did not want to upset Idra further, but she hadn't been happy since the adventure they had shared with Kuthan that morning. She didn't answer. Instead she continued to stare at the water.

"Enetheal didn't seem angry when he found us," Orin said reassuringly.

"I'm not upset about Enetheal." Now it was Orin's turn to frown.

"What are you upset about?" he asked. He sat down next to her. She turned her gaze back to him from the water.

"Kuthan's plan." She took a breath before adding, "I don't like it."

"It's scary," Orin admitted. "But I was thinking similar thoughts to his. I think it's important." She didn't meet his eyes as he talked. He wished she would, but instead she skipped another stone. She looked at the water again as she next spoke.

"It feels like we're betraying Namin, Lenya, and Ara by not telling them." She let out a breath.

"You're not going to tell them, are you?" Orin asked sharply. The idea was disturbing.

" 'Course not!" Idra reassured him. Orin relaxed and tossed another stone.

"I just wish there was another way to go about it," she added after a moment.

"Me too," Orin sighed. "But that would only cause more fighting."

"I know," Idra said quietly. "I couldn't stand the fighting today."

"I know," Orin echoed. They sat in silence looking at the water together. Orin put his foot next to hers, so that they were side by side. His feet were larger then hers, but not by much. Her skin was slightly darker as well, but somehow their feet did not seem so different side by side.

Orin heard movement away from their skipping cove. When they got up to join the others, they found Kuthan returning from his service. He looked pale, but he gave Orin a smile. Orin waved back in response.

"I should complete my service now," Orin said.

"I'll collect fruit and bring it to the cabins," Idra added. Orin was glad that they would both be busy.

Ara, Lenya, and Namin had been sitting separately from Idra, and Orin, but now they formed a full group once more.

"Should we?" Orin asked Enetheal, gesturing to the path. Enetheal nodded his assent, and they started towards the path.

"Hey, Ore?" He was caught off guard that Ara would call him by his nickname.

"Yes?"

"I need you to help me complete my service this evening." He looked into her green eyes for some hint of a joke. He found none.

"Help you?" Orin turned to Enetheal. Enetheal nodded, and held his hand out towards Ara. Orin took a few tentative steps away from Enetheal.

"Let's go," Ara encouraged firmly. Together they left along the trail. Orin was even more perplexed when Namin followed.

"You too?" he asked. Namin nodded. Bemused, Orin followed just behind Ara, with Namin a few footfalls behind them both. Soon the other three were silhouettes in the distance.

"Would you lead us to the Firefly Field?" Ara asked.

"Sure," Orin answered. He moved to the front so that he could navigate the paths, but it was clear Ara was still in control. As they wove through the pine woods he wondered, *Why would Ara want me?* Orin wasn't sure why. Every time he tried to do something, she would try to stop him, as when he had tried to help Idra find her stone that first day. Or when he had started to follow Kuthan during his service. Or even when he was just running around on paths when they were traveling as a group. He had learned to contain himself when she was around, because anything he did seemed to upset her. This morning she had rejected Kuthan's plan. What really upset Orin was that Ara was so sure of herself; of the rules, and of what needed to be done. *So why would Ara want to lead an adventure?*

They arrived at the Firefly Field. Stacked carefully at the edge of the clearing were lanterns. The only way to carry the flies around easily was to use these, so Orin had gotten in the habit of filling up a few of them as full as he could with fireflies and then distributing the flies around the island. It had worked so far. Capturing the lighted insects was wonderful, but the distribution could be tedious. Orin was glad that a lantern usually lasted a few nights before needing to be relit.

He forgot about Namin and Ara as he ran in the fields leaving a wake of trampled grass. Golden flashes streaked about him. The first few evenings he had only been able to catch a firefly once it had lit up right beside him. Now he could predict where each one was going, where it would land, and he could see a single fly even as it darkened and for a moment became nothing.

"Need any help?" Namin asked, as Orin exchanged one of the lit lanterns for an empty one. Ara answered before Orin could.

"It's probably best to let Orin do this alone." *Irritating, but predictable.* It was as if Ara couldn't help it. After a few more lanterns were filled, Orin stopped. The new lights shone in the darkness.

"I need you to light a specific path for me," Ara said seriously. "Can you do that?"

"Sure," he paused. Now was as good a time as any, so he asked: "What are we doing?" He braced himself for a reprimand, or an explanation of why she couldn't share the knowledge.

"I was told I must direct Namin to weave a web at a specific location," she said, looking between Namin and Orin. "To get there, we need the path to be lit because it's night."

He was caught off-guard by how straightforward her answer was. They started walking, each holding two lanterns filled with flies. It took him a moment to follow up on his question.

"Told by who?" It was now Ara's turn to pause. Namin and Orin looked at her intently .

"My service is to listen to the wind as it passes through the rocks." They were silent, so Ara continued. "You know, the rocks that make eerie noises …."

"The Shrieking Stones," Orin said quickly, eager for her to continue. He was pleased at his name for the rocks. Apparently Ara was too.

"My service is to listen to the wind as it shrieks through the stones," she affirmed. She stopped as they came upon a web in the path. Namin moved it aside, and they continued. "They speak," she said.

"Words?" Namin asked curiously.

"In a sense. I'm not really sure. It's hard to understand, but yes, I can make out words among the other noises."

"How come you didn't tell us when we discussed our tasks?" Orin asked. *Kuthan needs to hear this!*

"There was no need," she answered shortly.

There never is, is there Ara? he thought, but he remained silent. The path had awakened since darkness fell. The first part was already lit from last night's venture. Soon they reached an unlit path, and their progress slowed as Orin lighted the way.

"So where are we going?" he asked as he transferred a single fly to one of the lanterns at the edge of the path.

"The Shadowed Stair," Ara answered.

"Where Kuthan's service is performed?" Namin asked quietly.

"I think so," said Ara.

Their journey progressed slowly, though Orin was pleased with how quickly he was able to transfer the flies. As they walked, Namin hummed. The melody was soothing, but a faintly audible scuttling reminded Orin that spiders usually accompanied Namin's song. He wasn't scared of spiders, but the idea of them following Namin's voice unnerved him a little. Two by two, the empty lanterns along the path were transformed into flashing markers.

The path extended out to the partly submerged bedrock that led to the cave. The air had become warmer and wetter as they traveled. The coast was now misty and the path alien compared with the familiar trails Orin had discovered in his explorations. The dirt ended in front of them, but they continued to follow the lanterns into the water.

A splash and a "Whoa!" from Namin alerted them to the slipperiness of the rock.

"You alright?" Ara asked. Namin nodded and they continued, the firefly-flashes reflected in the black water. The mist held the light strangely as well, each flash becoming dimmer but lasting longer. The final pair of lanterns stood glowing on the dry rock just before the cave entrance. Orin stood back, looking at his handiwork. Behind him a curving path illuminated in golden bursts, reflecting off the water's surface, and continuing back into the dark recesses of the forest.

"Do you know what to do?" Ara asked.

"Uhh," Orin was about to voice his confusion when Namin answered "yes" quietly. The question had been for him. Orin and Ara sat down, and Orin was pleased to see that Ara seemed as excited as he was to watch Namin work.

Namin stood silently. Orin thought of asking him why he was waiting, but Ara looked sternly at him: now wasn't the time for questions. He looked around and his eyes settled on the darkness of the cave. It was a strange darkness. It seemed to penetrate further beyond the cave-entrance than it should, and Orin was glad for his lanterns.

He was brought to attention by the waves now splashing in against them. The water was uncomfortably cold despite the warmth of the mist. Orin felt impatient. He was about to tell Namin to hurry up when he heard the song. It started as a low hum, barely audible over the sound of the waves, but soon Namin's voice rose and fell gently. Orin had barely begun to settle and relax when something large and hairy scuttled over his resting hand.

"Ahh!" The shout burst out of him unbidden, but he choked it abruptly. His heart pounded in his chest. Unperturbed, Namin continued steadily. Orin tried to calm himself. He eyed his surroundings carefully. They rose up around them everywhere, large and small, scuttling from the cave and the surrounding rocks. It terrified him to see how suddenly they appeared. Were they always so close? Many were larger than his hands. They scurried about the entrance to the cave and started to weave. He became so caught up with their presence and number that at first he did not notice how they leapt and fell with the rising and lowering of Namin's voice; how the melodies and strands were interwoven. There were other spiders, too. Spiders that didn't jump and spin and leap. They remained in the shadows, revealed only by the flashing of Orin's lanterns.

He didn't like these quiet ones. He felt they were watching with something more than a desire to dance.

The song went on and on. It was graceful, but did not stop Orin from feeling wet and uncomfortable. And it was eerie as it echoed strangely across the water.

Orin was thankful when it ended. He and Ara stood up next to Namin. They all started the trek back to the forest. The water was cold, and Orin carefully placed his feet to avoid slipping, when suddenly the lanterns went out: There was now no hint of gold to light their way in the mist.

"What's going on?" Ara asked. Orin was surprised to hear a shaky edge to her voice—she was never unsure of herself. The mist and clouds obscured any light from stars or moon; darkness surrounded them. The noises of crickets, frogs, and owls had vanished along with the light.

"Let's be quiet a moment," Namin said, sounding calm. He took one of Orin's hands, and one of Ara's. They waited a moment. The water lapped unpleasantly around their ankles, and the trees whispered in the wind. There was no sound of the Shrieking Stones in the distance. They held hands in the darkness waiting ….

"There's light," Orin whispered. "Your web." A soft white glow shone from the web Namin had just sung. It grew brighter for a moment, and then faded once again, leaving them in darkness. But then a flash of gold penetrated the night, and then another and another until the path unfolded before them in blazes of gold. He wasn't sure whether it was because of their temporary absence, but the flashes now seemed more rapid and persistent than they had before the darkness.

They found their way carefully through the water, and into the forest. The trees seemed threatening as they loomed over the path. They traveled quickly, following the flashes back to Namin and Orin's cabin.

" 'Come in for a moment?" Namin asked. Ara nodded her agreement and followed them into the little shelter. Namin undid the web carefully, before closing it behind them. They brought the lanterns they had carried with them to the cave, and these now splashed the inside of the cabin with quavering golden light. It comforted Orin. On each of the beds was a small pile of fruit. They sat on the beds and ate in silence. They only began to talk again once they had finished.

"Have your lanterns ever gone out before this?" Ara asked Orin. He shook his head before turning to Namin.

"Do your webs always glow once they've been sung?" Orin asked.

"No. Only this time," Namin said. They grew quiet for a while, each lost in their own thoughts.

"Did the Shrieking Stones say anything about this?" Namin questioned.

Ara looked at them. "Only that you must weave a web over the cave tonight, and that I must make sure it is done."

"What did *you* say?" Orin asked pointedly.

"I didn't speak, I listened," Ara answered softly. She looked down at the floor while she spoke.

"The stones speak to you," Namin stated, calm as ever. "Can you speak to them?"

"I'm not sure," Ara whispered. "I'm still putting it together."

Namin touched them each lightly on their hands. "We all are," he said simply.

They walked Ara back to her cabin that night. Orin was glad to see that the cabin path he had lit the night before remained lighted. He was through lighting paths for tonight. The lanterns flashed as they usually did. The night was still wet, but the air was clearer along the cabin path than it had been near the water. Before parting from Ara they hugged each other. Namin made sure Ara had pulled the web-screen back into place before they left.

As they made their way back towards the cabin, Orin saw a golden flash in a bush next to the path. He paused. A lone firefly was struggling in a web. It's light flickered and it buzzed frantically. He thought to free it, but before he had a chance to act, a spider scuttled across the web, and wound the fly in silk. There was a last faint pulse of gold from within the snare, and then nothing.

"Let's keep going," came Namin's quiet voice. So they did. The firefly's struggle horrified Orin more than that earlier plunge into sudden darkness. They arrived at their cabin, quickly closed the screen behind them along with the door, and crossed over to their beds. The lanterns were still alight inside the cabin and Orin was thankful for that. Namin sat up near the foot of his bed, but Orin closed his eyes and lay back. Namin's gentle hum was soothing, but sleep did not come to Orin. The trapped firefly would not leave his mind. He imagined walking down paths that plunged into darkness. *And in that darkness are spiders that do not dance to song. In that darkness are spiders that just watch hungrily, waiting to swallow the light.*

KUTHAN - DAY FIVE

The rain was gentle. He didn't know when during the night it had begun, but Kuthan felt he owed his deep sleep to the rain. He wouldn't have woken that morning if it had not been for Idra's voice.

"Kuthan," she said. Her voice was surprisingly flat.

"I'm going," she said shortly, before closing the door behind her.

Not good was all he could think. Idra was upset. She had not approved of his idea to solve the island's mysteries as a separate team.

"We're not betraying the the others, we are helping them," he had told her last night. She had remained unconvinced, but had nothing to say. He could not bear her being upset with him, but there was nothing he could do to reason with her. Apart from 'feeling bad' Idra had little reason for not taking part in this mission. Her lack of support hurt him more than he would admit. At least Orin understood.

Ore had known from the beginning that the island must be explored.

Kuthan slipped off into sleep once more, but then awoke to Orin's voice.

" 'Morning," Orin said, as he and Namin walked in. They had become experts at arriving just before Idra returned.

"Hey," Kuthan managed. He felt more tired now than he had been when he had first woken. Namin and Orin sat on Idra's bed. Orin gave Kuthan an ill-concealed meaningful look, and Kuthan had to nod to stop him. But Namin seemed oblivious, his gaze turned to the window. The rain had slowed since Kuthan had first woken, and the day outside was brighter.

"Lots of frogs this morning," Orin commented.

"And last night," added Namin. Orin looked puzzled for a moment, and Kuthan filled the silence.

"Hope there's still some out there," he said. "I'd love to see them."

"I'll find one!" Orin said happily. He was gone before the others could say anything. Only moments later he returned with a large frog in his hands. Behind him walked Idra.

"Food," she said simply.

They walked up the path to Lenya and Ara's, Idra and Namin side by side, Kuthan deciding to join Orin as he surged ahead. The path was muddy, and they had to watch their footing. By the time they reached the cabin, the clouds had parted and the sun shone through. Orin pulled the web aside and knocked on the door. Ara opened, golden curls tangled, but eyes alert.

"I'll be back," she said, and gently shut the door. Namin and Idra caught up to Orin and Kuthan just as Ara and Lenya emerged from the cabin. Enetheal waited for them at the Welcome Table. Today's fruit was sunset red, its skin smooth and soft.

"Namin?" Idra smiled.

Namin smiled back before taking a large bite. Kuthan felt a twinge of annoyance. *Is she purposely ignoring me?* They ate together. Ara stood up first, and the rest followed. Enetheal stayed behind at the table, although Kuthan was sure he would follow as soon as they were out of sight.

Blue sky and warmth awaited them at the Stony Shores. Except for the damp stones, it was impossible to tell it had rained all night. Kuthan stared over the many stones. He didn't like how the Stony Shores divided them: Heads downcast, backs bent, they would follow their aimless, unmarked paths, each looking for a rock they could call special. He had started to feel the ache in his neck before he even started searching. His gaze shifted back and forth over the sea of pebbles.

Too grey, too small, too bright, too red, too angular, too smooth. He could think of reasons, but really he had no idea what made a stone the right one. Could he possibly find and work with a stone that would live up to the marvel he had created yesterday? He hoped so. He made sure not to become lost in his task. He made sure the others were in sight, and that Enetheal was not.

Where is Enetheal now? He couldn't be far. Or could he? What else did Enetheal have to do besides ensuring they accomplished their tasks? *Where does Enetheal go at night?* Kuthan was disturbed that he hadn't thought of this before. *Are there other cabins?* As he mulled this over, he noticed a dark grey rock with red patches. He considered it briefly and then moved on. He had just started wandering the shallows when he heard laughter.

"Stop," Idra giggled. Namin splashed her a second time, before diving under the water. Idra pursued, wading through the water.

"Where did he … Ahh!" she yelled, as Namin surfaced behind her with a large grin. She splashed him in the face, and he sank beneath the waves again, only to resurface out of Idra's splash-range.

Kuthan caught a glimpse of movement, and then Orin splashed past him, yelling. Namin turned his attention to Orin, but was taken by surprise when Idra joined the assault. A large douse of water was followed by a brief respite before all three resurfaced laughing.

"Stop it!" said Ara glaring ferociously at the trio. "What would Enetheal say?"

"He'd say the best rocks are out here where it's deep!" Namin called back.

"No he wouldn't!" Ara called back, outraged.

"He'd say the one who held their breath the longest wouldn't have to make a tribute stone today!" Orin shouted.

"No! …" Ara started to protest, but they were already submerged. Kuthan couldn't help but smile. There were bubbles, and then Orin shot out of the water, closely followed by Namin.

"That's not fair," Orin complained. Namin laughed. As a group they waited for Idra to surface. Kuthan had just started to worry when she emerged with a grin.

"No tribute stone for me?" she asked.

"Yes—there is!" Ara exclaimed in a tone both exasperated and threatening.

"I'll make one if you join us!" Idra called. Ara paused.

"Please?" Idra asked. Ara relented and waded out into the water. Kuthan joined in too, and finally Lenya, too, appeared among the waves. Every so often Kuthan glanced back toward the tree-line, and sometimes thought he saw movement. *Let him watch. Let him see that we are not just his puppets.*

When they were finished, each one of them had found a stone. They also found a large flat boulder to dry off on. The sun was warm and gentle. Ara started to rise and Kuthan chose not to object. Nevertheless, he groaned as he pushed himself to all fours.

"Enetheal would scorn our happiness; he'd tell us he was disgusted, and remind us we must finish our tasks," Kuthan said bitterly.

"Enetheal wouldn't say anything," Lenya said dreamily. Kuthan chuckled. It was true, but he hadn't expected it from Lenya. "He would smile," she finished.

For a moment he thought he had misheard her. The idea was absurd and revolting at the same time. Taken by surprise, his laughter escaped without restraint. Suddenly, they were all laughing together. It felt good.

They separated to decorate their stones, but this time the division was not in the group, only in their tasks. Kuthan decided the best place to complete this day's tribute was the Sapwood. He was surprised when Ara joined him, but he didn't object. As they drew near the wood they fell silent, even before the birds did. Just as before, the birds stilled, then the wind and the waves. Only the sound of their breathing remained. They passed the first tree. Kuthan had forgotten some of the details of the Sapwood. The bark of the trees seemed darker even than he remembered, and the twigs a more vibrant green. The streams of sap flowed more quickly than they had on the first day, but he could not tell if the silvery pools surrounding the trees were any larger.

They walked from tree to tree, looking into the sap-pools. Since picking the right stone was so important,

Kuthan felt that choosing the correct pool might also be important, only they all seemed the same. The pools had silver-clear surfaces, so calm and unbroken that he felt an urge to disturb the sap with his foot in order to see the perfection break. Reflected in each pool were sky, clouds, and the tree which rose from the center. If he leaned in close enough, Kuthan saw himself staring back. Finally, somewhere in the middle of the forest, he stopped. It wasn't that the pool he found was different from the others. It was simply time. Together he and Ara knelt by the side of the pool, and dipped their stones. Ripples spread from where the surface had been broken. They held their stones beneath until the ripples were gone, and then lifted them. The sap dried quickly so that the stones were now shiny and smooth, and only a little bit sticky. Holding their tributes carefully, with as little contact as possible, they turned back the way they had come. They continued to walk until they could hear waves, until the wind whispered, and finally until once again the birds sang.

Ara relaxed visibly, and Kuthan heard himself release a long breath as their own silence was now also broken.

"How can it be so peaceful and so stressful at the same time?" Kuthan asked.

Ara chuckled. "If we knew that, there wouldn't be much left to figure out, would there?" she said.

"I can think of a few things," he responded darkly.

"I'm sure you can." They did not speak again until they reached the slope, and began their ascent to the Welcome Table.

"Do you think Enetheal has rules?" Ara asked. Enetheal's cold grey eyes, tall frame, sharp nose, and blank expression jumped into Kuthan's mind. *Could he?* Enetheal was the one who enforced the rules—or at least watched until they were carried out. Why would he himself have rules?

"I don't know," he answered slowly. "But it would be good to find out."

"I think we all have a purpose," Ara said. "Enetheal, too." Kuthan was still mulling over her first question, and didn't comment further. They arrived at the table to find Lenya, Idra, Namin, and Orin awaiting them, fruit placed carefully for six.

It was wonderful until Enetheal joined them. Ara pulled out her completed tribute stone, placing it on the table. The others did as well. Kuthan's was rounded and grey with the slightest purple tinge. Enetheal nodded, and left silently.

"Do you think he wants us to work harder?" Ara asked, puzzled.

"We are quicker than we used to be," Idra said thoughtfully.

"I think we choose when we're done with our tributes," Namin said. "Maybe he was just saying 'hi'." He took another bite of fruit.

"Hi?" Kuthan asked sarcastically. "That's a strange way of saying 'hi'. As soon as we showed him our stones, he left. He was making sure we had our stones, and reminding us that we need to stay on task."

"Well, we should," Ara responded. "I can see why he'd be worried after what we did this morning."

They finished eating, journeyed to the altar, and deposited their stones. After Enetheal's interruption, the day went well. As a group, they walked to the Sandy Shores. Orin started to mold the island out of sand. Kuthan formed the cave, Lenya, the well. Ara molded the Shrieking Stones and the Welcome Table. Namin and Idra gathered sticks, and used them as trees. Idra placed the taller ones around the path at the foot of the slope.

"Still haven't visited them all," she said.

"We could do it now," Orin interjected, excitedly.

Idra looked up. "I like seeing them the first time they bear fruit." Orin returned to drawing paths, and puzzling over the model.

They never finished. The basic landmarks were there, but there were always more details to add. Orin kept altering and re-altering areas off the path, and Ara puzzled over the rocks that connected the island to the Shrieking Stones. The sky grew orange and pink, and Kuthan rose to stand.

"See you all later," he said.

"Bye," Namin answered, but no one looked up. Their services had become part of the natural rhythm, now anticipated and accepted. Kuthan did his best not to show trepidation. It was time for his service. Enetheal always got his way.

The sunset was glorious: gold, orange, and pink painted the sky better than Kuthan could ever hope to paint a tribute stone. A shimmering golden path approached his feet. *If only we could just walk away across that path.* And yet … the day had not been bad. It had been almost fun. He thought of when they had abandoned the tribute stones and swum together; when Lenya had said Enetheal would smile; his walk with Ara; the miniature island they had created in sand.

The sun was a red-orange flame as its last light touched the altar. When it was out of sight, Kuthan transferred the stones to the salver. It seemed only moments later that he was at the cave entrance. To his surprise, spider silk was embroidered in an elaborate pattern shielding the mouth of the cave. He felt a sudden burning urge to rip it down.

Instead, he retraced the careful motions Enetheal had demonstrated the first day. He delicately pulled at the outer strands of the web, moved it gently, and then put it back into place behind him.

Kuthan forgot about the web as soon as he came to the stairs and began to descend. Almost immediately, all light was extinguished: darkness, blindness, silence but for echoes. *Enetheal.* The image swam before his eyes. He had joined them for their midday meal as well as for their breakfast that day. No one had objected. No one had even truly acknowledged it! And how could they? Enetheal was taller. He knew the island. They were here under his rules. And now they were all accepting it.

Kuthan had watched the sunset alone that day. The others were lost, so lost in one beautiful moment, that they didn't even realize that so many beautiful moments were all being stolen. "No," he said aloud, breaking the silence. The word was muffled by the darkness, diminished so effectively that it barely reached his ears. Could the afterlight of sunset really still be somewhere behind him? He felt panic rise inside him and tried to think more thoughts, but none came. Stair after stair, nothing behind him or in front of him. He stopped, and then continued down. He held the stones close, as he had the last many days. Yesterday he had been able to become lost in the image on his stone. He couldn't with today's stone. It was done. He had put effort into choosing it, and it felt dear to him, but that was not enough.

Yesterday's stone shone again in his mind's eye: the shore, the slaves, Enetheal. Its image was an incontestable statement, just as the Welcome Table was. In front of him was a flicker of white light. The flicker grew, penetrating the darkness. Kuthan had made it.

He never could be sure how bright the light was—any light after the stair filled him with awe. It certainly was brighter than it had been on the first day. A steady drip came down from the stalactites. Kuthan walked towards the table. And then stopped.

There was something on the table, and the closer he drew to it, the more he became certain what it was. He put the salver with today's tributes onto the table and picked up his tribute from the day before. He allowed his eyes to feast on the image. *What can this mean? Has it been rejected?* He didn't know whether to be happy or afraid to have his tribute back. *But there is something wrong!* Every stone on the Stony Shores was in place, as were the trees and the waves. The figure of Enetheal still towered above the others. Only there was another figure. Hidden between the boulders of the painting was another dark silhouette. This one worked alongside the rest, and shared their frailty. However, unlike the others, it had one arm flung up in defiance to shield itself from the wrath of Enetheal.

His hands shook. He put the stone back onto the altar, fearing he might drop it. Blood pounded in his ears, and felt his heart pumping furiously. Slowly he turned for the stairs, leaving behind the new tribute stones alongside his old one. Step by step he climbed, but this time, the depth of the darkness and length of the stairway didn't slow him. His eyes were wet but he smiled. There was still so much more to understand. For now, though, for just a moment, it didn't matter. *We are not alone.* His footfalls echoed behind him as he climbed, but now they sounded comforting instead of eerie. With a small chuckle he whispered to himself in the darkness, "We are not alone."

IDRA - DAY SIX

"I'm going now," she told Kuthan.

He opened his eyes, told her thanks for waking him, and closed his eyes again. She glared at his unmoving form before leaving their cabin. What was the point in waking him if he was just going back to sleep! She placed the spiderweb screen behind her with a grace that did not match her mood. Then she turned and stamped her foot on the hardened earth of the path. She was angry, and not because he'd fallen back asleep. She didn't want to fight. She wanted Kuthan to apologize. She wanted him to agree that he was wrong, and that he had been foolish for suggesting they work separately from the others and keep secrets. She had told Kuthan, but he just didn't get it. It was infuriating! But she had nothing else to say. If he didn't understand, there was nothing she could do.

Idra shivered in the morning air. She had to get up earlier each day, because the walk was getting longer. She told herself that she would complete the loop as each successive tree bore the fruit. She had yet to see the last two trees. Enetheal joined her as she moved from the dirt path to the stone way that linked the trees. There was no eye-contact this time. He had finally learned that she didn't like looking at his eyes. She didn't like looking at him in general. They walked side by side without truly acknowledging one another. They passed the first tree in silence. She liked the familiarity of the path, and was glad that when the loop was completed she would come back to pick fruit at her first tree once more.

Each day her way around the loop became more familiar. She was now easily able to distinguish individual pine trees as well as specific rocks, and even some clumps of bushes or underbrush. They passed the second tree, and the third. By the time they reached the fourth tree the gold of the sun had spread through the forest, and the air was warmer. It was a long journey around the Welcome Table slope. She could have just gone over the slope, but this way felt right. Orin was pathmaster; he lit all the paths. But this one was hers. She might as well know it. She passed the fourth tree, and the fifth. The pines, rocks, roots, and brush were now unfamiliar. The way twisted and turned through trees. Left, then right, but always more left then right. That is how it needed to be for the loop to be completed.

But she had not closed her circuit yet. Suddenly alert, she realized that the birds had stopped singing. Then the wind died and the air was quiet and still. As she strained her ears she realized that she could no longer hear waves. Still, she continued to walk along the stone way. As the moments passed and she continued her journey, the stones grew further and further apart until they disappeared and the way was gone. Right ahead of her she saw an elaborate spiderweb crisscrossing between two trees, blocking her further passage. Beyond it was only the forest floor. The stone way had ended in the middle of nowhere. But it wasn't nowhere. The loop had led right into the Sapwood.

"I need to go in here?" she asked, turning to Enetheal for the first time. He remained motionless. Then he looked down at where the path ended, and beyond that, into the Sapwood. He slowly nodded. Idra hesitantly peeled back the web, and then began to walk. *This isn't right.* With no path to guide her she wasn't sure where to go. She looked around for a special tree. A large tree that bore fruit and grew tall. A tree full of life, and growth, and nourishment. All the trees looked the same in the Sapwood, and none of them bore fruit.

The bark had the same strange red tinge. The twigs were too green, the forest, too silent. Sap streamed into the pools soundlessly. No tree stood out. She followed the curve of the slope, just as if she were on her usual path, always cutting left more than right. *I should see it by now.* She looked around desperately. *I could be anywhere in the Sapwood—it all looks the same.* Trees loomed all about her, their shadows long, and their pools of sap sparkling in the sun. *What if I don't find it?* She remembered searching for her stone on the first day. Everyone had waited for her and she had broken down and given up. Her throat closed and her eyes grew wet. "No," she whispered hoarsely. Her whisper seemed loud in the silence of the Sapwood. She spun in a circle to face Enetheal. He started to look away in order to avoid her gaze.

"Look at me!" she demanded. When he did she had to stop her eyes from wandering to the empty pool of sap behind him. She refocused. His cold grey eyes stared back at her, unblinking.

"Do something!"

He continued to stare for a moment and then looked around, almost as if he were bored. Angrily, she scrutinized the trees in their immediate vicinity and then inspected the pools in which they sat. The Sapwood was hideous. *It should be here!* It was wrong. She turned from Enetheal, and continued to walk, but had the disconcerting feeling that they were moving away from her tree.

She stopped once again. She thought of the others. They would be waking soon. Again she turned to Enetheal, who had continued after her as if he were her shadow. "Please," she whimpered, her voice shaking. Enetheal shook his head slowly. Her legs started to shake, so she collapsed to her knees. Enetheal continued to stand, unmoving. A wisp of wind touched her cheek, and she realized with a start that they must be near the edge of the Sapwood. She rose to her feet, took a deep breath and moved on.

Birdcalls were audible now, and she started to run. *The stone way.* Her heart fluttered. The stone way was in front of her with its familiar curve to the left. And again there was a spiderweb, the twin of the first in its intricacy. Idra hurriedly pulled it aside, leaving Enetheal to replace it behind them. Surely the trail would lead to another tree. She raced along it. *I'm racing the sun*, she thought wildly. *There's still time to find fruit before they wake!* Her path cut in and out of trees. Frightened squirrels scampered off of it. Finally she reached the tree. There were no webs separating her from the clearing. She ran in eagerly.

For a moment she felt light, and a smile spread over her face. She blinked in the sunlight, gazing up into its branches. Then a cloud moved over the sun, and her eyes were undazzled. There were flowers in the tree, but no fruit. A hand gripped her shoulder, but she shrugged it off and ran for the trunk of the tree. She climbed away from

Enetheal, scrambling up the branches. In a sudden frenzy of frustration, she began to leap from branch to branch until she was high above the ground. She pushed aside leaves and flowers, but there was no fruit. Finally she sat still, perched on a slim leafy top branch, hugging one knee close.

Her breath was ragged. The foliage was thick enough that she couldn't see Enetheal. It was just as well: she didn't want to. *The others are waiting! Hurry!* she thought frantically. *There is no sixth tree!* She despaired. *Only a seventh.* Idra steadied herself on her branch. *It doesn't make sense. I don't understand.* She bit hard on her lower lip. It started to bleed. *Kuthan was right. Why didn't she listen?* She felt a tear slowly trickling down her cheek. She turned her head up to look at the sun. It was warm. *I can't stay here.* At first her hand wouldn't move, but finally she forced herself down. She descended one branch at a time until she was on the ground.

She stood beside the tree, her arms wrapped tightly around her chest, and suddenly realized she didn't know where she was going. *I can't go back to them empty handed!* Her throat started to close up again. She rubbed her blurry eyes, and focused on Enetheal. He stood almost casually, one arm up against the trunk of the tree. Idra spun around, turning back towards the Sapwood.

"Don't follow me," was all she could manage before running.

He was supposed to guide us. He didn't. She ran faster, taking care to keep her feet high so that she wouldn't trip on the stones or the roots that appeared unpredictably on the path. *He doesn't care.* Not that she had ever thought he did. She considered his grotesque form as she returned to the Sapwood, searching in that vast silent woodland once more. *On that first day when I couldn't find my stone, it wasn't Enetheal who helped me. And Enetheal won't help me now. Enetheal has betrayed me. Betrayed us.*

Her feet pounded the forest floor. The sound of her breath, her heart, and her thoughts seemed likes screams in the Sapwood. But in return, she heard only silence, emptiness. *I'm out of time,* she thought miserably. But she searched on until the sun was high in the sky above, before she left the Sapwood. Soon, she arrived once again at the seventh tree, the one that had only flowers. She pressed on along the stone way, looking frantically in case she had missed something. But she hadn't. Finally, before her stood the first tree. There were no other trees.

Idra arrived breathless to find her cabin empty. *They might be looking for their tribute stones already!* The thought horrified her. Instead of going to the Stony Shores, she sprinted up the slope. Her body was slick with sweat by the time she reached the top. Everyone was there. Ara, Lenya, Namin, Orin, Kuthan, and Enetheal were gathered around the table.

"I was unable to complete my service today," Idra said. At least her voice didn't shake. They stared at her uncomprehendingly. Amidst the alarmed and confused expressions, Kuthan's eyes met hers with purpose and understanding. "Kuthan could I talk to you alone for a moment?"

He got up, and they retreated down the slope together.

As soon as the others were out of sight, she broke down. She told him everything: the incomplete stone way, the Sapwood which held no sign of a sixth tree, the final tree on the stone way at the other side of the Sapwood which bore no fruit, and Enetheal, who had done nothing but step aside and watch her struggle. The whole time he watched her wordlessly, intently.

"I'm so sorry Kuthan," she cried. "I should have listened to you. You were right." She took in a deep shuddering breath. "I promise I'll do everything I can to help you and Ore. We need to understand. We need to take care of each other."

Kuthan wrapped his arms around her, pulling her into a tight embrace. "We will," he said emphatically. Idra laughed weakly.

"When can we start?" she asked.

"Now," Kuthan answered. He let her go, and took her hand as they climbed up the slope. The others were talking, but grew silent as Kuthan and Idra approached. Kuthan walked over to Enetheal, and looked into his cold grey eyes.

"Leave us." Kuthan said it very quietly, but distinctly. Enetheal blinked.

"Now," he added vehemently. Enetheal rose, and left them still gathered around the Welcome Table. Idra let out a breath of relief. Enetheal should never have come to the Welcome Table in the first place. After all, *he* wasn't hers to feed.

LENYA - DAY SIX

Starlight. She sensed it every time she closed her eyes now: the cold, the surge of life through her veins, the contentment of being whole, all of it emanating from fallen stars. Last night's star still burned in her mind. It had been a brilliant blue-white. When she had touched it, icy tendrils had shot up her arms and into her chest. She had gasped, but by the time Enetheal had rushed over to her she had lapsed into laughter. Every detail was perfect in her mind. Wisps of clouds blowing, the moon—almost half a circle— glowing, the sky-bound stars, the gentle lap of the waves, the wind whispering in the trees, the rocks, the sand, and the reflection of the fallen star in Enetheal's eyes.

But then Lenya's eyes were open, and it wasn't starshine in front of her, it was Ara. Her voice was distant.
"Lenya."
"Yes?" she heard herself answer.

"The others should be here by now," Ara said. Lenya hoped Ara wasn't annoyed with her. She knew that Ara had been upset at Lenya for 'not being here'.

"I'm here," she said, trying to reassure Ara. *"I make tribute stones, and eat fruit, and ... I'm here. My mind just wanders sometimes."* Ara scowled.

"But they aren't here," Ara replied. Lenya relaxed, realizing that Ara wasn't accusing her.

"They always come here to wake us by now," Ara continued. *"Maybe something is wrong."* She thought for a bit, her brow furrowed into a frown and finally said, *"Let's find Kuthan and Idra."* Lenya nodded in agreement, and followed Ara out the door.

Letting the star go had only been possible because of the promise of another star.

When they arrived, Ara peeled back the spiderweb and knocked sharply on the door. The door inside the cabin was thrust open. *"Hey,"* Orin grinned, but then he saw who had come, and his smile fell. Idra was not there.

"She should have returned a long time ago," Kuthan said, pacing back and forth.

"Which is why I should go out to look for her," Orin responded.

"Then two of us will be missing," Ara stated, *"and the day will take even longer to start."* She waited another moment. *"We need to stay together,"* she emphasized again.

"We'll find each other," Lenya added, trying to be reassuring. She sat on the bed next to Namin and lay back. Kuthan let out a discontented grunt, and Orin rolled his eyes.

"We should wait at the Welcome Table," Namin said quietly. *"That's where she'll go. She may have just had a

late start this morning. If we're there for too long, we will search for her."

It didn't dispel their worries, but doing something was better than doing nothing. Namin rose from the bed with Lenya, and the five of them left the cabin. When they reached the Welcome Table there was no fruit and no Idra. The others continued to talk about what they should do. Their voices were distressed. Lenya thought about stars.

Idra's task is the most like mine, Lenya thought. She gathers fruit by day, and I gather stars by night. She smiled, and imagined bringing a star to the Welcome Table. Starlight was overwhelming in a way that fruit could never be.

"But I cannot bring the stars," she thought sadly, "... only bear them to the well so that they can continue their descent."

Her thoughts stopped abruptly when the voices around her suddenly ceased. Idra had arrived, and looked at them, her teeth pressed firmly on her lower lip, her eyes flickering between each of them. She stopped biting her lip, and took a breath.

"I was unable to complete my service today," she said. Her words hung in the air. "Kuthan, could I talk to you alone for a moment?"

Wordlessly Kuthan arose and together they walked down the slope and out of sight. The silence at the table seemed loud, more audible than birds, waves, or the wind in the trees. They looked around at one another, but no words were spoken.

'Perhaps they are wondering what Idra is telling Kuthan,' Lenya thought. Lenya tried to understand why it was important, but her mind was moving slowly.

She closed her eyes so that she could see the stars again, just for a moment. Then, when she finally reopened her eyes. Kuthan and Idra had returned.

Kuthan strode towards the table purposefully. He avoided the questioning looks, saving his eyes for Enetheal.

"Leave us," Kuthan told Enetheal. His words seemed to echo. Enetheal remained motionless.

"Now," Kuthan added. Slowly Enetheal rose. He looked around at each of them, inclined his head slightly, and left.

Ara stared pointedly at Kuthan. Kuthan deliberately waited before speaking.

"Yes?" he asked. He said it as if nothing had happened. A dark expression flitted across Ara's face before she eased her composure.

"Explain," Ara demanded. Her eyes darted between Idra and Kuthan. Idra tensed, but it was Kuthan who answered:

"Idra couldn't complete her task today because Enetheal misled her." His voice swept over them loudly. "Enetheal has been hiding knowledge from us. Behind his mouthless mask he is a being who can think. Today Enetheal did not guide Idra to ripe fruit, but instead stood aside and watched her struggle. We do not know why he did this; only that he is using us to his own ends." He stopped to let his words settle. "Enetheal is not one of us. Far from it. It is time he left the Table."

"Enetheal upholds the rules that define our existence here," Ara said angrily. "And you would banish him from the table without consulting us? Without thinking of the repercussions?"

"We need to stand up for ourselves!" Kuthan's voice was almost a shout. "Today we go hungry because of Enetheal. You would defend him?"

"The rules must be upheld," Ara glared back, her jaw set.

"No rules were broken," Kuthan said. Orin and Idra nodded their agreement.

Ara's brow furrowed, but Namin answered before she did.

"The rules do not matter," Namin's voice was calm but cold. Ara motioned to protest, but Namin's eyes were for Kuthan. "That was wrong," he said quietly.

He departed, leaving the table and walking the same direction Enetheal had. The stillness that remained at the table was reminiscent of the Sapwood. They looked around, some eyes avoiding others, and some flitting away when they hesitantly met. The uneasy quiet continued. And continued. Finally Ara's voice interrupted the silence.

"We still need to make our tribute stones." Her words rang true. Orin and Idra rose quickly, and Lenya and Kuthan followed soon after. They parted at the Stony Shores, and resumed their daily search. *They all care so much*, Lenya thought looking at the grey sky and dark waves. Ara walked past, her gaze turned down to the stones below. Kuthan, Idra, and Orin were closer together, but were equally engaged in their private searches. *If I showed them the stars, would they understand?* The tribute she chose was a rough and grey stone that had dark red speckles. Despite their color, the speckles reminded her of stars.

Lenya felt herself pondering. Ara wanted her to "be here," to live for the rules and the tribute stones. Kuthan wanted them to take control, to escape the rules and Enetheal. Namin seemed to condemn both views. *But none of that matters in light of stars*, Lenya thought as she placed her stone carefully on the altar.

Lenya was alone as she followed the path to the Stargazing Beach. *They could share the light, could lose themselves in something that transcended their existence. Together they would feel infinitely small as the stars gazed down upon them, and infinitely large as they held a star in hand. Enveloped in rapture, they would take coldness into themselves, and pour warmth into a fallen living dream ....*

The beach was cold. Wind carried spray and sand. She walked past the point where they had first stepped onto the island. She remembered the fear, the uncertainty. She wasn't afraid now. Lenya looked up at the massive rock where they had first seen Enetheal, and then froze. He was there now, perched atop the great rock as he had been on the first day. She climbed, taking great care not to slip on the slick surface. She moved closer and closer to the stars until she was next to him. "Enetheal?" she asked. He turned his head, and all her thoughts of stars left her mind.

His face was expressionless, mouthless, and yet it had changed. Enetheal's grey eyes were wet with tears. They trickled down either side of his face in small streams, and down the length of his long nose, and along the smooth skin beneath. Enetheal slowly turned his gaze back to the horizon and the waves. *Perhaps he watches the horizon as I watch for stars to fall,* she thought, the stars pulling at her again. Lenya caught herself. She pushed starlight out of her mind, and took Enetheal by the hand.

They climbed down from the rock together and walked. The wind was cold, and they huddled close to one another for warmth. They wandered through the forest, across paths of dirt and stone, through the Sapwood, across the Firefly Field, and along the coast. When the sun started to set, Enetheal gently guided them back to paths and they returned to the Stargazing Beach. They lay close together, fingers interlocked, gazes turned upward. The stars were noticeably fewer than the first night, but the growing moon made up for the lost light. They watched its path across the sky. And then a star fell.

The star dropped from its seat in the sky, trailing silver-blue light. As it drew closer, the beach brightened and the water blazed with reflections. The reflected star raced upwards as the star shot down. They met with a huge splash in the shallows before them. Lenya smiled as droplets of water showered them.

She pulled Enetheal to his feet. Together they waded into the water. The radiance was dazzling as they drew near. Small movements in the water made the light ripple across their faces. She could already sense the cold of the star, and the water began to match its chill. Before she knew it, she was looking down on its brilliance. For the first time, she was frightened. Enetheal loosened his grip to let go of her hand, but she tightened her hold on him. Then she took a breath and reached down with her other hand.

Tendrils of ice surged up her arm and deep into her chest. Lenya heard herself cry out. Cold energy surged through her, and she heard herself laugh. But somewhere through the starshine, she recalled tears. She struggled to hold on to that thought, and gripped Enetheal's hand more tightly. *Enetheal.* She pulled them back to the beach. *Enetheal.* She pulled them up the cliffside stair. *Enetheal.* She pulled toward the well's edge. By the well she stopped. *Why am I doing this?* The question echoed insanely in her head. Both her hands shook as she stood at the edge ... and then the star tumbled into darkness.

Lenya fell to the ground, grasping for Enetheal and pulling him down with her. They lay side by side once again, and she stared into space above her. Her breaths came quickly and lightly, but soon they calmed. *I can't feel my hand,* she realized. Lenya stared at her hand, pulling the other free from Enetheal's. It hurt from gripping his so hard. She gave him a weak smile. His face was as blank as ever, but his eyes met hers, and she knew he understood.

ARA - DAY SIX

The wail was only a whisper now. If she listened carefully she could hear the dissonance of the different voices, but they weren't calling her. She was going to them. The first time they had cried her name and given her the message to listen. Afterwards, she had felt broken. She thought herself mad, insane, but she had listened. The second day she had waited to be called, and waited until the sun went down. When the sun had risen on the third day Ara had awakened to relief and guilt for her undone task. *Were the tasks not meant to be daily?* Apparently hers was not.

By the third day services were a routine for everyone except her. Each task save hers had a specific time of day in which it was performed and was performed in a specific manner. Why hadn't the stones called her again? *Have I done something wrong?* The idea horrified her, yet it seemed to be true. Why else would she not be called to serve? *Maybe it's because the others embrace their tasks!* Lenya certainly had taken to hers. Each day Lenya seemed to grow more distant, only truly paying attention if they talked of stars. Ara had tried to confide her worry to Lenya—her feeling of guilt for not completing a service, her concern about the reasons for this, her dread of the task itself. Lenya had answered with a dreamy smile.

"Things will work themselves out," she had said. She had not known what they were talking about, and failed to provide any other reassurance.

"It's like you're not even here!" Ara had told her angrily. Lenya had been oblivious to Ara's anger and to her own 'absence from the world'. They slept in separate beds that night. Lenya didn't notice.

The fourth day had dawned dark. Lenya was still distant, and when they finished their search for the daily tribute, Enetheal was missing. Perhaps he thought he could trust them to carry out their duties. Ara would have. If that was the case, then they were both wrong. As soon as Kuthan had noted Enetheal's absence he had spoken of mutiny.

How can they break a promise? Does Kuthan abandon faith so easily? With Enetheal gone, Ara had to defend the rules. And Kuthan was not alone in questioning the rules; she knew from their eyes. At least as a group they had heeded sense. They had parted ways, and Ara had been left with Lenya.

"How can they be so discontented in their labors while I can barely manage not having them!" she had questioned Lenya hopelessly at the Stargazing Beach. Lenya hadn't answered. Her eyes had been upward to the sky. They had decorated their stones with shells, and then finally, Ara's prayer, her nightmare, was answered.

"Arrraaaa!!!" An unnatural chill had accompanied the wind as it swept across the beach carrying the cry. Lenya had been oblivious. Ara had answered without question.

Leaving Lenya, she had journeyed across the island to the Shrieking Stones. The rocks had been slippery, but the journey was easier by day than it had been by night. Dread slowed her down, but she had been resolved to perform her task, even eager to confront and provide her service. This time when she entered the circle, each boulder seemed to cry with its own voice as the wind swept through cracks and holes in the rocks.

There was a howler and a wailer, a stone that both hummed and gave off a piercing whistle, a whisperer, a screecher, a sigher, and a stone that held silence—perhaps its noise was masked by the others. She had turned from stone to stone, eyes closed to their scarred surfaces, and forced herself not to cover her ears. She couldn't tell whether it was better or worse than it had been the first time.

The torrent of air had torn at her ears, but she knew to listen for the voice of the wind. Palms downward on stone, she had let the voices cry again and again. They cried and then grew silent. Ara had repeated what she heard and the wailing began again. The cacophony had gone on and on … and then stopped.

She had repeated the phrase: "Web the cave, block the Shadowed Stair." The silence had continued, and then she knew her task was done. Wearily she had risen to her feet, left the stone circle, and returned to Lenya. Lenya had not moved. At least Ara's own mind was now equally consumed by her service. That night would be the easy part ….

And now Ara wasn't being called. Today Ara was the caller. She emerged from the forest to a sight of the rocky coast and the Shrieking Stones. In front of her was the broken trail of rocks, the outcropping that led to the Shrieking Stones. The water was higher than it had been during her last journey and lapped dangerously at the rocks she had to cross.

Should this be done? The question came to her unbidden. *It must be done.* She answered herself angrily. It was the fear speaking; it was trepidation at the wind's onslaught. *Shouldn't I wait to be called? "Listen!," they had said.* Ara pushed the fear away again. There was no time to listen. Without pausing, she ran and then leapt to the first rock. She knew the rocks well, and would only know them better as she traveled.

I need guidance. I need answers. Kuthan was getting out of hand, and now even Namin was denouncing the rules. Idra belonged to Kuthan now. Lenya belonged to the stars. There was no way Ara could depend on Orin. *It's on me! I must preserve the rules, keep us obedient to them.* The rules had not been broken yet, but with Enetheal gone from the Welcome Table and the Stony Shores it would not be long until they were. *And then what?* There would be consequences, surely. Every time she visited the table, she recalled verses of its welcome:

> *You may choose to ever wander*
> *or remain and call this home*
> *If you stay, then you must honor*
> *rules engraved upon this stone ...*

> *Welcome, guest, to your new home*
> *for this is where you shall reside*
> *To be safe, to laugh, to grow*
> *by these rules you must abide*

Safety so long as we keep faith. If rules were broken they would no longer be welcome. If the rules were broken they would no longer be safe. But the rules would not be broken. *I will make sure of that.* The problem was the missing tree. She had talked to Idra at the Stony Shores while they looked for tribute stones. Idra hadn't wanted to talk long, but Ara was able to determine that the unfound tree was the source of the discord. A break between the group and Enetheal was the start of a break between the group and the rules. Enetheal didn't have any answers this time, but the Shrieking Stones just might.

She recalled Namin's words from the night they had sealed the cave:

"The stones speak to you." He had said it so simply. *"Can you speak to them?"*

Ara took the last leap and moved to the center of the Shrieking Stones. It was time to find out. The stones were cracked, and scarred. She caught sight of their grey-green reflections in the dark water, and felt her eyes lingering on their haunting dance, but she had not come for images. The wind whispered about her, each stone murmuring to the others. A low hum, a whistle, a wail. All were sounds of hushed voices. But try as she might to understand them, any meaning of the whispers was lost to her. As she listened to the stones she felt they were deep in a conversation in which she had no part.

"Ara is here." She added her whisper to theirs. The conversation around her continued, heedless of her words, indiscernible voices given power by a light breeze through the rocks. *They can't hear me.* Her stomach sank in disappointment, but her muscles relaxed. She would not be tormented today. *But they must be able to hear me: they speak and stop speaking to make sure I understand. I only need make myself heard.* This time she spoke loudly, clearly ....

"I am here, and I wish to speak to you!" Her voice echoed across the water "... *speak to you ... speak to you ....*" *It's not working.* Suddenly the wind came to a complete stop. The whispers died. Then a new wind rose, blowing from the island. The wind was cold and harsh, and it lashed the waves and tugged at her hair. Ara sat down in the middle of the stones. And the Shrieking Stones began their cacophony. Moaning, howling, whistling, humming, crying, they all melded together into one strained voice.

"*SPEEAAAKKK,*" the rocks and wind commanded. Ara grimaced at the invasion of her ears, her body, her mind. How could her bones even hold her body together against this onslaught? She must ask something, but what?

"What are you?" she spoke and thought the words at the same time. The wind grew immediately stronger. The torrent dashed the waves about so that icy froth flowed suddenly under her seated frame. Together the stones shrieked in an indiscernible howl. The wind struck at her back and slapped wet curls of hair across her cheeks and eyes. It screamed as it tried to push and pull her to the water. Unbidden, her hands rose to block the sound. She curled up into a ball, her ears covered, her eyes squeezed shut. The wind battered against her, and she found herself humming one of Namin's tunes until it finally calmed.

I could leave now. And yet she knew she could not. She considered how the voices inside her head conflicted with one another ... *just like the stones.* She closed her eyes again and thought: *When I hear them speak, some voices harmonize, others cause dissonance. I need to focus on one voice at a time.* She moved her hands away from her ears, took a deep breath, and repeated her question. "What are you?"

This time as the wind tore at her ears she crawled around the circle, taking turns to listen more carefully to some voices and to tune out others. Harmony and dissonance joined together, and now she could discern the words:

Echoes without call of voice
Reflections without casters
Choosers who never had a choice
Servants without masters

She couldn't be sure whether she had got it right, but it was close enough. Exhausted, she rose to her feet, and walked shakily to the edge of the circle. Her legs trembled, and she teetered briefly over the dark water, but caught her balance and steadied her limbs, preparing to leap. It was just as she was about to spring that she realized her mission was incomplete. *I haven't solved anything,* she realized with alarm. *I came here for answers. Answers that would explain what happened today. Answers that would help keep us happy, the rules upheld, the island safe.*

Miserably, she returned to the middle of the circle. She did not have to think long before she asked:

"Why is there no sixth fruit-bearing tree?" Again she tried to listen to the different sounds that made up the collective voice. *"IISSSSSSSS,"* the wind hissed.

"There is?" The wind stilled now so that she could hear the gentle lapping of waves. *Does it not answer because I got it right?*

"There is," she repeated, this time not in question. "Where?"

The wind rose again. Her head started to pound, the stones began to blur, and once again she closed her eyes. As before, they took turns. The wind tore at her; she answered, repeating back what she understood; and the wind rushed upon her again. Again and again she heard two answers and finally decided it was both of them:

Down in the sky
where low becomes high

Ara didn't try to figure out what this meant. When the wind subsided, she forced herself to her feet. Bones aching, she made her first leap out of the circle. Stone by stone she moved back towards the island. *I can talk to it.* She thought numbly. *I can talk to them.* Relief swept through her as she reached the island. She lay down as soon as she found soft earth and grass, and allowed her breathing to slow. The sounds of earth and gentle breeze were pleasant. How could the wind be so violent at the Shrieking Stones and so kind here? Delicate breaths of air touched the treetops. Birds sang and waves rolled softly. *It or them*? That was something else to ask if she could force herself to return. *They are many voices and one. Sometime I struggle to understand them all at once ... and yet only together are they understandable.* The pounding in her head became worse, and she tried to clear her mind. She focused on the softness of the grass, the slowness of her breaths, and the kindness of forest songs. She welcomed sleep when it came.

NAMIN - DAY SIX

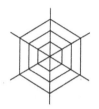

"*Behind his mouthless mask he is a thinking being.*"
That's what Kuthan had said. *He knows. He knows Enetheal is one of us, and he chooses to be cruel to him.* Enetheal was their guide. Enetheal had welcomed them to the island and showed them what they must do to live there. Enetheal was kind. Kuthan was cruel. *He knows Enetheal feels as we do, yet he hurts him all the same.* Enetheal didn't protect himself. He hadn't resisted. *He dedicates himself to us. Is this how we repay him?*

At first he had thought that Ara sided with him, but no. *She cares only about the rules.* She cared about Enetheal as a tool, not as a person. *Ara doesn't care for people. Does that make her worse than Kuthan?* Kuthan was cruel, but at least he cared for the others. *No. Kuthan is still worse.* He thought about the others. *Idra and Orin are too young to understand. Lenya too lost.* Only Namin had tried to remedy the wrong they had committed.

Enetheal had left; Namin had followed. Namin had started by walking down the slope but then realized he would have to run in order to catch Enetheal before he vanished down a side path. He hurried down the dirt path, following swiftly until it crossed the stone way that linked the fruit-trees. He looked down the stone ways on either side, and thinking he caught a glimpse of Enetheal to his right, pursued. He should have caught up to Enetheal by the time he reached the stone way. *Unless Enetheal is running too*. Namin's heart sank.

He ran. He passed a great tree with many flowers; he could only guess it was one of the fruit-bearers. A flicker of movement ahead caught his attention, but as he rounded a bend he found the end of the way. *The Sapwood*. He liked the Sapwood, but hated to disturb the quiet that enveloped it. Somehow it seemed discourteous. *No helping that now*. His pace increased as he ran between the trees. His breath became ragged, his heart beat fast, but his steps continued to pound on the forest floor. The sap flowed down the pine trees silently.

As he began to slow his pace, once again he saw movement, this time to his left. Again it was only a flicker out of the corner of his eye, but it was enough. He set off again towards the movement. He passed a small clump of trees and suddenly stopped. It wasn't Enetheal, but finding anything in the Sapwood was surprising enough to stop his search momentarily.

Before him lay large stones, atop of which was a slab with rounded edges. On the cracked, weathered surface of the slab were words. *Just like the Welcome Table*. Only it wasn't. It couldn't be. The Welcome Table was on the top of the slope. The Welcome Table was the center of the island. At least it felt like the center. This felt wrong. *It shouldn't be here.* But it was. Puzzled, he drew close. Remembering the Welcome Table, he placed his hands face down on the surface. Nothing happened. No voice or thought sounded in his mind. He walked around the table in a slow circle. *What can this mean?* Kuthan would undoubtedly want to know. *Kuthan doesn't need to know. The less he knows, the better.*

The chance of finding Enetheal was gone. Resigned, Namin sat by the table with one hand on its smooth surface. "Why did it have to come to this?" His whisper carried through sapwood. A soft echo was his only answer.

Sunlight shone in shifting rays through the vibrant green twigs, shimmering off the sap. As shadows lengthened and the sun's glow became more golden, Namin forced himself to leave. He had entered the Sapwood with his mind full of turmoil. Now it was empty. He did not realize he was lost until the Sapwood vanished behind him. He walked until he reached another path, and suddenly recognized where he was. *This is where we lay our tributes at the end of the day.* He passed the altar and then looked up at the sky. The sun was descending and the Stony Shores lay on the other side of the island. *Should I make a tribute today?* Ara would be upset if he didn't, but that wasn't necessarily a bad thing.

And yet I know I should. That thought pushed his feet along until he was stumbling upon pebbles at the Stony Shores. The coast was a sea of stones, crowned with a cloud-filled blue sky. Sounds of waves lapping the shore only emphasized its emptiness. Namin was glad it was empty. Beyond Enetheal, Namin craved no company. *Maybe Le-nya.* He thought of her smile, her eyes. *She is blameless.* His gaze swept over the stones. It took him a while to realize that he wasn't taking them in. He tried again, this time looking at each stone individually. He walked for a long time, but his mind kept wandering. *Is this how Lenya feels?*

He considered how she never seemed to focus on anything or hold a conversation at length.

Finally his eyes settled on a grey stone in the shallows. When he pulled it up, its form was egg-like. Holding it close, he walked away from the Stony Shores. He could paint it with berries, or fasten shells onto it in a spiral pattern. He'd seen Orin change one rock by hammering it with another. But these ideas did not appeal to him. Leaving his tribute decoration-free was an option, yet as he looked at the stone, he knew that it was incomplete. *The Sapwood*, he decided.

Even though he had been there earlier that day, the silence which filled the place caught him off guard. He knelt by a pool of sap, dipped the stone in, and took it out. *Still not done*. He frowned. *The stone doesn't need silence*, he realized. *It needs song*. The moment the thought occurred he knew it to be true. Not only should he sing, he *needed* to sing. He placed the rock on the ground, and began.

His voice seemed strange in the Sapwood. At first his song was the only sound, reverberating off the trees, echoing back to him. Then a scuttling sound joined his melody. Even here it seemed that the spiders had been waiting. It was odd to see them by daylight. They danced in the orange of the setting sun instead of the silver of the moon. They jumped and span, sunlight glinting off the silk strands. His fury, his disappointment, his sorrow, and his confusion all seeped into the song. When he was finished, the sun reflected off of the delicate web cocooning his stone egg, and brought it alive with orange light.

He walked through the Sapwood using the same route he had in the morning, passing the Other Table, and continuing until he reached the path near the Stone Altar. He walked to where the trees vanished, and to the rock itself.

More words were there. *So many stones. Stones with words, stones that shriek, stones that we make, stones that we walk on.* Kuthan was there too ....

"Close to sundown," he said. Namin didn't answer. Instead he held out his cocooned stone. Kuthan took it, a glint of curiosity in his eyes. He felt proud of his stone as Kuthan took it away. Perhaps Kuthan would feel what it held. *Then he could understand.* His thoughts of triumph ebbed away as soon as Kuthan was out of sight. The stone was now a tribute to the island. *But I didn't make it for the island!* he raged to himself. His stone was gone as well as the song that had coursed through its webs and brought it to life.

Namin turned again, not knowing where to go. *Back to the cabin?* He began to walk. An unmistakable splash stopped him in his tracks. He stopped, unsure of what he heard. Another distinctive splash sounded. He decided to investigate. Clambering over the rocks on the coast, he pursued the noise. Splash! It was getting louder. He heard laughter, moved around a rocky bend, and found the source.

Idra and Orin stood side by side at the water's edge. Several stones were at their feet. Idra skipped a flat rock so that it hopped over the water. Orin hurled a much larger rock out to intercept it with a large splash. *I should leave them.* There was no need to interrupt their fun.

But then Orin turned to find another large stone and saw Namin.

"Hey!" He called out.

"Hey, Ore," Namin returned. His voice was hoarse from not speaking all day. Idra turned and smiled.

"Namin," she beamed happily. "We were worried about you." She bent down to find another flat stone, and then straightened again. "You were gone all day," she added.

Should I bring up Enetheal? Would they understand? Idra is so happy again, and Ore is too. I would only make them uneasy. He chose his words carefully: "It was a distressing morning. I just needed time to think," he smiled to show them things were better. "I'm sorry I worried you."

"No problem!" Orin responded happily. He got ready with his stone. Namin turned to go, but Idra wasn't done.

"Want to join us?" she asked. Orin turned back, his eyes touching on Idra's before meeting Namin's and nodding his agreement.

"Alright." He couldn't refuse them. They showed him how to skip stones, but then Orin started hurling larger rocks as theirs skimmed across the water's surface. They took it in turns to skip or hurl rocks until dusk settled in. Finally, they stopped. Both Orin and Namin had been trying unsuccessfully to hit Idra's skipper.

"This is the perfect time to stop," Idra teased after her skipping stone narrowly evaded Orin's rock.

"Come on!" Orin complained.

"Nightfall won't wait," Idra persisted. Orin didn't resist. Their smile was shared as they walked the path to the Firefly Field.

" 'Shouldn't have much to do tonight," Orin said happily. "Most of the lanterns last a few days, and pretty much all the paths are lit."

" 'Think I might start setting up webs early then," Namin decided aloud.

"I'll come," Idra said brightly.

"And leave me to light lanterns alone?" Orin asked in mock distress.

"I trust you won't get lost," Idra poked back. Orin scowled, but it melted into a grin and a wave as Namin and Idra set off.

They walked without speaking for a time. Night was settling, but golden flashes held the dark at bay, allowing them to avoid rocks and roots on the path. Namin's stomach ached with hunger, but he knew better than to say anything to Idra. Somehow Orin had put a smile back on her face and Namin would not do anything that could take that away. They arrived at a flowering tree, and Namin remembered the night before.

Each night he put webs on either side of the tree next in line to bear fruit. The trees flowered the night before they were to produce. Only last night no tree had flowered. Instead, he had placed a web on either side of the Sapwood where the stone way disappeared. It had been a long journey to both ends of the stone way without journeying through the Sapwood. Enetheal had walked with him in silence, had watched intently as he sang. *But now Enetheal is gone.*

Namin stopped to sing at the entrance to the clearing. This time it was Idra who watched intently. She grabbed his arm tightly as the spiders began to scuttle forth, and held his arm close until it was clear that the little creatures were only there to weave. Her grip loosened slightly as she watched them dance, but she never let go. She continued to hold his arm as they moved to make the second web on the other side of the clearing.

When they finished, they moved to Kuthan's cave. In addition to replacing the spiderweb screens at the cabin doors, Namin had been visiting the cave ever since that first night at its entrance when his spiderweb had glowed. *It did something that night. Something important. It is essential that it can do that again—if it needs to.* Each of the services seemed to accomplish something. Because his webs were sung at the entrances to the cabins and the fruit-bearing trees he felt that they were protective. *Perhaps something in the cave needs protecting.*

He sang a melody similar to the one he had sung before, but new notes crept in and the spiders knew how to change the web. Idra still held him close as she watched. It felt good. They began to leave, and then the fireflies along the path stopped blinking. He had not noticed that the crickets had stopped chirping until the lights were gone.

"What?" Idra started to ask. But he cut her off with a "shhh!" She quieted instantly. He looked at the web expectantly and was not disappointed. For the second time he watched as a soft white glow emanated from the web. It wasn't as unnerving as it had been the first time. He just was puzzled. A flash of gold marked the return of the flies. The noises of the night returned, and they were on their way once more.

"What happened?" Idra asked. They walked close to one another in the darkness.

"I'm not sure," Namin answered. "It has happened once before, but I'm not sure what it means."

"Oh," Idra lapsed into silence again. "You sing beautifully," she said a few moments later.

"Thanks," said Namin, and he smiled.

"It's so comforting it almost made me forget …." She took a breath. "You're not scared of them?"

"Scared of what?"

"The spiders," she said quietly. "Orin mentioned they were scary, but I didn't know until I saw them."

"Oh," Namin said, not really sure of what to say. "I suppose not."

Silence fell between them again and they walked until they reached Idra's cabin. He decided to wait to sing the other webs until after she was safe inside. *She's probably seen enough spider-dancing tonight.* He walked up to the door and peeled the spiderweb-screen aside so that she could enter.

"Namin?" she asked. He turned.

"I know you're not happy with how things went today. I don't think anyone is. But we are still a family. We still care for one another." It took a moment for the full impact of the words to hit him.

"I know," he answered. "You understand that so well. You are right." She gave him a hug, and went inside. His thoughts were tangled. *Kuthan was so cruel. Ara so blind and heartless.* And yet Idra's words echoed through his mind.

He stood outside the cabin staring into the night before finally walking up the path to where Ara and Lenya slept. As he sang the webs in place, the faces of his family filled his mind. He could not prevent his anger with Kuthan and Ara from creeping into his song, and he felt guilty as his song and caring thoughts dwelled for so long upon Idra, Orin, and Lenya.

As he closed his eyes that night his thoughts returned to the tribute he had made earlier that day. *It wasn't for the island,* he remembered. *Why should I make tributes to the island? It's the people I care about.* He thought about Lenya's starry eyes and dreamy smile, Orin's laugh, Idra's warm brown eyes, ... and Enetheal. *It's people who are worth worshipping.*

ORIN - DAY SEVEN

He followed the path, a wide grin on his face, enjoying the gentle wind that blew his hair back. He did not know this path, which pleased him. The trails split before him, not into two or three paths, but into seven distinct ways. There was so much to explore. He was free! He drank in the different choices with his eyes. Which to choose? Before he could decide, a voice spoke.

"Lies," it said bitterly. The thought was not his own, and yet the voice sounded very much like his own. It was certainly familiar. It couldn't be one of the others, could it? Perhaps it was the voice from the Welcome Table, or....

"Are you content to accept the paths set before you? Is that why you smile?" His hands moved up to his face to find his smile gone. Where did the voice come from? He turned around to the solitary path behind him. It was empty but for a creeping darkness. The dark seemed to flow like rising water towards him. He returned his gaze to the paths in front of him. Which to choose? The dark was almost there.

"Don't look for paths. Look for revelation." This time he couldn't tell whether the words were spoken to him, or by him. Regardless, his eyes stung as the words washed over him, and then they burned. He closed them, allowing tears to sooth them, and then opened them again. The paths were no longer trails to follow; they were merely areas where plants did not grow. He was in the middle of darkening forest, but as he took in the entire wood he noticed lanterns.

They lined the paths, but were also cocooned within bushes, sheltered in crooks of trees, hanging from branches, and randomly arrayed across the forest floor. It was a wood now with no path, but no path was needed. The light of the lanterns grew brighter, and then there was yet more light, and fireflies flew freely, brightening the forest until it was daytime again and the whole wood was free for wandering ....

Orin awoke with sun in his eyes. He sat up, and felt his stomach groan. It rumbled loudly, reminding him of his hunger.

"You too?" Namin laughed. Namin always seemed to have awoken only moments after Orin did, ever since the first day when Orin had slipped off.

"Yeah," Orin agreed. Yesterday had been a struggle and he was glad for it to be over. Despite everything that had happened, it was his belly that made the loudest complaint. Lack of food had left him exhausted when he finally lay down the night before, and even now when he awoke, he was tired. Idra had voiced the idea of eating some of the berries they had used to paint tribute stones. It had helped, but it had not been nearly enough. *Couldn't let Idra know that, though.* She had been so happy to try and remedy what she had messed up. *"You did nothing wrong,"* he had told her. Orin hoped earnestly that things had gone well that morning for Idra's sake, and also for the sake of his belly.

Orin met Namin's eyes.

"Let's go."

Namin nodded his assent, and moments later they were in the filtered morning sunlight. They met Idra and Kuthan halfway between their two cabins. Idra had a huge smile on her face.

"Breakfast and lots of it," she said happily.

Kuthan put his hand on her head and mussed her hair.

"Hey!" she complained, but Kuthan only laughed. Then his eyes turned to Namin's. Orin felt the tension between them, and quickly skipped to Idra's side.

"Race you to Lenya and Ara's!" She started running before his words were fully out, but he was hot on her trail. They sped past her cabin. The distance between the two of them grew larger until he cut off the path to get in front of her.

"Rocks and roots!" she called. He stumbled, spotted a large rock, and leapt. They moved from rock to root and root to rock, until finally Orin arrived first with Idra just behind. Ara opened the door. Her eyebrows were drawn together, but she cracked a grin when Idra mentioned breakfast. As a threesome they hurried over to Lenya to rouse her.

"You'd think she'd be used to it by now," Ara said, rolling her eyes. Orin silently agreed.

"Lenya!" They took turns saying her name and poking at her. She moaned, and rolled away a few times, but they persisted until she opened her eyes. When she did, they seemed to flicker before focusing on their faces.

"Food is on the table," Idra proclaimed. Lenya seemed to struggle to find words.

"Oh," she blinked slowly. "That sounds very nice. Thank you."

"Let's go," Orin encouraged. The thought of the food made his mouth water.

Once Lenya was out of bed, she moved quickly. They hurried out the door to find Kuthan and Namin just arriving. Both had stony expressions, but were polite as they greeted Ara and Lenya. And then they were off up the slope. Although the tension between them was still palpable, all of them were unified in their hunger and eagerness to eat. They hurried up the slope and were well rewarded.

Idra beamed as they devoured the large pile of fruit she had laid upon the table. Namin had been chosen to take the first fruit that day. *She still hasn't picked me!* thought Orin. It was upsetting. *But Idra has her reasons.* They were a separate group now, Idra, Kuthan, and Orin. Idra understood the importance of what they were doing, but was still concerned for the others. She had been so upset yesterday. The three of them had spent much of the day together until Kuthan had left, and then Orin had been alone with her, talking, wandering, and skipping stones. By the end of their time together she was almost happy.

Besides the crisis of the missing tree, Namin had been on her mind, and the way he had vanished so angrily when she had returned fruitless. Kuthan had stood up for them, but Namin had thrown it aside. *He sides with Enetheal.* Kuthan had thought that too. *And he's right.* But still Idra had worried: she was so eager to have harmony among all six of them.

The tributes went well that day. Orin was proud to use some sticky sap to attach sand instead of shells. He used berries to paint over all of it. His tribute was beautiful: red, blue, purple, and yellow patches of painted sand transformed the stone into a thing of wonder.

By the time Orin lay his tribute on the altar, the sun was near setting. Idra and Kuthan had stayed close to each other during the day although they had been working separately on their tributes. Between work on the tribute stones, and the presence of Namin, Lenya, and Ara, there had not been enough time for planning.

"We'll talk when I return," Kuthan promised. They waited together until Ara placed her stone upon the Sunset Altar with the other five. Then, as a group, they watched the sun set. The sky was gold and yellow and pink as the sun came to meet its reflection. The shimmering path cast along the water dimmed as the sun sank beneath the waves. Kuthan grimaced as he began to walk away from them, holding the salver and the tributes close.

"We'll be skipping rocks," Orin announced. He made sure he said it loudly enough for Kuthan to hear.

"Come on, Idra," he added. They left, walking in the opposite direction of Kuthan's cave, towards the small cove. Clambering over rocks along the coast, it was a short journey, but fun. The water was calm in the cove and the rocks were easy jumpers. At first Orin and Idra didn't speak. They skipped their rocks in intersecting lines, trying to connect with each others'. Their throws seemed to take turns being mistimed and messed up: once Idra's stone even hopped over Orin's as it launched off a ripple in the surface.

"Things went well today," Orin ventured.

"Yeah," Idra answered, her stone skittering across the water eight times.

"No fighting, the tribute stones went well, the fruit was great, and Enetheal wasn't anywhere."

"Good. Let's hope he stays gone," she said sharply. Their stones weren't even close to one another, as they skipped upon the water. Idra sighed. "The fighting will return, and in six more days so will a fruitless day, unless we find the tree."

"You're sure there is one?" Orin asked. "All the trees in the Sapwood look the same—none of them look like fruit-bearers. Maybe going hungry once in a while is just part of how things are supposed to be."

"No. There must be a tree," Idra insisted. "I know there is. I can *feel* it. It's my responsibility to bring the fruit to our family, to feed *us*! What am I going to do?"

"What are *we* going to do," he corrected her with a smile. "We'll find your tree." *If there is one.* She returned his smile. They cast their slivers of rock, which made a small *clink* brushing past each other. After that they stopped skipping and just watched the water until Kuthan arrived. He joined them in silence, sat down behind them and fixed his gaze across the water as well.

"Would you return if you could?" Kuthan asked suddenly. "If we could go back and never have arrived here?"

"Nope," Orin answered.

Idra took longer, but finally said, "Maybe." She paused, then added, "You?"

"Naw," he chuckled. "This is what we are."

"You're right," Idra agreed. Orin glanced at the horizon nervously. It would be dark soon, and he had his task to complete.

"We need to start planning now," he said.

"Yes," Kuthan agreed. "I think our first step is to put together what we all know. The last few days have been confusing and we need to catch each other up." Orin nodded his agreement.

Kuthan continued, "So what do we know? What have we figured out?"

"I know that Ara doesn't have to do her task every day, and that when she listens to the Shrieking Stones they tell her things. They told her to use me and Namin to put a web at the entrance to the cave that you go into to deliver the tributes." He said it all in one breath, surprised that he'd forgotten to mention it earlier.

Kuthan's brow furrowed, his expression brooding.

"What does this mean?" he muttered. Orin could not be sure whether he was talking to himself or to them, but he decided to venture an answer. "It means we are not alone," Orin answered.

"No," Kuthan agreed. "We are not. That is for certain." He thought some more. "There is another ... presence I came across as well." He said it offhandedly. Orin and Idra answered him with stares, so he continued. "Just ... I think something, someone is receiving the tributes. One tribute was returned to me, two days ago. It was changed." Orin was surprised to hear the uncertainty in Kuthan's voice. "I think it, the someone, was trying to talk to me. It was my tribute and ...." Kuthan trailed off and then continued: "There was another one today. I'm sure it's trying to speak to me." A cold wind blew about them, and Orin shivered.

"Do you know what it was trying to say?" Idra asked.

"Maybe. Some .... It was hard to understand. I think it's like us. Someone who was made a slave by Enetheal ... but might have defied Enetheal, and was sent into the cave."

"A missing seventh person," Orin thought aloud.

"A missing seventh tree," Idra added, her eyes lighting up.

"Coincidence?" Kuthan asked. "We can't be sure. I'm trying to communicate with it through my tributes ...

though I still need to figure out how to understand more. All I have now are images that I create, which are then sent back changed."

They thought together in silence, and then Idra continued "So there is a missing tree, and a missing person you are communicating with. That connects our two tasks." She looked at Orin. He nodded his head, and she continued. "Namin thinks that his webs protect us somehow," she mused aloud.

"The webs block off the fruit trees, and the cave," Orin continued excitedly.

"As well as our cabins," Kuthan finished. "We know some of the connections, but we still don't understand the purposes of the tasks. If Namin is right about his webs, there doesn't seem to be anything that we need protecting from other than Enetheal, and the webs sure don't stop him."

"And we still don't understand Lenya's stars, Ara's voices, or Orin's paths." Idra added with a frown.

"The paths join the different parts of the island together at night," Orin cut in. He was upset that they couldn't understand how connected his task was. "And we need to walk the paths at night because … because …."

"Because that's when something important happens," Kuthan finished. "We just don't know what."

"But it connects to the other services," Orin continued, " by linking the cave, and the trees, and the webs. It allows us to travel to and from those places, even during the night." *And it's almost night now!* Some clouds still retained pink, but most of them were dark grey, even blue. The stars had begun to take over lighting the sky.

"Yes," Kuthan agreed. But he did not sound convinced.

"I need to go," Orin said, before the conversation could continue. Idra looked up at the sky worriedly, and Kuthan scowled.

"We'll talk more tomorrow," Kuthan promised. "And I'll have a plan. For now keep your eyes open. I think we're still far from having all the puzzle pieces, let alone putting them together." Orin agreed, and hurried off.

"Good luck!" Idra called after him. He smiled.

The paths would probably get him to the fields in time, but Orin knew his way around well enough to try another route. He cut across forest, weaving his way around plants and over rocks. An owl hooted, and the crickets began to chirp. Otherwise it was quiet.

He dodged around trees and bushes, making his own path through the foliage. The forest was darkening fast and the trees obscured most of the remaining light. Orin was running, just in case. He needn't have worried; the field appeared ahead almost immediately. Daylight still lingered there, and fireflies dipped and danced, both in the field and in the surrounding forest.

He was almost there when he saw someone. It was only a glimpse through the trees, but it was enough for him to change his course. *Who else knows their way around the island without the paths?* It wouldn't be Ara, especially with darkness falling. Kuthan and Idra were way too far behind.

"Namin? Lenya?" It couldn't be either of them. The figure was too short. That meant it couldn't be Enetheal either. For a moment Orin thought he had lost sight of it, but then he saw it moving away from the paths deeper into the woods. He sprinted after it. Just when he thought he had caught up, there was a bright golden flash. Initially he was blinded, but in the lingering afterlight there was nothing save dark, empty forest.

Orin swept his gaze around the forest, looking for movement, looking for a path. He found neither. It was dark. The deep blue sky was turning purple; the stars ruled the sky. He looked back from where he had come. *When did I turn?* He never made up his mind. Up ahead there was another flash of gold. He ran towards it, leaping over rocks and roots and weaving through bushes until he reached the spot. By then another golden flash sent him running. *I need to follow the light. The lights have always been the path.* His heart was pounding while he chased them, and suddenly he couldn't help laughing:

Never roam in dark of night
off the path of lantern's light

What was going to happen now? *Ara would be furious.* He grinned. "There are no paths," he said to the darkness, remembering his dream. But unlike his dream, the forest only got darker. The purple sky was blackening. A golden flash sent him in a new direction. And when he arrived, it flashed again. He slammed his cupped hands together around the fly.

It was then he noticed an expanse of darkness in front of him. The firefly flashed again and he saw the thing for what it was: *a cabin.* Now that he knew it was there, he considered it carefully, using the scant silvery light cast by the night sky. It was definitely a cabin. And yet no path had led to it.

Are there other people here? Is this where the fleeing figure went? Could this be where Enetheal lives? His mind was racing, and he could hear Kuthan's voice echoing in his mind: *"We're still far from having all the puzzle pieces, let alone putting them together."*

It was strange to see a doorway without a web in front of it. He walked to the door and pushed it open. The loud creak of the hinges made him jump back, but then he returned and stood at the threshold.

"Hello?" he called into the darkness. No one answered. *Maybe they're asleep.* He entered the cabin quietly, and held his breath. There were no sounds of another's breathing. *I should have brought a lantern.* A faint golden flash cast aside the darkness for an instant. There were no beds or windows inside the cabin, but there were lanterns. Hundreds of them were arranged upon shelves that lined the walls, some hung from the ceiling, and some were piled neatly on the floor.

"Pathmaster," he said to the room. And then a grin grew on his face. "Pathmaker," he said more loudly. The grin grew larger. He wished he could get started, but it seemed that darkness was destined to own the night a little longer. Excitement flooded through him as he sprinted back to the Firefly Field. Blackness blanketed the sky, but the stars and moon shone, and he was only really off the path for a short bit before he found his way to the field.

Kuthan was right about the puzzle pieces just starting to come together. He couldn't stop himself from smiling. *Now exploration would truly begin.* Orin lit the unlit lanterns around the island while he thought: *The night is ours now, and soon the island will have no more secrets. It's time to complete the circle; it's time to find Idra's tree.*

Namin was waiting for him when he returned to the cabin.

"How was it?" he asked pleasantly.

"It was a dream come true," Orin laughed.

LENYA - DAY EIGHT

She walked up the stone stairs. On one side was the cliff face of the plateau where the well was. On the other side and far below were dark waves which crashed against the rocks. The water extended out until it met the sky. The lanterns that bordered the stairs were dark, as was the sky above. Step by step she moved up the stairs. It was strange to make the climb without carrying a star. 'I just made this journey, only the stairs were bright with starfire.' The star she had held glowed with a purplish light, its flickering like that of flame. 'But I have no star now.' She reached the top of the plateau, only it had changed. Instead of a garden surrounding a well, there was a bridge. Like the plateau, the bridge was laced with moss and strewn with flowers. The leaves of the plants were silver and the flower-petals glowed white.

As she watched, they turned their heads towards the stars. Instead of being in their usual place in the heavens, the stars were gathered on one side of the bridge, watching her. She felt herself being pulled toward the starlight, mirroring the plants, stretching to the stars. They were calling her. She spread her wings, and then stopped. A drop of water had fallen on her cheek; she knew it wasn't rain. She turned her gaze, not up, but over to the other side of the bridge. They were watching her as well: Idra, Orin, Kuthan, Ara, and Namin stood in the darkness, their eyes calling her just as the stars did. Another drop of water fell. Her gaze shifted from one side of the bridge to the other and then back.

"I love you both, don't you see?" They continued to stare at her mutely. "We all belong together." They gave her no answer, so she walked along the bridge, the stars on one side, her companions on the other. Enetheal walked next to her. She hadn't noticed him join her, but now they held hands as they walked, and no more drops of water fell.

"Lenya," Ara's voice wasn't harsh; but neither was it gentle. Soft words would not awaken her; Ara's voice needed to be firm. When Lenya opened her eyes, Ara lifted her to a sitting position. Her dream slipped away even as she sat up. She hadn't been deep in sleep to begin with. Part of her mind was on the dream, the other still ached from the loss of last night's star. Its glow had been almost purple; its light had felt so cold that it was warm, or maybe so hot that it was cold. *It must have been cold. They are always alive with coldness.* And yet in her dream she had been uncertain of something. She was still uncertain. There was something else that was important, something that was not starlight.

"Lenya!" Ara's voice *was* harsh now and Lenya opened her eyes again. This time when she sat up she arose from her bed. The cabin was full, as it always was when she awoke. Kuthan waited by the door, Orin in the doorway, his arms reaching across it, pushing from side to side. Idra and Namin sat on Ara's empty bed, Idra lying across his lap. Ara now moved into the warm place Lenya had just left, wanting to be sure Lenya didn't lie down again. She wore a frown.

"You should go to bed earlier," Ara said quietly.

"Yes," Lenya answered sleepily. It was easier than arguing. Ara had been telling her that every day, before she went to bed, and after she got up.

"Lenya can choose when she goes to bed," Kuthan said, turning his attention from outside the cabin.

"Yes," Lenya agreed before Ara could respond. Lenya had no wish for a morning argument to break out. Fortunately neither Kuthan nor Ara pursued the issue further, and they journeyed to the Welcome Table without incident.

Ara was chosen to eat first, and she did so with vigor. Lenya bit into her own piece of fruit and once again remembered. Flavor burst in her mouth; she felt the strength of the wind as it gusted over the slope, the song of birds calling from different trees, the brightness of the sun, the scent of pines. But there was something else. *Starlight! Starlight does this and more!* But part of her pushed the thought aside and she thought again: *No ... starlight makes me forget something.* She looked down at the fruit in her hands, and then up at the people around her.

They weren't a pleasant sight: Kuthan, Ara, and Namin took turns glowering at each other and then looking at their fruit. Idra glanced between all three nervously. And Orin watched Idra with a frown. None of them watched Lenya. *Stars watch me, and I watch them.* She continued to eat, hoping it would help her think. *Tears.* That's what had turned her attention from the heavens. Last night's star burned so brightly in her mind that she had almost forgotten the one before. Enetheal had been with her. *Was it sorrow that turned me from joy? Why would anyone choose tears over laughter?* She looked before her again. Her companions were unchanged, save that they were eating more slowly. Neither tears nor laughter were in front of her. And yet it was the tears that would have captured her attention, she was sure. She took the last portion of her fruit, which filled her entire mouth. Juice burst once more, the tart flavor bringing her to full awareness. And she finished remembering: *It's not a choice between laughter and tears. The tears helped me remember the world.*

She closed her eyes and saw the glow of stars. Not one star, but all of them, just as they were before they had started to fall. *The stars ... so beautiful ... could they be dangerous?* The others were preparing to leave now; it was time for tributes. Yesterday she had speckled a stone with flecks of sand, to be the stars, and washed the other half in waves, to be tears. Today she would make something that didn't connect to either. She smiled, and Namin, catching her eye, returned the smile.

They arrived at the Stony Shores and she began to search for a stone. The day was unclouded, as the night had been. She looked around, lifting a single stone and then letting it drop. *It can't remind me of stars.* She ignored the round ones and the speckled ones. She let go of rocks that were cool to the touch and rocks that were bright. But even the warm dull stones seemed to carry hints of the heavens. *They have all tasted starlight.*

When the others began to gather near the entrance of the path, she thought of the night's task ahead. Usually the passage of time was comforting: time came and left with each fallen star, each night offering another wonder. The end and the beginning were written in the starshine. Lenya looked around. *Everything that exists ties me to them.* She threw away a cold dull yellow stone, and then picked it up again. She was done, that much she knew.

I need help, she decided as she walked over to her companions. Her eyes moved from one to another. Who could she confide in? Who could she tell she was scared of her task, and scared to be scared?

Ara would tell me I need to keep my head straight, perform my task because that is my job. They started walking back along the path. *Kuthan would be delighted to remove me from the stars; he would be eager to have someone else to fight the island.* She looked at Kuthan. He walked with Orin and Idra, side by side by side. He was whispering intently until Ara turned back to glare at him. He became mute. *I don't want to fight, I just need to think. I'm so confused.* They reached a fork in the path. Orin announced he was going to the Sapwood. Idra and Kuthan quickly chorused their plan to join him. Ara announced that she would paint with berries. Namin departed for the shells. *Everything is happening too fast!* She took a breath. *Namin*, she decided, remembering his smile.

She hurried after him. The wind seemed to sigh. Twigs and pine needles blew about as she ran down the slope. "Namin!" she called. The path curved and she turned off the path, shortcutting through bushes and pines. "Namin," she called again. And then there he was, waiting for her.

"Hey Lenya," he said simply. He seemed almost surprised. She blinked her eyes, and saw starlight once more before she opened them again.

"Can we talk?"

"Of course," he answered gently. She looked into his slate-colored eyes and saw concern. *I chose the right one.*

But then the right words didn't come. *How do I say this?* They walked side by side in silence. *He talks like Enetheal sometimes.* She couldn't help thinking of Enetheal as they passed the stone where he had shed tears. *That's where I started, but I can't tell Namin about that. It's not mine to say.* But what could she say?

"I ...." She stopped and then looked up at him. He nodded, so that she felt it was alright to continue.

"Could it be bad for me to love the stars?" This time his silence was more discomforting. She knew he was thinking hard. Now the forest had melded into the sand of the beach. Still they walked.

"I don't know," he said slowly. They stopped, and sat down together in the sand. His words were both frustrating and satisfying and she opened her mouth to agree, but he wasn't done. "I think it's wonderful that you love them, but also that you recognize your love for them has consequences."

"Yes," she heard herself whisper. "But I can't let go of them."

"No. But maybe you can hold on to other things too."

Please. "Yes," Lenya said again.

"What else do you want to hold on to?" He gave her a searching look, but the only answer she had was simple.

"Everything."

They spent the rest of the morning working on their tributes, attaching sea-shells and grains of sand with sap. As they worked, they laughed. The talked about the clouds and the strange soft noises they heard inside the shells. The stars didn't leave her mind, but she was able to talk about other things. They played with the sand, burying each other's legs and then trying to escape. Namin hummed happily. And then it was time to deliver their tributes. They walked together across the island, both deep in thought. *I can hold on to both.* She remembered Enetheal's hand in hers, the star clutched close to her chest in the other hand. And suddenly she realized something. *I remember now, but when I am with the stars, I forget.*

"Would you come with me tonight?" she asked Namin.

He thought for a moment, and then nodded once. "Yes," he added, and then once again, he began to hum. The tune brought her drowsiness and contentment, but sleep was still far off.

By nightfall a scant covering of clouds had moved in, but it did not hide the starshine. Namin noted that the moon was growing. She almost corrected him, pointing out that the stars were leaving, but then decided to agree.

She knew the star that would fall well before it moved. *I can feel them even down here.* It was a short walk this time, and the star had not fallen far from the path. It vibrated with energy. The star's light shone white and silver, the silver flowing like liquid over the glowing surface. When she touched it, iciness lanced up her arm, and once again she cried out, laughing at the same time. With effort she remembered Namin and turned to him, offering the star so that he could touch it too.

"Do you see? Do you see?!" she asked him, dancing with starshine inside her.

He smiled. "Yes, I see," he agreed. But his voice did not convey the joy she felt. She wondered if he really did.

Namin walked the rest of the journey with her, but her light went out with the star's when she released it into the blackness of the well, and he had to help her back to the cabin.

"Get some rest," he said as they parted at the cabin door. He walked away, but Lenya remained. Exhausted as she was, she stayed in the doorway, staring up into the heavens. Some of coldness remained inside her. She thought she knew which star would fall tomorrow.

A rustle in the bushes turned her gaze from the stars. It was Enetheal. *He only comes when Namin leaves,* she realized sadly.

"Do you see?" she smiled with exhaustion. He didn't have to say anything for her to know.

ORIN - DAY NINE

*T*onight! Orin couldn't help but shiver slightly. Sleep had come hard the night before. He was too excited to sleep. He had wanted to do it last night, but they had been delayed. Yesterday Orin, Idra, and Kuthan had worked to create Orin's new path. Kuthan's eyes filled with wonder when Orin described his idea. Orin's plan allowed them to explore the island in darkness. Orin's plan would reveal the secrets of the island, including the missing tree. The missing tree was where they had decided to start, and now the first path was nearly done.

If only I had caught the flies faster we might have fin-ished it! The broken loop of fruit- bearing trees was now completed by a new path. Orin's path. Yesterday they had placed lanterns through the Sapwood to complete the circle. But he had not caught enough flies to light the entire island *including* his new path. Kuthan had insisted they light the rest of the island first so as not to arouse suspicion. *Only one more day*, he had told himself, but he was impatient.

He would need to catch flies faster and catch more of them if he were to continue to blaze new paths. He clenched his teeth in frustration.

Today I will. There was still no sign of the tree, but the night might yield that secret. *It's only been at night that we've seen the webs glow. It was nighttime when I found these lanterns. The stars fall at night. And something else must happen, too—otherwise, why the rules?* Orin kicked off his blanket.

"Morning, Ore," Namin yawned.

I have to act normal, I mustn't give anything away. "Morning Namin," he answered brightly. "Ready when you are."

They left their cabin, and walked up the path towards Idra and Kuthan's. Orin continued to mull over ways to increase the number of flies he was catching, but no solution came to mind. Namin hummed while they walked. Maybe Namin would know. As soon as he thought it, Orin voiced his question:

"Can you think of a way I could get more flies faster?" The words poured out. *Idiot!* He waited for the answer, both dreading the response and eager for it. Namin avoided Orin's eyes while he thought.

"Not right now. I'll let you know if I come up with anything."

Orin sighed in relief. *Safe.*

"Why?"

"It's just … It's just that it's hard to catch enough flies to light the whole island when I catch them as slow as I do." Namin nodded. "I love my task, but it gets challenging at times," Orin added.

"I see," Namin said. Orin hoped he didn't. Namin closed his eyes for a moment, then opened them. They didn't talk again until they reached Kuthan and Idra's cabin. Idra was sitting on the doorstep when they arrived, and beamed when she saw them.

"Hurry up, Kuth!" she called through the open door. Kuthan emerged, his hair a mess from sleep, but his eyes bright and alert. They formed their usual foursome, moving up the path to gather Lenya and Ara. It was odd knowing what was in store for that night. Kuthan, Idra, and Orin all exchanged glances now and then, but Namin was oblivious. *It will feel better when Namin isn't alone in unawareness.* When Lenya and Ara joined them he did feel more relaxed. It was better to be two groups of three than to have one person left out.

The fruit was delicious, but Orin's mind was on his new path, and the missing tree. It could all be revealed tonight. The walk down to the Stony Shores was slow, the search even slower. He discarded stone after stone, and still couldn't find any that seemed worthy of special attention. Eventually Kuthan joined him. The others were far away, but nevertheless, he lowered his voice.

"Ready?" he murmured.

"Too ready. I can't pick a tribute."

"Just keep calm for a bit longer, we're almost there."

Kuthan left to continue his own search, leaving Orin alone once again. Just as Orin turned his head back down to the sea of stones he saw Ara watching. She gave him a severe look before turning away. *She can't know!* His heart hammered. There was no way she could know. *If she knew, she would have told us; she would have fought against us.* He made sure not to look up for a long time, and when he next raised his head she was a tiny figure in the distance. Even without talking Ara found a way to be mean. Orin's feet had carried him near the end of the shore. He would turn back in a moment, but he couldn't stop now. *No paths, no boundaries.* He reminded himself. *That's what today is about.* He continued past the end of the Stony Shores. He thought he heard Ara call after him, but fortunately the wind and waves would obscure a calling voice. He waded through reeds, and then into the brush and pines beyond.

Despite the coming night's adventure, he felt excitement. *I make my own path. Regardless of trails, regardless of Ara.* He wound his way through some ferns, over rocks, and then to some coastal boulders. *This is what the island is about,* he thought as he climbed. He clambered up a rock, and used a tree-branch to get down its other side.

And then he found his prize. The sun glinted off and through the stone. It was almost transparent, enhanced by the golden sunshine. He didn't know whether the light that shone from it came from the stone itself, or was merely reflected sun. He picked it up between his thumb and third finger. Somehow he wasn't surprised. *This is a real tribute. One that I had to find my way to. One that I had to discover. One that holds its own light.* He thought of fireflies, and held his tribute close.

The others were waiting when he returned. Kuthan looked smug. Ara looked angry.

"Where did you get your tribute from?" she asked.

Somehow he felt emboldened holding it tight in his hand. "That's not your concern," he said coolly.

"It *is* my concern. It concerns all of us!" she began to protest, but Orin had already started to travel up the path, not bothering to look to see if they followed. The footfalls behind them confirmed that they had, as he knew they would. Kuthan walked up next to him giving him a nod of approval, and Orin felt his stomach leap. *We're not so different, me and Kuth.* He smiled at the thought.

When it was time to part ways, he realized that for the first time since they had arrived at the island, there was nothing left to do. His tribute was perfect. He looked up at the others. Namin and Lenya left for the beach. Idra looked between Kuthan and Orin.

"Berries?" she asked.

"Sure," Orin answered, eager to go somewhere. To his horror Ara followed them. *At least she didn't mention the Sapwood. If Ara came there ....* They arrived at the Berry Grove. Ara started almost immediately, ran over to a nearby bush, and began plucking blackberries. After exchanging glances, Idra and Kuthan started picking their own berries. Orin did not even pretend. He sat under a bush in the shade, and watched the others. *Why can't the day move faster!* To make matters worse, Ara came over.

"Shouldn't you be working?" she asked.

"I did," Orin answered. "I'm done." Ara set her jaw, her arms crossed.

"Just because Enetheal isn't here doesn't mean we don't have to work. It's important to put effort into making these tributes, and that we make them the right way!" Orin looked beyond her. He wished Kuthan or Idra would intervene.

"Listen to me! You're making a mistake!" Ara intoned, forcing his attention away from the others. The joy of his newfound treasure and the upcoming nighttime adventure was quickly disappearing.

"The only mistake here is you!" Orin hurled the words at her. Ara started to speak, but her voice caught in her throat. Her eyes closed, and her hands moved to either side of her face brushing her ears. Then she turned and walked several paces away, returning her attention to her tribute.

Orin let out a sigh. *Why can't she just leave us all alone?* He squeezed his stone tight in hand, while his breaths slowed. *About time she got a clue.* He opened his palm to display his crystalline stone. It was perfect as it was; any change would blemish his discovery. Still, he wished he could do something. He played with the sun's light within his tribute stone until at long last the others emerged with their own tributes.

They went down to the beach to gather Lenya and Namin. There were several piles of sand around their tributes, and shells poked out of them decoratively. Their tributes looked remarkably unchanged. *And yet Ara doesn't scold them!* He kept the bitter thought to himself as they walked towards today's fruit tree. *Today should be a day of celebration,* he reminded himself, thinking of his glorious stone tribute and the night to come. *I can't let Ara ruin it.*

Soon they were gathered beneath the tree and Idra was scampering up. Orin could not help but be amazed at how quickly she moved from branch to branch. *Even the squirrels must be envious.* Coming down was harder. Once she reached the top and picked the fruits, she had only one hand free for climbing.

"Just throw them, Idra!" Kuthan called.

"In a moment," she laughed back. "I don't have a clear view through these branches. She descended a bit further. A piece of fruit started to roll from the pile in her arms and as she struggled to keep hold of it, her foot slipped.

"Idra!" Ore gasped, his heart lurching, but she had already caught herself. Kuthan cursed under his breath, and Namin had turned pale.

"I'm fine," she called down. After she moved a bit lower she tossed them each a fruit before descending gracefully to the ground.

"You're alright?" Namin asked.

"Yes," she laughed back. "Don't panic."

"You climb down holding our fruits every morning?" Namin asked.

"And haven't fallen even once, so stop worrying! We have food to eat." Ara gave Idra a hug, and even Lenya seemed relieved. That meal was the best they'd had in a while, and it seemed only moments later that the sun had fallen below the horizon, and that he and Idra were at their usual stone-skipping site. They both stared at the water's gentle waves lapping at the rocks. Neither of them ventured to skip a stone. Finally Idra broke the silence.

"Tonight," she spoke softly, in a half sigh, half whisper.

"Tonight," Orin echoed. He realized he sounded relieved. *It's time.* The wait for Kuthan was more pleasant than the seemingly endless day he had endured. They sat together, listening to one another breathe, their shoulders pressed up against each another. There wasn't anything to say, but that was how things were meant to be. Finally Kuthan returned from the cave. As always he looked shaken from his journey, but then his eyes met theirs and they stood up.

"It's time," he said simply.

The path was complete before the light was gone. It was dusk in the Sapwood. The sky was pale, the stars just starting to emerge. Around them were the pines, their bark blackening as the evening darkened. But even as the night deepened, the streams of sap trailing down the trees seemed to glow more brightly, and the pools in which the trees stood seemed to glow with their own light. Brighter still was what lay before them. *My dream!* Orin thought, his heart leaping.

Twinkling before them was the new path. Pairs of lanterns flanked it every ten paces. The fireflies took it in turns illuminating the sapwood in gold and plunging areas into darkness, but the trail was unmistakable for what it was.

"No rules broken," Kuthan grinned.

"Do you think we'll find my tree tonight?" Idra asked nervously.

"Yes," Orin said, excitement flowing through him.

"Something about this island changes at night," Kuthan said. "Someone is trying to hide something, maybe even your tree. Whatever happens, together we are about to learn more about how things work here."

As a threesome they paused at the edge of the makeshift path. The pale blue of the sky had become a dark blue by the end of their conversation. It slowly turned purple as they waited. The stars shone, the moon glowed, the sap flowed, and the flashes of gold grew brighter and brighter until the lanterns alone seemed to stand against the blackness.

It's my task, Orin thought, and broke the silence. "It will work," he said confidently. "Let's go."

They held hands as they stepped onto their makeshift path. He wondered if the sweat between their interlocked hands was his or theirs. Step by step they moved. The tree shadows shifted about them as they walked. Those made by moonlight held fast, but elsewhere the lanterns cast flitting forms. Despite all that interplay of dark and light, the wood was silent apart from the soft falls of their feet. The wood was silent, until they heard a single drip.

Idra gasped and Kuthan nearly stepped off the path.

"Relax," Orin hissed, although his heart was pounding. *I led them here, and I will lead them out.* Nothing more happened. Their heartbeats slowed.

"It must be the sap," said Idra.

"Yes," Orin agreed. "Everything's alright."

A flash of gold revealed the forest behind Idra for an instant, and Orin then saw him. He stood just off the path. His hair was dark, and his eyes, gold and wide. His gaze was fixed on Orin, his lips parted slightly. Then just as suddenly, he was gone. It was a full second later that Orin felt his heart lurch.

"What is it?" Kuthan whispered urgently as Idra gasped. Orin tightened his grip on both their hands. The strange boy's face still floated before him as he closed his eyes, the visage staring with an expression of wonder, sadness, and longing.

"I saw someone," Orin whispered.

"Who?" Kuthan and Idra asked together.

"I don't know. I think we should go now."

"Yes," Idra agreed nervously.

They moved along the path as quickly as they dared, trying to step softly so as not to shatter the silence of the Sapwood. Around them the trees stood black, long streams crawling horribly down their sides. They hurried along. To one side of the path glimmered an empty sap pool, gleaming with moonlight, but now only the flashes of gold mattered, not the silver of the sky. Finally they saw the edge of the wood. The familiar light and sounds beyond reassured them, and they slowed their pace. Orin could not help but look back. He wished he hadn't.

The figure was there again. Flashing lanterns held his image longer this time. It looked surprised. It raised both hands up, covering its eyes, and then slowly let them drop.

Orin stared, drawn inexplicably to it. Kuthan's sharp intake of breath, and Idra's audible gasp pulled him back to the present.

"Keep moving." It was Kuthan who urged them now. They ran the rest of the length of the path and out of the Sapwood. The night sky materialized and a sound of crickets filled the air. Their labored breathing quieted, finally giving way to slow deep breaths.

"You saw him?" Orin asked. They both nodded.

"What do we do now?" Idra asked. "We didn't find it. The tree is still missing!"

Kuthan and Orin exchanged glances.

"We go back," said Kuthan, answering Idra's question. "Not now," he added quickly, noting her alarm. "Tomorrow. But tonight was a success."

"Success?" Idra asked, incredulous. "How?"

Orin's voice shook when he spoke, but he was smiling. "It w-worked," he stuttered. He was grinning with excitement. "We were safe."

He drew a shuddering breath, but his voice didn't shake when he next spoke:

"No more boundaries. We make our own way."

Namin - Day Ten

*L*enya, *Idra, Orin.* They weren't just names, they were songs. Their melodies were interwoven in the webs on their doors and the dreams he had dreamt. They still lingered with him as he awoke to a new day. Kuthan and Ara had melodies too, but the tunes held bitterness and anger. *We are a family.* Idra's words came back to him. *She is so kind, and loves us all despite everything.* Her words *did* make him try to love Kuthan and Ara. Instead, though, he ended up thinking of Idra and his love for her. *She feeds us every day and delights in giving, in making us happy.* He remembered skipping stones with Idra and Orin. *He loves to be free, to share his freedom and his joy.* Orin wasn't person-focused like Idra was, but there was true beauty in his love of discovery. And Lenya: Lenya filled his mind most of all.

The night had been clear, each star shimmering with celestial light, the waxing moon glowing gently. It had been a night bathed in silver and shadows.

"Do you see? Do you see?!" she had asked. Her eyes had been wide, alive with starlight. Her whole being had glowed with joy, her smile spread across her face. Her up-turned palm cradled the silver-blue orb that chilled the air around them. She had held it out, offering it to him to hold.

"I see, Lenya," he said to himself. She had come to him for help. *Because she needs help. The stars are dangerous.* He could not imagine what she was feeling … *but whatever it is, it's tearing her apart.* They had walked back to the beach, up the stairs, to the well. The whole while Lenya had been dancing and laughing. Her skin had glowed as if she herself were becoming a star. And then, when it was time to release the star, she had stopped. She had grown still next to the well, her arms frozen over the gaping aperture. She had remained still, clinging to the star while Namin waited … and waited. But she could not let go. The moon had journeyed across the sky, yet eventually Lenya's only movements had been to sway gently as if with the breeze. Finally the star had dropped. Namin still wasn't sure whether she had actually let it go, or whether it had simply slipped between her fingertips. He had carried her back to her cabin placing her gently on the front step. When he waved goodbye, her gaze had already returned to the heavens. *I will help you Lenya,* Namin vowed to himself. Her song sounded in his mind. Every day she grew more distant, more a possession of the stars, less their sister. And when she let go of the stars as always happened, she was lost. *But I will find you.*

Then there was Enetheal. Enetheal who had welcomed them to the island, who had taken care of them, who had guided them and shown them what they must do to thrive there. Enetheal who was gone. *I have no melody for him.* Three days had passed since he had left the Welcome

Table. It was as if he had vanished. Namin had looked everywhere he could think of. The Sandy Shores, the Stony Shores, Lenya's well, the Shrieking Stones, Kuthan's cave, the Firefly Field, and the Sapwood. He had wandered off the path looking and had encountered only the pines, ferns, brambles, and boulders he was so familiar with. *Where are you?*

The others either did not care, or did not mention their concern. *Ara wouldn't care because rules have been up-held. Kuthan relishes Enetheal's absence. Lenya is lost in stars.* But Idra and Orin had not mentioned Enetheal either. Was he gone to them? Were they content with his absence? Since Enetheal had left there had been no arguing. But suspicion and resentment were even more pronounced in this new silence. Namin spoke very little around Kuthan and Ara. *There isn't much to say to them.*

Orin inhaled sharply and then sighed, and Namin knew that he was awake.

" 'Mornin', Ore." Orin took in a deep breath.

" 'Morning, Naim," he answered. The covers and sheets were tangled around him. Instead of springing from bed as he usually did, he pulled the blankets closer.

"You cold?" Namin asked. The night had been chilly, the wind strong. The Shrieking Stones had been audible from the cabin.

"Yes!" Orin answered quickly.

"Once we get up and move a bit, we'll warm up. Especially after some food." Namin sat up.

"Yes," Orin answered again. They were quiet for a bit, so Namin spoke again.

"How are the paths doing?" Namin asked.

"Ah …," Orin paused. "They are great."

"Good."

Something was on Orin's mind, but if he didn't want to share it, Namin wouldn't push; and when Namin got out of bed, Orin followed. The morning air was chilly and they jogged to Kuthan and Idra's cabin. By the time they arrived at the Welcome Table they were warmer. Breakfast was quiet again. As usual, Idra and Orin talked the most. Idra appeared distressed as she looked at the eyes around the table. *She wants this to be better*, Namin realized sadly. *But only those who caused the problem can remedy it.* Kuthan and Ara both sat back warily, eating slowly. Their eyes flickered at Namin occasionally, but it was clear that they each saw each other, not Namin, as their opponent.

It was a relief when they all left the table. It was uncomfortable to have all six of them together. The Stony Shores were windy. Orin quickly moved as far from Ara as possible, and Idra and Kuthan followed him. *At least they are still knit together.* Namin made sure Ara's gaze was downward before searching for his own tribute. He did not search for long. As he had yesterday, he looked among the plainest of rocks, and he found it quickly. The stone was near the forest's edge. It was rough to the touch, and angular in shape. A dull grey-brown coloration was evident on its surface and half of it was caked in mud. *There. A worthy gift for the island.* He settled down near the path's entrance for a bit, but soon stood up again. The others would be a while picking their stones and Namin had some *real* tributes to make.

He left quietly, making his way up the path. Just as he reached the spiderweb, Orin caught up with him.

"Hey, Ore, you finished?"

"Um, no," Orin answered sheepishly. "I was just wondering where you were off to?"

"Around," Namin answered. He wasn't sure exactly where he was going.

"Are you going to paint? Or paste on shells?"

"Probably not," Namin answered. Orin paled.

"You're not going to the Sapwood are you?" The way in which Orin said it made Namin pause.

"Might be," he answered thoughtfully.

"Oh," Orin said offhandedly. "I always find my best tributes are the decorated ones," he added.

"You should probably find a tribute to decorate then," Namin said hurriedly. *If Ara sees both of us are gone this early* .... Orin nodded and left. Namin was taken aback, but relieved that Ara had not noticed. That would have caused an argument, and Namin had no time for that. As he hiked across the island he refocused. It was still early in the day when he lay his stone at the altar.

It was interesting to see this side of the island, where the altar was, so early in the day. Namin had come to associate it with the orange sky and setting sun. Now the sky was bright blue and the water was dark except for glimmers of reflected sky. The day felt chilly despite the clear skies and sun. Namin turned away from the horizon, and walked back inland. Instead of following the paths, he cut across the forest until he reached the edge of the Sapwood. There was a clear line between the Sapwood and the other trees that filled the island. There was a small gap, as if the trees of the Sapwood avoided growing alongside normal trees. Sound deadened as soon as he entered.

Time did not appear to affect the Sapwood. The trees were still too vibrant. The bark was too red, the twigs too green, and the pools of sap at their bases too still. Streams of sap seeped down each tree and into the pools, all without a sound. Despite the uniformity of the wood, Namin was starting to get a feel for where he was in it. He did his best to walk toward the center. He passed the stone slab, the twin of the Welcome Table. The layers of lichen and moss on it were nearly enough to make him miss it, but it's shape was too well defined and circular, and the inscriptions on its surface still discernible. *It's as if it has been here longer than the Welcome Table.*

He continued on until he saw something else, something new. It was not obvious at first, but the pairs of lanterns that marked its edges made it unmistakable for what it was. *A path! A new path.* He stood stunned, as still as the trees around him. The sap continued to stream slowly into the pools. *Orin would be ....* His mind worked furiously. *Orin.* Then it struck home, and Namin laughed. *So this is what you have been doing, Ore.* It made sense now. Why Orin needed to catch more flies. And why he was alarmed to have Namin come near the Sapwood. And the lengths of time in which Orin, Kuthan, and Idra had vanished.

He walked along the path, admiring Orin's work. *He loves to discover.* The Sapwood seemed less foreboding with the path through it. Namin bent down to inspect one of the lanterns. It was solidly placed in the ground. *Why keep it secret though?* But for this answer, he did not have to ponder long. *Ara would be furious.* The idea tickled him and he couldn't help but let out a small laugh. Now, with the path present, the sound almost seemed to belong in the Sapwood. *He'll need to catch more flies. To make more paths.* Namin hummed to himself as he thought. And as his melody grew, it was Orin who filled his mind, and Orin's song filled the air. And then Namin knew what his tribute would be: a tribute not just to Orin, but for Orin. The melody grew louder; a new song was taking form. And then Namin wasn't alone. As if they had been waiting the whole while, his weavers scuttled around him, along the forest floor, down the trees, and from unseen webs. Soon they were spinning his song.

They rose and fell with his voice, his song and their dance becoming one. He still was not used to spinning webs by daylight. When he had made his earlier cocooned tribute, the webs had seemed to shimmer with sunlight. This time however, the sun was hidden by clouds casting the forest in shadow, and the web seemed to shimmer silver, as if it were surrounded by moonlight rather than daylight. A new web came forth, unlike any of the others Namin had made, and he knew that for the first time, webs and song would not be enough to make this tribute complete.

Their labor went on and on. Orin's melody was woven in and around the tribute's song. Namin worked with his hands as he sang, the webs glowing, the spiders dancing. They scuttled over his arms, his hands, and the web, trailing silk that glowed silver as they danced. And finally the melody ended. The spiders retreated slowly, as if to admire their work. Namin held it out at arm's length, breathing slow and deep. To finish the tribute, he dipped it in a pool of sap. It radiated as he pulled it out of the liquid and he felt fulfilled in a way he never had before: *Creation is worship.* He felt energy surge through him.

Namin almost began to walk away, but then knew he couldn't. Too much had happened for him simply to stand up and leave … but that was not quite the reason. *I'm not finished,* he realized. *Idra. Lenya.* His work—his creation, his worship—was incomplete. It was Idra who filled his mind first: her delight in nourishing her family. He remembered her graceful climb up the tree, and then her awkward descent with only one hand free for climbing as she clutched their fruit. Soon Idra's song filled the Sapwood, bringing it to life, and the spiders scuttled forth once more.

When he pulled his second tribute from the pool of sap, he was overcome again by joy and satisfaction. Yet once again his worship was incomplete.

The third melody soon slipped into the Sapwood, and so did thoughts of Lenya.

She is entranced by the stars, and yet still loves us enough to turn back to us. Her task has such a heavy price, but she pays it without losing sight of us. I will save you. The song ended, the third tribute now complete. He pulled it from the pool. The silky web glittered with its own light, refracting through the sap. And then, after only moments, all trace of surface stickiness was gone, the shining web was now dry and flexible.

Namin was alive with energy and empty of it. A deep contentment welled up inside him. He had never been able to devote himself to the island as they had agreed, nor did he want to. *But now I have given completely from myself. Lenya finds joy in the stars, Idra in bringing us fruit, Orin in lighting the darkness. Now I have found my purpose.*

He readied himself to leave the Sapwood. It was time to go. As he walked toward the edge of the wood, he paused to look at the great lichen-covered rock that was so like their Welcome Table. It stood near the Sapwood border, the place where silence gave way to song. A moment passed before he realized he was not alone. Just beyond the ancient slab stood Enetheal. Namin was stunned. After these last few days he had begun to wonder if Enetheal had vanished. He had looked and looked, combing the whole island. Finally he had given up hope of finding Enetheal. Yet here he was.

What can I say? What can I do to right what we have done?

Enetheal turned away as he approached.

"Enetheal!" Namin called after him, moving more quickly. Enetheal turned back, and their eyes met. Namin halted, suddenly unable to speak.

"I am sorry," he finally managed. "I am sorry for what we did." The words hung in the air between them. They sounded empty, inadequate. Behind Enetheal the sap flowed on as if nothing had happened. Enetheal continued to stare mutely. Namin took a breath and tried again, "I hope that you can forgive us." Once more their eyes held each other's. Enetheal's face remained as impassive as ever. Namin waited. But Enetheal showed no sign that he even understood.

"Thank you," Namin finally added. And then, remembering how Enetheal had guided each of them in their first days on the island, he went on: "... for all that you have done." He took another breath: "... for all that you do."

The words seemed useless; they did not remedy anything. He could not change what the others had done. But there was nothing else to say. After a few more moments Namin left. Enetheal remained by the lichen-strewn slab, one hand on its scarred surface, his eyes never leaving Namin's disappearing form.

KUTHAN - DAY TEN

The sky had grown dark during the day. Clouds covered the island in shadow, but just as the sun touched the horizon it broke through. The water suddenly shone, and the tribute stones were bathed in sunlight. *Is this important too? That the tribute stones are brought here first and then to the cave? It must be.* Idra and Orin were next to him, standing side by side, close to the water. *I should go. They'll still be here when I return, skipping stones, content.* Kuthan was not content, but that made him smile. *What would be my purpose if I were?*

The sun finished its descent. Kuthan arranged the stones on the salver, then picked it up and turned to look at the figure emerging from the forest. It was Namin. He walked towards them resolutely. *You're not welcome here.* Kuthan did not speak the words, but he hoped Namin felt them. In Namin's arms were shimmering structures of interwoven web and wood.

"You're too late if you wanted to catch the sunset," Kuthan said flatly. Namin didn't answer.

"Too late for tributes," Kuthan added, gesturing to the objects in Namin's arms. Namin glared.

"These aren't for you, and they aren't for the island." Namin said the words with contempt.

"Oh?" Kuthan asked. He was curious despite himself. He had said very little to Namin since Namin had betrayed them in favor of Enetheal.

"Don't you have a service to fulfill?" Namin asked. The words hurt, even coming from Namin. The journey through the darkness still terrified him. But he kept his voice cool.

"I do," he said shortly, and left. As he walked away he saw Namin approach Idra and Orin. Namin knelt before them so that their heads were level, holding out his gifts. *Is that supposed to upset me? Does he think to hurt me?* Kuthan splashed through the shallows, refusing to glance back again.

I must focus on what is in front of me. His stomach started to turn and he felt nauseated. *My task is to endure the darkness, but my sacrifice is well worth it.* Kuthan finally understood his task. *But I must keep it to myself. Idra and Orin have enough to do ... for now.* He wasn't sure why he hadn't told them. Perhaps because it seemed too private, too personal. It was Kuthan who had been chosen, not the others. *But we are a team. I will have to let them know eventually.*

Kuthan's thoughts were cut short at the top of the stair. He had finally learned not to pause before going down. If he stopped, it took him a lot longer. But that was not all. *Our friend is trapped down here. If he can endure this darkness all the time, surely I can brave it for a few moments.* His resolve strengthened. Step by step the darkness thickened about him until it was suffocating. Nothingness. Why was this nothingness so bad? *Because I am alone, completely alone.* His own footfalls were his only company and not enough to redirect his mind from the stair. Finally a faint flicker of white penetrated the darkness: Kuthan had reached the base.

A wave of emotion coursed through him as he approached the altar. He felt both laughter and tears as he swallowed. There *was* someone else here at the end of the stairs. Kuthan looked around, but whoever it was had never shown himself, and now was no exception. *Yet he shares this with me. He understands.* It wasn't just the dark stair and this room that they shared. Kuthan moved the salver onto the altar. However, he did not remove the tributes, not just yet.

Before him, illuminated in the flickering white light were the stones. And the stones were a story, a story he had been chosen to understand. "My tributes," he heard himself whisper. He touched each one in turn. The first still stood out to him, somehow more precious than the others. On its surface were images of the Stony Shores, Enetheal their slaver, and each of them working on the tributes. A seventh figure toiled alongside the six that Kuthan had drawn.

As soon as this tribute had come back changed, he had begun to paint each of his next offerings too. Once again he had let passion guide his painting, and he had not been disappointed. Conflict was in every line of his second masterpiece. His triumph over banishing Enetheal. His disgust with Ara and Namin. His passion for Idra who had returned to him, and for Orin who was steadfast and shared his vision. The painting had been of the Welcome Table. Orin and Idra were to either side of Kuthan. Kuthan held their hands, the three of them clearly unified. On the other side of the table were Enetheal, Ara, and Namin. None of them held hands, and darker colors were used for their silhouettes.

And this second masterpiece, likewise, had been returned. Kuthan had been jubilant. Again the seventh figure had been added. He stood beside Kuthan, Idra, and Orin, his hand resting on Kuthan's shoulder, making their number four, his colors as bright as theirs.

His third painting was designed to be returned. He had known that only through painting his tribute would he be able to ask questions that could be answered by his hidden friend. This third masterpiece had been of the seventh figure. To the figure's right he had drawn faint stairs. The question he meant to convey was, *Who are you? How did you get down here?* The returned tribute was altered more even than the other two. Kuthan's friend was now descending the stair, and standing at the top, his arm extended in an obvious gesture toward the darkness, was Enetheal.

Kuthan's breath came out unevenly when his fingers left the third painting as he reached for the fourth. The fourth stone had asked a different sort of question: *Why the rules? What purpose do they serve? To whose end?* Kuthan had drawn the Welcome Table. When the stone had been returned, Enetheal was back in it. He stood on top of the Welcome Table, above the rules with his usual perfect posture, his head held high, his beaklike nose protruding. Kuthan's fingers left the fourth stone for the newest piece to his puzzle. He took in a sharp breath ....

This fifth offering had been changed more than any of the other four. Kuthan blinked, then blinked again. Behind his closed lids he saw yesterday's image. Once again, he had drawn the stairs. The landing itself was swallowed by darkness, but as the stairs progressed upward, the scene became lighter. He had traced himself in orange, his friend in yellow. Kuthan held his friend's hand, leading him up the stair. It had been a dream of hope as well as a question. Only this time the image hadn't just changed, it was something else entirely. Kuthan opened his eyes. The stairs in the image were erased. The darkness vanished as well. Now his tribute revealed the Welcome Table, only it was broken. The table was split into two jagged halves. Kuthan stood side by side with his friend. This time Enetheal was gone as well, absent from the scene entirely.

Kuthan brushed his fingers across this new image hungrily. *My friend, my brother.* His gaze swept over the first two scenes. *He, too, defies Enetheal. And he stands with us ... with me, with Orin, with Idra.* His fingers moved across the third and fourth altered tributes. *The rules serve Enetheal. He controls us with them, and he alone stands above them. Is it with the rules that Enetheal cast my friend into darkness? Is that what happens to those who don't abide by them?* Surely that was why Enetheal had thrown his friend into the darkness.

Kuthan turned his attention once more to the fifth image, the one that had transformed completely. *I want to save him, to save all of us, to escape Enetheal's laws and judgment. Is this how?* He continued to trace his fingers along his tribute. It was only in this last image that Enetheal had no presence. In this fifth altered stone they were free.

But there is still so much more I need to understand! Too much more. One question a day, and no easy way to interpret the answers. The purpose of Kuthan's task was now clearer. Light had even been shed on the rules and on Enetheal. *But what about the paths and fruits, the stars and Shrieking Stones, and the webs? And what had happened last night?* They had created a path. Their own path. And they had seen something in the darkness. Something that was not trees, sap- streams, or flashing golden light. *It wasn't real.* But it had to be. There was yet another unknown presence on the island. *Every time I try to understand I get more confused.* Kuthan set down his most recent question, the Sapwood.

The Sapwood was hard to capture in an image. Earlier that day Kuthan had visited the Sapwood before returning to the Berry Grove to paint. Orin had been impatient, but Kuthan couldn't rush his paintings. Afterwards they had hurried back to the Sapwood to continue making paths. Orin wanted to continue making new paths, and Kuthan was happy to oblige. Idra was more hesitant, but she had helped put down the new lanterns as well. *Between the three of us we will figure out our three tasks as well as the purpose of the rules, but eventually we will need other ways to find answers.*

It's getting harder to leave, Kuthan thought suddenly. This had been his longest cave visit yet. Was it because he had more to think about? Or that he could not part with his tributes? Perhaps it was returning to the utter darkness of the stairs? *All three.* Kuthan turned for the stair, took a breath, and began his ascent. He felt an overwhelming hollowness. He was leaving himself behind again. The darkness pressed in around him, and he shrank inside himself, now focusing only upon the sound of his footsteps. They echoed behind him, louder than ever before. *It's as if someone else is walking with me.* He felt a weak smile spread across his face. *It's like my friend is with me.* He listened to the echoes until the darkness gave way to light.

Kuthan peeled the webs aside and emerged into the evening. But then, almost immediately, he felt a sinking feeling in his belly. *This isn't right.* He hated the darkness, and yet …. *I feel like I leave myself every time I come back.*

His eyes continued to adjust to the twilight as he splashed through shallows. *I hate it, but I am fulfilled by it. I am nothing without it.* Kuthan left the wetness for dry land, and hurried along the path. His eyes finished adapting to the light, and he considered again how long he had been in the darkness of the cave. He stopped short.

This doesn't make sense! When he had descended into the cave, the sun had just set. The sky had been pale blue with pink swirls of clouds. And now it still was. *It should be darker, maybe even past nightfall! I was gone for so long!* He searched the sky once more.

By the time he reached the Sunset Altar, indigo darkness had descended upon him. He clambered along the rocky coast until he reached the spot where he usually found Idra and Orin skipping stones, only they weren't to be found. Puzzled, he continued his trek along the coast. *They do like exploring.* Still, there was no sign. Finally he turned back and stepped onto a path.

The sky had darkened even more deeply during his search. *We were supposed to meet! Where are they?* His walked turned into a jog, which soon became a run. *They must be in the Firefly Field! It's getting dark.* He hurried along the forest path, leaping over stones and roots and cutting through the woods. A sporadic golden light up ahead told him that he had arrived. He burst into the open to find them. Not just Idra and Orin, but all of them.

Tonight the golden flashes were enough to brighten the field almost as if it were day. Orin ran through the long grass. Trailing behind him was a cloud of gold with silver glimmerings. Orin laughed as he ran. *It's a net*, Kuthan realized. The silver glimmerings were strands of web, and there was a visible wooden frame. Inside it was a swarm of golden flashing flies. *This is what Namin made.*

But Orin's net was not the only thing. Kuthan turned to the others. They had smiles that matched Orin's, although they were seated. In the middle of them was a basket. Once again, web and wood were woven together elaborately. Piled high within the basket was fruit. Idra, Namin, Lenya, and Ara were all seated around it, eating while they watched Orin run.

"Hey, Kuthan," Idra chirped when she noticed him. "Sit down with us!"

"Sure," he answered shortly. He made sure to sit at her other side, so that he wasn't close to Namin. Idra gave a contented sigh as he sat down. She deftly snagged a fruit from the basket, caressing its shape before handing it to Kuthan.

"Isn't it beautiful?" she asked. Happiness was evident in her voice.

"Yes," Kuthan answered. He took a bite. "And tasty too." The fruit was tasty, but he knew that it wasn't the fruit she was talking about.

"Not the fruit, the basket!" she laughed. Kuthan didn't meet her eyes. "Yes. It's wonderful," he managed.

Orin could not have stated his delight with his gift more plainly. His face was flushed, his golden eyes alive with joy as he rushed back and forth with his firefly-laden net. Kuthan looked down at his hands, and realized he had clenched them into fists without thinking. He loosened his fingers. *Is this it? Are my friends lost so easily?* He turned his gaze to Namin, but Namin was deliberately avoiding his gaze, instead watching Orin. A smile played across Namin's lips. *He knows I'm watching. He's enjoying this!* Kuthan turned his eyes sharply away, and towards Lenya.

He hadn't considered her much. She had become so distant that he sometimes forgot about her. So long as she didn't interfere with their goals he did not have a problem with her, but now even she held spun silver in her hands. *Not in her hands, on her hands!* The moment the thought came, he knew it to be true. Lenya's hands were covered with web-spun gloves. They, too, glowed in their beauty.

Finally he looked to Ara. There was no silver about her. *You can't be my ally, but you must understand.* Ara paid Kuthan no heed. Beyond that. She actually seemed more relaxed than usual. Her shoulders were down, and even she had a gentle smile as she watched Orin. Ara turned to Idra, tossing a piece of fruit. They started passing it around; Ara to Idra, Idra to Namin, Namin to Lenya, and Lenya back to Ara. When it went to Idra again, Kuthan made sure to be watching Orin. He didn't want the fruit coming his way. *I want no part in this.*

They passed around the fruit for what seemed like an age. All the while Orin ran back and forth laughing and catching more and more and more flies. *I should have stayed in the darkness,* Kuthan thought miserably. He was just about to leave on his own when the game ended. Orin stopped, too, and pinched off the top of his net, closing it neatly.

"I'll light your way back!" he told them excitedly. They moved slowly, but at least they were moving. When they stopped at Namin's cabin, the whole group exchanged hugs. Idra and Orin flung their arms around Namin, and he returned their embrace with a laugh. Next came Lenya, and Namin held her close. Ara gave Namin a nod. Kuthan met Namin's eyes with a glare. Namin raised his eyebrows, but said nothing. Kuthan didn't give him the satisfaction of responding to the unspoken taunt.

When they reached his and Idra's cabin Orin gave them a look: *"I'll be back."* For once Kuthan was not sure he wanted him to return. They entered the cabin, leaving Orin to lead the others onward. When the door shut behind them Kuthan collapsed on his bed face down. He wanted to be alone. But he wasn't alone.

"It's so beautiful," Idra was saying, as she had said over and over again that night. "So wonderful."

Kuthan grunted, still lying face down.

"Everything alright, Kuth?" Idra asked after a moment.

No. "Yes," he answered. *Enetheal is still in the shadows, our only real guide is a phantom buried in the depths of the island, and now my allies, my friends, are gone.*

"You sure?" she asked. He didn't have to look to know her face. Her eyes would hold concern, and she would be biting her lower lip. He could feel her at the edge of the bed. *My friends aren't just gone, but stolen!*

"No," he answered. The noise was muffled against the mattress. Idra sat on the bed. Putting a hand on Kuthan's back. For a moment he tensed, but then he allowed himself to relax.

"What's wrong?" Idra asked. *Such a direct question. If only I could give a direct answer.*

"Too much." The words were clearer this time. He had turned his head so that he spoke into air rather than into his sleeping pallet. Idra was quiet, and he knew she was waiting for more. He couldn't speak though, and it was she who broke the silence.

"It's not fair that the trials of some are harder than the trials of others. It's not something any of us can fix." She stopped, and he continued to listen. "But *we* can get through this together." She didn't say anything more, but she lay down next to him. At last he managed a "Thank you." They were quiet until Orin arrived.

"Ready?!" Orin asked excitedly as he opened the door. "We have some new paths to explore!"

How can he be so oblivious? Kuthan forced himself to smile. "Ready," he answered in what he hoped sounded like an enthusiastic voice. Idra took a deep breath, and stood up. But something made Kuthan pause. He looked at Idra, who had already gone over to her basket, and Orin who still held his net, alight with flies:

"I need to try something else tonight." And as he said it, he felt something rekindle inside him, a flame that had died down to embers flickered back to life.

"What?" Idra asked. She glanced at Orin quickly before adding. "If you're doing something, I think I'd prefer to join you. The paths frightened me last night." The figure from the night swam before Kuthan's eyes, and he knew it must be on Idra's mind as well.

"I can do the paths alone," Orin reassured them. Kuthan's mind was racing.

"Are you sure?" He had to clarify. Orin nodded with vigor.

"I think it's best all three of us go separate ways tonight. That way we can figure out the most."

"What are we figuring out?" Idra asked again. Kuthan smiled.

"We each have basic understandings of how our own tasks work, but we don't know anything about the others'. Tonight I want to fix that." They both stared at him intently. The flame inside him started to grow hotter. *They are mine!*

"Orin, you continue the illumination of the Sapwood and the search for our missing tree." Orin nodded, and Kuthan turned to Idra.

"Idra, you are right about us being one group. The others trust you—as they should. I need you to find out what Ara and Lenya know. What they know about the missing tree, what they know about their tasks."

Idra's expression turned to worry, but he continued. "What you are doing is important, not only so that we find out more, but also because it brings our whole group closer together. The more we know about one another the closer we can be." Idra glowed.

"What are you doing?" Orin asked.

"I'm going to find out more about Namin's service." Unconsciously they had gathered into a circle. They looked into each other's eyes. There was something right about each of them having a job to do, each one depending on the others. *Can I trust them?* Kuthan reproached himself for even thinking the question. They certainly trusted him. *But their loyalty is so uncertain.* His guilt resurfaced. *I haven't told them about the paintings.* Unbidden, the images of his altered tributes flashed before his eyes. *I will let them know, but now is not the time. Now we are parting ways.* They exited the cabin and Kuthan peeled back the web-screen delicately before closing it behind them. *Idra believes that the webs protect us,* he remembered. The night was thick, but Orin had done his job well, and their darkening world was illuminated with flashing gold.

Soon each of them was on a separate path, the darkness warded off by Orin's lanterns. Kuthan walked until he reached the stone path, passing the great trees until he came to the next day's fruit-bearer. He was satisfied to see the webs already in place. On the lower limbs of the tree there were still stray petal-clusters, young green fruit bulging from their centers. Around him fallen white petals were blown about by the evening breeze. They looked curious in the night's light. By tomorrow the tree would bear fruit. Kuthan swept his hand through the web. The motion was violent, but there was no resistance. The web broke apart, strands clinging to his hand. A spider scuttled across Kuthan's arm and he slapped the skittering creature, crushing it. The spider made a small crunching noise as it was flattened. He quickly traveled to the far side of the clearing and dispatched its web before moving on.

Kuthan washed his web-laced hands in the water that stood in front of the cave before arriving at its mouth. Looking into the darkness made his stomach clench, for the blackness beyond the opening was total. Starlight did not penetrate the cave. This time Kuthan worked with careful precision. He began on one side of the web, gently peeling it away before deftly lifting the other side. Once the whole of it was removed, he let the wind carry it out over the water. It glittered in the night, and Kuthan felt a deep hunger satiated.

Idra - Days Ten and Eleven

"Idra, you are right about us being one group. The others trust you—as they should. I need you to find out what Ara and Lenya know. What they know about the missing tree, what they know about their tasks. What you are doing is important, not only so that we find out more, but also because it brings our whole group closer together. The more we know about one another the closer we can be."

Her heart was beating fast by the time Kuthan had finished, and she could feel heat rising to her face. She couldn't help but smile. Could it be so easy? Nevertheless, the trust they put in her weighed upon her. *This is my fault—everyone fighting—it never would have happened if I had completed my task!* But now there was hope. They were going to find the tree, and *she* was going to bring everyone back together. *I will fix this. It is my job to take care of them.* She would find out what the others knew. She would find out how they thought, how they understood their tasks. *These tasks have become part of who we are.*

To understand and love one another we must understand each other's trials.

They gathered in a circle, and her thoughts leapt back to the present situation. *Please be safe!* She didn't say it aloud, but as her eyes touched upon Orin's, her heart lurched. Orin was so confident in what he was doing. "*Nothing happened!*" he had told her again and again that day. "*You're being silly, my paths work! They are just as real as the original ones.*" He was right, nothing had happened … but something about the figure they had seen made her afraid. They had run last night. What if tonight Orin couldn't get away? *But he knows what he's doing.* Orin always did.

It was time to leave. Orin led the way holding his glowing net close. Idra was tempted to take her basket. *But I won't need it.* Orin and Kuthan vanished down other paths, and she was alone. It was eerie walking the woods in darkness. Golden flashes prevented her from stumbling, but sometimes it was scary having bushes and small animals appear suddenly. *What if someone else appears?* But nobody did. Her thoughts returned to Namin and his gift. She thought of his song in the basket and the ease of carrying fruit in it. *Namin, if only I could spend more time with you.*

But it made her smile that she would be with Ara and Lenya. She arrived at their cabin door. Light flashing from nearby lanterns glimmered from the spiderweb as she peeled it back. *I hope they aren't sleeping.* She knocked quietly and waited. She didn't have to wait long.

"Idra, you're here," Ara smiled as she opened the door.

"Did you know I was coming?" She walked through the door.

"Who else?" Ara responded. She brushed her hair back and gestured to Lenya's bed.

"No Lenya tonight?" Idra asked as she sat down. She realized it had been a long time since she had been inside. Lenya's bed was a mess. Ara's was as tidy as usual.

"She's already with the stars," Ara sat down on her own bed, her eyes meeting Idra's. "Why have you come?"

Idra took a breath: "Can I come just to say hi?" The moment she said it, she wished she hadn't. Ara's smile became thinner, and her eyes narrowed.

"Is that why you are here?" Ara's tone was hard. Her eyes glittered green.

"No," she heard herself answer. She took a breath. *I shouldn't have expected it to be easy.* Some part of her had anticipated Lenya, or at least Lenya and Ara as a pair. Ara alone was a different matter. She waited expectantly, her eyes still narrowed in suspicion.

"I came for information. I want to know more about your task." Ara chuckled, but Idra glared at her until she stopped:

"I want the rift in our family to end."

Ara answered with a stare. Idra couldn't tell what it meant.

"I also came to say hi!" Idra added defiantly.

Ara moved so that her face was obscured in shadow.

"I'd like to believe that," she finally said. She paused, and Idra waited.

"I'm not blind," Ara added. "I have my own ways of knowing things, and I know that Kuthan, you, and Orin are up to something."

Careful. Kuthan would want her to say nothing. *But I need to. To be trusted I need to show trust.*

"Yes. We are trying to understand what is going on! We have to so we can live here and look out for one another!"

"Do you think I don't also seek answers?" Ara smiled her thin smile. "It's not the goal, but how it's achieved, and why we are achieving it." She sat forward, and her face became visible again. There was new intensity in her eyes.

Idra tasted blood on her lower lip. The scabs opened easily now, but she said nothing.

"What do you think my task is?" Ara asked.

Idra thought hard. *I don't know. That's why I'm here.* "You listen to the wind as it passes through rocks," Idra answered slowly. *But there's something more; there always is.* She knew her task and Orin's so well. They often journeyed together lighting paths, or visiting trees. *I know Namin too.* She had come with him once, and saw his song come alive with webs … she remembered the spiders. She thought of Kuthan's and Lenya's tasks. And then she realized something she hadn't until now. *I pick fruit, Orin catches fireflies, Kuthan delivers tributes, Lenya catches stars, and Namin sings webs.* But Ara didn't do anything that changed the island.

"And what do you think I hear?"

Idra tried, but couldn't think of anything to say. She didn't know.

"Answers," Ara answered her own question.

Idra's mind reeled. *Could we want the same thing? Why do we fight each other if our purpose is the same?* The missing tree had torn them apart, her uncompleted service, Enetheal, the unanswered questions. But it had started with the missing tree.

"Do you know where the tree is?" Idra asked. She couldn't help the eagerness in her voice. Ara's brow creased and she frowned.

"Why should I share my answers with you?" she asked coldly. Idra couldn't find words for a moment.

"Because that's your task!" she managed incredulously.

"I need to keep us safe. I need to uphold the rules. If I share what I know with you, you three will continue to put the rest of us in danger."

Idra's racing mind suddenly froze. "In danger?" The image from last night reappeared unbidden, and she thought of Orin, running down one of his 'paths' now. The golden flashes doing little to hold the darkness back.

"By these rules we must abide," Ara said irritably. "Don't tell me you've forgotten."

"No rules have been broken!" Idra exclaimed. But now there was doubt. Could what they were doing be wrong?

"No," Ara answered, " but they are breaking."

That doesn't make sense though! "How can they be breaking? They seem black and white," Idra protested.

"Yes," Ara sighed. "They do."

Idra frowned, perplexed. "But you just said ...."

"I know," Ara cut her off. Idra stopped. "I know," Ara echoed herself again. "I don't feel comfortable sharing anything. Can you understand that?"

Can I? Idra was forced to ask herself. Something stopped her from saying 'yes'. The tree was too important to keep hidden away. Everything could be fixed so easily if Ara would just cooperate. *But I don't understand her task like she does.* Then again, Ara didn't understand Idra's task, and the tree was *hers.*

"I know you and Kuthan don't see eye to eye. But you know that the last thing I want is to put us all in danger."

Ara's shoulders moved back and she let out a breath. But Idra wasn't done.

"My failure to find the tree started this whole problem. Can you help me fix it?" Their eyes met, and the light in Ara's faded into resignation. She nodded wearily.

"Down in the sky where low becomes high." She said it softly.

"Sorry?" Idra asked confused.

"That's what they tell me. The voices. Whenever I ask about the missing tree, that's the answer they give."

"Oh," Idra answered simply. Disappointment welled up inside her, and suddenly she felt very tired. Ara must have seen some of the disappointment in her face.

"I said they gave me answers, but that doesn't mean I understand them. I'm getting better though." Ara looked worried. There was something like a plea in her eyes.

She knows it's not what I wanted ... and she's used to causing dissatisfaction.

"Thanks for telling me, Ara." Idra did her best to sound grateful. *It's easy for me to be loved. It's easy for me to please others. I bring them fruit. I need to let her know she's appreciated.*

Ara smiled weakly.

"I'm going to bed now," Idra told her.

"Of course," Ara agreed. "I'm ready for some rest as well."

"Can I come with you to the Stones some time?" Idra asked. This time Ara's smile held uncharacteristic warmth.

"I'd like that," she answered simply.

Idra hugged her. A full second passed, and then Ara returned the embrace. The darkness did not seem so black as Idra traveled the path back to her cabin.

It seemed moments later that the next day dawned. The sky brightened, birdsong began, and Idra awoke. Part of her anticipated the morning even before it arrived, so that when it finally did she was already alert and ready.

She rose silently, put a hand on Kuthan's arm and murmured her goodbye.

"Hold on," Kuthan mumbled. She waited, but he didn't move. So she smiled, took her basket, and went out into the new day. It was bright. Her eyes took a few moments to get used to it. When they did, her smile widened. The day was gorgeous! The bark on the pine trees by their cabin seemed almost as colorful as that of the trees in the Sapwood; the wood seemed smoother, and the twigs a brighter green. A flock of birds rushed out of a tree, circled around, and then landed in another. Clusters of flowers beside the path were alive with a rainbow of colors, with butterflies, and with bees. As she walked past, she paused to breathe in their scents.

She skipped the whole way to today's tree. And as she danced along, she sang. It was one of Namin's tunes. But as she arrived her song died. The clearing was vibrant with morning life, but she sensed something wrong. She stepped over a fallen piece of fruit. *They don't fall until the end of the day.* She frowned and looked up into the branches. She felt a sudden tightening in her chest. Today's fruits had dark purple skin, but flesh had been ripped off the piece she was looking at, exposing the glistening orange on the inside. Flies darted about the exposed pulp. As her eyes followed the movement of the insects, she noticed more fruits that were missing large chunks. *How?* She was as confused as she was horrified. Her eyes darted from fruit to fruit. Some of the gashes were smaller than others, but not one fruit was left unscathed. Others were so damaged that only fragments remained.

For once she did not wish to climb. *But I must.* Her feet brought her to the trunk of the tree, and soon she was clambering up. *Maybe there are some undamaged fruits in the upper branches.* But the higher she climbed, the lower her heart sank. *What had happened?* She held one closer to inspect it, waving it about to scatter the flies. *Did an animal bite these?* She climbed higher. *What will I tell the others?* Near the top of the tree she picked some of the fruit, taking care to choose the pieces which were most whole, and even then only if they weren't fly-infested. She placed them delicately in her basket. *At least this time I did all I could.* But she wondered whether what she had picked was safe to eat.

She climbed down, and her throat started to ache, but this time she made sure there were no tears. *I couldn't have done anything differently. We'll figure this out.* But it was certainly another question to which they had no answer. *I need answers. I need Ara.* She reached the bottom of the tree, but it wasn't Ara she found there.

"Kuthan!" she gasped. "Something is wrong!" *I've let him down again.* "I don't know what happened!" She held out one of the fruits. Kuthan took it, then peered closely. *What is he thinking?* She hopped back and forth from one foot to another.

"I can explain." Kuthan looked up from the fruit.

"You can?" she looked up into his eyes, at once hopeful. But instead of reassurance, his eyes reflected her worry.

"This is my doing." He looked at her, but she was silent, so he continued to speak.

"We went separate paths last night, remember?" She nodded, and he went on. "Orin went to make new paths, to discover more about the Sapwood, to search for the missing tree. You went to Ara and Lenya to try to understand their services …."

"And you tried to figure out how Namin's task worked," Idra completed the thought as she looked to the entrance of the clearing. "You took away the webs."

"Yes," he answered.

"Why, though?"

"I wanted to know what would happen. I thought it was important to see."

"But you just messed up my service," she sighed, frustrated.

"It wasn't *your* task I was undoing. I didn't know that this would happen," Kuthan answered. There was a hint of exasperation in his voice.

"So it's okay to mess up Namin's task?"

Kuthan's expression darkened. There was a brief pause.

"No," he finally answered. "It is not okay to hurt each other. But these tasks aren't ours. They have been forced upon us." She nodded, and his expression grew softer.

"And now we have just figured out something very important, Idra." Kuthan smiled, and her spirits started to lift.

"Yes. Of course. I just want us all to be happy and safe."

" 'Course you do," Kuthan answered. "Did you figure out anything in your adventures?"

"Yes, and I'm going to find out more today." Idra felt energy building up inside her. "I think some answers are on the way."

"Let's hope so." They began to walk back to the cabin. *Orin and Namin will be there soon if they aren't already.*

"What will I tell the others?" Worry started to gnaw at her again. The last time her task hadn't worked out it had torn their group apart. *Enetheal tore us apart.*

"I'll take care of it," Kuthan smiled.

"Thanks." *Let's hope this time we can all agree.-*

Idra thought Kuthan would talk about the fruits before they arrived, but as they hiked up the slope as a group of six, she realized it wasn't going to happen until they all met at the table where she had left the fruit.

"What's going on?" Orin hissed in her ear as they walked up. He had been talking about his journey last night but Idra had stopped listening after he said nothing special happened. *He's safe. We are all safe.* After that, her thoughts had wandered with hazy forebodings of disagreement and discord. Orin had noticed she was on edge.

"You'll see," she answered back. He raised an eyebrow, but for once did not pursue the matter. He touched her lightly on the arm before running ahead to lead the way. By the time they had reached the top, all traces of sleepiness were gone. They sat around the table. In the center was Idra's basket, the fruit arranged so that only the unmarred sides were visible.

Namin's and Ara's eyes flickered to Kuthan for a moment. The distrust between the three of them seemed to amplify the more they didn't speak. *I can't let Kuthan do this,* she realized suddenly. *It will only make things worse.* They were all looking at her now, waiting for her to choose the eater of the first fruit. *Only I can hold us together now.* Kuthan cleared his throat, but she started to speak before he did.

"I'm going to eat first today."

Namin looked perplexed, and Lenya's eyes widened. Orin looked disappointed. *I still haven't picked him,* she suddenly realized. Ara alone seemed unsurprised. Idra took the topmost fruit from the basket, and turned it so that the mutilated side faced up. The fruit she had picked had been among the least blemished, but an unmistakable bite of fruit was missing.

She gave them a sad smile.

"They are all like this," she began. She gestured toward the fruit. Each person chose a piece of fruit to inspect.

"This is what happens when there are no webs guarding the fruit trees." She continued. Namin's eyes locked on Kuthan's.

Idra took a breath before finishing. "This was my doing."

Orin started to speak, to express his confusion, but Idra silenced him with a look. Namin's eyes stayed fixed on Kuthan. He cleared his throat.

"Did you stop to think what might happen to us if the webs from our doors were removed?" Namin spoke very quietly, but there was venom in his voice. He held his fruit out so that the absent chunk was emphasized.

"Only the webs from the clearing were removed. It won't happen again." Idra looked down at the table.

"I hope not," Namin said, his eyes focused on Kuthan. Again he spoke too quietly.

"What were you trying to do?" Ara asked.

"Find answers," Idra answered weakly. Ara's green eyes bored into Idra's. It was a searching look, but there was kindness and understanding there as well.

No one else said anything. *But that's so much better than another fight. Better that they are angry at me then at each other.* If Namin and Ara knew it was Kuthan the rift in the group could become larger, maybe even unfixable. Idra took the first bite. *Just in case there is something else wrong with it.* It didn't taste nearly as delicious as usual, but it was juicy and sugary, and satisfied her hunger. Idra allowed her mind to wander when it was clear that the conversation had moved on to the day's tributes.

ARA - DAY ELEVEN

"*A rrraaaa,*" the wind sighed. The voice was from the stones, but it came to her through leaves and twigs, mingling with the sounds of birds and waves. Still, her name was unmistakable. The hair on her skin rose, and she felt the familiar prickle of alertness rush through her. *They're calling me!*

"Here I am," she whispered, and turned so that she walked toward the voices instead of to the Berry Grove. Even the small mutterings of the stones were discernible at a distance now. *I am finally understanding.* If the others noticed her departure, they did not question it. They accepted her absences now. *But that's not completely true.* Idra had come last night. Idra saw Ara as one of *them*; thought of the group as a family. As a family they could uphold the *rules,* the world's foundation. Kuthan didn't understand the danger. Orin hated being restricted. But Idra … Idra *could* understand. She and Idra were the ones holding everything together. They were not alone.

Echoes without call of voice
Reflections without casters
Choosers who never had a choice
Servants without masters

That was all she knew of who the voices were, but now she better understood how the world worked. The murmurings of the wind were audible no matter where she walked now. And they were eager to share their secrets. But that did not make interpretation any easier. *And yet this is my task. To listen, to understand, to keep everything together.* Each day she visited them for as long she could bear it, and with each encounter she learned more before she was overwhelmed and turned away.

There were six voices and a silent seventh. When she asked a question, there were six responding utterances— shrieks and wails, moans, hums, whistles, and whispers. Together they drowned out all hope of understanding, and yet only together did they make sense. So she worked to listen to them individually, and then to put together the pieces.

And still I do not understand. I am understanding, but I do not understand. They spoke in verse some of the time, but at other times there was no rhyme or rhythm. *Why? Are they the ones who formed the rules?* The rules, too, were in verse. *But sometimes the voices just speak, like when they call my name.* It was vexing. It was easier to pick out words from verse because she could guess at what she missed. Without the pattern it took her longer to discern the individual words. The verses were also more easily committed to memory. Yet the verse came in riddles. And riddles needed interpretation. And interpretation allowed too many possibilities.

"What are the rules?" she had asked:

A cage that keeps us locked away
A light that keeps the dark at bay
A shield that holds against a storm
A frame that gives the world form

She did not know whether to feel triumphant or discouraged. Endless torrents of wind tearing at her ears yielded only what she already knew.

"What are we?" had been her next question. "What is the purpose of our tasks?"

Wanderer and weaver
The climber is retriever
Seeker and recaller
The dreamer is believer

Dreamer sees the end
Recaller looks behind
Weaver tries to mend
Seeker looks to find

Nourisher provides
Redeemer's teaching guides
Living light will find the way
by bringing night to day

She had sorted out the sounds and picked out words. She had considered the words until she could choose what they might mean. Then she pondered it all once more. *The descriptions refer to each of us, our titles, our names,* she finally decided, *our purposes.* Only there were too many.

More names than there are of us. *Do some of us have more than one purpose?* And then there were the tasks. *Maybe I can try and figure out which names belong to each of us based on our tasks.* She did her best but wasn't sure if she was right.

Her next question had been about the others: Kuthan, Orin, and Idra were not ignoring her, they were hiding something. When they didn't realize she was observing, she would catch a flicker of eyes, or hear a whisper that died as soon as she looked at them. Kuthan seemed intent on breaking rules eventually. Now that Enetheal wasn't present, it was up to Ara to hold things together, to uphold the rules. They were up to something. So she had asked:

"What are they doing? What secrets are they hiding?"

Ara wrestled with the wind. She hunched her shoulders and clenched her teeth, forcing her ears to accept the cacophony, forcing her mind to listen. They cried out their answer:

The living light has made a path
The living light will find the way
The living path completes the end
by bringing night to day

"Have the rules been broken?"

Rules that keep us breaking
followers forsaking
Seeker slowly learns
Weaver's worship turns

She tried to understand, but her head was throbbing. Single words and phrases continued to sound in the wind—

were these messages as well? But the fragments were without structure and Ara needed structure to remember. She needed to remember in order to put the pieces together, to make them make sense. And she needed for it all to make sense to keep order on the island.

The Shrieking Stones had made her strong. Ever since Enetheal had left, Kuthan and Orin, and even Namin, looked at Ara with disdain. *It's because I've replaced Enetheal.* Lenya was indifferent, *lost in her stars.* Idra hadn't seemed to care. Sometimes Ara was glad for the stones. They hurt her, but they did not ignore her, did not shun her. They answered her questions. The others gave cold glares and silence, or else they were absent. When she was alone, when the others slept and Lenya was with her stars, Ara shed tears. But when she listened to the wailing of the stones her sobs would quiet and she would fall asleep. *The Stones trust me, and I them. They help me to hold everything together.*

Everything had changed last night. *Idra.* Idra had come. *Only because Kuthan and Orin want information from me.* And yet Idra had seemed sincere. *She understands the danger we are in, the importance of keeping us together.* It was more than this. Idra seemed to care for her. *I can't depend on her, though. She still belongs to Kuthan, and if I let my strength waver ....* She didn't know the consequences. Only that she feared them, and that she had to make sure they would never occur.

She now arrived at the beginning of the stepping stones. Carefully she laid her unfinished tribute beneath a bush before beginning the journey. She was used to it now. The rocks used to cut her feet and leave bruises. Now her feet were calloused and safe. Her hands no longer had cuts from catching herself from stumbling. Her footing was firm, her balance steady. That did not mean she was incautious. The rocks could only be crossed with caution. They were jagged and slippery, and the closer one got to the Shrieking Stones, the more wildly the waves surged.

And then she was in their midst. Once again she sat in the center. It was here that she called to them. Now her desire burned even stronger. There were so many questions. What was the best way to make sure the rules were kept? What caused the fruits to be mutilated? Did the rules protect them from that same danger?

This very morning she had awoken before the others. She had come to the stones and asked about Idra's tree, when Idra would find it, and how it connected to their services. She was only given another confusing verse.

Come the night, the star and tree
Shall meet and sing a harmony
The climber climbs, completes the fall
The dreamer catches light for all

If only she had come after they had breakfasted, she could have asked about the mutilated fruits. She must know what had caused such desecration.

But now she did not call out to them. They had summoned her, and so she waited for them to speak to her. She did not have to wait long ….

"*Arrraaaa ….*"

"Here I am," she answered.

They began to speak. Their words did not come in verse this time. It was hard to make them out, and she worked and strained to understand. By the time they were finished, the day was nearly spent, but now there was no question about what she must do. Stone by stone she made her way back to the island.

She finished her tribute as quickly as she could while still putting her best effort into it. For Ara, the most important part of her tribute was in the choosing. Nevertheless, she marked the stone to complete her work. Then she laid it at the Sunset Altar, and went to find him, *the living light, the wanderer.*

He was in the Berry Grove, tracing his finger over his tribute.

"Orin," she called. If he heard her, he did not look up.

"Hey Orin," she called again. Still no answer. Ara suppressed a sigh, and walked over to him. She sat down next to him.

"Go away, Ara," he said. She let out a breath. *His harsh words are nothing compared to the wail of the wind*, she told herself. But still they hurt. His words from their last encounter in the Berry Grove still echoed in her mind. She took another breath, and her voice was calm as she continued to speak.

"I need you, Orin."

"No you don't!" He said each word slowly and distinctly.

"Yes I do, Orin, and you are going to help me," she insisted. She had to. The Stones had told her what must be done.

"I don't have to help if I don't want to, and I'm busy." He gestured to his tribute stone. It was finished in poor taste. Smears of color were splashed across a rounded yellow surface.

"I don't need you now, I need you tonight," Ara said. Orin's eyes widened for a second before narrowing.

"Sorry to disappoint," he said. "I'm busy tonight." A smile played around his lips, and at the corners of his eyes.

"Yes you are!" she said, making sure to emphasize each word. "Your service is to light paths at night. That's because we use travel by night to finish our tasks. Namin needs lighted paths to place his webs, Lenya needs them to gather stars, and now I need them!" She could hear the wind screaming in her ears, and yet none of the leaves moved. The strength of the wind and stones were inside her, and the command that had been spoken to her was now coming from her own lips. "You will fulfill your purpose! You will obey!"

Her voice had started low, but by the end it was almost a shout. Orin stared at her eyes while she spoke, and continued to gaze at her a moment afterword. He held his arms close to himself, shaking. But then he looked down, and Ara knew she had won.

"There is a bush somewhere on the island. It is special: on its branches are leaves of many colors. I do not know where it is, but you do. You will lead me there tonight, and you will light a path."

"There aren't any paths that lead there," Orin said softly, his eyes downcast.

"Then make one."

His gaze flickered upward to her face. In his eyes was a mixture of horror, fear, and shame. And then he was gone, sprinting away, but not before she saw the tears in his eyes.

Orin! She almost called after him. But she didn't. He would not have come back. And even if he had, she could not have made him feel better. He needed time to gather his thoughts. She could wait until tonight. Besides, he had a path to make.

She found herself at a loss for what to do. There was still time before sunset, and Orin would be in the Firefly Field. She was too exhausted to return to the Stones. Perhaps she could take a nap. Lately she had filled empty time with slumber. *But I can't risk sleeping through the evening.* Ara settled on going to the beach. *Lenya will probably be there.*

When she arrived, Ara found Namin and Lenya together. They had made a small trench in the sand, so that the water flowed in. Lining the channel were flowers that they must have found in the woods. Namin's smile turned into a scowl when she arrived, but Lenya's smile remained.

"Join us?" Lenya asked.

"Sure," Ara agreed. She sat down. They were quiet, and Ara wondered if she had interrupted a conversation. *Are they keeping secrets as well?* But then they started to talk, and Ara relaxed. At first she joined in, but she was tired from the stones and was able to appreciate the mindless act of lengthening and deepening the trench. For once Lenya seemed more engaged than Ara. She and Namin discussed whether the trench should lead to a mound, divide into multiple channels, or circle back to the water. Ara didn't really care and she told them that all three options sounded good. She couldn't decide if she was happy or sad when it was time to go. *Happy*, she decided. She did enjoy their company. *But also bored. There is so much more to be concerned about.* Maybe it just seemed like that because she was tired.

She felt energy surge back into her when she met Orin in the Fields.

"Is it ready?" she asked. He didn't meet her eyes, only nodded. Orin was quick at catching flies, and soon his net was full of golden light. He ambled up to her when he was done and they began to walk together along the path. At first she tried talking, but he answered with stony silence. They began on a main path. Most lanterns were still lit from Orin's previous ventures, but every so often they would come to a dark lantern. Orin's hand seemed only to brush these lanterns when suddenly they emitted golden flashes once more. *He's become so good at his task.* As they walked, the sky's pale blue began to darken. The stars began to appear, but the trees shielded most of their light, and Ara was glad for the lanterns. Finally Orin stopped.

"We're here," he said.

Ara looked around. It took a moment to notice. A flash of gold from the path they were on revealed other lanterns receding into the dark forest off the main path. But it didn't look right. The new path was uneven. There were rocks, and roots, and bushes. The ground wasn't clear. Even the lanterns weren't perfectly spaced.

"Follow my lead." There was something unpleasant in Orin's voice. Ara barely had time to register what he had said when suddenly Orin leapt onto the new path.

"Wait!" she called after him, but already he was running. Orin leapt to a clear patch of dirt between two patches of wildflowers, and then over rocks and roots and through a gap between thorny bushes. The thorns scratched Ara as she followed him. "Orin, slow down!" she called again. But Orin only sped up. The path was treacherous. She could only navigate it as long as she kept up with Orin. He knew where to leap or to duck and crawl under bushes, when to clamber over rocks. He knew where he had planted the lanterns that illuminated the way with their flashes of gold.

"Hold on Orin!" she called again. Then her foot caught in a tangle of roots. Her knees slammed down into the ground, and she couldn't help letting a cry of pain escape. Her right knee had hit a rock. She cradled it for a moment and the pain died, but when she was on her feet again Orin was nowhere in sight.

"Orin!" she called out. She was plunged into darkness for a moment, but then the light returned. *Coincidence. That's all.* Every so often flashes synchronized, making darkness complete for small moments. It happened periodically, but it made her uneasy when this synchrony occurred. But something seemed wrong. *This can't be allowed. This isn't a real path. I'm in the middle of the woods alone at night off the path. I have broken the rules.* But then she remembered that her voices had told about the rules breaking without being broken. *Maybe this is what they mean.* She refocused, and looked back the way she had come. The trail was not random. She could see it. It was rough, and newly hewn, but clearly a genuine lighted path.

Then suddenly, the fireflies seemed to flash at shorter intervals and the path brightened briefly, the light now spilling into the woods on either side. She caught movement and stared searchingly through the shifting shadows and illuminations. The rough-hewn path was not all she saw, there *was* someone. "Orin?" she called into the darkness. But the little figure wasn't Orin. He wasn't anyone she knew. He looked to be about Orin's size, his eyes the same golden-hazel, but his nose was sharper, his hair darker. It was hard to distinguish more than this, even with the regular flashing of the little lights. And as Ara peered into the flickering, changing darkness to get a better look, he backed away, a worried look on his face. He turned away from her, his face now concealed, and he beckoned furiously. Moments later another figure emerged behind him. She was a full head taller than the little dark-haired figure, and had deep green eyes and wild gold curls framing her frightened face.

"Hello?" Ara's voice faltered. She wanted to move her feet, but suddenly they seemed more firmly rooted to the ground than the trees bordering the path. The two figures approached her, leaping along the haphazard trail. Both seemed to know exactly where to place their feet. The boy led, the girl following closely behind. Ara's heart hammered as they drew near. *I thought we were safe on the path!*

"Hello …." Her greeting came out as a hoarse whisper. *The stones said nothing of this.* There was another moment of that horrible intermittent darkness before the figures were revealed again. There was something wrong with them—how they moved, the timing of their leaps and steps—but Ara could not think quite what. Instead she crouched at the side of the path, huddling under a bush. They were almost upon her. And then they were.

But they weren't. The boy leapt past her. The girl stopped for a moment, her deep green eyes seeming to look right into Ara's, but then she continued. *They can't see me,* Ara realized. Once again the lanterns plunged her into darkness, and then when the next flash of gold brightened the path, the figures were already moving quickly away.

Their footfalls are silent even as they meet the roots and the twig-strewn path. I see them only during the flashes of light—What if they only come into being during the flickers of lantern light? And she remembered the stones and the 'living light'. The danger was gone. *There was no danger, had never been danger.* Ara crawled out from under her hiding place and hurried after the two retreating figures.

Just as Orin had, the phantoms knew exactly where to place their feet on the uneven path. Ara followed closely behind them, but it was difficult. It wasn't just that they were hard to see when the lanterns flickered off; they flickered out of *being* when the light left. Ara couldn't help but worry that they would turn and see her, and then … she didn't know what. The path twisted and turned, weaving in and out between bushes, around trees, and through mud. As long as she kept up and watched their footfalls, she knew where to step. She followed her guides closely, with all her effort, focusing with such a single mind that she was startled and caught herself up abruptly when they stopped.

Why have they stopped moving? She barely had time to consider this when they turned around, facing her. Ara held her breath. But once again their eyes passed over her, through her, without seeing her. They gazed for a moment, and then turned their attention downward, kneeling beside a brightly colored bush, placing their hands onto the earth beneath it. In the next flash they were gone.

Ara waited, holding her breath. She let it out, and took another. Her surroundings were empty. In the distance she heard the waves, and as always, the wind. The stones. The stones were speaking. *The stones are always speaking. That is why I am here. I have listened to them; have trusted them to guide me.* It was hard to make anything out at night, but by the flashes Ara could distinguish variously colored leaves on the bush in front of her. Even in the limited light of the fireflies, she was mesmerized by this vibrant foliage. The lanterns were arranged in a wide circle around it. Slowly she approached the area where her phantom guides had knelt. Then she, too, sank to her knees.

"You found your way." He spoke behind her and she heard a sneer in his voice. Ara's heart leapt, and she flinched, but she did not turn to face him.

"No thanks to you," she answered coldly.

"Oh? You didn't like my path?"

"I didn't like being abandoned." Orin didn't answer. "You're still upset," Ara continued. "I'm sorry you feel that way. But we have bigger things to focus on now."

"Like what?"

Ara began to dig. Orin frowned, but then wordlessly joined her. It was tedious work. The earth was unyielding and chafed at her fingers, filling the crevasses under her fingernails unpleasantly. After they'd gone through the hard-packed surface-layer, however, their work became easier. They began to remove earth by handfuls. She paused as they uncovered some fist-sized stones. Orin removed a few, throwing them into a pile before continuing to dig. Ara lifted another and started to discard it just as a bright illumination of firefly light crossed its uneven surface. She stared. She could see that it was pale, and that shells were arranged in a little circle on one side. Another flash from the lantern lit the rock now cradled in her palm. Between the shells it was grey, but there were traces of a light pink-purple where it had once been painted.

"Just stones," Orin grunted as he pulled some more out.

"No. They're not," Ara said slowly.

"They're not?" Orin asked, curious despite his anger. "Then what are they?" Another flash revealed the pile of stones that they had unearthed, and she knew that now he did see.

"They're tribute stones."

Idra - Day Eleven

The sun was hot on Idra's neck as she searched the shores. It was bright, too, so that her eyes watered when she turned them away from the gentle darkness of the stones. An angular purple stone caught her attention. Most of the stones were rounded enough that they allowed for comfortable walking. This one wouldn't have. *Glad I didn't step on this one.* It had sharp corners, and a somewhat translucent sheen that played with the sunlight. *I'll decorate it with shells.* The shells looked particularly nice on the grey stones, but today they would work out nicely on purple.

She looked around. Most of the others still had their heads bent downwards. Except Lenya. Lenya walked along the shoreline gazing out towards the water. Idra's thoughts turned inward again. She couldn't believe how tangled things had gotten. Had she been blinded by her failed service? She hadn't talked to Lenya for … actually she didn't even know for how long. And before last night she hadn't had an open conversation with Ara since not finding the sixth tree. *But now we will be linked together again.*

Wordlessly she fell into step beside Lenya. Lenya wasn't looking at the stones. Her eyes were on the horizon.

"Do you ever wonder where we came from?" Lenya asked. They continued to walk while Idra thought.

"Well … there were the rules … we were on a boat before we were here …." She had forgotten until Lenya brought it up.

"I awoke to starlight and wind and waves. You were all sleeping. I don't remember anything before that, and yet I knew you. All of you. None of you was a stranger."

Idra closed her eyes trying to envision it. But it wasn't a sight that came into her mind. It was a sound. A song.

"I almost fell in. There was a song. When it stopped I was awake. And then we all waited to see where we were going …." They continued to climb over rocks until they were both knee-deep in the shallows.

"I know how it ends, just not how it begins."

"Oh?" she paused, hoping Lenya would say more. *Is she trying to confuse me?* "How does it end?"

"Come with me tonight," Lenya smiled "I'll show you."

The night came quickly. Orin and Kuthan left to explore forest paths. There was an unspoken agreement not to test the webs again. Idra left with Lenya. She realized she did not know the night. Lenya clearly did. She skipped along the path unafraid. *She loves this!* Idra loved the warmth of a new day, the excitement of a full day ahead, of living the day. Lenya turned and smiled. *Night has its own beauty too.* But it certainly was colder.

When they reached the beach she was surprised to see how bright it was. The moon was nearly round, yet beyond it the stars shone brightly. Their reflections danced in the water. The light also caught Lenya's hands in a peculiar way.

"Your gloves!" Idra exclaimed. Lenya moved her hands so that the webs caught the silvery light. Her hands shimmered.

"Yes," Lenya answered. "They're beautiful."

Side by side they lay down in the sand. For a time they were quiet. Cold seeped into Idra from the night sand and from the air, but Lenya seemed unaffected. She kept her gaze fixed on the sky, so Idra tried to do the same. Wind swept across the island carrying particles of sand and picking up water droplets.

"Is this what you do every night?" she asked, unable to continue the silence any longer.

"Yes." Lenya's eyes remained skyward. The stars were beautiful. They too seemed unaffected by the cold. They glowed brightly.

"Alone?" As beautiful as the sky was, silence and stars were not for Idra.

"No. Enetheal usually joins me. Namin's been here too."

"Oh." She had not thought of Enetheal all day. It was creepy knowing that he was still here somewhere.

"You watch stars with Enetheal?"

"Yes. I think he understands them—not like I do, but he understands them."

"What do you ...." She stopped in mid-sentence. A white silver arc trailed behind the star, shimmering in the nighttime sky. As the star fell, its light outshone that of the other stars; it even outshone the moonlight. The world seemed to darken because of its brilliance. Idra felt her stomach tighten.

"Let's go!" Lenya whispered excitedly. She pulled Idra up by the hand. Idra hadn't realized how numb she was from cold, but she didn't let it show. Together they raced for the path that would lead to the fallen star.

There were butterflies in her stomach as they ran, and she felt sick and giddy at the same time. *What's going to happen?* The lanterns flashed irregularly. Rushing through the forest made everything seem to shift about them, but Lenya didn't even seem to notice. *She has no fear of the night. This is her time.* Emboldened, Idra picked up her pace.

How does she know where to go? The star had been brilliant as it fell, but within the forest there was nothing to see but fireflies and the dim glow from the heaven-bound stars and moon. The dirt path met the stone circle, and then it was there, a faint silver glow. *I'm back.* This morning the tree had been abhorrent with its mutilated fruit. Now it filled Idra with awe.

It shone with starlight and the clearing around it was bathed in white silver. The bark shimmered as if lit from within. The leaves sent forth a piercing white. Even the needles of the surrounding pines seemed to glint. All traces of the mutilated fruit were gone. Their eyes wandered higher and higher following the light until ….

"There!" They said it together. In the topmost branches of the tree was the star.

"I've never found one fallen in a tree before," Lenya said. She smiled, her gaze still transported by the star.

"What are you going to do?" Idra asked.

"Me?" Lenya turned her smile so that Idra saw her in full. The light gleamed off Lenya's eyes. "This star wants to play with *you*."

It took Idra a moment to comprehend. Her stomach squirmed, but energy surged through her. She started for the tree.

"Wait." An icy hand clasped her wrist. Lenya's voice was serious.

"Don't touch it." Idra nodded, and began her climb. At first, the light made the climb easy. But the contrast between the glowing silver bark and the bright white leaves disoriented her. Coldness began to descend about half way up the tree. After that it became colder with each new tree limb. The branches began to thin, but she was almost there.

She paused to catch her breath and looked around. The sky was bright with specks of light, and the moon seemed even larger than it had from the ground. Glimmers of reflected light were visible on the waves in the distance. The rest of the island was dark. But that darkness was filled with sound. Owls hooted, crickets chirped, and somewhere in the distance was the wail of Ara's stones. *Are they speaking now?* She refocused her attention on Lenya's star so close and attainable.

She could not climb out to it; the little branches this high up could not hold her weight. She reached for the small limb, grasping as far from the trunk as she could. Then she began to shake it. It did not take much. The star tumbled from its cradle of leaves and twigs and fell down into Lenya's outstretched hands.

A wave of warmth seemed to flow around Idra as it fell.

"Ohhh." Her body suddenly ached with fatigue. It was difficult to climb down. She was even tempted to curl up on a bough and sleep in the tree, but she knew Lenya was waiting. As she neared the forest floor, the night air seemed to warm. When she finally reached the ground, Lenya was sitting cross-legged at the base of the tree. Held close to her in both gloved hands, was the star. Somehow it looked right with Lenya.

"Shall we go?" Idra asked.

"Yes," Lenya answered hesitantly. And then again with more certainty, "Yes."

She took Idra's hand in hers and carried her star with the other. Together they walked through the forest, Lenya holding the star in front of them, lighting the way. Uneasy thoughts intruded, and despite the cold, Idra leaned closer to Lenya.

What might be lurking beyond the path at night? Could Enetheal be out there in the darkness? Where does he go at night? Where is he now? He couldn't spend his whole night wandering paths.

Soon however they were back on the beach, the darkened forest and its mysteries behind them. Then they were climbing the stairs that led to the well. Idra was glad to have the starlight, if only so that she would not miss a step on the stairs. She doubted that lanterns alone could give her confidence to climb at night.

The night seemed closer at the top of the stairs, as if the stars and moon were not so far away. They began to walk towards the well. As they moved forward, the hair on the back of Idra's neck stood up and tiny bumps rose up on her arms. She paused. Lenya continued. *What was it?* She looked around for the thing that had made her uneasy. *The plants. The plants are watching us.* Yet it wasn't Idra they were watching. As Lenya proceeded across the plateau, the flowers turned so that their petals were facing her. And just like the tree that had been star-touched, they glowed. Yet they had not touched the star. Their light did not fade as Lenya moved away. At the edge of the well Lenya stopped, holding the star over the waiting abyss. She turned to Idra and beckoned. Idra hurried over, always keeping an eye on the plants.

"Ready?" Lenya asked.

"Yes," Idra encouraged. She was eager and also anxious. Lenya released the star and all the brightness suddenly vanished. Now the night was dark. *I can see nothing!* But then she blinked and she could just make out Lenya, who was still glowing faintly. Her hands radiated crisscrossing light. *The gloves!* Lenya didn't seem to notice.

"That is how it ends," she said sadly.

"What?"

"There are only so many stars." Lenya turned away from the well so that she and Idra faced each other. "That is why it is so important to treasure every moment, every star." She gave Idra's hand a squeeze. Idra didn't know what to say. Instead she looked blankly at the sky. It took her a moment to comprehend. And then she began to count the stars. She counted them once, and then again, and then a third time.

"Does that mean …." She said it slowly. "Are you saying there are only seventeen days left?"

"Well, seventeen stars. But it's best to think of each one as its own treasure. Don't worry about how many there are, just enjoy each one while it's here." Lenya's turned her eyes skyward, and her smile lost all sadness.

"Oh." Idra didn't know what else to say. "I need to think about that." She felt exhausted. The plants continued to watch them as they left the plateau. Without the stars Orin's fireflies were essential for finding their way.

"Thank you for coming tonight," Lenya said, and she smiled.

"Thank you!" Idra answered. "It was wonderful." They hugged each other outside her cabin before she entered.

When she closed the cabin door, all was dark, and except for Kuthan's regular breathing, all was still. She smiled in the quiet darkness. She was exhausted, yet energized. So much had happened in a short time. *We are becoming a family again. I've missed Ara and Lenya so much. And I understand the island better now, too. Webs, stones, stars... Kuthan will be so pleased. Things are finally fitting together.*

She lay in bed staring upward, but sleep did not come fast. *A star in my tree and I helped it to fall. Each day is such a treasure.* She closed her eyes. And yet she could still see ....

Before her was a great tree that extended into the heavens. Instead of fruit hanging from the branches, there were stars. She climbed higher and higher into the tree and finally chose the brightest of the stars. Far below Lenya waited. Idra was filled with joy as she tugged upon the bright star, held it for a moment, and then let it tumble down. Lenya smiled as she caught the star, briefly cradled it to her chest, and then released it down into the well.

ORIN - DAYS ELEVEN AND TWELVE

He had left Ara behind. She would get lost. Orin knew there was no easy way through these woods without his guidance. And when she needed him she would call out to him. And then she would apologize for her viciousness and beg him for help. *And for forgiveness.* He hadn't decided whether or not he would forgive her.

"Orin!" she called. But when she called he didn't go to her. *Not yet. Let her feel a little terror.* She called out once more. Orin smiled. *I will go on the third call. Then we will be even.* But the third call never came. Instead, he saw Ara hurrying along the path. Leading the way were two others.

Orin shivered. He knew one of them, the shorter one who had led Orin to the cabin full of lanterns, the one Orin had seen in the Sapwood on the new paths. *And now he has come to another of my paths.* It made him proud. *But he's helping Ara.* Orin did not know whether to be puzzled or frustrated. He did not know what to think of the second one. *I need to get a better look.* He crept behind them, heart hammering, until they arrived at the bush with many colored leaves. But Ara's rescuers had vanished.

Orin's heart paused for a moment. *I knew there was something weird about them.* Last night when he had seen the phantom, it had flickered with the lantern light. *They're not real*, he told himself. *Ara probably knows.* His anger returned. *I'll do what I came here to do.* He stepped up behind her.

"You found your way," he said coldly. Ara flinched.

"No thanks to you," she answered, with just as little warmth.

"Oh? You didn't like my path?" He was glad to see her discomfort.

"I didn't like being abandoned." Orin didn't know what to say. Part of him felt guilty, but he rejected it. *She deserved it. And she still found her way without me! It's not fair.*

"You are still upset," Ara continued. "I'm sorry you feel that way. But we have bigger things to focus on now." *Upset? She calls me upset!?*

"Like what?"

He tried to sound mocking, but if she noticed she ignored it. Instead she began to dig, and after a moment he joined. At first the earth was unyielding, but after they got past the surface Orin was able to pull away large chunks of earth. They started pulling out stones, casting them aside into a little pile. All at once Ara paused. She stared at the stone she had just pulled from their hole.

"Just stones!" he said impatiently.

"No … they're not," Ara said slowly.

"They're not?"

She didn't answer right away as she carefully placed the lumpy stone in her hand onto the pile.

Suddenly, he did know what they were. He just couldn't comprehend it. A surge of heat bubbled up in his chest. His toes and fingers tingled.

"They're tribute stones," she finished.

Orin's thoughts were jumbled, and it was hard to form words.

"But ... how?" *Why would there be tribute stones here?* "Unless someone ... someone moved them here."

Ara frowned: "Yes ... of course." She sounded unsure.

"Kuthan moves the stones after sunset," Orin said, thinking aloud.

"These aren't our stones, Ore," she said softly.

"No." She was right. He knew *their* tribute stones well. None of their stones looked like these.

Ara stood as if to leave. Orin looked at the stones.

"Aren't we going to do anything with these?"

"No. We just came here to find them. The Shrieking Stones said to come here and find them. Only I didn't know what we were going to find." Now she began retreating down the makeshift path. Orin quickly got to his feet and jogged to catch up with her.

"So you don't know why they're here?" The idea was aggravating. One moment Ara would pretend to know everything, flaunting her superiority, and then she would pretend she was just as confused as the rest of them.

"I'm working on it," she answered. *Ara enjoys her secrets.* Idra had told him about the tree, "*Down in the sky where low becomes high.*" Ara knew things, but she guarded her secrets jealously.

"People made these," Orin thought aloud. "And there aren't any other people here now."

"Which means there were people here before us," Ara continued matter-of-factly.

"Unless Enetheal made these stones." He was surprised to hear himself say it. He hadn't thought about Enetheal for a long time.

"No," Ara answered. "Enetheal doesn't make tributes."
They clambered out of the brush, and onto the main path.

"Maybe he used to," Orin replied. "Who else was here
before us, except for him?

"That might be it," said Ara, and Orin smiled involuntarily. But she continued, "but then why would he stop
making tributes?" Orin didn't have an answer. "I think he
was the protector of the rules," she said decisively.

Was. She considers herself the new protector.

"Maybe," Orin answered. He stared at her pointedly.
"Then there are others?"

"There *were* others," Ara corrected. But that didn't line
up. *Does she think I haven't seen the phantoms? She knows
they are here, but she hides her secrets.* Ara's voice grew
softer. "They aren't around any more. They aren't making
tributes now."

"Then something happened to them?" But it couldn't
be so simple. *They're still here—we can see them!*

"Yes. I think so," Ara said slowly. Somehow they had
arrived just outside Orin's door. The journey back had gone
so quickly. He had almost enjoyed talking to her. *What
could it all mean?*

"I hope you've *learned* something. We're meant to
work together! That's the only way to do what we need to
here." Her tone was belittling, proud, arrogant.

"The only thing I've learned is that the answers we
need to find are *not* on the paths."

Ara looked stunned. *That shut her up.* It was true. He
peeled back the web-screen, and opened the door.

"Good night, Ara."

He closed the door behind him.

It was a long time before he got to sleep. Vivid thoughts about phantoms, newly formed lantern paths, and buried tribute stones whirled in his mind. But as he struggled for rest that would not come, he heard song emerge from the night. Namin's voice was quiet and sad. Orin listened as the song grew louder and faster, almost anxious, then died down into a soothing melody. Whatever worries were out there would not trouble him here inside the cabin. He closed his eyes and this time sleep welcomed him.

"Orin." Namin nudged him awake. He was surprised to find himself groggy, but managed to shake the sleepiness off.

"Let's get moving," Namin encouraged. Orin's net lay beside him on his bed. He liked having it near him, but did not carry it during the day. Path-lighting was no longer time-consuming. His net allowed him to supply the island's paths in a single night. This even included his new paths, of which he now had many. Most of them ran through the Sapwood since he continued to look for Idra's missing tree, but he had made other paths as well. Orin felt a little guilty for the others, since he knew that Idra's tree was most important, but the Sapwood was loath to give up its secret, and he was sure there were other elusive mysteries that would be uncovered more easily.

Although he had created the paths, he had not really explored them. He wanted to, but other things—people— had come into his way. He thought over the last two nights.

Two nights ago Lenya had come to him to let him know there was a large section of path that had become dark, the lanterns in need of new fireflies.

"Another star has fallen, Ore," she had said. He had been surprised that she used his nickname. "I need you to light the way."

He had made the journey as quickly as possible, sprinting between lanterns as he lit them. Lenya had been excited to be part of the path-lighting, but Orin was only eager to finish and move on. Once he had connected the darkened path to a lit one, he had halted abruptly.

"I need to go, Lenya"

"You won't come to gather the star?"

"I can't, Lenya, I have exploring I need to do." He had been surprised to find his words truthful. Something about her always made him feel comfortable sharing.

"Maybe tomorrow?

"Maybe," he had offered.

Then he had returned to the Sapwood, feeling guilty for leaving Lenya. To make things worse, nothing had come of his exploration. He had traveled the paths and once, briefly, thought he had caught a glimpse of his phantom friend. When he had reached the spot, however, the shadow- child had disappeared. He had returned to his cabin exhausted and had fallen asleep almost as soon as he had laid himself down.

Then Ara had stolen away the next night. *I must do more night exploration! That's when things happen.* The phantoms seemed to come at night. And night was when stars fell and when Namin made his webs. *Why does it all happen at night?*

Namin gave Orin another nudge and Orin smiled. He wished Namin could join them, but he knew Kuthan would not be pleased. *At least I can just relax and have fun with Namin.* "Race you," Namin whispered in his ear. In an instant Orin was alert, already beginning to run before Namin had even finished speaking. Namin was close on his heels, though Orin managed to reach Idra and Kuthan's cabin before Namin did. But then Namin rushed on.

"All the way!" Namin laughed. Orin protested loudly, but surged onward. He was catching up, but they arrived at Ara and Lenya's cabin before Orin could close the gap.

"Not fair," Orin complained. Namin just laughed, brushing sweat off his brow. After a few moments, Namin peeled aside the web-screen and knocked.

For once, Lenya opened the door.

"Come in!" she said eagerly. Ara was sleeping.

"We'll wait for the others before waking her," Lenya said.

"Perfect," Namin answered. Orin just nodded, still catching his breath.

It was Lenya who was chosen to break their fast. Orin prickled slightly at Idra's choice. *At least it wasn't Ara*, he told himself. It was a warm, muggy day, but there was a pleasant breeze and clouds covered most of the sky. They returned to their daily ritual: breakfast first, then tributes. The search for the tributes seemed to be the only thing that was consistent.

That's how things were even before we got here. But even as he thought this, he wondered how there could have been a before. It was hard to imagine. Orin avoided the shallows. Without a strong sun, the stones didn't glitter, so he had started avoiding them on cloudy days. He was considering a little collection of green and blue stones when he heard Idra walking over.

"Hey, Id …."

"Hey, Ore." Idra was looking at him nervously, biting her lower lip.

"What's up?" Orin asked quietly. He stepped close to her, so they were eye to eye.

"It's tonight Ore! The sixth tree!" There were tears in her eyes. "We still haven't found it! I forgot—lost track of time—but now it's here!"

"Relax!" Orin put a hand on her shoulder, but she shrugged it off.

"Orin, this is when everything started to go wrong before. It's what started all the fighting between Kuthan and Ara and Namin! It's what split up our group."

"It wasn't just the tree, Idra." Orin tried to keep his voice calm. *Where did this come from?*

"It's my service, Orin! I need to complete it!"

"You will," Orin put his hand on her shoulder again. This time she didn't shrug it off. "Tonight I will complete my service, and find your tree."

"You will?" she sounded so hopeful that it both thrilled and terrified him. *What if I don't?* But he would. Orin was sure of it.

"I promise you, Idra. Tonight I'll find your tree."

Idra flung her arms around him in an embrace and Orin couldn't help but laugh. After a moment Idra joined in.

"I'll walk you to your tree in the morning," he reassured her again.

They finished their tribute search together. When it was time to decorate their stones they parted. Orin set off for the Stargazing Beach, Idra to the Sapwood. One wonderful thing about collecting shells is that you didn't have to pick only one. Orin dug a small hole, and wandered about the beach, bringing shells back to his little trove every time he found one. Lenya made a similar burrow next to his. They sat side by side, pasting tiny shells in little circular patterns on their tribute stones. The pine sap was sticky on his fingers, but he liked that. *Even that is different in the Sapwood. Sapwood sap isn't very sticky.*

"It's strange how your grounded lights lead me to my celestial lights." He hadn't noticed Lenya joining him as he worked.

"That is wonderful," he answered. He wasn't sure what to say.

"You should come with me Ore, you would love it! Each star is a new discovery!"

It did sound wonderful. *Paths are meant to lead somewhere.* So many of his new paths just connected to other paths, but all paths were meant to link destinations together.

"I'd love to, Lenya," he smiled. "I have another discovery to make tonight, but I would love to find a star with you." They continued working, pasting on shells. They helped each other to find some of the last ones. And then they were done. Just in time. The wind picked up enough so that the sand became irritating, and a light rain started to fall.

"It's going to be hard to see the sunset tonight," Orin said, looking up at the clouds.

"I'm more worried about seeing stars."

They hiked across the island. They could hear the Shrieking Stones wailing in the distance. *Is Ara there now? What are they telling her?* The rain grew heavier, but by the time they had reached Sunset Altar it slowed to a drizzle again.

"I'll see you later, Ore," said Lenya as she departed towards the cabins. Orin stayed, looking at their tributes until Idra arrived. Wordlessly they clambered over the slippery rocks, to their skipping site.

"Wish we could see a sunset," Idra said, looking at the clouds. The rain had stopped, but the sky was still a stormy grey.

"Well, we got plenty more in front of us," Orin grinned. Idra bit her lip nervously. "Don't worry, Id, things will work out tonight."

"Yes," she said, sounding unconvinced. "What do you think it means, '*Down in the sky where low becomes high*'?"

"I have no idea," Orin answered truthfully.

Idra looked out over the water again. "The horizon?" she asked.

"I don't think so. Your tree is in the Sapwood." Orin flicked a small flat stone and it skipped too many times to count, finally skidding into a little curve.

When they had finished, Orin knew she was still worried about her tree, but at least now she had a smile.

They returned to Sunset Altar, where they found Kuthan. He was staring at the tributes arranged neatly on the salver.

"We are finding the tree, tonight," Orin said with confidence. Kuthan nodded in affirmation.

"But first I need to deliver the stones. You and Idra collect fireflies and I'll meet you in the Sapwood afterwards," Kuthan said looking down at the tributes once more.

Idra smiled. "Perfect."

Suddenly Orin remembered his and Ara's discovery and realized it was something that needed to be shared.

"Umm ... I also found out something when I was with Ara last night." Kuthan and Idra looked up expectantly. "There were people here before us. They made tributes," Orin added. *Why didn't I tell them earlier?*

"What?" Kuthan exclaimed.

Maybe it was too much to throw at them without warning. "That's all I know," he added quickly. "But I think Ara knows more."

Kuthan's expression darkened. "My tribute stones have been coming back changed." He lifted his gaze from the stone-laden salver and stared across the water before continuing. "I think they are telling me about the past as well." He stopped for a breath. "We will find out. Ara *will* tell us." Now there was a note of fury in his voice.

"Please!" Idra said. "We mustn't fight one another. Ara is working hard to understand stuff too. We need to work together. Can we focus on the missing tree right now?"

"Yes," Orin answered before Kuthan could respond. Then he turned toward Kuthan, adding, "Meet you at the Sapwood."

But as his eyes left Kuthan's, he caught movement at his periphery. His heart stopped. Ara! How long has she been standing there? But if she had heard anything, she didn't show it. Maybe she had just arrived. Ara held out her tribute to Kuthan and then turned to Orin.

"We need to talk."

"No, we don't," Orin answered. "We've done too much talking!" He grabbed Idra's hand. "Let's go." Idra looked unhappy, but she didn't resist.

"Orin, wait!" Ara said angrily. She ran to catch up with him, and grabbed his free arm. "Just ...." Ara struggled to find words and there was a pleading tone mixed with the anger in her voice. "Just don't do anything stupid tonight! Okay?"

Orin yanked his arm back. "I'll do my best," he said angrily. "But sometimes I can't help it." He pulled Idra along.

"Be careful," Ara whispered. Orin pretended not to hear.

Idra and Orin walked until they were long out of earshot. Orin knew she was waiting for him to speak. "She is the worst!" he burst out.

"I think she's just trying to help," Idra responded.

"Don't you defend her. Not now." Idra was quiet. "We'll focus on your tree," he allowed after a moment.

"Thanks, Ore," Idra squeezed his hand. It made him love her more.

The Firefly Field was muddy when they arrived, but the little insects were swarming. Orin's net was full in moments.

"Most of the lanterns have healthy lights already," Orin said. "Not sure what I'm going to do with all of these."

"Could you fill some lanterns twice?" Idra suggested.

" 'Guess so." The fields had left Orin's feet muddy. He wiped his feet on some rocks, but they still felt caked and sticky. They lit lanterns, sometimes with three or four fireflies. The sky faded from light to dark blue, and they entered the Sapwood.

The rain had hardly affected the Sapwood. The twigs were a brighter green, the bark a deeper red, but the silence was the same. It engulfed them as they walked along the trail. There were multiple paths through the Sapwood now, many winding around sap pools. Orin was proud of them. When he had made the first new path it had seemed strange, as if it didn't belong. Now, though, with so many, they seemed right. Flashing firefly light caught the sap streams, turning their silver sheens to gold. The sap oozed slowly and silently. The sky still shed enough light that the lanterns were not yet necessary and Orin was able to run between trails to light the occasional darkened lanterns. However, as the evening dimmed, lantern light twinkled at constant intervals through large portions of the Sapwood, mingling with the stillness, giving the place a sense of awe.

Kuthan joined them just as the sky became black. They began as a threesome on the newest path, one looking right, one looking left, and one looking directly ahead. *The phantoms usually appear near the paths where they are visible in lantern light.* But Orin couldn't be sure. He thought he had seen someone when he had found the cabin full of lanterns—a phantom off the path.

They finished walking along that first path and moved methodically to a second. Idra was breathing fast, but Kuthan was focused. Now the sap glimmered with the lantern flashes, casting strange shadows. Orin was glad some of them had extra fireflies, because the stars were doing little to brighten the night. The sky was clouded and black. Orin had forgotten how dark the bark of the trees was at night. Gold flashes shone off the shiny black bark.

By the time they reached the third path Idra was biting her lip and blinking her eyes more rapidly than usual.

"Relax," Orin said slowly. "We know the tree is here, and we know we are looking for it at the right time."

"Do we?" Kuthan asked. "I'm starting to think that any tree would be easier to find in the day than in the night." Kuthan was so focused on squinting into the darkness that he did not see Idra's distraught face. "Maybe something else is happening at night that has nothing to do with trees."

By the time they reached the fourth path, Idra was breathing far too quickly, and it was clear that she was blinking back tears. Finally, Kuthan had caught on, but now it was too late to soften his words:

"It's not here. We would have seen it by now!" She began to sniffle, and then she was crying. Orin pulled her close in a hug, and Kuthan wrapped his long arms around them both.

"It'll be okay, Id. I promise." But now, for once, the lanterns were horribly irritating. The lights flashed on and off from random directions so that it was hard to see each other's faces clearly.

"Idra," Kuthan whispered. "We are going to do this." Idra's face was buried in Orin's shoulder. Orin and Kuthan exchanged a glance.

"Let's get you back to our cabin," Kuthan said softly.

Idra sniffled something incomprehensible.

"What did you say?" Kuthan asked.

"I c-can't leave you guys," Idra sobbed.

"You're just tired," Orin insisted. "Go get some rest. I'll take care of things here. You'll feel better tomorrow when we lead you to the tree." A flash of gold revealed Idra's teary-eyed smile. Kuthan gave Orin a nod:

"I'll be right back," Kuthan reassured him. He led her away.

"Not before I find the tree," Orin called after them playfully, but his voice rang hollow in the Sapwood.

He moved to the fifth path alone. He felt more tired now that the others were gone. It had been too many late nights in a row, and his eyelids were starting to feel heavy. His thoughts turned to Ara. *This is all Ara's* fault. *Ara and her secrets and her rules. She tries to keep us in the dark with riddles, always wanting to make herself seem smarter than we are. And she's nasty to everyone. She even tries to tell everyone else how to do their services. She thinks her service is better than ours. Poor Lenya ... Lenya is stuck living with her. No wonder she keeps to herself.* Enetheal hadn't been so bad. He had showed them how to follow the rules, but he had never insisted that they did. *Ara is the real tyrant. Why does she have to control us like that?*

The whole point of my service is to provide freedom. The paths allow us to go anywhere we please, unbounded, unconstrained.

He had made paths all through the island ... only in a way he was still was trapped, wasn't he?

*Never roam in dark of night
off the path of lantern's light*

Could the paths themselves be a trap? An extension of Ara's arm forcing him to some unknown purpose? He looked at the path before him with new eyes. "Lies," he whispered bitterly. And then he remembered his dream. "Don't look for paths, look for revelation." Again his voice was a whisper.

There was a flash of gold, and suddenly Orin saw the phantom. He was the same height as Orin, and eerily familiar, but the sporadic lantern flashes made it impossible to make out his features clearly. The little apparition left the path, but Orin could see him in the faint gold glimmerings as he darted between the trees. Orin scanned the flickering darkness off the path, straining to see where the figure was headed.

In the midst of the darkness there was a pool—a pool of sap he had passed many times before. But this time it was different. Its surface shimmered with reflected starlight. Orin turned his gaze upward. A blanket of clouds had turned the night sky to utter blackness. No stars shone through. He looked back at the pool, and instantly noticed something else. Every other pool in the Sapwood was formed around a tree and fed by sap streams. This pool was empty of any standing tree or stream. The phantom had vanished now that he was beyond lanterns' light, but Orin was sure he had been moving towards the strange pool.

He walked to the edge of the path, but the pool was still too far away and he felt uneasy. *Don't look for paths, look for revelation.* He had done it before, hadn't he? Been off the path at night? Surely it had grown dark before he had made it back that once, when he had seen his phantom friend that first time. And it had happened last night too. He had hidden away from the path so that Ara would lose her way. It was only a few steps off the path, but still, nothing had happened. *Lenya must leave the trail too sometimes. The stars don't all fall neatly along the paths.*

"The answers are off the paths," he whispered. Still, his feet remained rooted as he looked into the darkness.

Again he spoke aloud, as if voicing his conflict would aid its resolution. "No. My task is to provide freedom. My task is discovery."

He thought of Ara's rules, his mind racing to solve the puzzle. "The answers are *not* on the paths." His dream came back to him then, a forest full of lanterns, and without trails. "*Everywhere is a path.*" He was so relieved that he laughed. The idea that his task was an extension of Ara's was awful. "My task is to realize that boundaries do not exist. Everywhere is a path." And what about the lanterns? Surely there were other lanterns across the island. And between those lanterns and here was a path, perhaps a very wide path, but a path nonetheless. As long as he could imagine a path, then it was there.

What would Ara say? Orin smiled. Ara was so stupid. He carefully put his foot down, outside the line of lanterns which formed the path's border. Nothing happened. He took another step, and then another. There was only silence in the Sapwood. Stillness and flashes of gold. Had he expected something? *No, of course not.* He took several more steps toward the shimmering pool, now leaving the lantern light far behind. The forest truly was black, but the pool shimmered. He looked cautiously over its edge.

It was beautiful. Reflected downward into eternity was a tree. Its bark was black, as black as purest night. Its branches extended downward. And in its arms were stars. They shone brilliantly. *You were right, Lenya.* They were wondrous. There were so many. Endless stars. *So many more than our own sky has ever held. "Down in the sky where low becomes high."* It had made no sense before, but now the words took on meaning.

He gazed at the magnificent tree reaching downward toward the glittering stars, and all at once realized that something was missing. His own reflection was not there. He reached down, puzzled, and put a finger on the sap's surface. Circles rippled from the point he had touched growing larger as they traveled toward the edges of the pool. Somewhere he heard a drip. It sounded as if it came both from within the pool and from the surrounding woods. The ripple reached the edge of the sap. As if on cue, rain began to fall from above. The drizzling rain and reflected ripple distorted the sap's surface, but somewhere upon the distorted surface, Orin saw his reflection begin to form. He placed his hand gently onto the pool, extending his palms and fingers so that he touched the whole hand of his reflection.

But it wasn't a reflection. He did not know what It was at all.

Suddenly there was a splash. Orin saw the Thing beneath the surface move quickly. Before he could react, It reached out of the silvery pool and took hold of his hand.

Orin yanked his arm back, thankful for the slipperiness of the sap. Wrenching himself away from the pool, he pushed off from the needle-strewn earth, pine-debris sticking to the sap which clung to him. He leapt to his feet and began to run. Far in the distance he could just make out the lanterns flickering, marking the path's haven.

His feet hammered on the forest floor. He felt rather than heard the Thing behind him. *It's after me!* He was desperate. He felt It getting closer. *It's behind me!* All he could do was run. Trees blurred beside him. Time slowed. He felt his throat parched and strained as he struggled to breathe. But the flashes of gold seemed to be getting brighter, shimmering their assurance of safety up ahead. *Almost there.* He caught his foot on a root, but quickly regained his balance, still sprinting as he reached the golden flashes of sanctuary.

He dived onto the path, face down, breathing heavily. Hardly allowing himself to catch his breath, he scrambled to his feet, looking quickly away from the path. What he saw rooted him to the ground:

It was a Dark Figure. It moved towards Orin. As it reached the path's edge It hesitated, then crossed through the lantern's light and onto the path. A cry froze in Orin's throat. *Run!* his mind screamed. *Run!* But he could not run. He could not move. He could not fathom the Figure before his eyes … but then he did not need to. All of the lanterns flashed out, leaving him in utter darkness, and suddenly Orin broke free. And he ran.

His feet raced along the path. He wove in and out of trees, skirting their pools. The lights began to flicker once again, sickeningly, and he could see the soundless sap, now silver, now gold, gushing down the sides of the trees. Over his shoulder Something was coming. It moved like the phantoms, appearing, then vanishing … except that when

It vanished It seemed not like absence, but like the presence of absence. Orin's lanterns now flashed alarmingly fast, their golden light, pulsing desperately on and off. The rain now fell hard, warping the light, refracting it into hazy sparkles, but Orin could make out the form of his Pursuer with every flash, and with every flash It was closer.

"KUTHAN!" he shrieked, his voice shrill and ragged. But Kuthan was not there.

"NAMIN!" he called. "IDRA!" "LENYA!" But he was alone.

Ara was right. She was right. I was so stupid. Ara help me. Save me.

"ARRRRRAA!!" he cried out. But even she was gone. His voice was the only sound in the silence. No one heard.

Now the Sapwood was behind him. Yet each golden flash brought the Dark Figure closer. The silence had been terrifying, but now the noise was, too. The trees creaked around him, the sound of the pelting rain mixing with the howling of the Shrieking Stones. The Thing was ever closer.

He repeated their names, calling, pleading into the darkness, even as he saw his cabin up ahead.

"KUTHAN! IDRA! NAMIN! LENYA! ARRRRRRAAA!" he shrieked. He reached the door, and swiped at the web-screen to pull it off. Only it did not come off. Instead his hand stuck to the lacy spider-work. He grasped at the filmy screen with his other hand. But the web which had always been so delicate, so fragile, now tethered him with power. Pain like a terrible sound seared through his arms, resonating in his bones. And suddenly the web became brighter and brighter until it glowed. Orin thrashed, his arms and legs flailing frantically as he became more and more tangled in the web. The lanterns flickered more slowly now. The Dread approached, It's looming shape obscuring the light ten lanterns away. The world vanished and reappeared in the lantern's light and Its Dark Form was at the fifth lantern. And then the third. And then there. Orin's thoughts turned desperately to Enetheal. Enetheal who had shown them how the world worked. Enetheal who had guided Orin as he lit his paths in the beginning. Enetheal whom they had sent away. Enetheal.

"ENETHEAL!" Orin screamed.

The Former was there. Orin looked into Its Terrible Visage. The lanterns flashed one more brilliant flash of gold, then all was dark.

ARA - DAY TWELVE

When she finished her tribute, she went straight to the Shrieking Stones. They were calling her. Not by name, as they did when they had imparted their will to her. It was their murmuring that called her. By now she heard their voices from all places, but it was only when she went to them that they revealed their secrets. Their answers were calling her.

There were people here before us. Others who made Tributes. Perhaps others who performed our services. Unless ... could Kuthan have hidden them? But no. The buried tributes had a style that was different from any of theirs. Most days Ara got to see all of the tributes gathered before sunset. None of them resembled the buried ones.

So what were the tribute stones doing there? Even if there had been others before, wouldn't the rules have been the same? The stones were supposed to go to the cave. Kuthan's cave. *Why were these ones buried?* The only explanation she could think of was that they had been intentionally hidden. *Hidden from whom? Unless the stones were buried in order to be found?* Every question she asked gave rise to more questions.

What will I ask today? Idra had met her on the Stony Shores during that day's tribute search asking whether there was any more news about her tree. There hadn't been. Idra had looked distraught. *I could ask about the tree ....* But there were too many other important questions. They would just have to make sure to eat a lot of fruit for dinner. Another day without food. They could manage. She could ask about the mutilated fruit; but horrible as it was, that mystery could wait. Besides, it wouldn't happen again so long as webs were woven. Finally she decided that it was between the buried tribute stones and the shadow children. She would ask about one of them. They had to be connected.

The water lapped at her feet as she leapt from rock to rock. The outcropping of stepping stones jutted out from the island like an arm. Although she was still cautious, now even her feet knew the route so well that she would not have needed to be careful. The murmuring grew louder. *They know I'm coming.* Ara smiled.

When she finally reached the Stones they were quiet, almost respectful. Ara moved around the circle, touching their surfaces. Their faces were wet and scarred, weathered and cracked. But they waited for her. Waited for her to speak. *They are not trying to hurt me. They are trying to help.* She blinked, and in that blink she recalled a flash of gold from the night before. The phantom children had been terrifying, but they, too, were trying to help … and then Ara knew what she was going to ask. She addressed the stones:

"Echoes without call of voice
Reflections without casters

Choosers who never had a choice
Servants without Masters"

It was a statement, not a question. At her words, a breeze came across the water, and the stones hummed. It was an eerie noise, but not unpleasant. The hum died down, and Ara asked her question.

"What is an echo?"

The wind picked up and the eerie hum returned. It grew louder and louder, and the familiar cacophony returned: wailing, howling, screeching, moaning, whistling, whispering. Ara had learned not to cover her ears. She sat down and listened. It took her some time, but not as long as it once had. She concentrated on the dissonant sounds all together; then on each of their separate voices, repeating their answers in her mind until at last she heard the message for what it was:

Echoes are what stay behind
when voice no longer cries
a song that never ends
a life after it dies

The wind had died down once she understood, but for a few moments Ara still heard the voices continuing faintly over the sounds of the lapping water. Images of last night welled up in her mind. *The shadow children! The Shrieking Stones are their voices!* She was absolutely sure. *That is how they knew where the tributes were. That is how they know everything. They are 'echoes'! Echoes of what has already been.* She looked down at her hands. They were shaking. She mustn't stop now. Her head ached, her mouth was dry, she was cold and wet from wind-blown spray, and hunger was beginning to gnaw at her stomach, but she must not stop now. Again she called out:

"Why were the tributes hidden?"

And the voices answered her:

A hunger that we could not sate
A need to cry and raise our voice
A chance we took to shape our fate
A hopeless hope to make a choice

The wind carried bitterness as it died. The water grew calm. Ara was still shaking, but now she knew that it was cold, not excitement, that caused her to shiver. "Choice?" Her voice echoed out across the water: "Choice … choice … choice." What did they mean? *I need to ask.* But she was done. Her bones ached, and she had learned to recognize her limits. She stood up to leave, but then paused: *They weren't done ….*

"*… choice…choice… Choice …*" The wind carried her voice back with its own many voices. It began as a small gust, carrying a few rain droplets, but moments later it was a torrent that swept around, over and through the rocks. Now it was screaming and tearing at all of her senses. Ara clapped her hands over her ears, shut her eyes, and collapsed to her knees. *It has never been like this before!* She pulled her knees to her chest shielding herself against the onslaught. *I must be strong—even stronger.* The wind tore at her. She sat as still as she could while it pummeled against her. *It will not relent.* It engulfed her. She gasped for a breath. "I must be stronger; I am stronger," she told herself. Slowly she uncovered her ears. The voices were separate, interrupting and speaking over one another. She strained to listen through the relentless wind, and as she did so, she realized that, painful as the cacophony was, it was not difficult to understand the words:

Choose the living light
Choose the coming end
Choose the living path
Choose to keep your friend

She wasn't sure what it meant, but she knew she needed to go. She got to her feet, the stones still screaming around her, and leapt. The voices quieted as soon as she left the little stone ring, but they continued wailing softly until she reached the shore. Her head was ringing. *I have to choose.* The thought echoed numbly within her mind. It didn't seem like she had to choose. She cupped some water and splashed her face to clear her mind. It worked. She recalled another verse:

The living light has made a path
The living light will find the way
The living path completes the end
by bringing night to day

"The living light is Orin," she muttered, as she picked up her tribute stone. "And the living paths are the ones he lights with the fireflies." She began her walk towards Sunset Altar. *So if I choose him, will the end come? And if I choose the path, then I keep my friend?* Was Orin the friend? Or one of the others? Or maybe she was supposed to choose them all. She was not sure. She could not be sure of anything. The phrases had been overlapping and changing order. How could she extract a single meaning? Her head was beginning to pound.

She was pulled from her thoughts by voices. As she drew closer she recognized Idra's ….

"We mustn't fight one another. Ara is working hard to understand stuff too. We need to work together. Can we focus on the missing tree right now?" Ara's heart leapt. *They're talking about me ... and Idra's defending me, trying to keep us together. She does care.*

"Yes," Orin answered quickly. "Meet you at the Sapwood," he nodded to Kuthan. Orin and Idra exchanged a glance, and turned simultaneously. Ara tried to keep her face blank. Orin looked horrified to see her. *Why does he hate me so much?* If only they could reach some sort of understanding. *It doesn't matter how he feels, it just matters that he's okay.* Regardless of what exactly the Shrieking Stones meant, their message was clearly about Orin. She gave her stone to Kuthan, and addressed Orin:

"We need to talk," she told him, trying to impress how important it was by the tone of her voice.

"No, we don't!" Orin said vehemently. "We've done too much talking." He grabbed Idra's hand. "Let's go." Idra looked unhappy, but she didn't resist.

"Orin wait!" Ara called after him. *Why does he have to be so difficult?* She ran up to him, catching him by the arm so that he was forced to face her.

"Just ...." She didn't know what to say. She could see in his eyes that whatever she said, he wouldn't listen.

"Just don't do anything stupid tonight, okay?" She tried to say it gently, but knew instantly that she'd said the wrong words.

Orin yanked his arm back. "I'll do my best," he said angrily. "But sometimes I can't help it."

He pulled Idra away, and Ara was alone.

"Be careful," Ara said, but her voice came as a whisper and Orin was gone.

Ara's feet took her back to the cabin. She was exhausted. *What do I do now?* She thought. *What's going on with Orin?* She sat back on her bed thinking and stifled a yawn. *"Meet you at the Sapwood,"* he had said to Kuthan. That's where they were. Making paths. The Shrieking Stones had said that the rules were breaking, but Orin's makeshift paths seemed to work as well as the others. The Shrieking Stones seemed okay with it, and they had used one such path to find the buried tributes. *Is that breaking the rules?* It couldn't be. *I'll go to the Sapwood.* That's where they were. She would make sure things were alright. Then her eyes closed.

She woke up cold, her gold curls matted against her forehead and neck. The room was dark and her heart pounded in her chest. Her headache was gone, but she was still exhausted. The trees outside were swaying in the wind. When she peered out into the darkness, she could make out pine needles blowing across the path and she heard a light rain pattering softly on the roof. She heard a cry on the wind and strained her ears.

"ARRRRRRAAAA!!" The voice screamed from far across the island. *The Stones.* She had just left them, and already they were calling her back. "Here I am," she whispered. There was something different about them, but Ara didn't know what.

Lenya was away. *Waiting for the stars to fall.* She often wished for Lenya in the night, but she understood: they each had duties to fulfill.

Ara hurried down the path that led down to the Shrieking Stones. It was an unpleasant night. The rain was uncomfortable, and altered the light of the lanterns so that the path was hard to see. The Shrieking Stones were howling and wailing and humming. Ara paused to listen, but now she could not hear her name.

She thought she heard screams, but they were coming from the wrong direction. The wailing of the Shrieking Stones was coming from the open water, but the screams were from the other direction. She strained her ears. "ARRRRAAAAA!" the voice shrieked, the note of panic now almost palpable. Ara felt an icy surge fill her chest. The Stones were not calling. It was Orin.

"ORIN!" she called out, but her voice was swallowed by the wind. She squinted through the trees and the rain, searching in the direction of his voice. Flashes of gold were barely visible through the trees and brush. *That must be the path!* She could run. She could run now through the forest. She would reach Orin in moments. Behind her the Shrieking Stones were wailing, and somewhere in the wind she heard their verse again.

> *Choose the living light*
> *Choose the coming end*
> *Choose the living path*
> *Choose to keep your friend*

The many voices of the wind and Stones overlapped. Ara closed her eyes, and clapped her hands to her ears to block out the wind. "Choose!" she screamed at herself. She bit down on her lip and tasted blood.

Never roam in dark of night
off the path of lantern's light

That was when the world had started to make sense. The rules had provided them with purpose, a reason and a way to exist here. The rules had given them their services, which defined them, and the task of creating tributes which gave their days meaning. "Choose!" she screamed at herself again. Her heart skipped a beat, and she chose. *By these rules you must abide.* "I'm coming Ore!" And she ran, not through the woods, but along the path. The lanterns flashed furiously. She slipped on the mud, but still she rushed forward. Finally she found the right path.

"I'm coming, Ore!" she called, her feet slamming against the slippery wet earth between the lanterns.

"ENETHEAL!" she heard him cry out in terror. She was close. She was so close. Her footfalls pounded the earth. The path curved through the trees and connected to another. She followed the trail until she burst into the clearing. Ahead was Orin and Namin's cabin.

"Orin!" she shouted. But she could not see him. His lanterns flickered along each of the paths beyond the clearing. And then in the golden flashes, she saw movement by the cabin door.

"Orin?" She ran to him. Then she stopped and stared. An iciness filled her entire being. She could not move. The whole world seemed to have stilled except for Orin. The web-screen had been torn from the door, and ragged glistening strips hung limp and impotent. Kneeling at the threshold, covered by lacy shimmering web-fragments was Orin. His back was bowed, the muscles of his shoulders and arms working frantically. From her place in the clearing, she couldn't tell whether it was his skin giving off faint flickers of gold, or it was merely light reflected from the lanterns. She wrenched herself from her paralysis and moved quickly toward the writhing figure. And then once again she stopped to stare. Orin's hands scrambled across his face like spiders, running over the smooth skin where his eyes should have been.

KUTHAN - DAY TWELVE

Kuthan was having nightmares. Footsteps echoed in his dreams, and while he slept he was always hungry, even ravenous. Last night had been more vivid and terrible than the others. *They're getting worse.* His returned tributes had come alive in his mind.

His brother—the one who spoke through tributes in the cave—had been looking for him. In the dream he was free of the cave, and talking to Kuthan, trying to warn him of something. But the words had come out garbled and impossible to understand. Then, before they had become clear, Enetheal had appeared. The voice from the Welcome Table had filled the air around them, and Enetheal had stood there, pointing to the stairs, sentencing them both to the darkness, to the nothingness. *Is the voice Enetheal's?*

Throughout the day the dream had haunted him. He couldn't concentrate on eating or interacting with the others. His thoughts flitted between his dream and the changed tributes. Another tribute had changed. He had painted the

Sapwood, and it had come back with Enetheal in the midst of the woods. He was confident about his interpretations of the other changed tributes, but this most recent one confused him. *Is that where Enetheal is hiding? Or is Enetheal hiding something else in the Sapwood? The tree?* He needed more evidence. *Perhaps today....*

Yesterday he had painted one of the mutilated fruits. *Will my brother understand that it is a question? Will the answer make sense? Fit in with the others?* He hoped so. Today's stone had been very different. *I want to know who you are, at least to recognize you.* His brother was a friend without a face, and Kuthan planned to change that. He had drawn the outline of a face, a human face. But he tried to make it as simple as possible. *Let him fill in the details. Show me your face.* The most infuriating part about the process was waiting. *It was always yesterday's puzzle being solved, tomorrow's answer being anticipated.* It required patience.

It was near the end of the day when he finished. He decided to wait at the Sunset Altar until it was time to bring the tribute stones to the cave. There was no distinct sunset that day; the sky was overcast and grey. But Kuthan could *feel* it: the sun slowly sinking, the light dwindling. Lenya and Namin dropped off their tributes wordlessly. They were so different from his own. They were beautiful. Even Namin's. They didn't depict questions as Kuthan's did. They didn't show detail like Kuthan's. But they were beautiful. Lenya's had swirling patterns across it. And Namin's was a labyrinth of intricate lines. *Webs?* And then there was Kuthan's. His had color and illustration. Even Kuthan's simplest depictions described something, questioned it, begged to understand it.

He was so immersed in the tributes that he had not noticed when Orin and Idra arrived.

"We are finding the tree tonight." He heard Orin's voice, as if it was far off, yet he answered:

"But first I need to deliver the stones. You and Idra collect the flies and I'll meet you in the Sapwood afterward." *The Sapwood. Enetheal's territory.* That had to be where the secrets were.

"Perfect," Idra agreed.

"Umm ... I also found out something when I was with Ara last night," said Orin. Kuthan looked up, waiting for him to continue. "There were people here before us. They made tributes."

"What?" Kuthan answered sharply. Orin had said it so casually. *This changes everything. Made tributes? This is the story of my faceless friend, and Enetheal.* Did Orin understand how much this mattered?

"That's all I know," Orin continued. "But I think Ara knows more." Kuthan could hear an anger in Orin's voice that matched his own.

"My tribute stones have been coming back changed," Kuthan confessed. "I think they are telling me about the past as well." He hadn't said much about his service. *Because there is so little, I can't know for sure.* But it was also somehow personal. *I can't tell them more.* His tributes were his deepest, most intimate thoughts, concerns, conflicts. He couldn't share them so openly. Besides, he couldn't describe the experience even if he wanted to. But Ara ... Ara actually *knew things,* things that pertained to all of them with certainty. She was keeping them in the dark. Kuthan didn't like the dark. "We will find out. Ara *will* tell us." His voice trembled slightly.

"Please!" Idra pleaded. "We mustn't fight one another. Ara is working hard to understand stuff too. We need to work together. Can we focus on the missing tree right now?" *There are other things to focus on!* Kuthan loved Idra, and wanted to help her, but there were far greater things going on than her tree.

"Yes," Orin answered Idra before Kuthan could and then turned to Kuthan. "Meet you at the Sapwood." Orin turned to go. Kuthan was going to call them back, but then he froze. Ara was there. *How long has she been there?* Her eyes didn't meet Kuthan's as she handed him her tribute, but it wasn't because she was avoiding him. It was more like she didn't care. It was expected that he would just take it and deliver it for her. *She really does look down on us.*

"We need to talk," Ara told Orin.

"No, we don't," Orin answered. "We've done too much talking." He grabbed Idra's hand. "Let's go."

They left together, Ara in pursuit. Kuthan stood there for a few moments. He could go after them. He looked over at the salver, all the tribute stones were there now. *Answers await me, and a friend who cares who I am. A brother who understands.* They would meet in the Sapwood soon enough, and Orin and Idra could handle Ara for the time being ….

The stairs went on and on and on. It was still horrible, but Kuthan's mind had learned to go numb. *One step, another step, one step, another step….* He blocked out all other thoughts from his mind. If he did not, he would have to confront that which was not there. Finally a flicker of white brought him out of his trance. He rushed to the altar, and a deep satisfaction filled him.

He stared at his depiction of the bitten, mutilated fruit he had taken such care to portray. He remembered working diligently with the berry juices, trying to capture the hue of the fruit-skin, and the mutilated void where the flesh had been ripped from the rest of the fruit. It had taken a long time to dry in the sun. Kuthan noticed that his piece still had the same paint color and the same style, but the chunk that had been ripped out now looked different: Its outline was no longer bite-shaped. *It looks like a human.* A human silhouette was missing from the fruit. Kuthan's heart hammered, but he took a deep breath calming himself. *Think. Don't be overwhelmed. Think.* But emotions were part of thought. Namin's disdainful voice floated to the surface of his mind. *"Did you stop to think what might happen to us if the webs from our doors were removed?"* *Does my friend give me the same message?* His eyes flickered to Enetheal's image, ever present in Kuthan's other stones. Namin might be a traitor, but that didn't mean he wasn't right about some things. *What does Enetheal do if we break the rules?* He hoped they would never find out. *There must be a way to deal with him.* Except Enetheal was gone. Lurking in the shadows. *Waiting for us to slip. They have all forgotten him, but I have not.*

As usual he had lapsed into thought in the darkness of the cave. He had to push himself to go back to the stairs. "I need to think," he whispered as he climbed. But if he thought, then the nothingness would creep in. *Just walk. One step, one step, another step, another step, one step one step, another step, another step ....* Finally the dying daylight welcomed him from the darkness.

He looked back at the cave. He liked it better without the web. Namin had never fixed it, and it was better that way. The sky had hardly changed from when Kuthan entered the cave, but now, as he walked, it darkened. He hastened to the Sapwood to find the others.

They didn't last long in the Sapwood. Kuthan's mind had been on the tributes. He hadn't noticed when Idra started to break down. By the time he did it was too late.

"It's not here! We would have seen it by now!" Idra sobbed. Orin and Kuthan did their best to comfort her, but she was clearly done for the night. Kuthan met Orin's eyes. Unspoken they knew what had to be done. Idra had to be taken back. She wasn't happy, but she agreed.

"I'll be right back," Kuthan said, trying to reassure Orin.

"Not before I find the tree," Orin called as he left, attempting playfulness. Kuthan was unconvinced, but Idra smiled weakly.

Kuthan held Idra's hand as they walked back. He pulled her a little, encouraging her to walk quickly.

"Come on, Id. If I don't get back soon, Orin will beat me to the tree!"

She just nodded. By the time they made it out of the Sapwood she had found her voice again.

"I can go back now." Her voice did not shake. "I'm sorry I lost control."

"Yes," Kuthan agreed, looking her over. "You could go back, but I don't think it's a good idea."

When she looked up at him, he could tell he had been right. She was still on the brink of breaking down. She must have sensed it too, because she did not disagree. They walked amidst the golden flashes, and Kuthan gave her hand a reassuring squeeze. He was so focused on her that he didn't notice the melody on the air until they reached the cabin.

His voice is beautiful. Kuthan couldn't help but think it. He could feel Idra relax next to him as they walked closer. The sky was clouded, but the webs still held a silver sheen, and they could see strands forming and changing over the door. To actually see the spiders' dance Kuthan depended on lantern flashes. The little creatures rose, fell, and spun to Namin's voice. Even Kuthan fell into a trance until at last the melody slipped into the night. Only when spiders vanished into the darkness did Namin take notice of Kuthan and Idra.

"Hello," he said calmly, song still in his voice. He looked from Kuthan to Idra.

"What's wrong?" Suddenly the music was gone from his voice. Idra still had tears on her face, but she brushed them off.

"Nothing." Namin eyes were soft, but looked at her skeptically. "I was just … I'm just so scared about the missing tree," she admitted. Namin pulled her into an embrace, and she squeezed him tight. Something inside Kuthan tensed. When they broke apart, he spoke.

"We're going to take care of it, Idra," Kuthan said. Namin's eyes touched upon Kuthan's, and a flicker of emotion ran across Namin's face before it went blank again. Admiration? Praise? *It might not be too late for Namin. We might all want the same thing.* They shared a curt nod, before Namin turned to Idra.

"And I'll take care of you," Namin told Idra. He peeled aside the screen and opened it to let Idra in. She walked in. Kuthan didn't say anything, but he hoped that Namin could feel his thanks. "Be well," Namin said quietly. The web was fixed behind them, and the door closed. Kuthan breathed heavily. *Time for Orin.* He turned around and headed to the Sapwood.

Idra and Namin had gone inside just in time. The rain from earlier that day had come back, and far off Kuthan could hear the Shrieking Stones wailing. It was almost a relief to trade their wailing for the silence of the Sapwood. Even the rain quieted as it dropped into the pools of sap. "Orin?" he called. He looked around. The trees looked black, even when they were caught in the golden lantern flashes. He journeyed deeper into the Sapwood, calling out Orin's name again and again, but his voice was swallowed by the silence of the place.

He turned onto another makeshift path, this one seeming to head back toward the cabins. Out of the darkness he heard a shout. "Kuthan!" The voice was faint, but he could easily discern the fear in it. "Orin!" Kuthan called back. He began to run, straining to hear Orin's voice. The rain and flashing gold made running difficult, but the wet earth was even more of an impediment. Kuthan's feet slid on the muddy ground. "Orin!" he called again. He had reached the edge of the Sapwood. Now he looked around. In the flashing lantern light he saw muddy footprints leading away from the Sapwood and in the direction of Orin's cabin.

A feeling of dread came over him. *Why did he leave?* "KUTHAN!" He heard Orin again, this time his voice was a scream. Then Orin shouted the names of their other companions. And then most terrifying yet, "ENETHEAL!" Orin's shriek was pure terror. "Orin!!" Kuthan roared wildly. His mind was racing. *Enetheal's here! Enetheal has him!* But that could only mean one thing. Orin had broken the rules. "Orin!" he shouted at the top of his lungs. There was no reply. Kuthan hurtled along the path. "Orin!" He burst into the cabin's clearing. A flash of gold illuminated a silhouette.

"Orin!" Kuthan called out. He heard a sob in his voice. He was so relieved. Then came another flash of gold. The silhouette wasn't Orin. It was Ara. He felt his throat tighten as he flew to her.

"Where is he?"

Ara didn't say anything. Her body was shaking, her hand trembling as she stared unseeingly at the cabin door. There was nothing there but faintly glowing shards of web. He waited one moment, then two, then three. Ara remained mute.

"Where is Orin?" he demanded again. Ara just stared forward, her body shaking, her pupils dilated. *What's wrong with her?!*

"ARA!" Kuthan took hold of her shoulders, shouting into her face. "WHERE IS ORIN?!"

The smallest whisper of sound escaped her. "Enetheal." Her voice quavered. She pointed along the path that led around the slope to the other side of the island, her hand still unsteady. His heart seemed to stop and he felt rooted to the ground. *MOVE!* He shouted at himself. And suddenly, he broke free.

He tore across the clearing to the path, his feet slapping on the slippery mud. *Enetheal has taken him! What will Enetheal do to him? How could I have let this happen?* Kuthan had known Enetheal was still there. He had known Enetheal was still a threat. He had known Enetheal was waiting for his chance to impose the rules. *He wanted his rules to be broken!* And then the realization struck him. *This was my fault. I let my guard down. I let this happen.*

"Orin!!" Kuthan bellowed into the night. But of course there was no answer. Kuthan raced along the path, passing Idra's other trees. *Please! Please let me find him! Please let me save him!* Kuthan could not feel the ground with his feet; could not feel his body working. He just kept running. *Running where? Someone help me! Please! Where is Orin? Where is Enetheal?*

As if in answer, a brilliant blue-white glow emanated from the heavens, black clouds turning suddenly silver, and the star began to fall.

Kuthan had never seen anything so beautiful or so terrible. The whole night seemed to stop for the star. It curved over the island almost lazily, enveloping the land in piercing blue-white. Behind it trailed a shimmering silver tail. It captured Kuthan's eyes, demanding that he trace its path across the sky. And then Kuthan himself followed it. He ran through the forest, his gaze fixed upward. He couldn't look away from the magnificent light, or from its shimmering tail which remained etched in the sky—and then he tripped.

Together rock and root peeled away flesh. Kuthan scrambled back to his feet, not wanting to lose sight of the star. One of his hands brushed his leg and he felt a warm stickiness. He shook his head to clear his thoughts. He needed to move. *I'm coming, Orin.* He looked up again. The star had left the sky. It had landed. *It's near the beach where we arrived in the boat. The Stargazing Beach ... Lenya.* Kuthan knew where to go, and, even in the darkness, he knew how to get there.

He heard the sounds of the wind and waves as he reached the edge of the forest, and long before this he could see the water through the darkness of clouds and mist. He hurried toward the shoreline, but when he arrived at the beach, the star was nowhere to be seen. "Orin!" he called out once again. But there were only waves, sand, and shells.

This is not where the journey ends. On the far side of the beach were the stairs. They were cut into the cliff-side. The lanterns guided him up their curved path. *Orin. Orin. Orin.* He reached the top and looked out across the level toward the well. *Please.*

It was a perilous place—the sky somehow seemed very close—but Kuthan didn't have time to take in the eerie strangeness. He rushed over to the well. *I'm here.* Lenya was at the well, gazing into its depths. But there was no sign of Orin.

"Lenya! Where is he? Where is Orin!" Kuthan begged.

Lenya turned her face away from the well. She looked almost alien. Her skin glowed softly, and her hair. They both shone the same white-blue of the stars. Her hands shone most brilliantly of all, as if silver starlight was caught in the webs which encased them. But her eyes were still human. There was sadness in them.

"He's with the stars now."

Kuthan looked up, and then back to Lenya, not comprehending. But then he did understand. He had known it all along. He walked to the well's edge, and stared into the darkness.

Namin - Day Thirteen

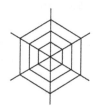

She was nestled close to him, but had long since fallen asleep. Namin continued to hum, singing without words, holding her close. At first Idra had clung to him tightly, but eventually her muscles had softened and sleep had taken her. Still his wordless music continued, soothing her, sheltering her, warding her sleep. For Idra the missing tree was the source of all their problems. Namin knew that the problem had never been the tree. The problem had been Kuthan. Kuthan had banished Enetheal, Enetheal who had done nothing but help them. Kuthan had divided the group, separating himself, Idra, and Orin from the others instead of allowing them to come to a decision as a group. Kuthan had mutilated the fruit by desecrating Namin's task. Even worse, he had made Idra lie for him. Somehow that hurt the most. Namin would never forgive Kuthan … and yet … *Kuthan wants to take care of Idra.*

He was out there now. Kuthan and Orin were both looking out for Idra. Namin would stay here until they got back. He hoped it would be soon; the night was moving on. Slowly he drifted into a half-sleep, still humming tones of calmness into the dark ….

And then Namin was in all places. He felt the wind blowing around him and through him, but his song held him together. It was music that he did not hear, a song that instead flowed through him. He was at once by the doors to each of the cabins, at the base of each fruit-bearing tree, and all over island. He felt strong. Whole. He was one with everything. Then Namin sensed an other. He recognized a familiar harmony, an old friend. But there was something else ... and then he felt it, sensed it like a wrongness. The other song. The unweaving. A strain which unraveled, which tore apart, which consumed. A threat. The song was forceful and insistent. The strains chased each other, fought against each other. But Namin's song was stronger. His was intricate, well formed, carefully woven. Namin's melody grew and filled the air; the other melodies grew fainter. Namin breathed long and low, and slipped into deep slumber.

Footsteps near the door awakened him. *They're back!* How long had he been sleeping? *Too long.* But it was still night. *Which means that they found it!* ... or that something had happened. Namin's stomach tightened as he remembered his dream. He heard the door-latch and shook Idra's shoulder gently. Then the door opened, letting in light. Lenya. She glowed softly, the woven webs on her hands brilliantly silver. Next to her was Kuthan's dark silhouette. They stood in the doorway, one light, one dark. Unmoving, unspeaking. The rain pattered softly behind them. Namin felt iciness fill his chest.

Whatever Namin felt, Idra was oblivious.

"Did you find it?" Namin put a hand around her. Orin wasn't there. But Namin would not voice this. Saying this aloud seemed awful, like it would make it so.

"Where is Orin?" Idra asked. The fear in her voice was plain. *Now we all know.*

"Gone," Kuthan whispered. They looked at Kuthan not comprehending. "Ask her," he gestured, turning to Lenya. Together, Namin and Idra turned to look at Lenya. She just nodded.

"What do you mean by gone?" Idra asked. Horror filled Namin.

"I mean he's not coming back, Idra," Lenya said softly.

"No," Idra answered slowly. She didn't believe it. It didn't seem real to Namin either. He felt like he was caught in fog or endless shadow.

"Where is Ara?" he heard himself ask. No one spoke. Finally Kuthan answered.

"She was at your cabin—but that was … was …." His voice trailed off. There was another lapse in time. Then Namin rose to his feet.

"I'll get her. You all stay here." No one argued. Namin walked past Lenya and Kuthan, closed the door, and carefully laid the web over the doorframe. He was glad to feel the rain on his face. He needed to collect his thoughts. He walked slowly to his cabin, his steps methodical and unnatural. He touched his cheek with his hand. Something was off about his sensation. Around him the lanterns flashed gold, enough so that the path was constantly illuminated. Namin closed his eyes so that the flashes flitted against his closed lids. When he opened them nothing had changed. He continued walking.

When he found her she was standing in the rain, her arms held closely to her body. She was shivering uncontrollably. Namin put his arm around her. Her skin was like ice.

"Come, Ara," he whispered hoarsely. "Let's go." It didn't even sound like him. Had he meant to say those words? When he helped her along the path, she didn't resist. They walked back together, his arm still circling her.

Kuthan and Lenya sat on Kuthan's bed. Namin wrapped Ara in Idra's blankets and Idra sat pressed against her, Namin sitting on the floor beside them. Again there was silence. They sat in the darkness, listening to each other's breathing, listening to the night around them. Finally, Namin broke the silence.

"What happened?" Again it didn't sound like his voice. Silence settled again, as if they were in the Sapwood.

"It was my fault," Idra whispered. "He was helping me find my tree with Kuthan." She let out a breath. "He promised me he would find it. He was trying to take care of me."

The silent moments resumed.

Then Kuthan took over. He cleared his throat. His voice was a monotone as he spoke.

"I took Idra back here. She was worried we wouldn't find the tree, so I brought her back here to calm down. I went back to help Orin, but I couldn't find him. Then I heard him scream. I left the Sapwood. I followed his screams … and then I found Ara." Kuthan turned to Ara. They all looked to her to continue the story. She didn't speak. And again the soundlessness lingered. They all waited, watching Ara as the silence enveloped them. Finally she found her voice.

"The Stones," she finally managed. "The Shrieking Stones tell me things. It's hard to understand what they say." Ara took a deep breath before continuing. "They told me to choose. But I didn't know what my choice was until it was too late. I thought the Stones had called me, but it was Orin. I could have saved him if I had broken the rules, left the path ... but I didn't ...." Her voice broke. They waited. She took several breaths, but still didn't continue.

"And then what?" Lenya asked gently.

"And then I found him ... tangled in the web ... his eyes ... he had no eyes ... Enetheal came ... Enetheal took him." She paused between each phrase."

"And then I found her," Kuthan completed when Ara did not. "And followed Enetheal until I reached Lenya."

They all looked at Lenya. Unlike the others, Lenya did not need time to gather herself.

"I was out looking for the star. Then it fell to me and I collected it. I brought it to the well. Enetheal came with Orin. Orin was almost gone. I dropped my star down the well, and Enetheal dropped Orin." There was sadness in her voice instead of emptiness.

"And you *let* him?" Kuthan asked.

"He was gone, Kuth." Kuthan didn't answer. None of them did. They just sat there. *I did nothing.* Namin thought. *I just sang my webs, sang to Idra ... and then I slept.*

"It wouldn't have happened if I hadn't been so stupid about the tree," Idra finally said into the darkness.

"Or if I had understood the Stones better ... and gotten Orin to understand." Ara's voice was hollow.

"If I had been more careful ...," Kuthan started.

"It did happen," Lenya said softly, but distinctly. "It isn't anyone's fault. But it *did* happen." Each of them tried to take in her words, but nothing felt real to them.

It is someone's fault. Namin's stomach turned. *Kuthan's.* Ara had struggled to understand the Stones. Idra needed her tree to provide her service. But the reason that

Orin had been taken was because he had broken the rules. *Kuthan had encouraged rule-breaking from the beginning. He drove off Enetheal who would have guided them. He divided the group. And Kuthan had left Orin alone.* But Namin couldn't speak. So like the others, he had lapsed into silence. He wanted to wake up. *This isn't real.* But it was, and the night went on and on. Until finally it started to grow light.

"It *is* someone's fault," Kuthan whispered. They could see him clearly now. "It always has been. Enetheal's." His voice had regained color and clarity.

"Kuthan ...," Lenya started.

"Orin didn't just vanish. Orin was stolen from us." Kuthan was talking to himself more than to any of them. They just watched him. None of them felt this fire, only emptiness

"I will END him," he choked out, tears in his eyes. He looked around at their blank faces and then walked out into the rain. None of them tried to stop him. The four of them stayed together, gazing listlessly at each other until the thin light of the cloud-covered day filtered into the cabin. Finally Ara got up.

"Where are you going?" Namin asked.

"To find my tribute," she said shortly. *Tribute?* The word sounded alien. Namin couldn't make sense of it. "Come," Ara added. Yet they were all getting up. Namin, too. And then they followed the path. Rain drizzled down from a grey sky. Far away they could hear Kuthan calling out for Enetheal.

"He needs time," Lenya said. Namin felt a flicker of annoyance towards her. *She's learning,* he told himself. *That makes one of us.*

When they reached the Stony Shores they all stopped. The water was dark. The sky was grey. Even the colored stones appeared dull. *What am I doing here?* Namin asked. The only response he heard was the rush of the waves, wind, and rain. He could see Ara several paces ahead, her golden curls glistening with mist. She was already starting the search for her tribute. Namin sat down on the wet rocks. A moment later Idra joined him. Lenya stood for awhile longer staring into the heavy clouds and then she, too, slipped down to sit beside them. Idra used her feet to shuffle around some stones, then picked one up randomly.

"How could he do this?" Idra finally voiced.

Orin must have broken the rules, Namin thought. *Had he found the tree? He wouldn't have known what leaving the path might mean.*

"I don't think he meant to," Namin answered. Idra gave him blank stare. "I mean, I don't think he knew what would happen."

"Not Orin! Enetheal!"

"Oh." Namin was at a loss for words. "I don't understand."

"There's not much to understand," Idra's voice cracked. "He took Orin ...." She didn't continue. She couldn't.

"I know Enetheal for what he is," Lenya said quietly. "And I think you do too," she directed this comment to Namin.

"And what is he?" Idra asked, incredulous.

"Our guide," Lenya answered simply. "He is still taking care of us."

"Our GUIDE?" Idra wore a mirthless smile. Namin had been taken aback, but then he understood:

"He's completing his service," Namin said slowly. "He is like us ... I can show you." It still didn't feel like anything was real, and yet he took a smooth stone, and rose to his feet. Lenya did the same, and moments later Idra joined them. Namin looked for Ara, and thought he could make her out in the distance. *She won't stop until she finds the right one.* Ara was dedicated, if nothing else. *She needs time alone as well.* That was one thing Namin did not need. He was empty. Confused. He knew that he did not understand. But he did not want solitude. Together the three of them headed for the Sapwood, Namin leading the way. *Orin always ran ahead ... He could be running ahead right now. Just out of sight.*

They arrived at the far end of the Sapwood, away from where Orin had laid his new paths, away from where the missing tree should have been. The rain came down steadily, trickling down their necks and backs despite the protective canopy of trees. Somehow it fell without a sound in the Sapwood, not splashing but making only silent ripples as it fell into the pools. The darkness of the day only enhanced the brightness of the twigs and bark so that the green and red stood out starkly against the grey of the mist. At least the rain was warm. Namin searched, afraid that he would not be able to find it. To him, the Sapwood had no direction. Everywhere seemed to be the center. Then, just as he was beginning to be concerned, there it was.

It was worn, and overgrown with moss and plants, but its resemblance to the Welcome Table was unmistakable.

"Enetheal's rules," Namin said. *If only I knew what they were. Then we could understand one another.*

A twig snapped and Idra gripped Namin's arm with a sudden tightness. He was here. Enetheal was here. He had once been a constant part of their days, but now the sight of him seemed unreal. Namin found himself unable to speak … and suddenly Enetheal ran.

"Enetheal, wait!" It was Lenya who called. To Namin's surprise Enetheal stopped. He was already several paces away, but when he turned, they could see him clearly. Namin found his voice.

"We know you had to do it! We don't blame you."

"Please let this end. Let us be a family again. Come back to us," Lenya begged. Namin felt the grip on his arm tighten. He looked down. Idra's face was white and tear strewn, her expression caught between fear and fury. Enetheal's eyes moved to Idra, and then he was gone.

"Idra," Lenya whispered.

"NO! Just no!" Idra hurled her stone into the nearby sap pool. It made a loud splash. And then Idra, too, ran. Lenya took hold of Namin's arm before he could start after her. Namin closed his eyes.

"It's just you and me, Len," he said sadly. Their eyes met, and he knew she understood. *It's just been us for a while.*

They watched the ripples in the sap pool where Idra had thrown her stone. Namin let his drop to the forest floor.

"There is no point in pretending," he said. After a moment, Lenya dropped hers, too.

They walked through the Sapwood until they reached Orin's paths. Then they followed the stone way that linked the trees. They no longer spoke, but they held hands. After walking past the fruit-bearing trees, they proceeded up the slope to the Welcome Table. There was no fruit on its surface, only the goblet, full, whether of rain or of sap—they could not tell. The words on the table curled around it in a spiral ….

"The rules seemed simple at first," Lenya said. Namin just nodded. They stayed at the table staring at the engraved letters, both deep in thought. To their surprise Ara arrived to find them there. She clutched her stone tightly.

"Are you two done with tributes?" she asked.

Lenya and Namin looked at one another, and then back at her.

"Yes," Namin answered for both of them, wondering whether Ara would understand. Ara closed her eyes. They stared at the table for a while longer before Ara broke the silence again:

"I'm going to finish up." She left in the direction of the Stony Shores. Together Lenya and Namin drifted to Lenya's cabin, and sat on her bed. Eventually they lay down and closed their eyes. It wasn't sleep, but it wasn't waking either. Their eyes were closed. When Ara came back, it was dark. The door creaked open.

"Namin?" Ara's voice was still hollow, but it also carried gentleness. "It's time for you to sing." Ara didn't address Lenya, but Lenya got up all the same. *I guess we're still completing our services,.* The webs were important. The song was important. *I must keep us safe.*

He went outside the cabin. The rain had stopped. It was strange to see the lanterns flickering. *It's as if Orin just lit them ... except soon they will stop. In a day, maybe two.* He watched the lanterns for a while before he began his service. Namin was silent at first. He didn't feel like it was the right time to sing, but he didn't know when that time would come. Then, when he did find his voice it felt forced and unnatural. At first it came out low and raspy. But then it began to rise. Still, something was different. There was something new in his voice. An emotion that had not yet touched him. As the spiders began to dance he closed his eyes. His tears burned hot against his closed lids. His voice rose and fell. *Lenya. Ara. Keep them safe. Orin* .... He could not untangle his thoughts, but he sang them all the same. And then he moved to Idra and Kuthan's cabin. The song began again. *Idra, please understand. Please be safe.* His melody was a prayer. But when his thoughts finally turned to Kuthan, the tears escaped his closed lids, and ran down his cheeks, and his song died.

LENYA - DAY FOURTEEN

Orin was gone. Enetheal had not watched the stars with her that night. *Did he know what was to come?* The star had arced across the island, revealing the land in silver-blue light, and landed on the beach. When she saw it rushing towards her, she had waited. It would not collide with her; it would fall before her. Her gloves had shone with silver as she touched the star. Lenya could feel the cold, but the icy pangs that shot through her were muted now. She could think. She could function. She could taste something other than starlight. *Thank you, Namin.* Part of her ached to take off her gloves, but she pushed that aside. *I am here now. This is where I belong.* She had borne her star up the steps, onto the plateau, and over to the well. Then she had let it fall.

She had looked down into the abyss. All her stars were there. Every one. When she had looked up again, Enetheal was there. He walked towards her and the well, but he did not carry a star. He carried Orin. Enetheal moved quickly.

In his arms, Orin writhed, his body convulsing, shaking, and emitting faint flickers of gold. It was as if he were connected to the fireflies he had used to light their way at night. Then Enetheal dropped Orin into the well. They held eyes for a moment, Lenya and Enetheal. Then Enetheal was gone.

Kuthan had arrived shortly after. When she told him, he had looked down the well, a mixture of hunger, horror, and disbelief lining his face.

That was last night. Now Lenya was on the beach again. Waiting. Her eyes were in the heavens, but for once it was not a star she waited for. She began to think he wouldn't come. Lenya heard wind in the trees, the waves, the sounds of frogs and crickets, but she did not notice him until he was standing over her.

"You came!" It was Enetheal. He did not lie down beside her, so she stood up. She took his hands in hers.

"Why did you run?" she asked, looking into his eyes. "Were you afraid?" He started to turn away, but her hands still held his, so he paused. "Next time don't run," she told him. He blinked in response.

Lenya decided on something new that night. Rather than watching from the beach, she led them up to the plateau. Without a star to hold, it was a long walk. The stairs went up and up and up, flashes of gold illuminating the way. *Orin is still here.* At the top they could see the whole island laid out before them; the heavens seemed close enough to touch. The moon was huge and round in the sky. Around it shone her stars. Each one was aflame with light. *Fifteen stars.* They watched until the island quieted and the wind grew still. The night held its breath with her … and then the next star fell. *Fourteen.*

Lenya began the journey. Enetheal lingered for a moment, his eyes resting on the well, but Lenya took him by the hand again. *Things have changed so much since our first night.* Lenya had been terrified then. The night had been dark, the island was scary … and Enetheal. She looked at him now. He had taught them the ways of the island, of tasks and tributes. *But his service is far from done. We still need our guide. What he did with Orin was important, I just don't know why.* Enetheal had been gone from the rest of them for so long. *Is it because he was hurt? Because he is scared? Or does he feel he can be a better guide if we don't know him?* That couldn't be true. *I would never have made it this far if Enetheal had not shared himself.*

She remembered his tears. There was no trace of tears now. His face was a mouthless mask. And yet somehow things had changed. Now *she* was leading him. And while he was still graceful, he seemed unsure of his steps. *I need to understand him. What is he thinking?* But her mind went blank when they arrived at the star ….

She had spotted it from a distance. This one was a deep dark blue. Rather than illuminating the surrounding forest, the star seemed to retain all of its light so that the woods seemed unusually dark near the star. Ordinarily the distance between the path and the star brimmed with light. Somehow this new darkness made her uneasy. What had happened to Orin? Had he left the paths? Lenya had left them before. They had followed the paths while they could, but the stars had never once fallen on them. *Is it part of my service? Does the light cast by stars provide the same protection the lanterns do?* But Orin had been in the midst of his lanterns when Ara found him. They hadn't protected him then. She looked back to Enetheal, her silent shadow. *He led me off the path the first night. My first star.* On the first night there had not even been lanterns. Yet now she felt afraid. The emotion was unfamiliar. She had not felt fear like this since the first night. She also felt a smile on her face, a strange energy.

Lenya took a breath, paused, and then ran. Branches and roots brushed against her as she sprinted into the darkness. Her heart pounded from fear as well as exertion, but the blue glow was hardly closer. She dodged low-hanging branches and leapt over the large roots and the stones she could see—she did not want to stumble. Suddenly she heard something like the snapping of twigs from the darkness just beyond. She felt a horrible thrill in her chest, and her heart raced again as she tried to pick up her pace still more. And then she was there, her hands clasped around her star.

It was cold and beautiful. She laughed weakly, but it was not from the star. From behind, she heard twigs snapping. She felt yet another rush of energy … but it was Enetheal who emerged from the bushes. She gave another weak laugh, and then felt the sudden heat of tears sting her eyes. It felt good. She looked up at Enetheal and her laughter stopped abruptly. All at once she felt sick. *What is wrong with me?* Orin was gone. Everything was falling apart. Why was she laughing?

Slowly, she understood. *I enjoyed being afraid. I have been so long without sleep. Orin is gone. I keep letting go of stars. Fear feels so much better than grief.* She looked down at her hands. Interlacing silver strands crisscrossed over them, the webs glowing faintly. *They protect me…I can feel without starlight.* But should she be able to feel at all? She had been gone for so long. She had never been close to Orin the way she wanted. *I will be here!* She promised herself. *It's too late to be here for Orin, but I will be here always!*

Enetheal was staring at her, his gaze flickering between the star and her eyes.

"I will not leave again," she promised him. His eyes fixed onto hers. "You don't need to worry. I am staying. I'm here for good now." Enetheal just stared. He watched her for so long that she began to feel uncomfortable. *What is he thinking?* Finally he broke the contact and they began their journey back to the plateau.

She stopped at the edge of the well when they arrived and looked into its chasm. She had dropped so many stars now, and Orin was there too. *Where? Where do the stars go? Where did Orin go?* It was always so hard to let go of stars, and yet this time was the easiest it had ever been.

"Fourteen more days, Ore."

When she looked up, Enetheal was still staring down the well.

"Enetheal?" He looked up. *How much do I really know him? How much of him have I just made up?* She looked into his eyes. Could she read emotion in them? Did she know Enetheal?

"I really don't blame you." She took a breath. He remained impassive as he continued to gaze into her face. "Please don't blame yourself either. We are all hurting, but we will come through this together." They held eyes a little longer. She pulled him close to her. For a moment he seemed unsure of what to do, and then he returned the embrace.

KUTHAN - DAYS THIRTEEN AND FOURTEEN

"ENETHEAL!" he bellowed into the rain. "ENETHE-AL!" he screamed. But Enetheal did not come. His only answer was a warm gentle rain that pattered softly on the ground. Kuthan wished that the winds were savage: he wanted a fight. But what would he do? What could he do if he found Enetheal? "ENETHEAL!" he shouted again. But Enetheal did not come. Enetheal did not answer. *"What would you do if he did?"* he asked himself. *"I would make him answer. I would make him bring Orin back!"* he reasoned.

Enetheal has the answer! "ENETHEAL!" his voice tore at his throat. "ENETHEAL!" They were Enetheal's rules. Enetheal enforced them. There had to be something Kuthan could do. *"We could make more tributes!"* he thought wildly. "We could make two a day, or three, or ten … as many as Enetheal needs."

"NO!" Kuthan realized he had been speaking aloud. *Enetheal can't be reasoned with. He must be stopped.*

"ENETHEAL!" Kuthan shouted. But only the rain replied. He searched desperately through the forests. *Where does Enetheal go during the days? Where does he go during the nights?* Kuthan journeyed off the path, not knowing or caring where he was. Eventually his steps took him to the Stony Shores. For a moment he didn't understand what the others were doing there. And then a horrible thought struck him. *They're searching for tributes!* How could they search for tributes now?! Kuthan wanted to go down there, to shout at them, to shove them and scream … "NO!" He turned away from the Stony Shores. "ENETHEAL!" he shouted again. *I must find Enetheal.* Did he not hear Kuthan calling?

Kuthan walked on and on. His throat burned from the shouting, but he continued to call out until his voice stopped working. He journeyed on and off the paths, switching back and forth between running and walking. He crossed the Stargazing Beach, and climbed up to the plateau with the well. He returned to the Stony Shores where Ara still labored to find her tribute. He walked the full circle around the slope that led to the Welcome Table, passing each fruit-bearing tree in turn and crossing the Sapwood. He stopped at the Welcome Table, staring at the rules before continuing to each of the cabins. He passed the Shrieking Stones, and went through the Firefly Field. The meadow was filled with frogs now, and not a glint of gold. His heart raced when he found a cabin off the path. He entered to find empty shelves. *It's where Orin got the lanterns.* Orin had never taken them there, but he had mentioned it. Orin would know where to look. Orin knew the whole island. Finally there was only one place left to go.

He stopped at the Sunset Altar. On its surface was the salver with five tribute stones. *One for each of the others. I am all alone.* He took the salver in hand. For a moment he considered throwing it away, but instead he began his walk to the Shadowed Stair. He entered the cave. The sense of entering nothingness returned, of a walk that would go on and on; but the horror of last night blotted out even this. And there was something else—How had he forgotten? He had seen the emptiness last night down the well. Suddenly the images from his changed tributes flashed through his mind:

His brother, his nameless friend who shared the darkness. He had tried to tell Kuthan. He had been sentenced to the darkness for defying the rules, and now Orin had joined him. *Orin!* Kuthan began his descent. He moved as quickly as he dared until there was nothing but his thoughts, his hammering heart, his quick breathing, and his footsteps. But he pressed on. The timelessness of the descent was lost on him this once. It didn't terrify him. It didn't matter whether a moment or an eternity passed. Kuthan reached the base of the stair.

"Orin!" he called. There was no answer. "Orin!" The flickering light was as bright as it had ever been. It caused the shadows cast by the stalactites to shift about, their reflections wavering in the water. The cave was empty. *No.* A horrible feeling filled him. Orin was gone. Without considering, Kuthan moved forward to put down the newest tributes. He placed them on the altar and started to turn away when he paused. *My own newest tribute.* He had made one yesterday, a lifetime ago, and yet he had not slept since he had left it there. *I wanted to see my brother's face,* he recalled. And some part of him still did. He turned and then froze.

Orin! The face staring out from the tribute was not that of a stranger. It was Orin's, caught in an expression between horror and despair. *"Orin!" he whispered in the darkness.* Kuthan blinked back tears. *He is here. He's trapped, but he is still here.* Kuthan could still save him. Save Orin and their nameless companion. *I can bring them both back!* Kuthan fell to his knees, his tears now spilling onto his cheeks. He dug the heels of his hands into his eyes roughly, wiping his tears away, wanting to see his tributes clearly.

There they were. Enetheal on the Stony Shores, demanding their obedience and slavery, their brother alone in his defiance. Enetheal being banished from the Welcome Table, their brother now joined by Kuthan, Idra, and Orin. Enetheal casting their brother into the darkness, pointing him down the stairs. Enetheal standing high upon the Welcome Table, dominating all of them with his rules.

His fifth stone was the most important. It was the first one in which Enetheal was absent. The Welcome Table was broken. Originally it had depicted Kuthan leading his friend up the stairs. *This one is it. The answer.* With Enetheal gone the rules would end. *With Enetheal gone we shall all be free. Orin will come back. I WILL bring him back.*

The sixth image had been a warning. Kuthan had asked about the mutilated fruit. Where the image had showed a piece missing from the fruit there was now a human silhouette. *If I had just understood then* …. But the seventh image was hope: Orin could still be saved.

"Orin! Orin, I will save you." Kuthan closed his fist around the rock. His hand shook. *Enetheal can't hide forever. And then the rules end. It will be a new world. We can make our own rules.* He smiled for a moment. He was shaking. He thought he was sweating, but when he touched his skin, it was dry. He couldn't tell whether he was full of

rage, or hope, happiness or despair. And then it was as if a voice whispered directly into his mind. *He is still gone. Enetheal has him. The rules have him.* He held the stone with Orin's face close to his chest.

"I will come back for you," Kuthan promised. *Can he hear me? Can they both hear me?* He spoke aloud to the brother with no face. The brother with no voice:

"Guide me. Help me do what I must!" Then he put the stone back on the altar and turned toward the stairs.

Eternity in nothingness meant nothing, even more so. *I will bring Orin back. And I'm not alone.* He felt his brother next to him. Together they walked up the stairs. Two distinct sets of footsteps; no echo. *We are together.*

He found Idra where he knew she would be. She wasn't skipping stones. She just stared.

"Kuth- ...," she whispered hoarsely, "I never let Orin eat first ...."

"Idra!" he cut her off. "We're not done yet." She looked up into his eyes, and he saw her despair.

"Orin's gone, Kuth," she whispered.

"NO HE ISN'T!" Kuthan grasped her shoulders, giving her a shake. *She needs to understand.* "No he isn't," he said again, his hands falling to his sides. He could not bear to hear her say it. *It could become true.* He brought his face close to Idra so he could feel her breath.

"Enetheal stole Orin. He's hiding him. We WILL get Orin back. We must!"

"Kuthan," she sobbed, her voice was full of despair and incredulity. *She doesn't believe me. How could she? She has not seen what I have.* Kuthan needed to make her understand. So he told her.

"My tribute came back changed." But he heard the self-doubt in his own voice.

"Doesn't it always!" Idra cut him off.

"Listen! My tribute came back changed. Orin's face was on it. Orin was trying to speak!"

"No more lies, Kuthan. Lenya and Namin have deceived themselves to think Enetheal is helping us by getting rid of Orin. I fooled myself pretending there was another tree. And you are deluding yourself now. ORIN IS GONE!"

"NO!" Kuthan shouted. "HE IS NOT!" His words hung in the air. He could hear the desperate self-delusion in his own voice and it made him angry. Idra turned away. Kuthan wanted to shake her again, but he restrained himself. *It is Enetheal who must answer.*

"Where is Enetheal?" he asked, as much for himself as for Idra. Yet to his surprise, she answered.

"I'll show you." They walked together without speaking. Once they entered the Sapwood even their footfalls joined the silence. As they walked the sky began to darken. Kuthan looked around but there was no sign of him. *Enetheal is gone ... and so is Orin.* But he rejected his own thought. He had found the answer in the cave.

"This is it," Idra said. Kuthan looked around, but saw only a large, flat, moss-covered rock. It was very like the Welcome Table, but there was no sign of Enetheal.

"What?"

"He's not here. I think he only comes when Lenya and Namin are around." She stopped for a moment. They slipped into silence again.

"How could they!" Idra burst out without warning. "How could they care for Enetheal now!" Kuthan didn't answer. *And yet somehow you still made a tribute,* Kuthan thought darkly. *You still fulfilled his rules.*

"There has to be something we can do," she finally said. Kuthan began to walk towards the cabins.

"There is," he said quietly. They arrived just before nightfall. They lay in their separate beds, Kuthan deep in thought, Idra drifting into a light slumber. Kuthan closed his eyes. He was exhausted, but he would not sleep. Outside, the spiderweb screen gave off a dying flash of silver. He did not sleep, but he did dream. It was his old dream, but this time there was clarity ....

The world was vivid, alive beyond reality. And his tributes, all of the tributes were alive. There were the colors of sunset and starshine, trees and sap, flowers and waves. And there were the sounds of wind and rain, song and laughter. There were the textures of waves and sand, bark and flesh. Somehow he was both relaxed and full of energy all at once. He felt more fulfilled than he ever had.

And then there was Enetheal. Where Enetheal walked the world darkened and a mist covered the land. Until it was just Kuthan, Enetheal, and the Welcome Table ... only the Welcome Table was not as it normally was. Now it was formed from tribute stones. Around the table there arose faded forms ... silhouettes that Kuthan knew to be his companions. One by one, each emerged from the mist around the table, laid another stone, and then returned into the mist. And with each added tribute stone Enetheal looked more menacing. His form grew larger, his nose more beaklike, his shadow longer. Kuthan could feel his own form shrinking.

Then a voice spoke.

"A Tribute there must be. A Tribute to end all tributes. A Tribute that defies the rules. A Tribute that brings the table crumbling down. Defy the rules. Defy Enetheal. Undo Enetheal. Undo the rules."

And then his brother was there. He placed a rock in Kuthan's hand. And in Kuthan's hand was a Tribute. Kuthan hurled his Tribute at the Welcome table with all of his strength. The table crumbled. Enetheal crumbled. And emerging from the rubble was Orin. The mist disappeared. And the world melted back into Paradise.

Then the dream was gone, and Orin with it. Once again the world was without hope. *But I am still here.* Kuthan thought. *I will not accept this world. I will not accept the rules upon which it has been built. I will not accept rules that would take Orin way. I will not accept a world without Orin.*

"A Tribute there must be," he whispered. He blinked back tears. "A Tribute to end all tributes."

Breakfast was silent. Idra divided the first fruit into five parts. *Orin's fruit.* Kuthan knew this, but he did not say it. Then they each ate their own full fruit as well. Finally, at the end of their meal, Ara spoke.

"Tributes."

Kuthan was the first to get up.

It was a beautiful day that awaited them at the Stony Shores. The sun was bright and gold. It shone off the water, its reflection dazzling. Its warmth filled the day. The sky was a brilliant, piercing blue; the breeze was gentle. They spread out to find their tributes. Kuthan moved back and forth over the shore of stones. He looked near the forest's edge, the shallows, and everywhere in-between. He knew he would find it. And he did. It was buried under a few others, but he knew it was the one. It alone felt real, as real as the world he had dreamed. It fit his outstretched hand perfectly. It was grey and rounded, but it was rough to the touch. *There would be no decoration. This is it. This is my Tribute.*

He walked to the Welcome Table, and then waited. He reread the rules over and over. He relived his dream. He relived their time on the island. He relived Orin. As he saw the sun was drifting toward the horizon, Kuthan got up. It was time to find the others.

"Come," he said to Ara, and Ara followed.

"Come," he said to Lenya, and Lenya followed.

"Come," he said to Namin, and Namin followed.

"Come," he said to Idra, and Idra followed.

Kuthan led them. And they followed Kuthan. He led them from the world of sound into the silent world of the Sapwood. The bark was alive with redness, the twigs a brilliant green. The sky was blue, and the sun gold. Sap flowed into the pools, the pools which reflected all. But all was reflected in silence. Kuthan's breaths were slow. His heart beat, steady and strong. His skin prickled. He felt too hot and too cold at the same time. But part of him lived outside of his body as he walked. He led them far from Orin's paths, to the far end of the Sapwood. There he found Enetheal's table ... and he found Enetheal.

Enetheal was staring at the ancient stone fixture. *What does it mean to him?* But then he stopped. The time for questions was over. His choice was made. He would not go back now. He would not succumb to indecision and fear. Enetheal began to turn away, but Lenya called out to him.

"Enetheal." She said it quietly. Endearingly. Enetheal turned back. "No more running." Enetheal turned so that he was facing them.

Kuthan blinked. It seemed like an eternity ago that he had chased after Enetheal, arriving at the well's edge too late. An endless time in which he had searched the island, screaming for Enetheal. An endless time in which he had entered the cave below the island, still hoping that Orin could return. And now at eternity's end he held the last Tribute. Orin was gone. But the rules had to end. Enetheal had to end.

Kuthan's body was beginning to betray him. He felt unsteady. His shoulders and arms were shaking. He must be strong. Enetheal had ended Orin. Kuthan must end Enetheal. For Orin. Around them the sap coursed relentlessly down the trees.

Kuthan leapt forward. In his hand he held the last Tribute. He raised his arm, rock held high. Enetheal lifted his hand, shielding his face. Kuthan smashed his tribute onto Enetheal's head. There was a horrible thud of rock meeting bone, and both figures collapsed to the forest floor. Kuthan brought the rock down again and again, not stopping until all of it was covered in blood. Until Enetheal was still.

The others remained silent, unmoving. And then, as they stood, the stillness of the Sapwood transformed into sound. Sap gurgled now as it coursed down the trees. And as they listened the gurgling became trickling, the trickling became dripping, and finally the dripping slowed to a single drop, and then, once again, to silence.

Don't stop. Kuthan turned and ran, leaving the little group, still unmoving, behind. *Let it be done. Please let it be done.*

Around him sap-sounds whispered back to life. It was a gentle trickle this time, only a murmur of liquid washing over bark. He stared as he passed the trees, seeing now that the sap seemed to rise upwards from the pools, flowing up the trunks, up into the trees. Kuthan forced himself to continue, knowing that he must not pause, not even to try to understand what he was seeing.

Please let it be done. Tears streamed from his eyes, blurring his vision, but still he did not stop. The blood on his tribute caught the last light of the sun as Kuthan reached the stairs. He stumbled down into the darkness, his face streaked with sweat and tears, his body smeared with blood. But it would not end. The stairs would not end. *Please let it be done.* And then he reached the landing. Kuthan collapsed at the altar, and laid down the last Tribute.

PART TWO - REAWAKENING

The world was broken. And yet time went on. Enetheal's blood started as a gush, but soon slowed to a stream. As it entered the clear sap-pool next to where he had fallen, its redness expanded like a cloud. At first it was bright, but the red darkened and thickened as more blood pulsed in. It spread across the pool until the tree was surrounded in crimson.

Sound had entered the Sapwood. It was not the trickling of blood. It was sap. Now it made noise as it entered the pools. But as the flow of blood slowed, so did the flow of sap. And when the blood finally thickened and stopped, the sound also ceased, and sap flowed no more. Silence again filled the Sapwood. Unlike before, this quiet seemed as if it were holding its breath. Then, ever so slowly, the sap began to trickle upwards.

"What … have we done?" Ara asked.

"He didn't do it," Idra said. There was something off about her eyes. They were glassy, and distant. "He didn't do it" she said again.

Namin and Lenya stood motionless.

None of them had moved to stop Kuthan. They had not understood what was about to take place. They had not known it could be; could not fathom it even as it occurred before their eyes. They were going to find Enetheal, to try to understand what had happened to Orin, but now Enetheal was gone. Their questions, their thoughts, their feelings were suddenly absent. Their minds were a void.

"What have we done?" Ara asked again and again.
"He didn't do it," Idra repeated like a chant.

As time seeped on, it began to appear as if all the sap-pools were darkening. Then it became clear that it was the sky: Twilight was passing quickly, unnaturally, as if light was being sucked from the world.

"We need to leave," Lenya said slowly, but she did not move.

"But he didn't do it," Idra answered.

"The sky is almost dark," Lenya continued. But it didn't seem like Lenya. Namin was silent.

Ara found herself. She was used to losing herself and finding herself again. The Shrieking Stones had taught her that much. She took Lenya's hand, and placed it in Namin's. Then she placed Namin's free hand in Idra's. Finally she took Idra's free hand into her own and began to lead them through the Sapwood. As she walked a dream floated up to the surface of her mind. It was a dream in which Enetheal was leading them and yet they all ended up lost. A dream in which the Shrieking Stones had the answer that Enetheal did not. Could they have an answer? Surely there was none. Her mind was numb.

Twilight melted into dusk as they moved. And dusk began to darken. The stars made themselves visible, and through the trees they could make out a large full moon. The light did little to ward off the dusk, so they hurried on while darkness settled about them. Just as it became hard to see, a silver light shone from their midst. It was Lenya. Her gloves were glowing. And as moments passed, they began to glow more brightly.

Behind them there was something wrong about the sound of the woods. Kuthan? But it was not noise that followed them. It was almost a lack of sound, a stillness that pursued. It was as if the world behind them were deadening. Lenya's gloves began to glow even more brightly. Behind them Ara could make out a silhouette.

"Enetheal?" she whispered. The form was too tall to be Kuthan. And something was wrong with it. Its form was grey, the color of dusk ... and she couldn't make out any features.

Idra's voice broke. "He's come for us!" she cried out softly, her voice full of terror. "It's over, Enetheal has come for us."

"It's not Enetheal," Lenya started ... but her voice betrayed her uncertainty.

"Quiet," Namin hissed. It was definitely coming for them.

"Move! Now!" Ara whispered hoarsely. Somehow, despite everything, they had energy. They ran. Their feet echoed against the forest floor. They wound between trees, and bushes, leaping over fallen forest debris. "Faster," she pushed. It was getting hard to see. They struggled to avoid tripping over roots or running into bushes and trees. Exhaustion was catching up to them. They could only sprint for so long before they collapsed, legs burning from exertion.

"Hide," Idra whimpered. They crawled under a small clump of bushes, wrestling with the sharp, stiff branches that scratched at their faces and shoulders until they were safe inside, hidden behind leaves. They struggled to contain their rapid, heavy breathing.

"Did we make it?" Idra panted in a whisper. Ara peeked through the bushes. She didn't see anything.

"I don't know," she answered quietly.

"He knows we broke the rules," Idra said, fear in her voice.

"But we didn't," Ara said.

"We didn't deliver tributes," Lenya explained, shaking her head slowly.

"But I did," Ara whispered frantically, trying to contain the terror in her own voice ... "for all of us."

"It's still nighttime," Namin said, his voice dead. "The paths will be gone tonight."

"We could go to the cabins" Lenya suggested. "We would be qui- ...."

But her voice fell silent. Lenya's gloves had begun to glow silver once again.

"Hide them!" Ara commanded. Lenya was fast. She held her hands close to her belly, shielding them with her arms, curling around them, but she couldn't hide the glowing light that leaked through. Idra peered through the leaves. For a moment the forest seemed empty ... and then she saw It.

The Former knew that they had broken the rules. They knew without looking at each other that they could not face the Terror. They must remain hidden.

Its shape was human, but It was pale grey, Its edges blurred. It was tall, like Enetheal, and like Enetheal, It was thin. The Former had Enetheal's graceful loping gait as well. But that is where the similarity ended. This Figure was without a nose, or eyes, or ears. Even worse was the mouth. As It approached, a great gaping hole opened up where a mouth should have been, vanishing and reforming, so that there seemed to be nothing else about the Figure save this one horrific chasm.

The sound which came from the Former could have been called a low whisper, a hiss, or a croak, but none of these names would have captured its essence.

When It spoke they were overcome with dread. The Former's voice was horrible not in its sound, but in its familiarity. It was more familiar than waves on rocks, or wind in trees. More known to them that the light of the sun, stars, or moon, or even the darkness. Easier to recognize than warmth or coldness, than hunger or thirst. The voice was as their own heartbeats, their very breath. It penetrated their minds as it had when they had first encountered the rules.

Rules by which you must abide
Rules besmirched and cast aside
Now the children try to run
Now the children seek to hide

The Former drew closer. And where It walked, the world seemed to shimmer and fade even as Its own dark-ness grew more distinct. They looked around, desperate for absolution. Perhaps there was a path nearby. Perhaps Orin's dying lanterns could still protect them:

No longer safe in lantern's light
No longer safe in dark of night
The paths are gone, and gone the sun
And now the days forever done

They shrank even further, clinging hopelessly to one another as the Former approached. But none of them could shield the others from judgment:

In light of sun you were to lay
a gift of thanks a gift of praise
But falsely made and falsely laid
your gifts have brought the end of days

Its voice had grown louder as it drew nearer. And faster. Every word was distinct:

You had a service to provide
but every service was defiled
Now you've sacrificed your guide
Your acts cannot be reconciled

The Former spoke neither with sorrow nor with regret. It spoke with triumph, with desire, with hunger:

Foolish children thought to play
to cast aside the Former's laws
Now lost is night and lost the day
and gone your lives, your dreams, your flaws

The mouthlike space opened even wider. The Former's voice could not be resisted. The Former was the voice of Truth. The voice of Being. It seemed right to draw near to the voice. A relief to embrace Its Judgment. A wrongness to do anything but to accept their fate.

They fell down before the Former … but Namin stood in front of the others. The voice of the Former carried *the Unweaving, the Unmaking, the End.* And Namin *rejected* It. His voice, his prayer, had always belonged to his family. Namin raised his voice against the Former, crying out his defiance, crying out for creation, crying out for all of them.

The Former moved to devour them, but Namin's prayer had been heard. They came from the trees around them. They came from the bushes, plants, and forest floor. They came from the world which shimmered around and underneath the Former. The spiders came. They leapt about the children, rising with Namin's voice, spinning silvery silk strands all about and over them. The silken webs glowed with energy.

The Former raged in hunger and desperation. But Its screams did not quell Namin's song. Namin sang on and on and on, the webs forming about them, shielding them, protecting them. The Former searched for a weakness, circling and shifting about them, frantically trying to reach them. But Namin sang until the children were surrounded by webs. Until the Former was no longer there. Until they were safe. And even then he still sang.

NAMIN - DAYS FIFTEEN TO SEVENTEEN

Namin sang. He sang for all that had been, all that was, all that might be. He sang against the Unweaving, against the song that would undo and consume the world. The others clung to him. They held close to his body, his voice, his prayer. The song came forth from Namin, until he did not know whether it was he who sang, or whether he was merely the way by which the song entered the world. The air around them howled, as tree-limbs and bushes were battered by the wind. The trees groaned, and the Shrieking Stones added their voices to the cacophony. But Namin's voice was stronger, and the winds finally calmed. High above them the moon hung in the sky, large and serene, spreading soft white light over the island. Even in the glow of the full moon, they did not fail to notice the star. It seemed to pull the moon's light with it when it arced down from the heavens, so that an aura of moonbeams trailed in its wake. Namin felt the others tracing the star's path as well—Lenya more attentively than the others. But when it landed far across the island, they huddled against Namin once again.

Ara was the first to succumb to sleep. Soon Idra's eyes closed as well, her head against Namin's shoulder. Lenya lasted longer, her gaze out to where her star lay waiting, yet she remained still, until finally even she closed her eyes. Namin sang, and the night went on. When a pale light that was not moon or stars began to fill the sky, Namin took a deep breath and then released it very slowly.

The others woke moments after his voice was still.

"The day came," Idra said incredulously. She smiled weakly. A bird chirped, and then another. Slowly the land started to awaken. And despite the horror of the last night, the world still held beauty.

"What do we do now?' Ara asked.

"I need to get my star. Now," Lenya said hurriedly.

"What?" Ara exhaled in disbelief. Namin's brow creased, but he remained silent.

"Don't you see?" Lenya gestured to the webs about them. "Our services still matter! Our world still matters. We still matter." No one answered her.

"Help me out," she said, gesturing to the webs. And they did. It wasn't until they were completely free of the webs that they realized that the world had transformed.

Wherever they looked there was contrast. There were dead trees, fallen, rotting. But sprouting up from them were tiny silver shoots and brilliant wildflowers. The bushes, too, were affected; some barren and decayed, others covered with leaves and silver-white flowers. Where there was new life there were strokes of silver. Sounds were the same, though; the waves washing in the distance, and the wind in the trees. Even the way branches swayed in the breeze was unchanged. And the birds sang the same songs.

As soon as they were free of the webs Lenya set off. The others looked at Namin. He smiled, pulling them both into a close embrace. He didn't speak. To speak would be to end the song, and the song was not done. Lenya was right, the services did still matter. The world still mattered. They still mattered. *By my voice we were delivered—my voice will bring deliverance.* Namin began to walk, and as he walked he sang. This time his voice was more purposeful. As he moved, the spiders followed his song.

He traveled until he found a path, and then started to follow it. Spiders jumped between the trees alongside, spinning strands of web along the way. They spun webs over and between the lanterns. Namin walked along the path connecting the cabins. At each clearing he wove strands around the circle of trees and renewed the web screens at the entrance before continuing to the path on the other side.

When he had finished with the cabin paths, he moved to the stone circle. He protected the stone ways and the great fruit-bearing trees from which Idra brought food. As he sang, Idra offered him fruit, but he shook his head and continued. The sun arced across the sky, its gold shining magnificently on the silver-strewn world. He walked around the loop, and through Orin's makeshift paths in the Sapwood, walling them in with strands of web. He webbed the path to the cave. He wove a new web over the stairway opening.

Namin sang along the path to the Sunset Altar, catching the last light of the day, before continuing. The spiders followed him to Orin's Firefly Field. As dusk settled, the fireflies arose from it, emitting brilliant flashes of gold. Orin's song was woven into the webs, and the fireflies followed Namin's voice as he continued to sing. They zigzagged, becoming caught in Namin's web. Namin saw the little insects struggle, and moved on, luring them into his snares. *My world. Orin's world. A world of life and death side by side.* Sometimes a spider paused her spinning to eat a firefly, but there were many of the tiny living lights so that the paths were illuminated in gold once more. *Were our services always the same? Did they both provide protection? Or were they opposite? Did Orin's lanterns allow for safe passage, and my webs prevent passage?* This song would do both.

If the Former was anywhere, it was far from Namin's voice. And Namin's voice was everywhere. The others would be safely webbed into their cabins. The island paths and all the special places would be safely webbed as well. There would be no place for the Former. Namin sang into the darkness letting his eyes close as he walked. His song was his guide.

He found another of Orin's paths, and webbed it in in silver silk, the golden flashes from the trapped fireflies lighting the trail behind him. It seemed as if the world moved with him. The stars and moon, the gentle breeze, the spiders, the fireflies. And these were not the only ones. As he sang, he felt the others join to walk with him. They traveled beside him, only becoming visible in the flashing golden light of the fireflies. Although he knew he had never seen them, they were familiar to him. They appeared singly, yet as he looked carefully, he saw that there were little groups of them. And then he realized that Enetheal was there too; Enetheal was walking with him. He was there and he had a mouth. It was strange to see him with a mouth. Enetheal did not speak, but he walked with Namin along the path now lined with flashing golden webs. All of them were there. *Only in Orin's light. Orin is here too.* All of them were there. The whole world was one: that which was, is, and would be. Namin wove it together. *So long as the Former is separate from the world these strands will hold this existence together.*

By the time dawn came, Namin had webbed the paths to the Stargazing Beach, the plateau with the well, the Stony Shores, and the Shrieking Stones. The trails and where they led had crisscrossing spider silk all about them. But still Namin sang. He began to walk off of the paths. The new webs did not protect all of the island, but they held it together. Night fell, and day came again. Namin sang. On the third morning of his singing he arrived at the Welcome Table. It was there that he finally allowed his song to end. Wordlessly the others joined him. Idra gave him the first fruit. When Namin saw their eyes he wanted to continue, to never stop singing. But the song was finished.

Namin ate. He had never tasted anything so delicious. And then he slept.

LENYA - DAYS FIFTEEN TO SEVENTEEN

"*No more running,*" she had told him. He hadn't run. He had stayed for her. *Because he trusted me. And then ...* and then Kuthan .... The Sapwood had transformed. The pools of sap had started to drain upward, but for them, time had stopped. *Because he trusted me. Because I told him to stay.* She had heard herself trying to get the others to move as the light vanished from the world, but her heart hadn't been in it. The Former had come. It seemed they had been waiting for the Former a long time. When It had spoken there was starlight in Its voice. But when Namin had sung, she had heard her own promise in his song. *"I will be here always."*

The star had fallen in the middle of the night. She had yearned to retrieve it, but she knew she must wait. They held onto Namin through the night, clinging to his body, to his voice. Around them, sheltering them, were the webs, and outside was the Former. They waited. The night went on and on and on. Yet despite everything, dawn crept into the world. When Namin's voice stopped, Lenya had opened her eyes. She rose to her feet.

"The day came," Idra sighed with wonder.

"What do we do now?" Ara asked, turning to Namin.

But Lenya answered, "I need to get my star. Now."

"What?" The disgust in Ara's voice was plain.

She knows what I was. But not what I am now.

"Don't you see?" Lenya gestured to the webs about them. "Our services still matter! Our world still matters. We still matter." No one answered her. If they didn't understand now, they would soon. But right now she had to get out of their webbed sanctuary. She had to retrieve her star before it was too late.

"Help me out," she pleaded desperately. They did. As soon as the webs had been moved aside, Lenya sprang through. *Our services still matter.* Namin's song had proved that. *Our services are our protection. A way to take care of one another. A sacrifice. A promise of making things new.* They had to continue.

The world had transformed. Around her was death and ruin, but there was also life and renewal. The sun filled the air with warmth, but the ground was cool. Not just cool. The ground was cold. And then she felt its energy. It surged up through her in a sensation of joy and dread.

Lenya began to run. As she drew nearer, the effect of the fallen star was more evident. The land itself was silver-strewn, as well as the bushes, and trees, even the birds. When the gold of the sun entered the world, the light was brilliant but horrifying.

Lenya drew even closer. The brush grew thicker. The trees and grass grew taller. The young bushes bore flowers with silver petals and silver thorns. As she grew nearer to her star, Lenya was careful of the sharpness of the new growth; it was hard not to get tangled. In the shade of the trees the bushes were denser, stronger, more apt to cause difficulty with passage, so she tried to cut through treeless areas where the sun shone.

Finally, in the midst of the foliage, she found her star. Branches and roots had ensnared it and she wrestled with them for a time, but the star was for her, and finally she wrenched it free. *I waited too long. Now the world has tasted starlight.* There would be no going back. She looked down at her gloved hands. Far off she could hear Namin singing.

A new world. Lenya looked to the life around her, the new saplings shooting from the earth, the foliage which had grown about and around the star, even the birds ... all strewn with silver. *No. An old world. Clinging to song and starlight.* Lenya moved quickly. The longer the star was here, the worse it would be for this world.

Lenya ran, holding the star close, fleeing from the new day which rose up behind her. *This is wrong. Night and day should dance, but they should never become one.* The star stole from the newborn day, and the day stole back from the star. *Is this how my service was defiled? Did The Former know what was to come?* When Lenya reached the beach she paused to look down at the star in her hands.

Its glow was hard to see in the daylight. A thin layer of silk crossed between her hands and the star. *Perhaps I was meant to fall prey to the stars.* She still longed to tear off the gloves, to become one with it. *Namin's gift, my life, my promise.* Lenya continued. The stairs rose along the cliff. She had never climbed them so quickly. By the time she reached the top her legs were burning. The well stood waiting. In the sunlight the star was beautiful. The silver and gold shone as one light. It was dazzling. *But it must not be.* Lenya lifted the star and then released it into the darkness. She felt dread and relief all at once, and knew that the day was now right.

Yet still there was sorrow, regret in letting go of another star. *I must not look back.* It was hard not to think back on her stars, on all of them she had let go, the days between them, the things she might have done differently. What if she had not been so captivated by them? What if she had been more present? Things would have happened differently. *No.* She was here now. She would not look back.

During that day, she prepared herself for her next star. And when it fell, she was swifter than she had ever been. She did not slow during her journey, or even when she returned to the well. It was only after she dropped it into the abyss that she gazed into the darkness after it.

When she next dropped a star, she left the plateau the moment its light was gone.

IDRA - DAYS FIFTEEN TO SEVENTEEN

Now it was just Idra and Ara. Namin had returned to his song, and Lenya to her starlight. But Idra and Ara had no songs to sing, nor stars to carry. They began to walk. It was strange leaving the sanctuary Namin had made them. Their first few steps were unsteady. Idra reached to clasp Ara's hand. Ara tensed, but then she held on tightly. Together they entered the new world. The landscape was transformed. The night's storm had altered everything. There was decay, but also life. And the land seemed to glow. *The star.* Idra remembered the night she had accompanied Lenya, and the way the star had transformed the tree when it had fallen into its branches.

But when she looked into Ara's eyes she realized ... *Orin's gone. Enetheal's gone. Kuthan's gone ... and Ara's gone. Am I gone?* She knew neither what she was nor who she was. *I get the fruit,* she remembered. *Is that who I am?* The warmth of the sun now touched the trees around them. Slowly Idra guided them. They didn't say anything. There was nothing to say. Ara understood the blessing that silence was, and now she did too. They drifted along the paths. The sun was pleasant. It did not change anything, but it felt good to feel warmth in the world. They reached Idra's cabin. Ara stood back while Idra pulled aside the web. Idra was quick. She went in, came out, now with her basket, and took Ara's hand again. Wordlessly they continued their journey.

The tree had borne fruit as if nothing had happened. It had remained unchanged. Idra climbed. Ara waited, and Idra came down, her basket full of fruit. Then they continued their journey and soon arrived at the Welcome Table. Idra put the basket down between them. They stared at it for a while, neither of them making a move to eat. Neither of them spoke. The sun moved across the sky. Finally, Idra could not stay any longer. She picked up the basket and waited for Ara to get up, too. Ara remained unmoving, so Idra turned and left.

She did not know where her feet would take her, only that if she kept them moving they would take her somewhere. *Like Orin.* Except Orin had revelled in going somewhere. It gave him purpose. *But I don't understand going anywhere. I don't understand why time still passes.* If the world had just stopped, it would have been easier. But it went on. And she could not sit still. She heard Namin singing. Without being aware of it, she moved towards the song.

He was beautiful. He strode forth with purpose, his voice strong. The whole world listened. She offered him one of the fruits from her basket, but he shook his head and continued to sing. It hurt. She knew he had to continue, but it hurt all the same. Soon his song faded through the trees and Idra was alone once more. Once again her feet started to move. At first they moved her nowhere in particular, but then they seemed to know where she needed to go. She arrived at Sunset Altar, and then along the rocky coast until she finally reached her destination.

She looked at flat stones which they had once collected, and then slowly picked one up. She sent it skipping over the water. The surface was smooth and it hopped seven times before sinking. Each landing place left a growing ring. These ripples expanded outward, flattening until they faded into the stillness.

Idra closed her eyes. In her mind Orin was still there. Still next to her. Laughing. Smiling. Complaining. Comforting her. She remembered Kuthan crying out to her that Orin was still here. And for just a moment, Orin was there. She heard him sigh.

"Hi, Ore," Idra whispered. But when she opened her eyes, he was gone.

She took another rock. This time instead of skipping it, she hurled it into the water. It made a loud splash. The ripples were larger, and there were more of them, and still they expanded outward into an ever widening circle, until again, they waned to nothing. No more ripple. No Orin.

She reached for another rock, flinging it, too, into the water. And this ripple again died away to nothing. She took another, and another, hurling them one after another until the water was broken up about her, and there were ripples everywhere. But then they were all gone.

"How could you?" Idra whispered. "How could you leave!??" Her voice echoed "… leave … leave … leave." But then it, too, diminished to nothing. She threw the rest of the rocks with fury. Then she started to throw pieces of fruit. She tossed the fruit until the basket was almost empty. The fruits bobbed up and down in the water, mocking and ridiculous. She grasped the last fruit, brought it to her mouth and ripped out a chunk with her teeth.

An explosion of flavor filled her mouth; tears filled her eyes. She closed them and then, against her closed lids, there was color. And Orin was hers.

"I'm so sorry Ore," she wept. He didn't answer. She knew he couldn't speak. But it felt as if he was there.

"It was my fault. It has always been my fault." The tears began to flow freely.

"I couldn't complete my service. I was the first to fall." Her voice shook. Orin's eyes stayed fixed on hers.

"I was a coward. I couldn't face it on my own. So I pulled you in. And now you are gone." She began to sob. He gestured to the fruit in her hands. She took another bite. Again sweetness filled her mouth. And Orin seemed more solid. She kept her eyes closed.

"I told Kuthan where to find Enetheal. I didn't know what was going to happen. I didn't think about it." It was hard for her to make out her own words as she choked up on tears and fruit. But Orin understood.

"Kuthan … Enetheal … my fault. All my fault. And you. You're not even here." Her lids flashed gold. Her eyes opened. And for a second, just a second, Orin was there.

Her tears stopped. Her breath caught. "Orin," she sighed. He was already gone. But she was sure that she had seen him. Sure that he had been there. Sure he was there now. "Orin?" There was no answer. Far away she could hear the wind calling through the Shrieking Stones.

There was another flash of gold. And then another. But neither of the golden flickerings brought back her friend. *He was here. He is here.* "Bring me Orin," she told the fireflies. She waited for him to appear in a flash of gold. She wanted to cry. There was a flicker, but no sign of Orin. The tears started silently. *And I told Kuthan not to delude himself.* The fireflies continued to blink and flash, off and on, another and then another. Each flash was further away. There were no lanterns and yet there seemed to be a path of sorts.

The sun was setting, but Idra didn't care. There would be time before the sky was completely dark, and besides, now the dark held no secrets. No more terror. She followed the path. She hesitated when the golden illuminations continued into the Sapwood. *This is where it all happened. Where Orin left the path. Where Kuthan murdered Enetheal. Where the Former came to devour all of us.* Nonetheless she entered, following the flashing lights until she was near the heart of the wood. The flashing seemed to pause, making her aware of the depth of the darkness. There was still a paleness in the sky, but the forest knew that night was soon to come. She looked around for more firefly light, but there was nothing. Just empty forest. And then she looked down.

On the forest floor was Orin's net. She looked around for another flash of gold. But still there was none. *He led me to his net.* She bent down and picked it up. She was surprised by how light it was. Her basket was much heavier. She held them side by side. *One for holding fruit, and one for holding fireflies*—then, remembering Lenya's gloves—*and one for holding stars.* Namin's gifts. It seemed strange. She thought of the three services. Each was essential. But hers seemed most important. Whatever the lights of gold or silver did, how could they compare with her service? Her task was to nurture the others, to bring them the sustenance to live and laugh and thrive.

"This is still my service," she said, looking down at the basket. Her gaze moved to the net. "And this is all I have that is left of you." He must have lost it while searching for her tree. "I've made so many mistakes. But our services still do matter. I will find our tree, Orin. For both of us."

She could feel hot tears on her face but her voice was steady now. "It was always my task. I will never forgive myself for placing it on you. But I *will* complete my service," she vowed to Orin, holding his net tightly.

The sky was darkening quickly now, so it was with haste that Idra left the Sapwood. Namin's webs were spun alongside the paths she walked. She found Ara at the Welcome Table. Together they went to Ara's cabin. Ara was silent. Idra too. She thought of everything she knew about how the island worked. *Where is the sixth tree?* Ara and Idra slept together, holding hands. Somewhere in the darkness Namin sang, spinning the world together, and Lenya watched the night waiting to catch a star. But in Ara's cabin they just held each other, their eyes closed, waiting for the solace of sleep to come.

When Idra awoke, the sun was high and the day was bright. Memories of the last few days seeped through her confusion and she sat up, suddenly alert. She looked at Ara, who was now curled into Lenya, their hands clasped even in sleep. She had not felt Lenya join them in the night. *I have a service to complete.* Idra had to move quietly to avoid waking either of them. When she left the cabin she had to squint her eyes from the bright sun, but as they adjusted she welcomed the white daylight. She ran along the path, the strong sun now warming her face, so that by the time she reached her tree she was full of energy. She climbed, filled her basket, and came down. Leaping from branch to branch no longer gave her the same thrill, but it did make her feel good. She brought the basket to the Welcome Table and went to get the others.

Lenya awoke quickly. She even managed a smile and Idra was surprised to find that she herself was able to reflect that smile. It wasn't so much an expression of happiness that they exchanged, but of affection. Ara took longer to rouse. At first she didn't open her eyes. Once her eyes were open, she didn't move. Eventually, Idra and Lenya each took one of her hands, and she got up. They led her up the hill to the Welcome Table and sat down together. Idra gestured to Lenya, who took the first fruit. Together they ate, but Ara just watched. When Lenya finished, she touched each of them lightly before leaving.

Idra stood up and took the basket of fruit, touching Ara's arm gently. Ara remained unmoving.

"Please come, Ara," she said quietly. Then, rather than waiting for her, Idra began to leave. It worked. Ara followed. They wound their way through the woods silently until they reached the Sunset Altar. Idra led Ara along the coastline until they reached the rock. There were stones to skip, but that was not why they had come. *Our services mean everything now.*

She offered a piece of fruit to Ara, but still Ara did not eat. Idra took a bite instead, and then threw the bitten fruit in the water. It splashed, before bobbing to the surface, ripples extending out from it.

"He might be gone, Ara, but what he has done, how he has changed the world, has changed us. That still matters. He still affects us." Idra took another piece fruit from the basket, offering it to Ara. Again she refused. Idra took another bite and threw this one into the water too. It made a splash, and the resulting ripples pushed the first piece slowly to the side.

"He still affects us," Idra repeated, "and we owe him the best. He would not want us to waste away." Ara remained mute.

"The world still matters. We still matter. Our services still matter," said Idra, echoing Lenya's words. She offered a third fruit to Ara. Ara accepted it, staring at it for a moment with a troubled expression, and then finally took a bite. *I have to push her.*

"Have you visited the Stones?" Idra asked. She looked over. Ara was chewing the fruit slowly, but it was having an effect. Tears were welling up in her eyes now. She swallowed.

"The Stones?" She turned her wet eyes to Idra. "What answer could they possibly have that could justify this? What answer have they ever had? I went to them. I went to them after Orin was taken. They have no answers!" She began to cry.

"Ara," Idra said softly.

But Ara continued as if she hadn't spoken. "Don't you get it? The rules were made to be broken! Your tree was made to never be found! The paths were made so that we would leave them at night! The stars were made to steal Lenya from us! The stones were made to break me!"

Idra just watched. Ara waited a moment, but when Idra said nothing she continued.

"And they have been broken. All of this has. I don't know what the cave did to Kuthan, or what the webs have done to Namin, but I know they have been broken! Everything was designed that way. Do you think that Enetheal's blood would have been spilled had the rules not forbidden it? Or that we would have neglected to make tributes had they not been commanded? The rules were made so that we would fail!"

She is right that we all were broken in different ways. But we will heal in different ways too. Maybe we can help each other heal.

"You might be right, Ara," Idra said. "Maybe the rules were made to be broken. But the service each one of us provides can save us. We have already seen it begin. If it was all fate, then we have also been delivered by fate." There was hunger in Ara's eyes. *She wants to believe me.*

She continued, the words for herself as much as for Ara. "Either way, we now have a chance to shape our future. It would be a mistake to throw that chance away. I'm scared. I think you are too. But we both have services to fulfill. And there is still much to live for."

When she finished, tears glazed her cheeks. *Did I convince her?*

They huddled together, staring out at the fading ripples in the water, eating fruit. They watched the sun set together and when darkness settled in, sleep took them dreamlessly.

The next morning came and the sun held life. Namin finished his song at the Welcome Table. Idra awaited with Ara, Lenya, and a basket. They ate as a foursome, Namin devouring piece after piece of the delicious fruit. Despite his exhaustion, Namin smiled. Once it was clear that he was finished, Lenya led him away. Ara and Idra looked at each other and rose up together. Then Ara left for her Stones and Idra began her search.

ARA - DAYS FIFTEEN TO SEVENTEEN

*A*rrraaaa!" the Stones shrieked. *"Arrraaaa!"* Ara heard them, but she did not reply. Why should she? They had no answers for her. Where had they been when she called? Ara did not speak. She did not eat. She did not want to be. She wasn't meant to be. And yet somehow she perceived and recognized the ripple ....

> *Echoes are what stay behind*
> *when voice no longer cries*
> *a song that never ends*
> *a life after it dies*

The ripple spread from where Idra had thrown the fruit. The ripples seemed more real than Idra's voice. But she could still hear Idra speaking. Ara wished she would stop. She was tired of listening.

"He might be gone, Ara, but what he's done, how he has changed the world, has changed us. That still matters.

He still affects us." *But Orin isn't here.* Ara looked. Idra offered her fruit again. When Ara turned away, Idra threw it into the water. It splashed, resulting in waves which expanded outward, pushing the first fruit aside. "He still affects us," Idra repeated, "and we owe him the best. He would not want us to waste away." Ara did her best to say nothing. *She doesn't know. She can't know.*

It wasn't Orin alone, but creation itself. The world had been created false. The world had been created to end. To fall. Idra had not mentioned Kuthan. Or Enetheal. She had not mentioned the Former. Or the rules. Idra only talked of Orin. *Does she not understand the joke that our existence is?* Perhaps this was Idra's way of coping: If so, Ara would not take it away. Idra's voice returned. Ara listened. She had learned to listen, no matter what the pain.

"The world still matters. We still matter. Our services still matter." The words were nothing new. *Lenya's words. And they speak nothing of what Lenya is.* Lenya was still gone. They all were. That was the point. Ara blinked. In front of her, Idra offered another fruit. *Take it. She will not stop until you do.* Ara took the fruit and brought it to her lips, and the flavor in her mouth was as repulsive as it was rejuvenating. It tasted of happiness even when she knew that happiness to be false.

"Have you visited the Stones?" Idra asked. Ara chewed slowly. The fruit weakened her: she could contain herself no longer.

The Stones' betrayal had been worst of all. Her own service had broken her. When Orin had gone she had come to them. She had begged them for Orin. "Where is Orin? Where is his echo?" Yet there had been no answer. The only echo she had heard was her own voice. *It wasn't just for me.* The others had needed the answer too. There had to be a reason. "Why?" she had cried over and over. "What can we do?" By the end the only sounds, the only wailing, was her own.

They had not given her guidance. Nor had Enetheal. Like the Stones, he was absent. It had been her choice to believe that there had been a reason behind the events which had taken place. It had been her choice to design her tribute when the others had not, hers to create additional tributes to substitute for those the others had neglected. These, she believed, would continue to uphold the rules despite everything. But her faith had been answered with betrayal. The Former's rules had been made to be broken. Its voice rang with triumph. And mingled along with it were the voices of the Stones. The Former had spoken in verse just as the Stones always had. And she had received her answer.

Now the sweetness of the fruit made it hurt all the more. In her mouth she tasted the world that was a lie. A beautiful lie. But it was the truth that came pouring out of her. Truth and tears. Ara told Idra of the Stones. She told Idra of the world that had betrayed them. But unlike the Stones, Idra did not answer with silence.

"You might be right, Ara. Maybe the rules were made to be broken. But the service each one of us provides can save us. We have already seen it begin. If it was all fate, then we have also been delivered by fate." As Idra spoke, Ara took another bite. And this time joy did not taste so false. *The Former formed us with the ability to resist. To shape our own fate. It could not be an accident.*

Idra continued. "Either way, we now have a chance to create our future. It would be a mistake to throw that chance aside. I'm scared. I think you are too. But we both have services to fulfill. And there is still much to live for." Tears were in both their eyes when Idra finished. They watched the setting sun. They did not have joy, but they knew that joy had a place in the world, and that the world was not made that they must fail. *The Stones may have answers yet.*

They ate together at the Welcome Table the next day. Four of them were still there to shape the world. *The others are still here. I will listen.* Ara left for her Stones.

"ARRRAAAA ..." Their voices grew louder as she drew nearer. *They know I'm getting closer. Why are they so desperate?* She stopped at the water's edge. Before her stretched the outcropping of rocks. Leap after leap would take her further from the island. *Further from what is. Closer to what was. Orin.* The gaps between the stones seemed to have moved further apart.

The first few leaps were still effortless for Ara. But as the Shrieking Stones loomed nearer the steps became more difficult. Ara leapt, barely managing to make her landing on the next rock. *Had they always been so far apart? Perhaps they only seemed further apart now because she did not want to go.* But that was certainly not the case. *They may have let me down, but now they must redeem themselves. There is still purpose.* If that wasn't true ... but it was, so the alternative was not worth considering. She had learned long ago that you had to commit to your jump. *No half measures.* The last jump was the longest of all. Ara leapt. A wave licked her foot, but she landed safely on the little islet.

The Stones watched her, now in silence. "Here I am," she told them. She could not disguise the anger in her voice. *And yet I still have faith.* The winds began to whisper about her. Ara walked to her usual spot in the middle. "We need guidance. And I will listen." The whispers died around her. She closed her eyes. "Please."

"Ara." A single voice surrounded her. She had heard them all before. Each voice had sounded, as a scream, a whisper, a wail, a moan, a hum, a whistle, a shriek. They had overlapped and clashed with one another. But it was one voice that spoke now with calmness and clarity. "Here I am."

Ara felt suddenly cold. Her breathing quickened and her heart began to race. Never had the Stones been so intelligible. *I'm talking to someone.* Understanding was no struggle now. The words were filled with sorrow. *There really is someone here.* Some part of her had always doubted the reality of this communion; listening to and speaking with the wind, with a part of the world. It seemed unlikely. She could have been making the whole thing up. The last time, when silence had been her only answer, she had wondered if she had suddenly become sane, and if it was the sanity that broke her.

Now there was clarity. Now they could speak freely. Ara was filled with questions.

"Who are you?" she blurted out. The answer was one she had already heard.

"Echoes without call of voice, reflections without casters," the wind murmured. *"Choosers who never had a choice, servants without masters."* The wind died down and for a moment Ara's heart plunged. *It can't be gone already.* But the voice returned, again sounding almost human. *"That is who we are; it is what we are."*

"Where were you?" she asked. Before arriving she had wanted to berate them for their silence, but now … might they have answers? "Where were you when …." She could not finish.

"I was too late to save Orin in this world. I was too slow to stop Kuthan." The air sighed and for a moment wind and water swirled up about her:

It was my task to be your guide
I felt that I'd been cast away
and so I chose to run and hide
and so I led you all astray

It couldn't be. It didn't make sense. Enetheal had walked among them. Could he be here with the Stones as well?

"Enetheal?"

Sad and serene, it answered. *"Yes. No. We are many echoes. Enetheal's is the newest, the clearest."*

"So there must have been others. Before. And only Enetheal survived." It was a statement, not a question, but still the voice answered.

"No survivors. Only echoes. Even though one wore flesh." The voice was filled with regret, but, but there was no more time for this. Ara closed her eyes and took a breath:

"What must we do now? You and your world are gone. We will soon be gone as well unless we receive guidance." She looked around at the Stones imploringly.

"The old worlds must be washed away completely. Our voices must sound no more. Only then can a new world arise. Bring us our tributes. We will tell you how to release us. We will leave you with one last gift: a new covenant."

"Thank you," Ara whispered, and then once again, more softly, "Thank you so much." There was a pause. She walked around the circle touching each of the Stones. She paused at the one which had once been silent, the one which she now knew to be Enetheal's. The voice spoke once more:

"You will succeed where we did not."

Ara nodded and started for the edge, but then something made her pause once again. A twisting in her stomach. A question that had to be answered:

"Echoes are what stay behind when voice no longer cries, a song that never ends, a life after it dies," Ara told them. "You told me that once."

The Stones were silent.

"Orin? Orin's echo? ... and Kuthan's? Are they still here?" Her voice echoed ironically. "After all, you are," she added when there was no answer. She waited.

"Leave the past. Learn from it. Accept that it shapes you. Accept that it was, that it lives on in you. It must be let go if you are to become more."

"I will," Ara answered. She knew that there would be no more answers. She took a breath, collected herself and leapt from the ring of echoes.

The space between the stones leading shoreward still seemed longer than before, but she leapt with resolution now and the distance to the island melted before her. Despite the chill of wind and water as it splashed her Ara felt warmth inside herself. *I have always had to pretend that I knew for the sake of the others. That was what was expected of me. But not anymore.* Now her service was nearly complete. No more riddles. Their path was clear.

She began her journey across the island. Enetheal. She did not know what to think of him. When they had met, she had been fearful, but also eager to please him. The rules, their labors gave them purpose. She wanted to succeed in her task and for him to appreciate her competence. But Enetheal had left them, and Ara had been left to guide them in Enetheal's absence. *He betrayed us.* But he hadn't.

Not really. He still had guided them, still helped them to understand the island.

In return, they had murdered him. *Kuthan had.* Ara felt the heavy weight of guilt. Yet having spoken to the Stones, she felt Enetheal's forgiveness. And more than this, his faith in them. It made her feel alive again.

Ara returned. She brought their tribute stones to the edge of the island near the Shrieking Stones. And when they were all gathered, she brought them across, leap by leap. Finally, she placed the tributes in the center of the circle of Stones.

"Here I am," Ara said. *"Here I am, I am, am, am,"* echoed her voice across the quiet water. But then the wind returned, and the Stones spoke:

The circle turns
"Be more be one, be more be one"
The circle learns
"What's formed's undone, what's formed's undone"

To grow the circle ends
To be the circle mends
Leave the will you've woken
Leave incomplete and broken

The living light has made a path
The living light has found the way
The wanderer has led you there
by bringing night to day

The seeker sought to find
The Former was unbound

The seeker must be sought
The seeker must be found

Weaver soon redeemer
Shall sing a song of making
Woven dreams make up the seams
that halt the world's breaking

Recaller brings our voice
a world they will create
Recaller brings them choice
the tools to shape their fate

Fruit collected from each tree
Their seeds shall help the world grow
Each fallen star has fallen far
Their light shall help the world know

Tributes made for world new
Tributes made that were unclaimed
Tributes with the maker's mark
Tributes show the maker maimed

Will shall make the world be
Song shall make the world feel
Wandering shall make us free
Heart shall know where it may heal

Nurturers, believers
dreamers, all retrievers
seeker and recaller
weaver, all redeemers

Now is the time to mend
Begin by bringing end
You are the circle broken
You are the world woken

There was no goodbye. Nor were there more questions. The wind died as the tributes sank beneath the water. Ara left the circle in silence.

IDRA - DAYS SEVENTEEN TO NINETEEN

Down in the sky
where low becomes high

Golden light gleamed off the pools of sap. The bark was a deep red, redder than it ever had been. The twigs shone green. The Sapwood had remained unchanged: all color, no sound. Above, the sky was a piercing blue, clouds drifting slowly across. *Down in the sky,* Idra thought again, her gaze upward. But then she turned her head toward the forest floor. *Where low becomes high.* The words no longer instilled dread; she was at peace with them now. *The Sapwood is mine, as is its riddle.* She had left her basket and Orin's net behind. But she had brought something else: the stone goblet, the one which they had drunk from on the first day. It had always been full when they arrived at the Welcome Table. They had never thought anything of it, they had only drunk. "Enetheal's task," she whispered.

One of them anyway. And now it is mine to fill. But where to fill it?

Around her were the pools of sap. In each pool was a tree. Ripples of sap slowly moved back towards the trees where they oozed upward. *Draining the world.* But there was still plenty of sap left. She knelt down by one of the pools, dipping the goblet beneath the surface and then bringing it back up, now full of sap. She looked around. Tranquility. Timelessness. It was at the same time both soothing and unsettling. She stood carefully, holding the goblet steadily as she turned away from the pool. It was time to leave the Sapwood and bring her gift to the others. Already, fruit was waiting at the Welcome Table. And now she brought them drink.

She re-entered the world of sound and song. Insects buzzed around her and birds sang. Sweat beaded on her face as she climbed to the Welcome Table. The others would be coming as well, but she was the first to arrive. She set the goblet in the middle of the table, arranging the fruit around it, and closed her eyes to wait. *I'm getting closer to the tree. I feel it.* Soon she heard voices. *Lenya, Namin.* They spoke calmly but without emptiness. *We're all moving on.* It wasn't as if they had a choice, but nevertheless, Idra felt proud. Then Ara was there, too.

"I have listened," Ara told them, "and I have heard our answer." She sat down. "I bring a new covenant to this table." And then she spoke. She was confident and strong, and they felt this in her voice. It was not the voice that had sounded inside of them on the first day. But there was truth and hope in her words.

They were quiet after she finished. Then they drank, as they had done once before. *We accept as one.* The sap was warm and somewhat thicker than water. Next they partook of the fruit. A gentle sweetness overcame their senses. Eventually they allowed their thoughts to dwell upon what they had learned.

Ara smiled. "I listened. I heard. I did not say I understood. I think we should come to understand this together."

Idra thought aloud: "Fruit collected from each tree. Their seeds shall help the world grow."

Lenya continued: "Each fallen star has fallen far. Their light shall help the world know."

Idra and Lenya looked at one another.

"That's us, " Idra finished. "Lenya and me."

"I'm the Weaver," Namin said softly. "To sing a song of making." They turned to Ara.

"And I'm Recaller," Ara added. "Bringing you their voice." They stopped for a moment.

"So that's us." Ara continued. "But then there is the circle and the tributes."

There is only one circle. "The trees," Idra stated. "The broken circle." She looked around for agreement. Lenya was gazing upward and Ara's eyes were fixed on the Welcome Table, both of them lost in thought. Namin, however, met her eyes and nodded slowly. A cloud moved across the sun placing the table in sudden shadow, and a breeze picked up, blowing pine needles about.

"But it sounds like the circle can think," Ara added, both for the others and for herself. "The circle turns: 'Be more be one, be more be one.' The circle learns: 'What's formed's undone, what's formed's undone.'" Ara said it slowly. "To grow the circle ends. To be the circle mends. Leave the will you've woken. Leave incomplete and broken."

I will understand! Idra thought desperately. The circle had to be hers.

"And what about the tributes?" Namin asked. "Kuthan brought them to the Former. We are making new tributes now for the new world." He did not sound pleased.

"Yes," Ara said, "more tributes. But where do we bring them?" she looked to Idra and Namin, but it was Lenya who answered the question.

"The well," she said serenely. "That's where the gathered stars are. That's where Idra will bring the fruit. The tributes, the song, the seeds, the stars."

They were astounded at Lenya's insight. But Idra's voice interrupted their celebration.

"The circle …," she said softly, aware she was draining away their excitement. "Are we supposed to leave it incomplete and broken? The circle of trees is broken, but it must not be left that way."

"Why not?" Namin asked.

"Because," Idra answered slowly, "we need fruit from the missing tree. That will complete the circle." *She knew it was true. The tree is everything.*

"We've ended *one* circle already," Ara said. She continued to answer their questioning gazes. "There were others before us. They were consumed by the Former. We have escaped that fate … or we will make sure that we do. The circle of creation and unmaking will end, and no one will be left behind."

"But that's not the circle of trees!" Idra exclaimed. *How could they not see?*

"It could be," Namin said. "It could be both."

"It could mean both? Or be both?" Idra asked. No one answered. "Either way we need fruit from every tree."

"Yes," said Lenya reassuringly.

"Tributes made for world new. Tributes made that were unclaimed. Tributes with the maker's mark. Tributes show the maker maimed," Ara reiterated. "We need more tributes."

"I understand the first," Namin said. "but what of the others?"

"The circle isn't clear to me either," Idra said, confusion in her voice. They paused once more, allowing thoughts to flow. The wind picked up again, cooling the heat of the day.

"We don't need to know," Lenya said. Ara opened her mouth to object, but Lenya continued: "Not now. Not immediately. We'll continue to talk and discover more as time goes on, but we cannot know everything now. We do not need to know how it ends. Just how it begins."

"And how is that?" Idra asked.

Namin answered ironically, Ara assuredly. They spoke together: "Tributes."

Despite Namin's reluctance, the world seemed more peaceful than it ever had been as they began to gather. They wandered over stones and searched in the shallows. *Now no one is commanding us to find tributes but ourselves. This is our choice.* Idra found one stone she liked and then another. Rather than choose only one, she took them both. She noticed the others continuing to search. She went over to ask them to meet her at the beach when they were done, and then she left with her basket. Later, when she arrived at the beach, her basket had not only fruit but also branches from the berry grove with unpicked berries. Together they painted their stones and decorated them with shells and beach findings. Namin's had pine needles and sand. Lenya's was caked with mud and berry juice. Ara's was speckled in shells. One of Idra's had wildflowers woven about it; the other, a single shell in the center.

When they were finished they made the new pilgrimage together. It was not far from the beach to the well. Lenya laughed as they came closer. The top of the plateau, the top of the world, was before them, and the well was in the center. One by one they released their tributes. It was difficult for Idra. But at the same time, for once it was *hers* to let go of. *This truly is mine to give. A gift should not be demanded or expected. It must be made by the self for the other.*

"This is for you, New World," she said into the well. Then she dropped both of her tributes.

The next day she felt more of herself return. She looked across the room to where Lenya and Namin lay asleep, their arms entwined around one another. Ara's question about the rules being made to break them came back to her. *If we had all been able to sleep together from the beginning ....* but there were too many ifs. Idra cleared her throat and left for the new day.

The day was beautiful. The wind was stronger, the air cooler. It was bracing. Idra ran until she reached the circular stone way, and then picked up her pace so that she was sprinting. She was eager to get to the Sapwood. But first she had to climb. The first tree she passed was skeletal, naked, but it gleamed in the sun. The next had leaves of orange, green, red, and brown. When she reached the third she stopped and climbed. She loved the feeling of bark on her hands and feet. Her ascent was quick and smooth and almost immediately she was leaping, then gathering. Her basket was soon full. She almost missed the challenge of climbing with her arms full of fruit. She descended and continued along the stone way. One more tree was alive with flowers, but still fruitless. Then she was there. Time stopped. Sound stopped. And Idra searched.

She looked about her, tranquility filling her mind. She thought of the sap that used to flow downward. *As if it were rain, or as if sunlight had become sap or life somehow.*

Around each tree was a clear silvery pool that caught the sun. *Now the sap flows upward. It cannot come from above.* She thought of the roots extending downward like branches, the tree continuing down; she stared into a pool and saw the reflected sun. It was time to go; Idra felt it. Once the sun was high enough to reflect in the pool, Namin, Ara and Lenya would be awake.

Idra filled the goblet with sap and brought it to the Welcome Table along with her basket. She arranged the fruit, and traveled down the slope to get the others. As she had predicted, they were awake. "Breakfast is ready," she told them. Now that the others were with her, the day felt new again. They ate together. She no longer picked one of them to begin: the point was being together; choosing one to eat first was separation.

"Did you bring a fruit to the well?" Ara asked.

"No," Idra answered. "I'm going to start with the fruit that we have not yet taken." There was question in their eyes, so she continued: "I've thought more about the circle of trees. I think it's important to take the fruits one by one, and to stop at the seventh." She took a deep breath. *It might not make sense to them, but it does to me.* "Since that's how I'm doing it, it's important that I start with the tree that has been giving us the most trouble. That way, if I'm not successful retrieving that fruit right away, I can get it at the end of the next cycle.

"Have you found it?" Ara asked eagerly.

"No," Idra answered, "but I'm almost there." She knew it to be true. They finished and again went to make tributes. The silence, stillness, and color of the Sapwood filled Idra's mind while she searched and even while she worked. *I can feel it.*

When the sun disappeared, sleep did not arrive quickly. But eventually it did come. Soon after came dreams:

"Why wait for stars to fall when you can climb to them yourself?" she asked Lenya.
"Why climb to fruit when you can fall to them yourself?" Lenya answered.

Suddenly she was awake: the same waking that had come to her on the boat so long ago. She smiled. It was still dark, but she could feel the day approaching. Next to her Lenya lay deep in sleep. "Thank you, Lenya," she whispered.

Despite the darkness, Idra was unafraid. Namin's webs had spun the island together, sheltering and shielding. *We are safe now.* Idra closed the cabin door and started along the path. This time instead of walking all the way around the ring, she turned towards the Sapwood. It did not take long to find the stone way, and she walked methodically along it.

Down in the sky where low becomes high

The world was still. There was no wind to blow the strands of webs that crisscrossed between the trees. Even the silver of morning dew seemed to glint more than shine. Just as Idra entered the Sapwood, light crept into the sky. She passed tree after tree, each with its own pool of sap. Light continued to seep into the world. She left Orin's path, and paused. The early day caressed the world with gold. Before her was a pool. A pool without a tree. She had passed it before. *But now I see it.* The morning's dawn descended to twilight beneath its surface, growing into a new day. In its light was a tree that extended downward to the eternal deep. Her eyes turned toward fruit buds that shone gold as the sun. A sliver of sunlight peeked over the horizon, and a single drop of golden sap fell from the tree, upward, toward the pool's surface. Ripples appeared as it broke upon that liquid, and the tree shimmered into nothingness, the pool now silver and empty.

Ara - Days Nineteen and Twenty

Tributes made for world new
Tributes made that were unclaimed
Tributes with the maker's mark
Tributes show the maker maimed

Idra had found the tree. Only two tasks remained: discovering the nature of the different kinds of tributes, and Orin. The morning had begun unlike any other.

"Ara! Lenya! Namin!" Idra had called, elated. She had led them to the Sapwood, to the empty pool where the tree grew. "It's here at night! Only at night!"

"Brilliant, Id!" Namin mussed up her hair, but Idra was too excited to care. They celebrated at the Welcome Table. They drank the sap from the newfound pool and ate the new day's fruit.

"When should I collect it, though?" Idra wondered aloud. Ara didn't understand, but Idra elaborated. "I harvest fruit from the other trees in the morning. Should I gather it from this one the night before or the night after?"

Smiles dissolved into looks of confusion and contemplation.

"I think I'm going to try tonight," Idra finally answered for herself. "If it were a normal tree, the fruit would be there tomorrow morning and would grow the night before."

Ara nodded. *This is Idra's task*, she reminded herself.

"Perfect," Lenya agreed.

"Careful," Namin said quietly. "Let's not get ahead of ourselves."

"What do you mean?" Idra asked. Her voice was calm, but Ara saw a glint of annoyance in her eyes.

"I mean we should approach this cautiously," Namin answered.

"Your webs protect us at night, Namin. They spread across the island now. We are safe."

But Ara understood what Namin meant.

"If we are with you … if Namin is with you, then nothing can happen. His voice has delivered us before, and it will again if anything goes wrong," she told Idra.

Idra's tone grew fiercer. "And what would go wrong? I can complete my service on my own, and this time no one will be put in danger!"

"No they won't," Lenya agreed calmly. "Your service is yours. You will complete it. But this goes beyond services." Idra closed her eyes, but then she nodded.

Idra blames herself for Orin as I blame myself, Ara realized.

The rest of the day was dedicated to tributes. All of their feelings and thoughts poured into the their stones: happiness, thankfulness, tranquility, sadness, anger, excitement, and contemplation. As they worked clouds rolled in, but they labored on. Ever present was the weight of time, the night drawing nearer. At last, Ara put down her latest tribute.

"My final for today," she told the others. Then, one by one, they finished. Finally they began the ascent to the well.

As they climbed the rain began to fall. It was warm. Ara could not decide if it made her comfortable or uncomfortable. They reached the top just as she decided it was not comfortable. They dropped their tributes down the well and then moved to the Welcome Table to eat. When they had finished they walked to the Sunset Altar, and clambered on top of it. Deep within the clouds they could just make out the red-orange glow of the sun. Ara could not help but think of Kuthan. He had loved to watch the sunset, although he had dreaded what came next. *Now we also must face darkness.* But this was different. Even though Orin's lights no longer lit the way, Namin's webs and Namin's song would protect them, would guide them.

The rain finally stopped, but their skin remained soaked. Ara looked over to Idra, who kept fidgeting. *We wouldn't have made it this far if it wasn't for her… I wouldn't have.* "The hardest part is waiting," Ara told her. Idra nodded her thanks, but Ara wasn't sure that her reassurances helped much.

"Let's go," she told them. The four of them climbed off the rock, and turned toward the forest. Their journey to the well had been rainy, though the paths and scenery had been clearly visible; but now the rain had become mist and fog which obscured the land and muffled the island sounds. Only the distant washing of waves and the occasional birdcall intruded upon this quiet. Even those sounds, however, were silenced at the edge of the Sapwood.

Night, mist, and silence were their companions as they walked past the tall trees and empty pool. The Sapwood, always uncannily vibrant, now seemed like a dead place. Dark trees loomed out of the mist and vanished as they passed them by.

"Keep close," Namin cautioned unnecessarily. Lenya, Ara, and Idra were already huddled around him as they walked.

"Where are we?" Ara asked after a while.

No one answered for a long time, but finally Namin whispered, "I think we're trying to figure that out."

Their eyes darted around, waiting for the Former to emerge from the mist. But the only thing they saw were faintly glowing strands of web. *They keep us safe,* Ara reminded herself. Although the webs glowed gently in the darkness, they cast no light, so the travellers kept stumbling.

"Ah!" Lenya yelped when she stepped into a pool with a splash. She quieted almost instantly, but it was a long time before any of them moved again.

"What if the Former … made this happen?" Idra whispered.

"It would have come by now," Ara reassured her. "Maybe It's scared." But Ara knew she hadn't even convinced herself, and they squeezed even more tightly together.

"Namin," Idra asked suddenly. "Could you sing for us?"

Namin didn't answer at first, but then he began to hum.

Just like when I sleep, Ara thought.

The girls weren't the only ones who found Namin's voice comforting. None could see them, but they could sense when the spiders came.

Namin led them through the forest. He stretched out his arms, spreading his long fingers delicately to either side as he sang. He led them in a path meandering between the trees. Ara could not imagine what he was doing. They followed his voice. What or who guided him they did not know. *But we will follow him.*

They knew the pool as soon as they found it. Its surface glowed softly in the night. Without a visible moon or stars to contend with, its gentle gleam shone. Ara saw Namin's face by the sheen of the dim pool: his eyes were closed. He walked around the pool, the little group following, letting his hands ruffle gently over web strands like the scuttling of spiders. Only when he completed the circle did he open his eyes.

"We are here," he told them. Only then did they step away from him. As one they crept to the pool's edge. Ara gasped. That morning there had been nothing but the reflections of clouds. Now the tree was clear before them. Darker than night. And large. So large. *Endless.* Its branches spanned out over the Sapwood, encompassing all of it. *Under the Sapwood,* Ara corrected herself.

Idra laughed softly in excitement.

"Are those …?" Namin began to ask

"Stars?" Lenya finished. Hanging from the branches of the tree were stars. Each one a brilliant piercing blue white, shimmering, alive, eternal.

"But that's not right," Idra said. "Stars are yours," she said to Lenya. Lenya lapsed into silence. They all did. They stared into the pool. Beneath them were endless stars. Above them, shrouded in clouds and mist, there were nine. Ara glanced to Lenya whose eyes were wide. *She's hungry.* Ara realized. But when Lenya spoke her voice was calm:

"They look like stars now, but I don't think they are finished yet."

"What do you mean?" Idra asked.

"Normally you don't get to watch the fruit grow. It grows during the night so it's ready for the next day."

"I can go down while they grow!" Idra said impatiently.

"No." Ara and Namin said it together, both a little too loudly.

They all looked around, but the forest was silent. *We'll be safe.* Web strands hung between all the trees. *And Namin is here.*

"Why not?!" Idra said under her breath so as not to disturb the silence once more. Ara and Namin exchanged a glance. *We are of one mind in this,* Ara thought. It was a relief to have Namin on her side.

"We're being safe, remember?" Namin explained softly. "We're finding out more before we do anything. We'll watch to see if the fruit ripens. It's a long climb. It looks too long! We must not risk anything just now."

"This is my service and I'm going to do it!" Idra whispered vehemently.

Ara and Namin shared another glance, before Ara took over:

"I know it's hard. My service is nothing like yours, Id, but waiting and struggling to understand, and failing to do what I thought I needed to do … I've been through this. It's been awful. You told me we had a chance to choose our destiny, and you were right. We can't risk throwing it away by being reckless." Idra took a breath, and nodded.

Ara finished, "There is still something here we don't understand." Again Idra nodded.

"You're right. I just …" Idra's voice caught in her throat. The night held its breath. As one they looked up as silver illuminated the overcast sky. The star arced over the Sapwood, its brilliant piercing blue light flickering between trees, touching upon sap pools, casting shadows and reflections everywhere. The mist came alive with light … and then it was gone.

"That's me," Lenya smiled. Without another word she left. Namin took a step after her, and then stopped himself.

"She doesn't need protection?" Idra asked.

"The star is not in the Sapwood," Namin answered. "And this tree has given us more reason to be cautious."

Lenya has been traveling at night for stars long before the webs spanned the island, Ara reminded herself.

They lapsed into another silence; this came upon them naturally in the sapwood. Ara looked into the pool. Were the stars changing? They seemed more solid, their shimmering now a steady glow. The little group continued to stare downward, occasionally glancing up at one another as if to gauge each other's understanding of the scene below. Ara didn't want to say they were changing until she was sure. *I mustn't get Idra's hopes up.* Namin constantly looked over his shoulder and at the near surroundings to be sure they were alone. Ara was on the point of mentioning the changing stars, but Namin cut her off.

"Look!" he whispered excitedly, pointing. A great radiance was coming through the trees. *Lenya.* They gathered together, uneasy. But it *was* Lenya. She emerged, wearing an apologetic smile, her skin glowing faintly."I think I'm going to need help with this star."

Ara looked to Idra, who smiled; exhaustion was apparent in her shoulders and eyes.

"It's not time," Idra said, and gestured to the tree. "I know that now. The first time this tree bore fruit I was unable to understand: I blamed Enetheal. The second time I was too afraid: Orin tried to take care of it. This time I was too eager to conquer the service and my fear. But it isn't time. Things have happened too fast. I need more time to think, and I have it, too. Seven more days. I will be ready then. She looked carefully into the eyes of each of them to show them the truth in her words.

"We never doubted you, Idra," Ara reassured her.

"Your star?" Namin asked Lenya quietly.

Lenya turned to Ara with a smile. "The Stones."

The night continued as they walked through woods. The sound of lapping waves was audible once they left the Sapwood. As they approached the edge of the island the mist glowed blue. Soon they were at the island's rocky edge. Before them, mostly obscured by the thick mist, was the rocky outcrop that led to Ara's Stones. Blue starlight clung to the mist but did little to help them see the rocks better, and little to provide comfort. Where the mist in the Sapwood had been warm, here it was cool.

"I don't like it, " Namin said. "What if this is some sort of trap? To take you away from me, and my webs?"

Lenya laid her hands on Namin's chest briefly.

"It's ok, Naim," she told him. Namin didn't reflect Lenya's smile. Ara understood:

"This is the only way, Namin, but I don't think we are in any danger." The Former is somewhere on the island, probably trapped by your webs or waiting for us to be separated from you. But if you were on the shore, you would shield us from It ever reaching us." Namin nodded unhappily.

Idra held Namin's arm, pulling him away from the other two. "They'll be fine."

"We have no choice but to be fine," Ara added.

"Let's go," Lenya said impatiently.

Ara made the first leap, a small one. She held out a hand to guide Lenya. Lenya leapt, landing gracefully. Ara took the next jump, and again guided Lenya. *Once Enetheal leapt and guided, and I was the follower.* She led Lenya further into the mist. After the third jump, Idra and Namin were just silhouettes, and after the fourth they were gone all together. Leap by leap they made their way deeper into the blue mist.

The water seemed to quiet below them. Usually it crashed upon the rocks as the wind howled about her. Now all was still, the water dark and silent beneath them. *But it's hungry too.* Ara leapt into mist and darkness. *My feet know where to go.* The landing was slippery but she was prepared.

"Here, Lenya," she called back into the dark haze. One leap away from her, Lenya was enshrouded by mist. Ara prepared herself, but Lenya did not come.

"Here I am Len. I'm ready for you," she called again. *"Ready for you ... for you,"* came her echo.

"Okay," Lenya answered. But still she did not come.

"On three," Ara told her. "One," she said slowly. "Two. Three!" *"Three."*

Lenya emerged from the mist. Ara caught her just as her feet touched the rock. They crouched together, breathing heavily. After a moment, Ara stood. She put a hand on Lenya's shoulder reassuringly, released it, and leapt.

"Ah!" Ara gasped as she landed, her foot sliding down the curved edge of the rock. She managed to right herself without slipping off and falling backwards. *They have been moving further apart! I'm not just blinded by mist and night!* Could the Stones be moving? Ara took a deep breath. *Be calm. You are in control. Lenya needs to see that.*

"Ready Len!' she called back. "This one's a bigger jump! About half again as long as the last one! But you can do it!"

"Do it," called her echo. Ara counted for her again. On three Lenya emerged, leaping towards Ara's voice. They both shrieked, but once more, Ara caught Lenya and steadied her. *She's graceful in the air.* They did it again and again. Each leap seemed longer than the last. *Is the island still there behind us?* All was mist, and Lenya.

Lenya became more sure of herself as they proceeded. They had started out slowly, but now they were moving from rock to rock more quickly.

"We're almost there," Ara told Lenya. "Just a few more leaps. This is where the echoes spoke to me."

Lenya stopped, a small frown on her face.

"Ara? What is an echo?" Lenya asked her. Her voice carried across the water. Ara answered almost instinctively. She had the verse committed to mind, so it was part of her.

"Echoes are what stay behind when voice no longer cries, a song that never ends, a life after it dies."

"Oh," Lenya answered. They leapt again.

"Is the wind an echo then? You said the wind spoke to you as it passed through rocks."

I never did get to share. None of them truly had shared. Their services were their own burdens to bear, impossible truly to share, but still, she did want to ….

"I never could solve everything. I just knew that what I heard were fragments of what was. I pieced them together the best I could." Lenya continued to stare, so Ara continued to speak. "What was clear was that there was some sort of … echo. There was a 'before' which happened prior to the 'now' that affected the world. And if I could piece it together, and if I could listen well, I would be able to guide us. But it wasn't just an echo. It—no, they—were alive. They didn't want us to follow their footsteps, just to listen. The wind was their voice I think. Yes."

Ara got ready to leap again, but Lenya put out a hand to stop her.

"They were more than just voices," Lenya said. "The others and you have *seen* echoes."

"Yes," Ara agreed. "There are mysteries yet to solve. And I will solve them."

"We will," Lenya agreed softly.

They leapt again. And again. The water had been dark and silent beneath them, but now it began to glimmer with starlight. The shadows of the Stones came closer, until finally …. "Stay," Ara told Lenya. Lenya nodded. Ara turned to the Stones. Despite the light of the shimmering star, she wasn't sure of the leap. *One.* The distances between rocks were longer, and this was the longest jump yet. *Two.* Her heart was pounding, but she could feel the exhaustion in her body.

"Wait!" Lenya whispered. Ara froze, leg muscles taut, heart hammering.

"What?" Ara whispered back.

"If anything happens, come right back, okay?" Frustration welled up inside Ara, but she held it in. She took a breath.

"Nothing's going to happen, Len." *Three.* She gave Lenya's hand a squeeze, turned, and hurled herself into the mist before she could pause again. The jump was long. But Ara's leap was strong, landing her just beyond the edge. She bent her knees to absorb the impact but then straightened quickly.

The star had fallen in the center. *As if it knew where to land.* But the center of the circle did not hold her interest.

The Stones were still and silent. *Like the Sapwood.* The thought was unsettling. *How could the voices not be here anymore?* They couldn't just leave! *He must be here!*

"Ara!" Lenya called out.

"Here!" Ara said loudly, silently berating herself for not speaking instantly. "Everything is okay."

She guided Lenya with her voice and then her arms as Lenya landed in the circle. Lenya, like Ara, paused. But while Ara could not take her eyes from the Stones, Lenya's eyes were fixed on her star. Ara looked at Lenya, and at the star, but there was nothing in the circle. She turned her gaze back when movement caught her eye. She squeezed Lenya's arm, but Lenya didn't seem to notice. To the far side of each Stone, fleeing away from the flickering starlight, was a shadow. Her eyes traced its path as it leapt from behind one Stone to another, a flicker of its reflection on the water. *It's him. It must be.* She started to move toward the Stones.

"Ara," Lenya whispered. The light dimmed. Ara turned. The blue glow had diminished, but it now spread through the strands of silk around Lenya's hands, and over her skin. "Let's move on."

"Yes," Ara agreed. "Move on," she echoed. This time starlight moved with them, and although the mist slowed them, the light was reassuring, their path now more clear. Ara still leapt first, still steadied Lenya as she followed, but they no longer faltered. The shore came into view first, but it was only when they were two jumps away that Ara saw the silhouettes and let out a breath of relief. The four of them embraced when they returned to shore, but no one dared challenge the quiet.

The next day Ara returned to the Stones. "The answers are off the paths," he had told her. Small waves lapped the rocks now, and the sun shone hazily through clouds, but far brighter than the starshine had. The breeze was there, but it was gentle and the Stones were mute. *I'm not the listener now. I'm the caller. I need to hear an answer.* Ara filled her lungs with breath. "Orrrrin!!"

LENYA - DAYS TWENTY AND TWENTY-ONE

No time, or endless time. Did stars have echoes? And did she trust them? The sun shone now but Lenya still wore the gloves on her hands. *The mark of my distrust. Do they allow me to complete my task? Or prevent me from completing it?* Perhaps neither. Perhaps both. The stars had not been leaving. They were leading. *They always have been. But if they hold the answer, then why do I not bear them directly, close to my hands and heart, as I am meant to? And if I am meant to carry them, and let them go, does the Former want us to leave? The Former wants to consume us. But Ara's service, and Namin's ... our services have been our protection, our salvation.*

The stars had misled her before. Stolen her away. What were they doing now? Why had one fallen in such an unlikely place? Such a difficult place?

The room grew lighter while she thought, but she only became aware of the world once she heard Idra stir. They looked at each other for a moment. Idra was huddled in close to Namin, Ara on his other side. Lenya moved over quietly, and Idra carefully shifted away from Namin and Ara. Namin's brow furrowed, but his breathing was still slow and deep. Lenya cracked open the door and Idra peeled back the web. Then they were outside. When the door was fastened behind them they began to walk.

"Sapwood?" Lenya asked.

"Yes," Idra answered.

"What do you hope to find?" Lenya asked.

"A peaceful place," Idra answered solemnly. Two steps later Idra let out a small laugh.

She's joking, Lenya realized with a smile. And then they were both laughing.

"You mean it, don't you?" Lenya asked when she took a breath.

"A bit," Idra said. And then they were laughing once again. This time though, when they stopped, their laughter didn't return.

"Our services have us confused," Lenya said after a moment.

"You?" Idra said ironically. But Lenya sensed serious-ness too. "I thought you were set! If it weren't for you … well if it weren't for you, I don't think we would have kept completing them."

"Thanks Id, but they own each one of us too much for us to let them go."

Idra paused, and for a moment the birds took over the conversation. Finally Idra looked over to Lenya and asked, "So what's confusing about your stars?"

"Oh, the stars are wonderful …." Lenya hesitated. She did not want to burden Idra.

"The problem is mine. I love the stars ... but I thought they were stealing me away. Namin helped," Lenya held up her web-spun hands. "And I have come back, but now it seems the stars were leading us right all along."

"You talk about them as if they are people," Idra said quietly.

"Yes! I do! I'm confused. Especially after last night. I've never thought about where they landed before. But it can't be chance that a star landed at the Shrieking Stones or in the tree that night. Were they trying to avoid me? Or meet you? But each star is different ...."

"Lenya, slow down." Idra took her by the hands. Lenya realized her voice had been coming out tense and loud. "Take a breath with me." For a moment Lenya resisted, but Idra's eyes told her otherwise. Together they filled their lungs, deep and slow, and gently exhaled.

"Another one," Idra insisted, "eyes closed." They did it again. When they opened their eyes, Lenya recognized that they had reached the Sapwood. In fact they were well inside. Enetheal and Kuthan filled her mind. "One more," Idra whispered. Somehow by the third breath she was calm

"We don't need to know this moment," said Idra quietly. Lenya knew her own words were being used. But Idra offered more: "Maybe it only seems like they have misled you."

Lenya took a breath. Her body ached for starshine. *When I take off my gloves, we will be one once more.* Even the memory of starshine filled her with joy.

"Perhaps they fall in places where they can be safely re-trieved," Idra said, unaware that Lenya's thoughts had shifted.

"Or maybe what they do, and where they fall is an acci-dent," Idra continued. Lenya closed her eyes, remembering last night's star.

"It makes no difference." The words were painful, but they jolted Lenya back to the present. "We need them and we need you," Idra told her.

Lenya smiled for Idra's sake. *But can we trust them?* Instead of asking, she turned her gaze down to Idra's tree. In its branches, impossibly far away, were fruits of silver-gold. But as the stars vanished and the sun rose, the pool shimmered and the tree was gone.

"What are you going to do?" Lenya asked. "They are so far away."

"I'll get the fruit," Idra said simply. "This is the path Orin made for us."

They didn't leave the Sapwood right away. They wandered between the pools, letting their eyes drink in the colors, reflections, and the flow of sap. They allowed their heartbeats to slow, their breathing to calm, and their minds to empty. Eventually Idra took Lenya's hand and they returned to the others.

Another day ... another night ... another star. Lenya shivered with excitement.

They tried to eat the fruit Idra had collected the day before, but could not. It was like wood, stiff and tasteless and without juice. Then they began to work in silence. "We're tired," Idra told no-one in particular as she stained her tribute with berry juice. But it was more than that. *They're unnerved too. By the star.* Idra tried to start conversations a few times, but soon gave up. Eventually Ara disappeared, and Namin contented himself by humming as he worked. When they finished, they delivered their tributes to the well, watched the sunset from the plateau, and then returned to the cabin long before darkness touched the sky. Just before they entered, Namin pulled Lenya aside.

"Should I come with you tonight?" he asked quietly.

"Wha ...? No!" she answered, pulling away from him. Namin looked at her incredulously. She took a breath. *I shouldn't be upset. I'm just unnerved.* When she spoke next her voice was calm.

"What happened last night was strange, but I can handle the stars. You should get some rest."

"Rest? Rest isn't as important as safety! Ara and Idra are safe here!" His hands fluttered over the web screen. "But you. You're alone out there! Unprotected!"

"Kuth ... Namin," she quickly amended. His eyes flickered in annoyance. Lenya didn't know why Kuthan's name had slipped out, but she continued: "We are safe on the island because of your webs. You know that's true. I will be fine. You need rest and I need to be alone tonight. "

Namin opened his mouth to speak, but she cut him off.

"If anything happens I'll come right back and get help." Namin took a breath, then nodded in resignation.

"Thanks Naim," she smiled, and left him at the entrance to the cabin. She sympathized with Idra. *She should have gotten the fruit last night. Being too cautious can be a problem ....*

But it was more than that. Namin was scared of the stars, of how they affected her. *He separated us!* If their paths were to join together once again, Namin would only get in the way. *He may have helped me, but I'm the one who must decide what to do with stars.* Her body trembled for a moment, but then she was fine.

She walked to the beach and paused. *The plateau is closer to the stars. But Enetheal wanted me here.* Here she was closer to the waves, the ground, the noises of the night. Had Enetheal wanted her near the ground, further from the stars? *I thought I was done making this choice.* But she would be soon enough. There were eight stars in the sky.

And then, all at once, there were only seven.

The star arced downward faster than any of the others had. It was gone before she realized it was falling. No trail of light followed its descent. *Are they playing again?* Lenya got up, looking into the nearby woods. The breeze picked up, swirling sand about her. Above her, the waning crescent moon painted the waves and beach with silver. Lenya's body trembled again, yet she found herself smiling.

"I'll play!" she told the far-off star. Lenya ran. The trees blurred before her as she rushed down one path and then another. Silver moonlight leaked between branches shining upon webs, lighting her path through the woods. Lenya ran to the Welcome Table, then to the Stony Shores. She rushed to the Firefly Field, and then combed the surrounding woods. Finally she sprinted through the Sapwood, and then to Ara's Stones. She continued to run. But she found no starshine. At last exhaustion caught up with her. She brushed at the damp skin on her brow. *Cold. Like the stars.*

"Where are you?" she called out softly. But her hidden star did not answer. "Where do you hide that I cannot see your light?"

She lay down again, and looked up at the sky from the forest floor. None of the others stars moved, but they glimmered. Lenya realized she had never looked back to the stars above once one had fallen. She watched them for a time as her breathing slowed. "Will you tell me where your sister has fallen?" Lenya looked up at the stars, the moon, and then to the darkness in between.

Slowly, she rose to her feet, and began to walk. Excitement coursed through her, but now it was laced with terror. She remembered Namin's words from the night before. *"What if this is some sort of trap? To take you away from me ... and my webs?"* But Lenya pressed on, past the Sunset Altar, along the island coast, through the shallows, up to the entrance of Kuthan's cave, until finally she reached the top of the stair. Her eyes drank in the stars above her one last time. *I could still go back. Namin would want me to. But then he wouldn't let me go. He would think it too dangerous. Besides, there isn't enough time.* Lenya moved the web aside and began to descend.

I must not hesitate. The stars lead me forward. No holding back. Step by step she moved down the stairs. Her skin glowed, but its light was insignificant in the darkness that swallowed her. Blackness pressed her from all sides. It consumed her light. It pushed into her thoughts. *I should not be here. This isn't my task! This is where the Former lives.* But another voice was stronger. *This is your task! The star must be down here.*

Down and down went the stairs. And down and down she climbed. *They seem unending, like the stars.* And yet unlike the stars, the darkness demanded to be filled. Lenya walked on and on. Until all at once, she saw light. She began to rush down the stairs, two, then three at a time.

Then she was there. In a shallow pool of water was her star. She reached for it and felt ice in her hands as her fingers closed around it. But her touch was not close enough. Her gloves glowed bright, and she knew their connection was diminished. She looked about her. *No one would stop her if she took them off.* Her eyes moved around the cave. It was big. There was a blackness in it that was not repelled by starlight. Somewhere nearby she heard a small splash. She squinted into the darkness, and realized with horror that she was not alone. She held her star close. She took a step, and then another, and then she saw.

KUTHAN - DAY TWENTY-ONE

There was a flicker—a flicker of thought! *No.* He pushed it away. Thoughts like that could do horrible things. *Darkness.* He laughed and wept. He was finally home. *Nothingness.* It was neither dark nor light. It was nothing. No sight. No sound. No smell, taste, or feel. Thought started to return, but he pushed it away again. *No.* He held on, hugging his knees. Between his chest and knees there was a small lump. *A forgotten tribute, like me.* But again he pushed the thought away. He reminded himself that some things must be forgotten. Then he quickly forgot that as well. It was easy to forget what did not exist. No past. No present. No future. *Your service.* The voice came back into his mind, but he shoved it away angrily. And then let go of the anger, too. No service. No thought. Had he laughed? Had he cried? He felt nothing now. *I'm almost gone.* But then he felt disappointment at having that thought. How could he vanish if he was aware of vanishing? He began again.

No. Nothing. Without. Gone. Breath, heartbeat, heat, leaving, dissipating, gone. But then something terrible happened. Nothing vanished, and there was light. Kuthan's eyes snapped shut, but silver burned through his lids. He moaned and scrambled down the stairs away from the light. It was falling down the stairs after him, chasing him as he ran. It wasn't far. The flickering pools were around him. Stalactites, stalagmites. Reflections. Light. Kuthan shuddered, and retreated to where it was darker. He had never truly explored the cave, but he knew its darkness. *My home. Where I am safe.* The light coming down the stairs was far brighter than the glinting of the pools. *I need to hide!* Kuthan searched desperately. At last he settled in a corner. Lying down, he pressed his body against the cave wall.

But it was too late. Thoughts were coming back, memories returning:

Please let it be done. The Tribute to end all tributes. Enetheal's blood. Enetheal's corpse. Blood and sap flowing, becoming one. The endless stairs, the flickering light beneath the world. A tall, lean figure, with long arms ending in a twisted frenzy of elongated fingers. So dark It was almost a silhouette. Both triumph and despair had swept over Kuthan while It devoured the last tribute. Was this his emotion? Or did the feeling come from It?

Kuthan had prayed, had begged with his mind and soul for the Former to take him next. But the Former did not devour Kuthan. Kuthan had stumbled, had fallen down. *Please.* His hands had scrambled over the ground around him, had felt for one last piece of the world to hold on to ... and found the forgotten tribute.

I thought it was over. But more memories flooded back. Orin gone, taken by Enetheal. The promise he had found in his tributes. The new world he had glimpsed. A friend to save them, to guide them. *But I forced myself to believe it.* Because he had to believe in something, in purpose, in hope, in a perfection that had been denied them, a perfection which could be achieved ....

This world had betrayed them. But that wasn't true. *It gave me nothing. And nothing is what I've always wanted.* So Kuthan embraced the stairs ... but now even *nothing* was not his. The star had chased even that away. The light grew closer and closer. *I can fight it!* Kuthan thought wildly. It was a feeble hope. And then the light grew nearer yet, and Kuthan turned to face it.

The Creator! Kuthan thought wildly for a moment. She was beautiful. Her skin glowed blue-white. Her hair shone even brighter. Her hands were crisscrossed in silver. In one of them she held light. He shrank away, but then she touched him, touched his chest. He felt a searing pain, deep and alive within him. It was cold, and sharp ... and good.

Sound returned. He heard her breathing. Heard his own breathing.

"Kuthan," she whispered. He felt tears sliding down his face, but he didn't say anything.

"Oh Kuthan," she said again. He realized that she too was weeping.

She knelt beside him, letting the star slip to the stone floor, and placing her free hand gently on his shoulder. He looked to her eyes. *Lenya's eyes.* They were soft and they glistened with tears. It wasn't disgust. There was pity, sadness, and something even worse. Nausea welled up inside of him, and he twisted away.

"Leave me!" he rasped. He meant it as a shout, but it sounded small, with a faint echo that quickly died.

"Kuth, you need to come with me," she told him. His tears continued. He shook his head.

"Don't you see Lenya?" he choked out. He gathered his voice again. "This is my service."

"Your service?" Lenya asked. Kuthan did not answer. He looked at the wall, but the star had ruined the darkness, so he closed his eyes. Even still, it was too bright. The silence went on, but the light remained. Lenya stayed.

"I always wanted Orin's task," he said finally. "To vanquish darkness! But my task has always been to embrace it." His voice shook with anger, with hatred, with shame. He took a breath, and tried to let go. "So I have."

She said nothing. "So leave me be!" Kuthan added. He waited. And waited. And waited longer. But the light did not flicker or falter. It was steady and bright, and Lenya's hands were still upon him. He felt anger well up inside of him, but he would not speak. If he spoke it would go on. *She can't stay forever.*

"We need you, Kuth" she whispered softly. The words sounded wrong. Kuthan had to think before making sense of them.

"No," he told her, "you don't."

"Yes, we do," Lenya insisted. They lapsed into silence again.

"We are making a new world, Kuth," she told him. He said nothing.

She stood up, now looking down at him. "But to do that we need you. You bring our thoughts into the emptiness, bring them into existence, an existence tangible beyond what they were as mere thought. You were right. This world was formed flawed. Our creations, our tributes, were devoured. We need you. We need you to help shape the new world. Help us, Kuthan!"

He had never heard her raise her voice before. His heart seemed to catch and something came alive in him just for a moment. But then there was nothing. Lenya smiled at him. In it there was uncertainty and hope.

Kuthan wanted to look at her. He yearned to see happiness in her eyes, to help mend everything. He longed for Orin. For Enetheal. He longed to undo everything and start over. But it was too late. How could she ask for what was impossible?

"Lenya," he croaked. His throat closed. The tears returned.

"I never asked for this," he told her, his voice shaking, and cracked. "I never asked to be. But existence was thrust upon me—a debt I could never repay; and I tried my best with it." He looked up to her eyes, her image blurry through his tears. "I wanted to understand the world, to love it. I think I do understand now: I hate it. I don't care about this world or any world. Nothingness is all I wish for. You were wrong, Len: we never had a choice." He continued to look up at her, hoping she would understand and let him go. But there was no absolution in her eyes.

"You do not hate the world, Kuthan," she told him. "You care so much it hurts. You care more than I ever did. I woke up looking at stars and loving them. Loving them before I saw you, the others, the world. But you, when the warmth of the world touched your face, you were alive. You needed to understand *because* you care." He waited. *Please.* She took a breath and continued:

"You love. And yes, you hate. But you care. Your tribute stones were always the most vivid, the most detailed. The reason emptiness is so hard for you is because it is the opposite of what you are. You know emptiness, and you fill it. You create. Please. Help us shape the new world, Kuthan."

Lenya pulled him to his feet and embraced him. He felt his legs shaking. Without another word she bent down, picked up her star, and walked toward the stairs. Her words still hung in the air. A sudden panic took hold of Kuthan as she reached the first step, but then she turned to face him once more, holding out a hand to him.

"We do have a choice, Kuthan," she whispered. He remained rooted to the cave floor a moment longer, and then all at once he stumbled towards the light, towards her. She smiled.

He reached her at the base of the stairs and they began to climb, step by step, Lenya in the lead.

NAMIN - DAY TWENTY-ONE

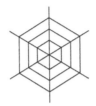

Where are You? He searched. Searched without eyes, sound, or scent. He felt. Of course, Ara and Idra were the easiest to find. They lay on either side of him, their breathing deep, their bodies warm. *Lenya.* Far away he felt her too. But the webs seemed weaker than when he had first woven them. *They need song*, he thought, but he could not leave Idra and Ara. He had always let Lenya go. Maybe because he and Lenya had always shared the night. Like Namin, Lenya seemed safe after sundown. *The stars are dangerous, but her gloves keep her safe from them now.* The night before, when the star had fallen outside of his reach, he had felt her vulnerability. She and Ara had left his protective webs, which only spanned the island. But she had returned, and he would know if she left again. He felt the breeze coming from the beach, from the Stony Shore. He felt the absence of wind in the Sapwood. He felt *them* scrambling over strands of web. Every now and then they would weave their own webs. It made him nervous.

He could not feel theirs. Was the Former singing It's own song? *Where are you?* Idra's trees were safe. Orin's fields were sheltered. The table and the woods were protected. Everywhere he knew. Where besides Ara's Stones did his webs not touch? *Where are You hiding!??*

There must be somewhere else. Somewhere untouched by his webs. And the Former would emerge to claim what was his. Idra rolled over. The waning half moon moved across the sky. Ara mumbled in her sleep. But still he did not feel the Former. *Where are You?* He felt where the webs were stronger and more numerous, where they were weaker and fewer. But there was nothing strange. He felt the occasional flap of wings, the shuffling of night creatures, insects becoming trapped on strands. But these things were not unusual. He realized it all at once, dread suddenly overwhelming him: Lenya was gone. But how could that be?

He refocused. He closed his eyes, slowed his breathing, and carefully remembered where he had last felt contact. It was in the woods near the Sunset Altar. Why could he not feel her always? His webs were upon her hands. Was it because the stars did something to the webs? But then, he considered, he had never felt Idra's basket or Orin's net. He took another deep breath. He had to focus, had to think! He had not felt the Former emerge. He had merely stopped feeling Lenya. Maybe the star had fallen into the shallows, where her body and her breath would not shake the strands. Perhaps the star had fallen once again onto the Shrieking Stones. Or maybe there was somewhere else he hadn't considered .... She had promised she would come back if anything happened. Namin waited, but still he did not feel her. *There's nothing I can do without knowing more,* he realized.

It didn't matter. If she was in danger, he was going. He hated to leave Idra and Ara, but he could not let anything happen to Lenya. Then, just as he relinquished contact, he felt something. *It's Lenya! It must be.* This was infuriating, but once again, he forced himself to become calm. Taking in a deep breath, he exhaled, humming the melody that coursed through his webs. Then his sight was gone, and although he felt his voice reverberating, he no longer heard it. As always, the contact was faint. But they were there. *Two of them. Together.* His mind went blank in utter confusion. *Who?* He reached out to feel, but then he stopped. There was only one person it could be. Revulsion welled up within him and he withdrew from the contact, fully allowing wakefulness to take him. Sight returned, along with the sounds of the night and the smell of the pines. But he did not focus on his senses.

How could this be? Kuthan was gone. They all knew this. But then Namin thought bitterly how Kuthan would, no doubt, have answers when he returned. He wondered why Lenya was with him, but then realized she must have gone down the stairs. *Where the Former lives.* The star must have fallen there. Another misfallen star could not be a coincidence. And once more, Namin wondered if it was a trap.

"Be safe," he whispered. Ara and Idra remained motionless. Careful not to wake Idra, Namin climbed over her sleeping body, walked to the door and opened it slowly, thankful for its silent hinges. He breathed deeply. Between him and the night was a thin web-screen. So delicate. So fragile. The webs. The world. But it would hold. *It must.* Gently he peeled it aside, then secured it back into place behind him. He began to hum, the sound little more than a vibration at first, but soon it began to penetrate the night as the spiders answered his call. They danced across the door frame, leaping and weaving until the screen was thicker and more elaborate than ever. Then he walked around the cabin as well, the spiders following him, spinning and weaving until the entire cabin was wrapped in a sheath of webs. The spiders stared at him when he finished. *They're hungry. They want more.* But Namin had finished singing. He turned away from them, walked to the front step of the cabin and sat down.

Clouds covered the moon, cloaking the world in near darkness, but he saw them approach by the glowing form of Lenya and the faint light of the stars. *She's brighter than they are now.* But Lenya's light was not his concern. In fact, it was not Lenya at all who caught his gaze, but the shadowy silhouette at her side.

Namin stood up. "You've returned," he said curtly. Kuthan shrank behind Lenya, who stepped forward.

"Yes. We have." *She's defending him. After everything he's done.*

"I thought you were gone," Namin told Kuthan. *It would have been easier.* Kuthan's eyes remained downcast.

"I found him," Lenya answered. Kuthan remained mute, bowed behind her.

"And you brought him here? After everything he's done?!" Namin struggled to control his voice as he spoke. He heard a clicking sound behind him. He turned. The spiders were still watching. *Ready to protect us if need be.* Angrily, he turned back to Kuthan.

"I can find another cabin," Kuthan whispered hoarsely.

You can slink back down to your cave and spend eternity there!

"We could find another cabin," Lenya agreed firmly.

Namin couldn't believe it! *There has to be a reason.* His mind raced wildly, with confusion, fear, and outrage. *The stars.* The stars still had her, confused her, had penetrated her mind. *I thought I had freed you. You were supposed to come back to me, and instead you went down the stairs? For a star? They never stopped owning you,* Namin realized sadly. *I must protect her ....*

Lenya watched him, her eyes wide, her expression blank.

Does she care what I say? What could he do? *I could bind him. With song and webs.* But then what would Lenya do?

He did not have much choice. Lenya was going where Kuthan was, and there was no way he could leave Lenya alone with him.

"No," Namin said slowly, carefully keeping the fury from his voice. The next words came with difficulty. "One roof." He took a breath. "For all of us."

"Good," Lenya said softly and she put a hand on Namin's arm. He resisted the impulse to shrug it off. Lenya walked to the web- screen.

"Wait." Namin's voice was soft but he spoke with authority. "Kuthan does it." Kuthan and Lenya both turned to him in surprise, but Namin did not back down. "Kuthan does it," he repeated again, watching carefully. Gently, Kuthan peeled aside the web-screen. The web didn't glow, nor did it burn Kuthan or stop his passage. Namin clenched and unclenched his fists, and then, finally, took a breath. They entered as a threesome. Kuthan walked over to the far bed, away from Idra and Ara. *Good.* But after a moment Lenya joined him. *What have the stars done to her?* Again he stopped, but there was no way to argue. Instead he crawled into bed with Idra and Ara, but sat up so as to not fall asleep. Kuthan fell asleep instantly. Namin and Lenya stared at one another until Namin tired of staring. He closed his eyes.

Morning came too soon. Namin woke up, shaken by Idra, and saw that Ara was being roused as well.

"Wha—?" Ara yawned, but stopped in mid-yawn. Across the room were the sleeping forms of Lenya and Kuthan.

"What happened?" Idra asked. Her voice carried dread and confusion. *Good question.* But Namin had to provide the answer. Idra and Ara looked at him expectantly. He responded by inclining his head towards the door. As soon as they were outside he began to talk.

"Lenya brought him back last night."

"And?" Ara prompted.

"And that's all," Namin answered, irritation in his voice. He saw Ara was upset. "Sorry," he added. "We need to talk together. As a group." His throat itched, so he swallowed before continuing. "Last night wasn't the time. We couldn't speak then. But we will now." He swallowed again and turned to Idra.

"Could you two get us fruit?" They continued to look at him expectantly. "I'll bring the others to the Welcome Table," he added.

"Yes," Idra added after a moment. "Of course." But Namin could tell that they too were deeply unsettled. *Why did I let him in?* Namin asked himself. *Because there was nothing else to do.*

But it was wrong. Kuthan's presence was a poison. *Lenya,* he thought bitterly. *Why?* He returned to the cabin. She was waiting for him; somehow he wasn't surprised. Kuthan lay next to her, still asleep.

For a moment they just held eyes. Namin wanted to scream. *We are supposed to be the protectors! To hold everything together when it's falling apart! How can you betray me? Betray us?* Why had she brought him back? Instead he took a deep breath, allowing a calmness in his voice that was denied to his mind.

"Hey, Len."

"Hey, Naim." She said it normally, as if nothing was wrong, but then she continued. "You're upset." She looked at him.

"Yes," he answered.

"Don't be," she said simply. The words were aggravating.

"Don't be?" he snapped, again struggling to control his voice. "How could I not be? Why wouldn't I be?"

She held a finger to her lips, nodding her head toward Kuthan's sleeping form, and when she spoke, she was quiet.

"How? Only you can know. Why? Because he's one of us."

"He is not! Not after Orin! Not after Enetheal! And we cannot let this happen. I need you, Lenya. I need you on my side!"

"We all need each other. Now more than ever."

Namin didn't answer. She was beyond reason. He closed his eyes and let the time crawl by. It was painful.

"It's time," he finally decided. He strode to the door.

"Kuthan," Lenya whispered. She shook him gently. Kuthan opened his eyes slowly. "It's time."

Kuthan took a moment, and then rose to his feet. Without another word they began to walk to the Welcome Table. Namin took the lead. Behind him Lenya led Kuthan by the hand.

Idra and Ara awaited them with a basket full of fruit, and the goblet of sap. Namin sat down between them. Moments later, Lenya and Kuthan sat opposite them. The only voices were those of the wind and trees.

"I found him," Lenya said. "Kuthan has come home." No one said anything. "The seeker has been found," Lenya added. *She's right,* he realized with horror. *It doesn't change anything though. Ara's prophecy.*

"Not only do we *need* him to shape the new world. We *want* him because we love him."

"No!" Namin and Kuthan exclaimed together. Namin wished he could end Kuthan by staring at him. He was at a loss for words. But Kuthan spoke, his voice low, quiet, and steady.

"I don't want love. I don't want forgiveness. I want what I deserve." He took turns meeting each of them in the eye. "My actions are beyond forgiveness, beyond undoing. I was lost. Confused. I wanted the world to end—the world in which Orin could be taken from us, the world in which our lives were not our own. I fooled myself into thinking that ending Enetheal was the only path, and hate overcame me. He cleared his throat:

"There is no reconciliation. My evil cannot be undone. That is as it is. But I will do what I can to help you build a new world, if you will have me."

His words hung on the air. Even Namin was stunned. *How could you even hope we would consider building something with you?*

But Idra spoke first:

"Eat."

"What?" Kuthan answered, confused.

"Eat. You must be starving." Idra said again. She did not smile, but she was serious, sincere.

Hesitantly Kuthan took one of the fruits. *No!* Namin winced. Lenya took one next. Then Idra and Ara. Finally

Namin took one. Ara began to speak: She told Kuthan of the new covenant spoken to them by echoes, wind, and stone. The new world that was to be. Idra told Kuthan that they had found the tree, the tree which reflected downward in the Sapwood. He listened intently and nodded. Namin wished for fruit with no flavor. When they were finished eating Ara told them it was time for tributes. She and Idra got up. Lenya gave Kuthan a smile and followed. Kuthan started to get up, but Namin stopped him short.

He came close to Kuthan so that they were eye to eye.

"I did not save this world for you." His voice was fierce and low so that the others wouldn't hear.

"I do not plan on creating one for me," Kuthan answered. Namin blinked. They both rose, and joined the others.

Maybe. Maybe this can work.

KUTHAN - DAYS TWENTY-ONE AND TWENTY-TWO

We never had a choice. The world was different from when he had last walked these paths. There were traces of starshine and strands of web. *We are all broken. The world, too. How can something whole emerge from something broken?* They were to make a new world. He remembered the Former, the shapes of the forgotten tributes, and her, *Lenya.* He stumbled after her, blind to all else. *I'll make a world for you, Len.* The others spread out over the Stony Shores. Kuthan stumbled over stones to keep close to Lenya. But he did not look for tributes. *A new world. How? Why?* We can only exist as broken forms. Kuthan remembered the beginning. *We were all the same before we were broken. Only now are we who we are.* His mind returned to the cave, to the last Tribute, to Enetheal.

He had dreamt of Enetheal the night before. They had been alone in the Sapwood. *The sun arced across the sky with alarming speed. "Kill me!" he begged Enetheal. But Enetheal didn't move. "Kill me!" he urged again. He gazed up at the sun anxiously. Time was running out. "Quickly!" But Enetheal didn't move. Kuthan watched himself enter the clearing, followed by the others, watched himself raise the last tribute, and watched Enetheal's blood as it drained into the pools of sap. The others vanished, and he was alone with Enetheal's corpse.*

Kuthan found the cup. He filled it with Enetheal's blood, now tainted with sap, and poured it into Enetheal's mouth. "Please come back," he pleaded. And then Enetheal was choking: "Kill me," Enetheal begged. Kuthan had awoken. Had remembered darkness and light. Had remembered Lenya.

"Enetheal didn't have a mouth," he reminded himself. He touched his own mouth as he followed Lenya into the shallows. Finally Lenya found a stone and they began their way back. The others glanced at Kuthan as they walked. Their eyes darted to his empty hands, but they said nothing. *Silence.* Kuthan was glad for it. *They would not be quiet if I wasn't here.* But he was here, so silence belonged.

He watched Lenya trace over her tribute, her finger covered in berry juice. He watched its color change, watched her put leaves on it. It rained lightly as they worked. *Too much rain*, Kuthan thought. *I lost Orin in the rain.* Why should they be out here? They could be in the cabin together. The door would be shut and they would be warm and comfortable. They could close their eyes.

Lenya began to climb stairs, and Kuthan followed, briefly remembering the last time he had climbed up that plateau before returning his attention to Lenya. *Len's stairs. Hers go up, mine go down, but we always return to the earth between.* They reached the top. One by one they let the day's tributes follow the rain into the well. When Kuthan reached the well he had nothing to add to its emptiness. He looked down into the darkness. *It must lead to the cave. One big circle.* But then why was there no sunlight? And what was the light down there? Moonlight? *The time for questions is done.* He pushed the thoughts aside.

"Look!" Idra shouted. But he did not look. *The darkness is right here. Maybe I should tell them to look.* But then Lenya put a hand on him, so he had to look. Slowly, he turned. The rain had picked up, but at the horizon the sun burst through the clouds. A golden light spread across the whole island, reflecting off the world, illuminating the trees, the rocks, the paths, the cabins, and shining off the water. He saw the Welcome Table at the hill, Idra's great trees, the Stony Shores, the Shrieking Stones, the Sapwood, the beach, and even where Orin's field and the Sunset Altar must be.

And he saw *them*. Not just Lenya, but Idra, Ara, and Namin. The sun shone off of them too. Idra directed their gaze away from the sun to the rainbow which shone with brilliant colors over the Stony Shores. Above it there was a faint echo, another rainbow. His eyes stung with tears. He turned back to the sun, its light, its glow. *I can do this,* he realized. And he told them.

"I can do this."

They stared at him, not comprehending. But Kuthan felt himself smile, even though he was crying.

"I will do this."

Idra smiled too. It was not the smile he remembered, but it was hers. She put down her basket. In it were stones big and small, berries, sand, and fruit. Carefully wedged among them, so that sap would not spill, was the goblet.

"Let me know if you need anything," Idra said, and then she was gone. Lenya put her hand on his shoulder, pressed gently, and went after Idra. Ara nodded her approval. Namin looked at him, and then turned away. Kuthan began. He took out the stones and began to paint.

He started with the sun. And then he painted the sun again. And again. And each time he painted, it was different. It was big, it was small, it was gold, yellow, orange, red. It was hot. It was warm. It was cold. It was high. It was low. It was gone. He painted the sky. Again. And again. And again. The clouds changed each time. And the light, and the mood. He painted with water and with wind. With passion and with tranquility. Night fell. Idra quietly brought more stones. More berries. More of everything. Kuthan ate and drank, but it was brief and he never stopped. Kuthan painted the night. The stars. The crescent moon above him as it was, as it used to be, and as it would be. He painted it full. He painted it gone. He painted the water and wind again, now at night. And began painting the land as he saw it in darkness. He painted the falling star that Lenya had gone to retrieve. And then he painted the other stars. He painted the quiet of night and the silver that shifted with the clouds. Morning came, and Kuthan painted the day again. He painted the island, both as he could see it and as he had seen it. Idra brought him food, and drink.

"Do you want to pick tributes?" she asked. He didn't stop but he answered:

"Pick them for me, I trust you. All of you."

They brought him stones and materials and he continued to paint. Animals. Trees. Flowers. Plants. Sand. Dirt. Mud.

He painted everything his mind touched upon. Again and again and again. And every time he went to the well, he dropped his tributes, filling the darkness with his mind.

Kuthan started to paint anew. Not what he saw or had seen, but what was not yet present—lands that had never been, things that could be, that should be.

"How can we help?" Ara asked.

"Paint with me," he told them.

And they painted together. Idra painted living things. Lenya, sky. Ara, stone. Namin, the changing world. Kuthan guided them. He told them what was needed. Sometimes they would tell each other what to paint as well. Like Kuthan, they gave shape to things that had never been. Kuthan painted with calmness, and he painted passionately. The others would take it in turns to leave and gather rocks into Idra's basket, but not Kuthan. Kuthan could not leave. He painted his dream. He painted Paradise.

ARA - DAYS TWENTY-TWO AND TWENTY-THREE

Ara's hands shook with excitement. *We are doing it! They were shaping a new world together. *This is what we were all meant for. Orin too. We need him. We need him for our new world.* But for now they all focused, working with purpose and determination. They painted. They ate and drank. They gathered stones. Sometimes they slept. They did this all in turns.

I need to tell him. She had listened, and brought them an answer. It was working. They were making a new world. But there were parts that were missing. It was hard to speak to him. They listened to him. Worked alongside him. But she had not yet spoken to him apart from asking about her tributes and twice directing him on his. *This isn't that different.*

"Kuthan," she said softly. The others stopped working. Kuthan's hands continued moving, his eyes remaining fixed on the world between his hands. Then his hands became motionless and he blinked.

"Ara," he answered, as if not trusting his voice with her name.

"You have heard the new covenant, the one I brought from the Stones. And now we are creating a new world with tributes."

"Yes," he answered. His eyes met hers and she struggled not to look away.

"We need four kinds of tributes: 'Tributes made for world new. Tributes made that were unclaimed. Tributes with the maker's mark. Tributes show the maker maimed.'" Ara recited the passage carefully. She saw that he understood, but finished her thought:

"We've been making the first kind. What about the others?" Sudden dread filled her. "The only unclaimed tributes I can think of are the ones left behind by the echoes. And I dropped those into the water."

"You didn't," Kuthan answered. "I mean, I'm sure you did. But those are not the unclaimed ones spoken of." He took a breath and looked over the edge of the plateau. He looked up at the sun and then back at her. "They are down the stairs." he said softly. "I never told you. Some of the tributes that I brought down were not taken."

"Oh," she thought out loud.

"Don't worry," Kuthan said evenly. She realized he was talking to everyone now: "I'll get them." She stared at him, pondering his words. She wasn't alone.

"Now?" she asked.

"No," he answered. "First I finish here. Then I'll finish there. And then .... Then I'll be done." He said it calmly, almost happily.

"Oh." They returned to work. They ate. They drank. The sun moved across the sky. And then Ara resumed her questioning:

"And what about the others? Tributes that have the maker's mark? Tributes that show the maker maimed?"

"I wouldn't worry about those," Kuthan answered. "Our mark is on everything we touch. I could never make a tribute such as you have. Nor could you mimic mine." He smiled. "And I'm sure that each of us has delivered a tribute that showed we were maimed." They returned to work once more, speaking only of the new world. At long last the sun began to set.

That night they slept on the plateau, although they did not sleep much. Kuthan woke them when he needed them, and this was often. Ara worked, finished, dozed off, and then worked anew. She began painting paths, and looked across the island to the Sapwood where Orin's paths used to be.

They walked together. She and Orin. There were trees, and a bright sky. But mostly there was Orin. They held hands.

"I love your paths," Ara told him.

"Good," Orin answered. They reached a fork, and he squeezed her hand gently as they paused. He turned his face up to her and she pulled away in horror. His eyes were gone. In their place was an expanse of flat smooth skin.

"This path is for you," he told her, gesturing with his hand. She walked, and as she walked the world became beautiful. And then she realized Orin wasn't there. Horrified, she turned back, and started running, trying to retrace her steps. He couldn't see! How could she forget he couldn't see?! She arrived at the fork, but Orin had disappeared.

"Ara."

"Didn't I tell you? The answers are off the paths." She turned.

"Ara." It was Kuthan. Ara brushed the wet from her eyes. It was too dark for them to see her tears. They worked on a tribute together. All of them. And then she worked on another with Lenya and Namin. Then one with Idra and Namin. And then the sun began to rise.

That day they moved. They made tributes in the woods, in the cabins, along the coasts. They didn't just use rocks. They used bark, and flowers, and leaves. They used anything that seemed right to use. The day passed more quickly than the last, and then, once again, the sun began to set.

"Let's watch it from our old place," Kuthan offered. So they did. They hiked across the island to Sunset Altar and watched the sun sink beneath the waves. They ate fruit while they watched. Ara threw a piece in and watched the ripples catch the last of the sun's light.

"Tonight we'll sleep," Kuthan stated, and no one contradicted him. They started back to the cabin. As they passed the path to the Firefly Field Ara had an idea.

"I'll catch up," she called out. Namin glowered, but she cut him off: "One more tribute. I'll be quick. Back long before nightfall," she promised. Idra gave her the basket full of materials and they went separate ways.

The fields were silent when she arrived. Dusk was settling. She knew how to capture an image better than she ever had before. There was a flash of gold. And then another. Her mind remembered, and her hands brought it back. Orin. Orin in the field. Orin with the fireflies, the lanterns, his net, his face, his smile. *He's here.* She finished just as the wind began to grow cold. *Orin's task really was right between day and night.* She began her walk back but then paused as she saw the Shrieking Stones far away. There was wind now, but the Stones were still silent. She walked past Namin and Orin's cabin where she had found Orin too late. Enetheal had been there. He had been too late as well. She closed her eyes, and saw his mouthless form. *Did you leave the paths when you came? Did you choose as I did?* But Ara opened her eyes again. No Enetheal. No Orin. The night was blacker without his lanterns. She continued past Idra and Kuthan's cabin. Finally she arrived at their cabin. Namin stood outside.

"You're late," he told her.

"Yes," she answered. "Sorry." They hugged.

Together they entered the cabin. On one side Kuthan was deep in sleep, his head against Lenya. Kuthan's brow was furrowed and his lips formed a thin line. Lenya slept lightly, her eyes fluttering. The moonlight did not touch Idra, but Ara brushed against her sleeping form as she crawled into bed. Namin took his usual place in between them. Together they allowed their breathing to slow and quiet, until the wind's breathing was louder than their own.

"Will Lenya wake for her star?" Ara whispered.

"I think so." Namin answered. "Somehow she always finds the stars."

Ara laughed quietly, "We all find a way to do what we need to."

"What we want to do," Namin added. They were quiet. Ara felt sleep pulling her inward, but she desired to talk. There was too much working. She missed speaking of other things.

"What do you think we'll do afterward?" she asked Namin. He took so long to respond that at first she thought he was asleep. But then, just as she was drifting off he answered.

"Love. Laugh. Sing." He started to trail off. "Swim. Run. Climb. Eat. Drink … Sleep."

Ara smiled and held him close.

"ARRRAAAA!!" Ara jolted awake, wiping the tears from her eyes. He was here. She had listened. *I knew it. I knew!* She laughed through her tears. The wind was back. His voice was back. *His and mine.* Quickly and carefully, she crawled over Namin and Idra.

"ARRRAAAA!" She unlatched the door. The wind thrust it open, but she caught it before it slammed against the wall. Ara undid the web, closed the door behind her, and replaced it.

Nothing was left to chance. It was a painful world. *But a beautiful one. Nothing left to chance.* She laughed as she ran with the wind.

"Echoes are what stay behind when voice no longer cries, a song that never ends, a life after it dies!" She laughed. She wept. She ran. Trees flew by her. Echoes had come back before, and now Orin was back. She had fed the hope, but she had denied herself true belief. *Because it would be too painful if it wasn't true.* But it was.

"ARRRAAAA!!" he called again.

"My living light you made a path, my living light you found our way. My living light come dance with me, and bring this night to day!" The answers had always been around them. In the very fabric of reality. They had made the world too complex when really, it was simple.

"We live in a world of circles, ripples, echoes, and reflections." She whispered it to herself.

"ARRRAAAA!!!" There was urgency in his voice now.

I choose the living light. I choose the coming end. I choose the living path. I choose to keep my friend. He was both now. The light and the path.

She reached the edge of the island, where the chain of rocks led outward. Above, clouds raced across the sky. A glimmer of moonlight shone briefly, and then was gone. The wind was stronger than ever. The waves rose high, crashing over the rocks, and rushing onto the shore. The stepping stones were farther apart than they had ever been. *As if that could stop me.*

"ARRRAAAA!!" he shrieked. Her blood ran cold, joy extinguished. It was the same shriek that she had heard the night they had lost him. *Not again! Not this time.* She knew her choice now as she never had before. *The answers are off the paths.* That had always been the way. And *her* stones were certainly far from the path. Ara leapt. The rock was slippery, but she righted herself instantly. She gritted her teeth, and leapt again.

"ARRRAAAA!" he shrieked again, his voice higher this time. *I can't stop.* "Here I am!" she shouted into the wind. She leapt again and again without pause. Waves crashed against the rock. The spray was cold. Her feet slid and scraped against the rocks' surface. They had never been so far apart, or so slippery. Her shins slammed down painfully but she stood again immediately.

"ARRRAAAA!" He is so close.

"ORRRRIN!!" She yelled back. She jumped again, and again. And then she was there. The wind howled and moaned, but Orin's voice rang out above all else. She ran to the middle of the ring. "I'm here Orin!"

She looked desperately around the circle of stones. Which one was his? All of them? None of them? The wind?

"Please," she begged the stones, begged the wind. "Orin. Orin come back to me."

"ARRRAAAA" The wind swirled around her. She heard the voice shriek and moan, whistle and hum, sigh and howl and whisper. But the voice was wrong. And it wasn't just around her; it was inside her. Ara clamped her hands about her ears, but the Voice reverberated in her very bones. The wind stung her eyes, blurred the world. She could not see the island, nor even the Stones before her. *I must leave.* Blindly she stumbled towards the edge, toward home, but the wind which had first tried to blow her away, now caged her. On and on it swirled about her.

I can't breathe, she realized with panic. She tried to exhale, but instead more air rushed in. It poured into her, forcing its way into her throat and lungs. She tried to scream, but the voice that came out was not her own. She fell to her knees. The world swam before her, blurring, darkening. *Orin.* She saw a path. Not lined with golden lights, but a path nonetheless. She crawled. Crawled away from the standing stones, out of the circle.

The water was cold. She couldn't breathe. Above, the wind howled and shrieked. But Ara sank into silence.

NAMIN - DAY TWENTY-FOUR

His sleep was deep. Not just deep, but dark. It wasn't that he didn't dream. The dream itself was soundless, lightless, and slow. He was not frantic in the darkness. Nor was he calm. He just was. But there was something he was anticipating. It would happen. The assuredness that it would happen made the 'when' irrelevant.

"I am supposed to anticipate something." There was something he had missed. Something wrong. And then there was panic. And dread.

Suddenly there were hands on him.

"Namin!" Idra whispered frantically, her hand on his shoulder. "Where's Ara?"

"What?" he blurted, trying to shake the sleepiness and the dread. Why was he so tired? Idra pointed. On Namin's other side was the indent Ara normally filled, and a single tribute stone. It was Orin. Orin in the field. Orin's eyes and smile. He was surrounded by golden light. The dread returned.

"Come," he told Idra. She heard the forced calm in his voice.

"What's wrong?" she asked. Namin ignored her.

"Lenya. Kuthan. Get up." He didn't shout, but they heard him. *Lenya must know.*

"Lenya. Did you talk to Ara last night? Did you see her?" Lenya paused, considering. *She always needs to think. Has to sift through the starlight in her mind. Speak!* His frustration remained unvoiced, however, and finally she answered:

"No. I did not see her," Lenya said quietly. "When I came back from the star I didn't see anything. I just went to sleep." How could she not notice? *Stars again. Stars always.*

"Come with me," he told them. No one questioned him. They hurried down the path, past where Kuthan and Idra used to sleep. Past his and Orin's cabin. Through trees and bushes. The day was just becoming warm, and a misty sun shone through an overcast sky, casting a haze on the world. Sweat beaded on his skin and he paused to wipe his face before he continued. The Shrieking Stones seemed distant when they arrived. Unnaturally far from the island. The waves between the shore and the Stones frothed and heaved. Namin stopped and squinted, trying to make out Ara's form.

"Do you see her?" Idra asked, staring desperately out towards the rocks.

"No," Lenya said sadly. They stared a moment longer, but saw only waves and rocks. When they strained, they could hear the faint whisper of wind in the trees over the constant ebb and flow of the water, but the sounds of insects and birds were gone. And Ara wasn't anywhere ….

"Yes," Kuthan blurted out suddenly. "There!"

On the shore, just where rock met water, lay an unmoving form.

Namin felt his heart grow cold. As one, they rushed over to her. *Please,* he thought desperately. Perhaps she had risen early just to watch the waves? Or had fallen asleep after visiting the Stones?

"Ara!" Namin didn't know whether he or Idra shouted first. The two of them knelt beside her, Kuthan and Lenya standing close behind. Idra brought her hand to Ara's chest, feeling for a heartbeat. Namin grasped Ara's hand and shook her still form. "Ara!" he screamed again. But if she heard she didn't answer. He looked over her desperately, searching her limp body for an explanation. *Why didn't I feel her leave? Why did she leave? What was she thinking?* He paused as he examined her ears. A thin membrane stretched over them. *Just like ....* He closed his eyes and took a breath, then opened them once more. His mind was still racing. There had to be something.

Idra pressed down on Ara's chest. Suddenly Ara coughed. There was a horrible gurgling sound. Namin got behind her head, hoisted her onto his lap, and squeezed his arms around her chest and belly forcefully. Ara coughed again, and this time water came out. Namin repeated the move once more, and then Ara was coughing on her own.

"Come on, Ara!" Idra shrieked. Ara got on all fours, vomited, and then rolled over, collapsing onto her back, face up once again.

"Ara, we're here. Talk to us," Lenya said.

Namin moved around, running his hand over her form. The air was heavy and hot. Sweat beaded uncomfortably on his skin, but Ara's skin was cold and dry. He bent down beside her ears again, running his fingers over the membrane. Ara's eyes opened. Her pupils had shrunken within her green irises.

She took in a ragged breath, but as she tried to exhale, what came out was a choking, rasping hiss:

Tributes stolen bleed me
but every action feeds me
All that is, is in my name
All that is, is mine to claim

They froze. It was the Former's voice. But it was also Ara's. They stared at her in terror. Her body trembled as she spoke, but the words came with horrible clarity:

Plants and trees
roots and leaves
all that fly and swim and run
stars and moon and earth and sun

"Hold her down!" Namin shouted. Idra was the first to act, and she quickly grasped Ara's other arm.

stone and wind, warmth and cold
voice and thought, young and old

Kuthan and Lenya each took hold of a leg, but as they held Ara's body, she only writhed more. Her voice grew stronger, louder. There was undeniable certainty to the words:

Stars shall steal your light away
Weaver's web shall be undone
Fruit of life shall be unclaimed
Circle mended, circle one

"The water," Namin spluttered, struggling with Ara's flailing arm. They listened and they followed. As one they carried her.

You cannot steal away your fate
You cannot take what I create
I gifted blood, I gifted breath
You dined on life, now drink on death

With a splash they brought her body just beyond the shallows, forcing her beneath the water. The Former's voice, her voice, was submerged. They looked to Namin, their eyes wide, their bodies shaking. *It's me. It needs to be me now. Ever since I sang to shield them. I need to stay strong.*

"Pull her out," he said, his voice not wavering. Ara coughed up more water, and then shuddered violently before emitting a long slow breath. In the soft noise was the shrieking of Ara's stones, and another voice, more familiar and terrible.

The others looked back and forth between Namin and Ara. They were waiting for something more to happen, but Namin was not going to wait.

"With me," he said. They walked together, supporting her weight without speaking so that the only sounds were their footsteps and Ara's splutters and coughing. They moved along the path and across the Stargazing Beach. Ara struggled as they climbed the stairs that led up to the plateau. The others looked to Namin again when they reached the top.

Namin avoided their eyes, looking purposefully at the well. He moved, and they followed. As they approached the well Ara's eyes fixed on its opening, and her body became still.

Ara breathed in once more as they reached the well. Her pupils were now large and dark, but her gaze was unfocused. They held her over the opening, and Namin looked back at them, at their trembling limbs, their widened eyes, and at the sweat that streamed down their bodies.

"Let her go," Namin said. But none of them did. Not even Namin. There were tears. *How can I ask them to do this?* But he was not asking them to do anything he wouldn't do. *This is the only way.*

"We'll do it together," he said slowly. "On Three." *They must know I am certain, so that they may be.*

"One." They looked at each other and then quickly back to Namin. "Two." He tried to keep his voice calm, but it shook as he said, "Three." They let go. Ara's body plummeted into the darkness.

They were still there, somehow, and time went on. The world had not stopped for Orin. It had not stopped for Enetheal. And it did not stop now. It was a long time before any of them moved. Kuthan was the first to stir. He walked slowly away from the well and looked out over the island. Idra was next, following after Kuthan and taking his hand in hers. Namin looked at Lenya. She returned his gaze from across the well. They blinked, but continued to share eyes.

Finally Namin found his voice. He turned his eyes away from the island and out upon the endless waves. Somewhere out there was where this had all started. They had been a group of six. They had known only sky and water, their vessel, and each other. They had not chosen a path. They had not made a path. The waves had brought them here.

And they had chosen to stay. What would have happened if they had not? Starvation? Thirst? Another land?

Lenya walked beside him, weaving her web-laced fingers between his own. Their fingers interlocked. *Are her eyes on the same horizon? Or on the stars that have yet to rise?* Namin closed his eyes. Maybe she was still here with him. His lids burned with tears and he took a breath. *I need to hold us together.* He took another breath, and opened his eyes again. Lenya turned to him, and then pulled him toward her, holding him close. A wave of cold energy rushed through him. He held on. And then they broke apart. Lenya's eyes met his. *She is here.* He glanced away from her and saw Kuthan and Idra approaching. They were looking at him for direction. Lenya too. *I will sing for them.*

Namin stepped to the edge of the well, and stared into the darkness. Somewhere in there were all their hopes. His voice emerged from deep within, unbroken. He sang of Ara, who was gone. Her smile. Her eyes. Her stubbornness. Her laughter. Her sorrow. Her anger. Her regret. Her fears. Her hopes. All the nights he had sung for her were in his melody. But the song grew greater still. His voice echoed down the well, and echoed back from deep within. He sang of Enetheal next, and then of Orin. Then he lifted his eyes from the depths and let his gaze rest on Lenya. The change in his tune was as subtle as it was ethereal. His melody and voice shifted as his eyes moved on to Kuthan. Something inside him twisted, but Namin felt stronger as his song finally turned to Idra. Then, at last, he sang for the new world. *I only hope there are spiders there to weave.*

LENYA - DAYS TWENTY-FOUR AND TWENTY-FIVE

Ara had been the first to notice when the stars were claiming Lenya. She had been the most upset to find Lenya 'drifting away'. But now she wasn't here. *You were supposed to finish building the new world with us,* Lenya protested, ... but it was not to the real Ara; it was only to the Ara in her mind. Lenya had never seen an 'echo' as the others had. What now?

She refocused. Above her were four stars. Not long now. Lenya smiled to herself. They have always pulled me away. But my place is here. It hurt to desire both. She was watching from the beach. *I remember why I am here.* She could hear the insect noises from the forest and the waves washing against the shore. She could feel the grains of sand beneath her body, the water lapping at her feet, the wind on her skin. Once it had felt cold to her. Now it all felt warm.

Enetheal had lain beside her here. And Ara. And then Orin as well. But then she refocused on the stars. No sooner had her eyes touched upon them than another fell. *Only three left.* This one had a halo that moved with it. *It's brighter than the sun.* The whole island came to life in its light. *The Sapwood.* She always knew exactly where they landed now.

She began to run. *Where are you leading me? Why do I follow?* They needed the stars. They did not know what had happened to Orin. Or to Ara. *It must have been their services that undid them, so what do I do about the stars?* There were webs everywhere. They were eerie. Lenya missed the island as it had been before it was laced with webs. Every so often she would purposely brush a finger across a strand.

Namin had accomplished his task. *But he's barely holding things together.* And so it was for each of them. What they had done with Ara was the only thing they could do. And yet Lenya found herself running faster to her star. The Sapwood was silent, but the webs were everywhere. *I am safe except for the starlight, but the stars are my deliverance.*

It had made a small indent in the earth. Sap had trickled from a nearby pool, encircling it. Even earthbound, it retained its halo. She picked it up. "With or without you, I will never be free," she told her star. But she knew what she would do, and no longer hesitated or clung to it. She ran through the woods, across the beach, and up the stairs as she clutched her star.

Waiting at the top was the well. Its opening seemed impatient. Lenya paused. The well wasn't the only thing waiting. The garden was alive. The silvery petals of the flowers turned towards her. *Eyes that drink.* Lenya smiled.

They are as torn as I am, rooted in the earth to eat, faces towards the sky, praying that their thirst for starlight might be quenched.

Carefully she walked to a cluster of flowers. They seemed eager to leave the soil. When she brought their roots to her star, they entwined themselves around the light hungrily. She added soil and pebbles, packing them carefully around the root-encased star. *Earth, star, and something torn between.* She did not hesitate, but released them into the well. Nothing would be hard to let go of ever again after today. "Goodbye Ara," she whispered.

IDRA - DAY TWENTY-FIVE

Idra sat before the empty pool. All around her were trees, silent and tall, all with sap trickling up their trunks from the pools in which they stood. Reflected in the pools around her were treetops, and a sky that was just beginning to fill with gold. Within the empty pool of sap in front of her was the Tree. It's branches were great and thick. They forked again and again and again, until they were out of sight.

Idra closed her eyes, and took a breath. When she opened them the tree was gone. One day. One night. One day. And then it would be time. She rose to her feet. Once she had relished her morning climbs as a challenge, a welcome to the day. Although climbing still marked the beginning of the day, now the task was effortless. Her body moved on its own. Without hesitation. Without fatigue. No longer did she consider each of her movements. Now she leapt from branch to branch, or spread her weight between branches without conscious thought. The island was beautiful from the treetops. The sun and wind were completely hers up there.

When her basket was full, she returned to the world. She moved across the island and climbed Lenya's stairs. At the top, the well waited. She took a piece of fruit from her basket and held it carefully over the center of the well. *If it hits the side it will be bruised.* Then she released it. Every day she had brought fruit to the well. *Fruit collected from each tree. Their seeds shall help the world grow.*

Then she left the well, climbed down the stairs, crossed the beach, and headed for the Welcome Table. Once, there, she arranged the remaining fruits around the table, placing the goblet, brimming with thick sap, in the center.

There is still time. And the others need to sleep. It would be better to let them rest. They had been through so much. Idra sat down, allowing her breathing to slow. About her the wind in the trees was gentle, the birds alive with song. It still didn't feel real. Idra closed her eyes and an image of Ara swam in front of her: Ara's eyes open wide, her pupils so small that they were almost gone, vowing that all was hopeless. *But you had already given us hope that could not be taken away.*

They had dragged her struggling form and thrown it into the well. Idra wondered if there would be a new world. *Hopes of the hopeless.*

Namin had sung for the new world and had saved them once again. On the first day of tributes Idra had been the last to find hers. She had panicked. And then again, when she could not find the tree. She knew that she would not panic now. She felt only calm. How could she be calm after what they had done to Ara? *But I accept what has happened and what I will do.*

She returned to the others. The inside of the cabin was still dark. *How are they still asleep?* But she found herself smiling. She crawled next to Namin, huddling up to him. She closed her eyes.

They woke late. The sun had shifted. Idra didn't know when the others had awoken, but she knew that they were awake. They were all still lying in. *Ara would have had us up and moving, making Tributes. I'm one who gets us moving, too,* Idra reminded herself. She used Namin to prop herself up.

"Time to get up," she told him. She climbed out of bed. "Kuthan. Lenya. Namin." One by one they looked at her. "Let's go." The air smelled of pine needles and fallen leaves and there was a warm breeze. They ate and drank at the table.

Her heart rose when they began to eat. They didn't smile, but their eyes grew brighter, their breathing deeper. After they ate, they walked together along the Stony Shores. The stones there were not as bright as they had once been. They took turns filling Idra's basket. They brought berries, too. Sticky sap. Sand. Leaves. They climbed the stairs. The wind grew colder and stronger, but their exertion kept them warm. Atop the plateau they began to work.

They worked separately that day. Idra painted one stone, and then another. But on the third stone she stopped. *I can't concentrate.* To either side of her Namin and Lenya were busy painting. She walked to Kuthan, who was scowling thoughtfully at his work.

"Do you need me?" she asked. Kuthan shook his head, his brow still furrowed.

"I'll be back," she told him. She took her basket with her. Namin looked up, a questioning expression in his eyes, but she showed him her basket. He nodded and Idra left.

She gathered fruit and stones. Even as she finished, her feet continued, and she found herself wandering. Her eyes watched the lanterns now. They were empty and lightless. They had never flashed during the day. However, they had made the night come to life. Idra squinted. The sun glinted off of the lanterns, and if she closed her eyes half way, she could pretend there were fireflies. The sun felt good with her eyes half-closed. She let the wind guide her down the path, following the flashes.

And then she was back at the cabin. She hesitated before entering, but peeled back the web, and went inside. She opened the windows, straightened Lenya and Kuthan's bed, and turned to their own. And there he was. *Orin.*

"I'm losing my mind," she whispered. But she smiled. *Orin and Ara.* It was Ara's tribute. The one she had made the night before she left them. And it was Orin too. *Did he lead me here?* She looked about the room. It was dark enough that a flash of gold seemed like it would belong, but there were no fireflies. She turned back to the stone. "You did not leave us empty handed, Ara."

"Tributes show the maker maimed," Idra said aloud. "I was so fragile before. But I don't feel broken now. So how do I show myself 'maimed?'" Ara did not answer. Orin did not answer. But she imagined they were there considering with her. Idra's eyes fell upon Orin's net. She remembered picking it up in the Sapwood. She closed her eyes as memories flowed through her. *I know where my tribute is.* She reached for Orin's net and holding it close, began to walk.

Her feet brought her to the Sapwood. The sap was flowing quickly, as it had been in the morning. In one hand she carried Ara's last tribute. In the other was Orin's net. Despite the many times she had been here, it still appeared vast, still endless. She walked away from Orin's paths.

On and on she journeyed. It no longer seemed like a place where she could get lost. *If every place is the same and it goes on forever, then I am already where I need to be.* She found it. The table. *Enetheal's Table.* She walked up to it. It was still crumbling and overgrown with moss. She put her hand on the uneven surface. There were letters here that meant something to Enetheal. Was it by these rules he had cast Orin into the well? By these rules brought us sap to drink and showed us the island? Were those his own choices? Had he broken the rules? Or was he perhaps the only one that had kept them long ago? *I'm not here for the table,* Idra reminded herself, although it was unnerving still to have such mysteries.

She walked over to the pool. *This at least I know is what must be done.* She leaned over. Pine branches from neighboring trees were reflected in it. They were reflected almost too well, it seemed. She could not see past the pool's surface. Staring back into her face was her own reflection. *Here I go.* She dipped Orin's net, breaking the surface. Her heart lurched. There was sound. The sap was rushing up the trees and she could hear it. It took a moment for her breathing to calm. She gazed carefully at her surroundings. *Nothing but woods and tranquility.* She returned her attention to the pool. The sap rippled outwards from where the net had broken the surface. But broken as it was, she could now see into its depths. At the bottom of the pool lay her tribute, waiting.

She leaned forward, dipping the net downward until it touched the bottom. *Come on!* And then she had it. She pulled up the net. It was a lot of trouble to go through for a stone. *But I've put far more time into other tributes.* This was it. The tribute she had thrown away when she rejected the world. *I was so angry.* Idra took it out of the net, and held it in her palm. It was wet, but aside from that, it was a plain stone. *Not to me.* She closed her hand tightly around it. *I wasn't ready then. Am I now?* The remaining ripples in the pool stilled along with sound. The forest returned to silence.

She returned to Enetheal's table. *I blamed him for everything. Fault never had anything to do with it.* Sorrow began to well up inside her. Regret for what she had done, and for what she had not done. She took a breath, closed her eyes, and clutched the stone even more tightly. When she opened her eyes some of her burden had lifted. She touched the table. "I'm sorry, Enetheal," she whispered.

"Where were you?" Namin asked when she returned to the plateau.

She held up the net, Ara's stone, and her own lost tribute in answer.

"Orin." She dropped the net down the well. "Ara." She dropped Ara's stone. "Me." She dropped her own lost tribute.

"And tomorrow night I will retrieve the last fruit," she said.

"Yes," Lenya whispered softly, her eyes wide. Namin nodded. Kuthan smiled.

"Which means everything is ready," Kuthan said softly. "It's time for me to go."

KUTHAN - DAY TWENTY-FIVE

"What?" Idra asked.

She's the only one who is surprised. Kuthan felt a twinge of something. *Satisfaction? Do I want to be mourned?* He glanced to Lenya. Sad but understanding. She had expected it. And Namin. Namin had been waiting for this. *He won't want me to return.* His eyes returned to Idra. Shock. Even hurt. *Yes. I do want them to miss me.* He shrugged off the thought.

"Tributes made for world new. Tributes made that were unclaimed. Tributes with the maker's mark. Tributes show the maker maimed." He chanted it almost like a song, then wished he hadn't. The others did not even hint at a smile.

"I need to retrieve the unclaimed tributes," he said softly. He waited, hoping someone would say something. Something to stop him. Or simply to say they cared about him. *Why do I think I deserve their care now?* In his mind's eye he saw Enetheal. His hand raised. Raised to defend himself. *What sort of monster am I?* He would leave. He would leave now. *It starts with one step.* He took the step.

"Kuthan?" Idra asked.

"Yes?" he replied too quickly.

"One more tribute?"

All four of them worked. They chose a large stone. They painted, stuck on sand and shells, twigs, and the petals of flowers. They kept working, adding more and more. It felt so good to be together. It was Kuthan who had to stop them.

"It's beautiful," he said, smiling. Together they took it to the well's edge. Together they let it go. And then together they walked down the stairs, across the beach, across the island. They stopped at that day's tree. Idra climbed easily to retrieve the fruit. Kuthan didn't feel like eating, but for her sake he accepted, and realized that it was delicious. Even more so because he could see her joy. Finally they reached the entrance to the stairs.

"We lost Orin on the new paths. We lost Ara to her Shrieking Stones." Kuthan took a breath. "And I know that this is the Former's Cave."

"We could think of a plan …," Idra said, a pleading note in her voice.

"No plan," Kuthan answered. "I know there is only one way. I just want to say goodbye." He was surprised to find his throat closing. He took a breath.

He turned to Idra first.

"Thank you Idra. You made life joyful." She ran forward and hugged him. When he tried to break apart she held on to him longer. Then finally she let go.

"I do love existence, Len. You were right." Lenya, too, hugged him. It was a long hug, but not prolonged. They let go together.

And then it was time for Namin. He was surprised to find Namin's eyes confused.

"I won't be joining you in your new world. But I have given everything I have to it. It will be beautiful. I promise," Kuthan whispered. Namin blinked. Kuthan started to turn away.

"Kuthan," Namin said. They held eyes. He didn't say anything for a moment. But then Namin found his voice. "We'll be waiting for you."

Namin turned his eyes away. Kuthan looked around at them. *The stairs have only ever become more difficult.* Across the water the sun was setting. They watched it together. It sank beneath the horizon and Kuthan took his first step. *We're both descending now.*

One step. Then another. Then another. The light grew dimmer and dimmer. Or maybe it was the darkness growing thicker. He could feel it now. First it was as a warm wind. Then a heavy mist. Then a blanket of darkness all around him. And then it was the only thing. It wrapped itself around his mind as well as his body. Until it was all. *No time. This is all. No past. Not even a now. Nothing. But I am here! I can create. I can think thoughts that are separate from myself. I have created a world separate from myself.*

"I love," he said into the darkness. "I love existence. I love Lenya. I love Idra. I love Orin. I love Ara. I love Namin. I love Enetheal. He felt nothingness. But he felt somethingness too. And the somethingness was stronger. And then he was there.

There was light. *The stairs are my service.* Kuthan took a breath. How could it be the same place? When he looked at it, it felt different. He knew what the Former was. And now Lenya had been here too. The walls had been touched by her light. But now there was something else here. There was dripping, from the stalactites to the stalagmites, and reflected back from the stalagmites to the stalactites. And there were ripples. Now the stones seemed like the tips of branches, their shadows dancing across the wall … *branches … or roots?*

Kuthan walked to the altar. His tributes were still there. Orin's stone was there too, the one that played with the light of the sun. And also Namin's tribute, cocooned in webs, the stone that Kuthan had held close all those days of darkness when the Former had been ever-present. It too had remained. *All here. All unclaimed.* Kuthan looked around. *I must not hesitate.* Kuthan grasped the salver. Light faded into nothing. *I'm used to darkness,* Kuthan reminded himself. He kept his breathing even.

"You freed me." He heard the voice out of the darkness. It carried across the water, echoing off the walls.

"You freed us." Now the voice seemed to come from a single direction. Kuthan stepped away from it.

"The rules were broken, as we decided they would be." Slowly Kuthan gathered the tributes. He knew them by touch. He counted every one of them.

"And you can create the world as it should be by your own hands." Kuthan gathered up Orin's stone and then Namin's cocooned tribute.

"But why run, dear friend? We are brothers. Together we were bound by rules. Together we were banished to the darkness. Together we escaped. Together we are free." Kuthan carefully headed to the stairs.

"You want them back." Kuthan closed his eyes, but it did not silence the sound of the Former's voice, nor the sound of the dripping.

"Do you want to create them again? Create them better? We are still bound as long as this world remains, but once we break it down, once we rejoin, once it is *us*, then we can do what we will." His foot reached the first step.

"You think to walk away from me? Every step you walk away is a step you walk closer to me." But Kuthan began to climb the stairs.

"*Look* at me," Enetheal demanded from behind him. Kuthan recognized Enetheal's voice from his dream. But he did not turn back. "Was I sacrificed for nothing?" His voice filled the cavern. Kuthan continued to climb.

"I can't see," he heard Orin say in the darkness behind him.

"Kuthan will come back," Ara reassured him.

But Kuthan continued, step by step. He heard their footfalls behind him: Enetheal, Orin, Ara, the Former. And his own.

"Abandon this world? Abandon us? Run from all that is? To embrace nothingness?" The stairs were empty. The same darkness as in the well. They had been playing. Just playing. Tossing stones down a well. Make-believing a new world. Would he trade everything for a fantasy? For every step he made, he heard many behind him. They told him to turn around, to look at them. They whispered. They pleaded. They shouted. They screamed. But Kuthan continued to climb. Up. Up the stairs. *Ara looked back. We have all looked back. But now I'm looking forward.* He heard the footsteps behind him. But he saw the steps in front of him. He saw where he was going to place his feet. *I can see,* he realized.

There was still sunlight left in the day when he emerged. The footsteps were still behind him. "Kuthan!"

they shouted. Now there were other voices. Lenya's. Idra's. Namin's.

"Kuthan ... stop!" But Kuthan did not stop. He walked. They walked around him and behind him. But the path in front of him remained clear.

"Kuthan!" Another step. Another step. And yet another step. More stairs. *I will climb.* Higher, and higher. Never had his legs burned like this. His body protested. The voices shrieked in his head for him to stop. But Kuthan would not stop. He reached the summit, crossed the plateau, and followed the tributes into the well.

Idra - Days Twenty-Five to Twenty-Seven

His skin was pale when he emerged from the darkness, his steps slow and methodical. Before him he carried the salver upon which were the unclaimed tributes.

"Kuthan!" Idra shouted. Namin held out a hand in warning, but she ran forward to greet him. Kuthan looked straight past her. His eyes were bright, glassy, and fixed beyond them.

"Kuthan?" Idra asked. Kuthan continued to walk, moving one step at a time. When she touched him, his skin was covered in icy sweat.

Namin pulled her back as Kuthan's deliberate movements continued. "Kuthan!" Namin shouted after him. Kuthan did not pause.

"Kuthan!" Even Lenya shouted now. But he did not respond. They walked with him, talking to him, but he took no notice.

"Should we?" Namin asked. Idra took a breath.

"No. But we'll walk with him now." They walked across the island. Lenya, Idra, and Namin were silent. Kuthan continued, unreachable. They arrived at the Starward Stairs, yet Kuthan's pace did not falter as he began to climb.

"Kuthan, slow down," Lenya pleaded. But his movements were relentless and soon they all reached the top.

"We're here Kuthan! You can stop!" Namin cried out, breathless after the climb. "Kuthan!" he shouted. But Kuthan did not stop. He approached the well at that same steady pace, still not slowing as he reached the well's edge, then tilted abruptly and toppled into the darkness, still bearing the salver and the unclaimed tributes.

"No." It was just a small gasp that escaped Idra. She blinked, and then blinked again. "Not like that." It came out as a whisper. It couldn't have happened. "Not like that." This time she choked. She did not know if tears had caused her to choke. She took in a slow breath and then another. How could it be that she smelled pine trees up here? Somehow, though, their scent was strong. Idra closed her eyes and took another deep breath.

She inhaled through her nose and exhaled slowly through her mouth. *I'm in the Sapwood. There is no here. There is no there. There is no up. No down. There is no path. It is all path. Kuthan and Orin knew where to put lanterns. But I knew they weren't needed. Nothing has changed. Nothing can change. Nothing will change.* She smiled and opened her eyes. The world was still there. The world was changed. Namin and Lenya sat with her, each of them staring at the other's eyes. Idra closed hers again. *We can wait now.* But then she thought about it. *Not waiting. We can share this time together.* The sky's orange and pink faded into pale blue. The blue darkened and became purple. The purple became black.

It was only after the sky was black that Namin rose to his feet. He placed both his hands along the edge of the well, staring into the darkness. *He is going to sing.* She realized that she did not want to hear him sing. And then he didn't. But it was worse. The silence dragged on. Namin cleared his throat and took a few breaths. Still there was no song. Her heart seemed to pause. *Please.*

Her thought was answered as soon as it came. A low hum emerged from Namin, and then gained strength until it blossomed into song. They watched him and listened. Lenya, Idra, even the flowers turned their faces toward the song.

The spiders came. They danced. They leapt back and forth over the well. When they were finished, the opening was covered in a crisscrossing silk web. Namin's voice diminished into a soft hum and finally became inaudible. The spiders scuttled away through the grass. Namin's gaze followed them until they were out of sight. Then his eyes found Idra's. He sat down, breathing and resting. Finally, after a while, the three of them lay down together and watched the sky.

The star was beautiful. It was bright and silvery white, but surrounding it was a pink halo and pinkness trailed behind it. They walked together, taking their time, holding hands. When they returned with it, Namin peeled off the web screen from the well, and Lenya released it. The three of them lay down once more, and closed their eyes.

The sun rose. They saw its gold come across the water, shimmering as it touched the waves.

"Tonight is the night," Idra told them. They drank sap, ate fruit, and wandered together. They visited each special place on the island. Idra led them to the little cove where she and Orin had skipped stones. They walked off the paths, too, and visited the Welcome Table and each of Idra's trees. They talked to each other and laughed. It was easy to laugh. They splashed in the shallows and swam off the beach where they had first arrived. The waves were surprisingly warm. They even fetched tributes from the Stony Shores. They did not decorate these, but they chose them. Namin's was deep blue, Idra's red-brown, and Lenya's green. They brought them to the well and let them tumble down.

"Just a few more tributes," Idra smiled. Suddenly she picked up her basket. "Thank you, Namin. This was a wonderful gift." Namin blinked, taken aback. But then he nodded. The basket brushed the side of the well as it fell. Lenya's hand moved to her wrist. Namin quickly caught it. Idra took in a sharp breath, but Lenya just stared. Then Namin knelt down and slowly smoothed her loosened glove back into place, wrapped his arms around her and held her close.

"We're going to need these until the end," he said softly. Lenya nodded.

"It's time," Idra said, looking at the sun.

"Yes," Lenya echoed. "It is time."

It did not take them long to find the pool in the Sapwood. Lenya took Idra's hand as they approached. Idra's heart began to beat faster and her breathing sounded loud in the Sapwood's familiar stillness. But the noises belonged. Together they stared at the pool's reflective surface. Namin began to sing. He walked about the pool, brushing his hands over the trees. Spiders danced, and silver strands crisscrossed between them.

"To keep you safe," Namin whispered. Suddenly he wrapped his arms around Idra and she smiled, returning his embrace. Then she was hugging Lenya, her smile now a grin. When they broke apart, Idra looked into the surprised faces of her two friends and could not help but laugh.

"I love you," she told them. They echoed her with one voice. She saw the uncertainty in their eyes. "And I will see you soon," she reassured them. She turned away so that they would not see her joy. It would only hurt them. *Down in the sky where low becomes high.* The last of the sun dipped beneath the horizon. A ripple shimmered across the pool. And her tree was there. Eternal. Bearing fruits that shone with the gold of the sun. Idra stepped into the pool. The world righted itself. And Idra began to climb.

She was not surprised, but elation filled her. *It's real. The world below us is above us. The world behind us is before us. We have followed and have been followed.* The bark was alive beneath her fingers as if the tree itself were humming, and its song reverberated in her bones. It was a joyful song. It spoke of peace and timelessness. The humming was soft. *It's the Sapwood's song. The song we never heard before.* There were large stretches between the branches near the base of the tree, but nonetheless, she climbed with ease. *This tree was created to be climbed.* She looked at the many branches and was again amazed to notice that the tree extended up endlessly. *Down endlessly.* But there was something else, something that did not quite make sense.

"The light!" She had been so lost in the tree that she had not thought to observe the sky. It was night. But it was also day. The light was a faint silver gold about her. *Where is it coming from?* She looked toward the trunk now below her, and her stomach lurched.

There was no reflective pool. No sign of Lenya and Namin. No earth. No roots. Instead the tree continued, the trunk widening beneath her, and then narrowing once again. The tree below sprouted branches identical to the ones she climbed, and far far below were fruits that shone with starlight as brilliant as the ones above. *A reflection.* Only there was no pool.

She blinked, and then she closed her eyes, suddenly nauseated. Her stomach turned and she took a sharp breath, clinging close to the humming tree.

Which one was the reflection? If she had entered a reflection, then wouldn't the tree beneath her be the real one? The tree that completed the circle? *Is the fruit the same?*

Was there a real tree? This one was surely as real as the other.

"I have all the time I need to decide," she tried to reassure herself. But then her eyes found the source of the light. *The sun. The sun is rising.* And it was not just the sun. Far below her she saw the full moon as well. As the sun rose towards the branches above, the moon sank towards the branches below. *They are circling one another.*

"Circle," she whispered aloud. The word sparked a memory. Ara's new covenant that gave them hope of a new world:

Now is the time to mend
Begin by bringing end
You are the circle broken
You are the world woken

Idra climbed. *This is the one,* she told herself. *Fruit taken from each tree, and yet the circle is incomplete.* After that, all thought ceased. Her body climbed. She heard blood pounding in her ears, noticed her breaths quickening. She felt the scrape of bark upon her skin. But most of all she felt the constant humming of the tree. It was a slow climb, seemingly endless. *Like Kuthan's stairs.* And yet she could tell that she was making progress. *The humming.* She laughed. The change was slow, but it was happening. The notes were growing higher, the reverberations stronger. There were leaves all about her now, but the fruits were much higher. *They* were in the heavens. So she continued to climb.

As fast as she climbed, the sun climbed faster. Soon it was level with her; then it passed her. She felt a chill go through her as it touched the topmost branches of the tree. When she realized that it had begun its descent, she felt her throat tighten. *I'm not even half-way there! What if ...* But she could not even consider that possibility, so she simply moved. She leapt from branch to branch. Sometimes to get to the next branch she would have to leave the tree's central stem, running along one branch, then jumping up to the next, and finally returning to the stem. And still the tree rose higher. The light of the moon grew stronger than the light of the sun, yet she continued to climb.

She looked down toward the base of the tree. *The sun has already set.* She hadn't noticed the moment it happened. Without any earth to hide behind she did not feel its light vanish; she only realized its position because the moon was getting closer.

A coldness settled about her. It was not the cold of a distant sun, nor was it that of a rising moon. Her heart skipped. *The stars. I'm getting close to the stars.* But they couldn't be stars. The stars were for Lenya. *Fruit,* Idra reminded herself. *Or is my task different this time?* The branches grew thin as she continued her climb, and without the sun, the branch-tips were freezing. *Is it the sap that freezes?* The moon was right next to her now. She could stretch out her hand and touch it. But it wasn't the moon that she reached for.

It shone. Shone as a star might. But it wasn't starlight and it wasn't cold. It wasn't warm either. *Kissed by both sun and moon.* Idra thought. She hesitated for a moment and then pressed her own lips to the fruit.

Alive. Alive with everything that life was. She stopped. The sun shone. Shone from far below, blinding her vision of the tree beneath her. *Is she as alive as I am? Did my reflection far below kiss a star? Does she consider taking it for herself?*

Idra hoped not. Her heart pounded. *My service is to carry, not consume.*

Now the moon began to descend, and so did Idra. *It's a race.* But climbing down had always been harder than climbing up. The moon passed her. Soon it traveled beyond where the horizon would have been. Idra moved down as quickly as she dared. She was well-practiced. Sometimes she leapt without using her hands. She moved from branch to branch. *I must not miss a step.* The sun came closer. The world grew warmer. Then, as the sun and moon each approached the horizon, she saw something move far below.

My reflection. The sun and moon seemed to stop. Idra looked down at her reflection. So far away and yet somehow their eyes met one another's. The humming stopped, just for a moment, like a sharp intake of breath. And then the whole world rippled. The tree. The sky. The sun and moon. Her reflection. Herself. All were distorted. She felt the dissonance in the hum of the tree as it returned. The fruit alone remained untouched. Idra gazed down, staring. She held fast to the tree, but far beneath her, her reflection continued to move.

No. It couldn't be. Now she descended with abandon. Her feet propelled her from one branch to the next, her free hand scraping the bark to slow her down. She couldn't help but look down. Had the figure, her reflection, been leaping as she had? It was now moving slowly, calmly working its way toward her. *Only because I have stopped. The ripple behind is always faster than the one in front.* She continued to leap down. I can beat it. I must.

Somehow she had climbed up the massive trunk without the aid of branches. *But how can I get down?* She could not drop down. Below her there was no earth, only tree and sky. Besides, with one of her hands clutching the fruit, climbing down the trunk would be impossible. The sun was nearing its peak above her; the moon below her. Never had sun and moon danced their circle so quickly. But now her reflection was motionless.

Her heart paused. Her breaths were as absent as wind in the Sapwood. Her panic died. *The reflection is waiting where the two trees become one.* Her mind raced to figure out why. *What must I do?* The sun and moon continued to circle them with unnatural speed. It is waiting. Waiting for time to run out. *But the sun is on my side. It is night in the Sapwood. The last night. My last chance to return.* Could she return? There was no sign of the pool. Nor any sign of Lenya and Namin. Perhaps she could only return when night reached her side of the tree. *No. Otherwise It would not be waiting.*

Did It know that It had won? Was that why It had stopped? She stared. Her reflection looked back at her. *The Former wants me.* But Its eyes flickered to her hand. *No. It wants the fruit!* The Former must want both me and the fruit. The sun and moon continued to race. Slowly Idra crept down the tree, hugging the trunk with her body and legs until she was at its base. She felt the gnarled beginnings of roots, and her feet found purchase.

The Former watched, the hunger in Its eyes undisguised. She reached her hand down, the fruit clutched tightly. Slowly, the Former stretched its own arm toward her. *No.* She pulled back the fruit. Why doesn't It just take me and the fruit? Could It? Did the Former's rules bind the Former? *It wants me to give It the fruit!* The sun and moon drew ever nearer to the horizon. *There has to be a way!* She looked frantically for the pool. Then, all at once, she understood.

She looked down, desperately to where she knew the others waited. The Former looked up. "Take it," she whispered. *Please,* she thought. She begged them to understand. Idra extended her arm downward. The Former extended Its arm upward. She reached out her hand, offering the fruit. "Take it!" she pleaded again. The fruit was suspended, a hair's breadth from Its fingertips. Their eyes met. But she did not look away. The Former rippled in front of her, Its figure distorting. A hand reached forth from the scattered light, grasped the fruit, and Idra let go.

NAMIN - DAYS TWENTY-SIX TO TWENTY-EIGHT

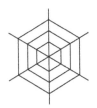

Idra and Lenya. *My everything. My all.* He paused, yet they continued on to the pool's edge, hand in hand. *I need to sing for them. I will sing for them. For Idra.* But he struggled to find his voice. Idra was leaving. *But she will come back.* Kuthan and Ara would not. *Why did you do it, Ara!? How could you be so stupid!* She had left them, alone, in the middle of the night. *Left us for a service already finished.* Had the Former forced her? *No.* Ara had left willingly. Away from the sanctuary of Namin's webs.

Kuthan was different. *He meant to leave. To escape into his world. To leave us in this one.* Kuthan had promised. Promised them that the new world was not for him. He had promised to help them. But Kuthan had abandoned them. He had brought this world crashing down, and had left them to ruin.

No. Namin took a breath, allowing his mind to clear. *Orin. Ara. Kuthan.* They had been lured away from the safety of Namin's webs by a song sweeter than his own. *But that will not be Idra's fate.* Namin found his voice. He sang. The spiders came slowly, almost lazily. They rose up from beneath the twigs of the forest floor. They scuttled down the length of the trees of the Sapwood. But they did not dance. Instead they watched him with many dark eyes. *I will lead and they will follow,* Namin reassured himself. He walked around the perimeter of the empty pool, around Lenya and Idra. As he walked he sang, and his voice commanded the web to be woven. When he was finished, he opened his eyes to find the three of them enclosed by walls of silk.

He was drained of energy. *But it's only a little longer. I will find the strength.* He turned to Idra. "To keep you safe," he whispered. He hugged her, and she pushed her body against his. He held her tight. *I don't have to let go. I can hold her here. She is safe in my embrace. Safe in my webs.* But he took a breath and let go.

Idra was smiling. Not a sad smile, but a smile of joy. She turned to Lenya. By the time they broke apart a wide grin spread across her face and she laughed.

"I love you," Idra told them.

How can she smile? "I love you," Namin told her. Did she know what that meant? *You are my world. The only one who cared about us as a family. The only one who didn't get lost in your service. You make my songs come to life.* But he didn't say any more.

"And I will see you soon," Idra said.

Come back, Namin wanted to say, but again he restrained himself. *Stay here.* Another unspoken thought. The sun sank beneath the horizon, and Idra stepped into the pool.

"Goodbye," Namin said. But it was too late. Idra was no longer here. Idra was there. The heavens extended downward as a great tree, darker than night. And in its branches were stars. Endless stars. Above Namin and Lenya were only two. Idra began her climb a short way up, before turning her gaze down. Namin waved and shouted, but Idra didn't respond. Her face was confused and anxious, but her eyes never met theirs. She looked around, then up, and then down. Then she continued to climb.

"She can't see us, Len," he whispered.

"No," Lenya answered. "That's probably for the best."

They sat cross-legged at the edge of the pool, holding hands and watching Idra. She grew smaller and smaller as she moved further away, but the tree continued to rise on and on.

"She's not moving fast enough," Namin said, trying to keep his voice even.

"She's moving as fast as she can," Lenya answered. "It has to be fast enough."

Lenya got up. "I need to get my star."

"Your star?" Namin asked, confused. "Yes. Yes of course," he said after a moment and returned his gaze to the pool. *How could she even notice the star? Idra needs us here!*

Lenya left the enclosure, but Namin kept his eyes focused beneath the pool.

"Hurry, Idra," he said softly. She was out of sight now. Far far away. *But she will come back. She must come back.* He barely noticed Lenya return. But he felt her hand slip into his. It was gentle, smooth, and cold.

"Lenya," he whispered. "I'm scared."

"We both are," she answered.

The night went on. They held more tightly to each other's hands. They stared into the pool. Above them, the moon a small sliver in the sky. Finally the dawn came, but there was no sign of Idra. The sun rose, and the image of the tree vanished from the pool. Namin could feel his heart begin to pound in his chest.

"What now?" he whispered.

"More waiting," Lenya answered. So they waited.

"She will have her fruit, you, your star, and together we walk to the well." He didn't know whether he was speaking to Lenya or to himself. "We will walk carefully. Slowly. And I will sing."

"Yes," Lenya answered. "We will carry and we will sing."

How does she remain so calm? He started to answer himself, but he pushed the thought away.

"You're here, Len?" he asked her.

"Yes," she answered, her voice sounding concerned. "You?"

"Yes," he answered. They shared eyes. He wanted to believe her. There was so much there. Love. Fear. Determination. Distance.

"Rest," She told him. "Not sleep," she said quickly before he could protest. "Just rest. I will watch."

Namin gazed at her face a moment longer. Then he slowly laid himself down, resting his head in her lap. He looked up. Trees. Rivers of sap flowing up the trees towards the sky. The sky was beautiful and blue. The sun shone gold high above them. And somewhere far below them was Idra. Did she see the same sun? Was it always night where she was? Namin closed his eyes, letting the sun warm his lids. He breathed in the Sapwood, Lenya, and pine needles. He kept his eyes closed, trying to listen for a song. He concentrated on slowing his breaths, his heartbeat. Gradually the sun shifted across the sky. And then Lenya began to sing. It began as a hum, but soon her voice was free. She caressed his hair as she sang, and soon his mind was swept into the song. When she was finished, his face was wet with tears.

"Your turn, Len," he said hoarsely.

She smiled, and they shifted, moving so that her head now rested on his chest. Namin hummed, running his hands over her. *Rest Len. Rest in my voice.* He placed a hand on her forehead, stroked her hair. One hand moved down her arm … and then stopped. *It's gone.* His voice stopped for just a moment, but then continued. Lenya didn't seem to notice. He moved gently, keeping her head cradled and undisturbed. He sang and he saw: the other one was missing too. Now as his hands ran over hers, they were smooth and cold. Her gloves were gone. *She threw them down the well, with last night's star.* He had been so focused on Idra that he hadn't felt Lenya let them go, hadn't noticed that they were gone when she returned. He pictured her, a smile illuminating her face as her gloves caught the last breath of wind and drifted into darkness. His mind began to race, but his song continued, steady and true. *Don't think about it.* The sun began to set. As it touched the horizon, his song became a quiet hum and then, almost imperceptibly, just a breath. He held Lenya close as they stared into the pool. As they watched, it rippled. And then, suddenly, Idra was there.

She was frightened. She looked directly at them and they saw terror in her eyes.

"Something's wrong, Lenya," Namin whispered. She held his hand tightly.

"Wait," said Lenya, once again, calm. Idra leapt from branch to branch. The pool rippled again, distorting her image. When the ripples cleared she was much closer.

"It's too dark to see." Namin's voice was steady as he tried to mirror Lenya's calmness.

"She's coming, Namin." She held his hand even more tightly.

"We need to be ready to go in if she needs us!" The pool rippled again, and suddenly Idra was climbing down the trunk. They held their breath. And then Idra stopped.

"Lenya?"

"Hold on, we just need to …." Lenya stopped. Her hand suddenly let go of his. Above them the sky was blackness, except for the single star above them. Silver white it shone. And silver white it fell. It didn't arc as the other stars had. It plummeted straight down.

"Lenya!"

But she was gone.

"Idra!" In the star's light Namin could now see Idra's face plainly. Her eyes met his, terrified as only she had been when they encountered the Former. She reached towards the pool, the fruit in her hand, offering. But then suddenly she yanked her hand away as if it had been burned. Idra's eyes didn't leave his. She reached out once more, the piece of fruit at her fingertips. "Take it," she mouthed. Namin's mind went blank. Yet still she held out the fruit, her eyes fixed on his, now desperate. All at once he understood.

No. You can't ask this of me.

"Take it," she mouthed again, hope and terror mingling in her eyes. Her fruit-laden hand moved closer until it was just under the pool's surface.

I'm taking you, Idra. He reached past the fruit to grab her wrist, but he found only the fruit. The moment his fingers closed, the surface of the pool rippled. He caught only a glimpse of her smile before her image vanished. *No. She was here. She IS here. I reached for her!* Namin leapt into the pool, but now it was shallow. He splashed the water about. "Idra!" he screamed. The Sapwood muffled the scream. He did not scream again. Idra was no longer there.

Idra was gone. If he had reached down further to grab her wrist … if he had entered the pool sooner … if he had never let her go down … if he had caught Kuthan before he had gone down the well … if he had noticed Ara slipping out from their cabin that last night … had stayed Kuthan's arm before he brought it down on Enetheal with the last Tribute, had walked with Orin that night to sing away any dangers … but he hadn't. The past was set in stone.

He looked about their enclosure. The spiders were dancing again. But as they danced, the webs were peeling apart and vanishing into the faint light. He looked at the sap flowing up the trees. And then he looked at Lenya.

She held her star in her hands. She was alive with starlight. Silver white flickered across her bare skin, traveling back and forth between her and her star. And she was smiling. Smiling as she never had during the day, during her time with them.

Namin had sung. He had sung for Orin. For Enetheal. For Ara. Even for Kuthan. He had sung against the unweaving. He had sung to protect the others. *I need to sing now.* It was his worship. He had worshipped people. Not this world. Not some new world. Orin. Enetheal. Ara. Kuthan. Idra. Lenya. *They are my world.* But they were gone. *Lenya is gone too.* She always had been. *I have to let her go, too. She has always belonged to the stars.*

Then, from amidst the light, he heard her voice. "Namin," she whispered. "Namin. I need you to sing." *Sing. Yes. The Former was coming.* He looked down at his hands in which he held a piece of fruit. It looked plain. As plain as the stones they had once carried across the island. *I hold this instead of Idra?* There is no one left, no reason to sing.

"Namin," he heard Lenya whisper again.

He swallowed. Darkness was pressing in. The moon had not risen tonight. Every night it had been a smaller sliver and now it was no more. Even Lenya's light was fading. Slowly all the light was being swallowed by the darkness. *The world is fading.* Namin closed his eyes. Tears burned against his lids. It was a croaking rasp that escaped him. He tried again, and a choked whisper of sound came forth. He opened his eyes. They were there. They were waiting. Many legs, and many eyes. *My salvation.* They kept to the shadows, away from Lenya's starlight. Lenya didn't notice them. Lenya noticed only her star. Namin tried again. It wasn't even a whisper now. But the spiders came. They came for him.

The Unweaving was in his voice, even in the soundless utterance. The spiders scuttled over his flesh. They covered his skin, his eyes, his mouth. He had never minded the feeling of their legs scuttling over him, but they had not bitten him before now. He fell to the ground. Yet somehow the pain seemed far away. They were weaving all to nothingness. *I need to sing the world away. I need to sing myself away.* The spiders danced and wove. Their webs cut him off from the world, sealed his lips together, taking away his breath, taking away his song.

LENYA - DAY TWENTY-EIGHT

Life, light, and eternity. It pulsed into her, through her, and back into the star. Idra's fruit had been delivered to them. Her star had come down. How had she forgotten wholeness? How had she forgotten purpose? The world was darkness. *But we are light. We are energy. We are Being.* The star fought to own her, but Lenya's own voice and thought rose beyond that oneness.

The Former is here for the star! The Former is here for us!

Her body would not move. Somewhere, close by, Namin was there. *I'm still here, Namin*, she thought frantically. Her body was still and breathless. Then she began to tremble. She gasped.

"Namin." She tried again. "Namin. I need you to sing." His song would deliver them from the Former. Deliver her from the star. It had before. But she sensed the Former drawing closer, and once again her body would not move. The star has me. *I always wanted the star to have me.* But another whisper escaped her. "Namin?" she asked. She felt It drawing closer. Slowly. *Does the Former stifle Its hunger as I have stifled mine? Does It want us like I want my star? To be complete? For Being to be complete?*

Then she heard him. At first she was not sure it was him. She did not recognize his voice. But it was Namin.

His eyes were closed, and yet tears escaped. A horrible croaking rasp came from his mouth. Then even worse, silence. Lenya felt her light begin to darken. She stared at him, pleading with her eyes.

Namin. No. Not this. Not now. A choked noise came from him. Then she saw the spiders. So many she could not count them. They scuttled from the shadows, keeping to the edge of her light. Like a dark river they came, flowing quickly and quietly, now encircling his limp form. Then they swarmed over him.

"Namin!" she shrieked. The starlight was cast from her mind as she ran to his side.

The spiders danced about him as they had once danced his webs into being. His voice had asked for end, had uttered the Unweaving. And so the spiders had silenced him, silenced his voice, silenced his song. Namin's body was still when she reached him.

As she knelt beside him, the light of her star shone on him, and her eyes widened as she looked upon his face. Just under his nose streched an intricate web, forming smooth skin where his mouth should have been. She saw the spiders slip quietyly away, back into the night from which they had come. The star slipped from her fingers and fell beside his outstretched body. Lenya leaned over, resting her head upon Namin's chest.

He was here. But now he was gone. He had chosen to leave. To undo himself. To undo them. To destroy everything they had been working for. He had been their protector. Their guide. Namin had held the world together as he had held them together. Held Lenya together.

Once again she could not move, could not think, could not feel. What was left? They were supposed to do something now. But she had forgotten. *What was my purpose?* Stars. Stars had tied her to this world. But somehow that answer seemed wrong. She lifted herself up, and again she looked at Namin's still form. In his hand he still clasped Idra's last fruit. *That is Idra's. Surely the star is mine.* She turned her gaze to the glowing shape beside them and reached out hesitantly towards it, but when she took it up, the familiar pull of cold energy was gone. Gently she loosened the silvery-gold piece of fruit from Namin's grasp. Then, lifting it carefully, she held it, held both the fruit and the star, one in each hand.

She did not see the Former. But she felt It. *The time has come. I wanted to be whole. I thought I could do this through stars, but true wholeness can only happen if the Former consumes us, if all becomes one, all separation ends.* Slowly she rose to her feet, and turned.

The Former was farther away than she had thought. Where It walked, the sap stopped flowing. In one hand she held the fruit that had cost them so much. In the other she held the star. But the light of the star was no longer separate from her, and the star no longer claimed her.

"Come to me," she said to the Former. And the Former came. As It approached, she watched and waited to be consumed.

But then a hand caught her wrist. The shock of it was stronger than any star.

"Enetheal!" she gasped. He stood over her, his eyes a piercing slate grey, his face covered by a membranous sheen where his mouth should be. But he could not answer. Once that face had been a mask through which she could see no emotion. But now she saw his form as she had never seen it before. Enetheal was great, and beautiful, and enlivened with fury.

"Are you an echo?" she heard herself ask. And then she laughed.

The Former did not matter anymore. She laughed again. She knew that she was safe, that she was separate, and that all was well. She felt her purpose and her will.

Enetheal took the star from her hand, entwining his fingers in hers. And then they were running. Running through the darkness. Running as all around them spiders unwove the world. Behind them the Former approached. But none of that mattered. Enetheal was with her. Their feet found earth to support them as they raced forward, hand in hand. They were together! She laughed again. Their feet pounded against the forest floor, across paths they no longer knew, and saw only dimly from the light of the star in his hand.

Had the star weakened? Was it dying with this world? *No, the star isn't dim. I am bright. I am brighter than starlight.* The stones and roots before them could not have been lit by the small star alone. Lenya glanced down at their linked hands and saw her own, shining and folded within the dark shape of his.

Then she looked at her other hand, the hand that still clutched Idra's last piece of silver-gold fruit. Together they pressed forward. The dark was thick, yet they were able to make out their path ahead.

Suddenly her laughter died, and she pulled against Enetheal's hand, bringing them both to a stop. There was song behind them. It was not the Unweaving. It was gentle, and sad. *Namin's song. He's still here.* She started to turn them towards the music, but Enetheal resisted. When she tried to break free, he shook his head in warning. She understood. *It isn't Namin.* It was the Former, and It was drawing closer. Dread came upon her, and they ran for fear of the Unmaking. The voice came closer, but while they could not see clearly through the darkness, their feet found sand. *The beach... the well!*

How could I have forgotten the well? It had seemed like an endless run. There was no wind, no waves, and no world behind them. Only the Former with Namin's song, and ... Enetheal. And then there were the stairs. They climbed. The song followed close behind, chasing them, until they were at the top of the plateau, the well a dark silhouette ahead of them.

The garden was overgrown as never before. And now not just the petals of the flowers and leaves shone silver white, the stalks and stems glowed too. The two of them moved quickly, across the plateau towards the well, but as they ran Lenya felt something pulling her feet: the flowers. Their silver stems wrapped around her ankles, tripping her as she ran, slowing her, but still she would not stop. She continued to push ahead, tearing plants from the earth with each labored step. And then she stumbled.

"Enetheal!" He did not hesitate: In one smooth motion he turned, caught her up, and tore her from the plants' grasp. They closed the distance to the well's edge. It was without preparation or thought that the two of them dropped the fruit and the star into the open well. They did not stare into the vast darkness as the last glow of the star vanished, but when Lenya turned toward Enetheal, he had taken a step away.

"Hurry!" she said. But he did not move. Instead his eyes moved between her and the edge of the well. Behind him she heard Namin's melody, but she could also hear the Unweaving, joining and mixing with that song. "Enetheal! Come!"

He remained motionless and she followed his gaze. Then she noticed the web draped over the well's edge. *The covering to the well. The door must be closed.*

And Lenya understood. She rushed to him, pulling him towards her, her cheek against his heart. But she knew what he had to do. Their embrace was close and quick. When she released him there were tears in his eyes. Then he pushed her towards the well's edge.

There was a horrible ache in her chest, but somehow her body moved. She put her hands on the well's edge to climb over, but the Former's voice stopped her:

"Lenya." The Former spoke calmly, endearingly. "Light of my children. Star among stars." Lenya looked in the direction of Its voice, but could only see the darkness of the starless, moonless world. "Become one with me and bring forth a world greater than any other. A world without separation, without end. A world of perfection."

My echo. It has caught up with me.

It would be easy. To become one with eternity, to become whole—like holding on to all the stars and never letting go.

Lenya gazed into the darkness toward the voice, but could see nothing. Then her eye caught movement, and she turned to see Enetheal, her own glow the only light remaining to illuminate him. He reached to his face. Carefully, he pulled a single strand of web. In its shimmering she saw a song, a life, a person she loved. And as he reached over the edge of the well, the shining semblance dangling from his hand, she now could see his features: It was Namin.

And then she saw the shadows that he cast. There were six of them, and they flickered just beyond his form as he released the shimmering strand into the well. And she knew what her choice must be.

"No," she whispered. And she turned and stepped off the edge.

The fall was faster than she had imagined. Down, down, down into darkness. Like the last falling star of this world, she plummeted, never nearing the well's rough inside wall. As she looked up, she could only see black emptiness. *He has shut the way*, she thought. There is no going back. He is lost to me forever.

It seemed all of time and no time at all that she fell, or flew, or moved, or none of these. There was darkness, but there was also the light that shone from her. She closed her eyes. She could still feel his embrace, and then his hands in hers, and against her closed lids she saw him falling with her. When she opened her eyes she thought she could still see his eyes, even his mouth, and she was not sure who he was, only that she loved him. Their hands were together as they fell. But then there was new light, the image before her faded, and in her grasp was nothing but empty air.

She blinked, looked down, and she saw:

Stars. They were gathered beneath a smooth surface of liquid, illuminating a world. She rushed towards it. A thrill of excitement filled her, and then she broke the surface. The stars scattered away in all directions, outward. *I will never touch them again.* And at once both a piercing sadness and a gentle joy filled her. Everything spun around her, expanding outward. There was light, rippling out in all directions, and there was a song. *Namin's song.*

And then she was there.

The new world was beautiful. But Lenya had eyes only for the people. Orin. Ara. Kuthan. Idra. Namin. She didn't understand. She didn't need to understand. She laughed, and she cried. They all did. Tears and laughter together. The first sounds of the new world. It was more vibrant, more full of life than they had ever dreamed or painted. They held onto each other, crying and laughing until they could do so no more. Even then, they could not look away from one another for a long time.

Finally, Lenya glanced at the sky. The stars looked more distant now. More knowledgeable. Less forgiving. If they felt betrayed, then they were not alone. There were endless stars now. *Eternity.* But none of them moved.

When the golden light of the sun entered the world, Lenya closed her eyes. She knew the stars would not close theirs.

EPILOGUE

When the Former rose again to consume the world, the created beings defied It, for the ability to endure and to create had been given to them. And as they beheld the world with its brokenness, they saw the beauty of a separation that was in harmony with itself.

The Former worked against each of them. It sought to use their gifts against them. For the Former knew that if creation gave itself up to It, then Being could be entire and without relation once more.

The Former encountered them, and was able to devour part of the essence of each.

But the children had cast their essence far beyond themselves. It was in the world they touched and in the tributes they had made, in their laughter, song, and tears, their joy, resolve, and remorse. It was ever expanding beyond them.

And so, with their gifts and essences, the children made a new world, a world untouchable by the Former.

Each child ascended, and each was consumed in part.

And as each was consumed in part by the Former, a greater portion of each became part of the new world. The world they created had beings like themselves, echoes of echoes, holding essences of the past.

They were not the same. Nor would they be unchanging. They would be ever changing, and the world ever living:

A world of echoes, ripples, circles, and reflections. A world with and without end. A world of separation, and of harmony.

ABOUT THE AUTHOR

S am Frykenberg grew up as the middle of three brothers in Andover, Massachusetts, and has loved listening to and telling stories his whole life. He studied biology at Stonehill College, where he began to write short pieces of fiction, including the young adult novella *Water's Shadow*. He has served as a volunteer in Kentucky, and is currently completing medical school.

CPSIA information can be obtained
at www.ICGtesting.com
Printed in the USA
JSHW040210300421
14153JS00001B/3